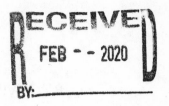
PLAGUE PITS & RIVER BONES

ALSO BY KAREN CHARLTON

The Detective Lavender Mysteries

The Heiress of Linn Hagh
The Sans Pareil Mystery
The Sculthorpe Murder

Individual Works

Catching the Eagle
Seeking Our Eagle (non-fiction)
The Mystery of the Skelton Diamonds (short story)
The Piccadilly Pickpocket (short story)

KAREN CHARLTON

PLAGUE PITS & RIVER BONES

THE DETECTIVE LAVENDER MYSTERIES

THOMAS & MERCER

Text copyright © 2018 by Karen Charlton
All rights reserved.

No part of this book may be reproduced, or stored in a retrieval system, or transmitted in any form or by any means, electronic, mechanical, photocopying, recording, or otherwise, without express written permission of the publisher.

Published by Thomas & Mercer, Seattle

www.apub.com

Amazon, the Amazon logo, and Thomas & Mercer are trademarks of Amazon.com, Inc., or its affiliates.

ISBN-13: 9781542048392
ISBN-10: 1542048397

Cover design by Lisa Horton

Printed in the United States of America

For
THE HISTORICAL (HYSTERICAL)
FICTIONAIRES
Babs Morton, Jean Gill, Jane G. Harlond, Kristin
Gleeson and Claire Stibbe.
Thank you for your love, help and friendship.
xxxx

Chapter One

G awd's teeth!'
Constable Ned Woods pulled his hat firmly down over his close-cropped greying head, yanked on his left rein, dug his heels into the flank of his horse and sped towards the river. The cold wind from the Thames whipped his face as he thundered through the central square of the Royal Hospital for Seamen towards the embankment. He heard the clatter of a second set of hooves on the flagged path close behind. The sharp-eyed young Constable Barnaby must also have seen the scrawny body cavorting on the esplanade ahead.

Woods and Barnaby drew near and reined in their horses. The crowd of pedestrians parted hastily with a murmur of surprise, revealing the figure.

The prancing man was completely naked. Through a curtain of long, lank hair that half covered his scowling face, madness shone in his dark eyes. A flash of recognition jolted through Woods; he'd met this lunatic somewhere before.

At the sight of Woods and Barnaby swinging out of their saddles, the fellow gave a blood-curdling shriek, vaulted over the railings and began to dance a jig on the muddy shingles.

Barnaby was laughing as he tied his horse to the railings beside Woods. 'Well, this beats chasin' footpads on Blackheath!'

Behind the prancing madman, the river was crowded with ships, lightermen and rowing boats. A three-masted East Indiaman glided gracefully past in full sail, her teak hull gleaming in the weak sunlight. Further downstream, the bulbous oak hull of a prison ship loomed out of the river like an impenetrable floating fortress. On the far bank, low-lying mist shrouded the uninhabited and mysterious Isle of Dogs. Its marshes and treacherous bogs lay below the level of the tidal river; folks said the peninsula was haunted by the ghosts of huge dogs that wailed at the full moon.

Four men from the crowd joined the officers. Two were well-dressed middle-aged gentlemen in smart topcoats and hats.

'Thank the Lord you're here, Constable!' said one of the men.

'It's a disgrace!' exclaimed his indignant companion. 'My wife is quite overcome with the vapours.'

Woods glanced back at the women in the crowd. A couple of them clutched each other in shock, but the rest didn't look like they were overcome with anything except curiosity.

The other men who'd joined him and Barnaby were elderly and hunched. They wore the antiquated, dark-blue uniform of the retired seamen from the hospital. One had an empty sleeve with the yellow trim of a former boatswain on its flapping cuff. A wooden stump protruded from the flared bottom of the other's trouser leg. Both had wide, toothless grins stretched across their brown, weathered faces.

Down on the beach, a gang of ragged, barefoot youngsters left their mudlarking and ran shrieking towards the naked man.

'Who is he?' Barnaby asked.

'He claims he's the Prophet Isaiah, the son of Amoz,' said one of the gentlemen in an indignant tone.

When the wretch twirled around to face the river, Woods suddenly remembered the man and groaned. 'He's Rabbie Waverley, an escaped Bedlamite.'

'Well, the asylum needs to welcome him back!'

'Arrest him, officer!'

Woods nodded and climbed over the railings. 'Follow me, Barnaby. We'll try to grab him before he decides to take a dip in the Thames.'

Waverley eyed them warily when they approached.

'Come on now, Rabbie,' Woods said gently. 'You've had your fun but you're causin' a disturbance of the peace. It's time to go home now.'

'No!' shrieked the madman. 'I'm Isaiah! Naked and barefoot, with buttocks uncovered.'

The wind picked up Waverley's high-pitched shriek, carrying his words to the ears of the gawping young beach-scavengers, who howled with laughter.

A tall, carrot-pated lad of about thirteen yelled: 'Are yer fishin' for tiddlers with yer lobcock for bait, mister?'

'You're a foolish saphead,' Woods said to Waverley. 'You've left a string of faintin' ladies up on the embankment. Now come along, quiet, like.'

'You get him, Constable Woods!' shouted the ginger-headed boy.

But Waverley had no intention of surrendering to the police constables. 'So shall the King of Assyria lead away the Egyptian captives and the Cushite exiles!' he yelled, turning to streak into the freezing river.

'Damn it!' Barnaby cursed. 'He's tryin' to kill himself!'

The shock of the cold water stopped Waverley within a few feet of the shoreline. He paused, thigh-high in the swirling water, and shouted to a flat-bottomed barge heaped high with coal: 'Loose the sackcloth from your waist and take off your sandals from your feet!'

The startled lighterman glanced over at the naked lunatic and nearly dropped his oars.

Waverley opened his mouth to shout again but lost his footing on the slimy mud and disappeared beneath the surface. Woods and Barnaby reached the water's edge as he surfaced, gasping like a fish for air.

'Can Waverley swim?' Constable Barnaby asked Woods.

'I don't know,' Woods replied. 'Can you swim, Barnaby?'

'Yes.'

'Well, in you go, son.'

Woods' instruction wiped the smile from the lad's handsome young face, but he only hesitated for a second before he unbuttoned his blue overcoat, threw it down on the muddy sand and pulled off his boots. As he entered the freezing river he swore and recoiled in shock.

'Now, now, lad,' Woods shouted. 'We'll have less of that language; there's ladies and nippers about.'

Waverley resisted Barnaby's first attempts to grasp his slippery limbs, lashing out and thrashing against the water, but he was no match for the strong and angry young officer, who, step by step, hauled him out of the river.

Barnaby was swearing like an infantryman when Woods reached his side.

'Tut, tut, what would your ma say if she heard you now, Constable?' Woods grabbed Waverley's flailing arms and clapped his handcuffs around the thin wrists.

'I'm sure my ma will have a few choice words to say when she sees the state of my uniform!' Barnaby pushed a lock of dripping hair out of his eyes and hugged himself for warmth. His wet shirtsleeves clung to his arms like a second skin.

Woods grinned. 'We'll borrow a pair of dry breeches from the Seamen's Hospital to get you home.'

'I'm frozen,' Barnaby complained. 'Why isn't that saphead feelin' the cold?'

The fight had finally left their prisoner. Waverley had dropped to his knees on the shingle and was swaying and moaning in a meditative trance. He didn't shiver or seem to notice the bleeding cuts on his filthy feet.

'God protects his prophets,' Woods said with a wink. 'So do you still think this is more fun than chasin' footpads on Blackheath, son?'

Barnaby scowled and his teeth chattered. 'I'd rather risk a tobyman's musket ball than go back in that flamin' river!'

Woods laughed. 'Get your boots on. I'll ask the old fellahs to get you some dry clothes.'

While Barnaby pulled on his boots over his wet trousers, Woods regarded their naked prisoner thoughtfully. 'What are we goin' to do with you, Rabbie?' he said.

'I'm Isaiah! Naked and barefoot, with buttocks uncovered.'

'Yes, yes, of course you are.'

Woods took off his own coat and hauled the manacled prisoner to his feet. He tied the arms around Waverley's waist, covering his nakedness. When the wind rose, it lifted the dangling arms at the back; it wasn't perfect, but it would do for the moment. The ragged urchins lost interest and returned to their beach-scavenging.

Barnaby scrambled back up to his feet. 'How shall we get him back to the asylum?'

This was a problem Woods hadn't considered. Normally, they would have dragged the prisoner behind their horses for the five-mile return trip to the city. 'We'll get a hackney carriage and tie my horse behind it. We'll take him back to Bow Street and let the asylum collect him from there.'

Barnaby leaned down and brushed the mud and sand off his trousers. 'How the hell did he escape from Bedlam anyway?'

Woods grinned. 'When the asylum reported him missing, they said he'd climbed inside the slurry in the night-dirt cart. It was ages before they noticed he'd gone.'

Barnaby grimaced. 'Urgh! Has the man no sense of smell?'

Woods pushed Waverley further up the beach. 'He'll not get back over those railings now he's cuffed. We'll take him back up the steps.'

The movement seemed to jolt Waverley out of his trance. He shivered, whimpered and stumbled along the shingle in his bare feet.

'I didn't know you couldn't swim, Constable Woods,' Barnaby said.

'Who said I couldn't swim?' Woods winked. 'Come on – let's get this jingle brains back to Bow Street before he catches his death.' He gave Waverley's scrawny frame a good shove before stopping in surprise as something caught his eye.

A battered and torn old boot lay half buried in the stones and weeds. Four blackened toe bones protruded at grotesque angles from a gaping hole at its end.

Frowning, Woods dropped to his haunches and cleared away the dried weeds and broken shells surrounding the boot. Two bleached-white bones poked jauntily out of the boot's ankle. Woods recognised the faint, sickly sweet smell of rotting flesh and his broad nose wrinkled in disgust. 'Gawd's teeth!'

'What the devil . . . ?' Barnaby crouched down beside him, his blue eyes wide with horror.

'It's a severed foot,' Woods said. 'A man's foot, judgin' by its size.'

A congealed mass of stinking flesh was just visible inside the top of the boot. Most of the bones had been picked clean by the river fish and other scavengers. It looked as though tiny teeth had nibbled away at the leather of the footwear in a desperate attempt to reach the rotting sinew and tissue within.

Barnaby grimaced and stood up hastily. 'How did it get here?'

'It's been washed up by the tide, I think.'

'Where's the rest of him?'

Woods stood up and glanced around the tranquil beach. Nothing.

'And where's it come from?' Barnaby shivered again. He needed dry clothes.

'You ask a lot of questions, son, and I don't always know the answers.' Woods reached down, thankful for his gloves, and lifted the boot and its grisly contents. The waterlogged flesh and bones made it surprisingly heavy.

'What are you going to do with it?'

Woods held the odorous limb out at arm's length and nodded to the promenade above. 'You go ahead and fetch the horses. I'll bring Waverley – and this thing. There's a rag in my saddlebag. I'll wrap the boot in it and take it back to Bow Street.'

'Why?'

'Because, son, although I don't know the answers to your questions, we both know a man who'd revel in a mystery like this.'

Barnaby grinned. 'Has Detective Lavender returned from Bristol?'

'Last night, I believe.'

The young man's eyes brightened and he smiled.

'He'll put his best foot forward to solve this riddle,' Woods said.

Barnaby groaned at the joke, then set off up the steps to the promenade.

Woods prodded Waverley in the back. 'Come on, Isaiah, son of Amoz; follow Constable Barnaby up those steps. It's time for you to return to your home in the hospital of Bethlehem.'

Chapter Two

Stephen Lavender walked along the alley behind Bow Street Magistrates' Court and Police Office and grimaced when he heard the shouts and crashing over the wall in the stable yard. He'd forgotten the building work was due to commence in his absence. A large horse-drawn cart full of rubble, mud and wet clay swung out of the yard and forced him back against the wall. He paused beneath the arched entrance to survey the chaos.

For years Bow Street had used the cellar of a local tavern as an extra cell for their prisoners. Now Magistrate Read had decided to extend the police premises. He'd acquired the lease of the property next door and commissioned builders to knock the two houses and yards into one. The dividing wall had been demolished and the cobbles stripped away. An army of mud-splattered, burly workmen were digging the foundations for the new cell blocks and courthouse.

Or rather, they were trying to dig them. The spring had been unseasonably wet and the ground was saturated. The old stables, morgue and crumbling cell blocks stood in craters of mud and brackish water. Wooden planks criss-crossed the yard over the waterlogged trenches. Sweating men with spades and pickaxes hacked away at the sodden earth and struggled to shovel the sloppy mud into wheelbarrows, their shoulder muscles bulging beneath their filthy jackets. The yard echoed with the dull thud and scrape of their tools.

Lavender sighed and wished he'd used the front entrance. It would be impossible to traverse this mess without ruining his gleaming boots.

'Oi, yous! Take yer eyes off me tewls!' A short, bald man with bulging blue eyes stomped across the mud towards Lavender. He gripped a smoking pipe between his bared teeth.

Lavender eyed him coldly. 'I can assure you, my good fellow, I have no intention of stealing your tools.'

'So what do yous want 'ere?' The man's voice was peppered with the nasal tone and distinctive rise and fall of the north-west, and his shirtsleeves were rolled back above his elbows, revealing a colourful array of tattoos on his forearms.

'I'm Detective Stephen Lavender, a Principal Officer with the Bow Street Police Office. I work here.'

The eyes of the fierce little man narrowed. He stretched out his neck and stared up into Lavender's face. 'I 'aven't seen yous before – and some light-fingered cove filched two of me spades and a barrer last week.'

Lavender felt strangely wrong-footed. The foreman's aggressive stance and attitude made him feel irrationally guilty. Three of the nearby workers paused to lean on their spades and watch. One of them, a straggly-haired fellow, looked nervous about the confrontation, but broad grins spread across the grimy faces of the other two. Both stockily built and covered in tattoos, they looked a right pair of rogues. A vivid scar ran down the face of the one with the widest grin.

'I've been away on police business these last two weeks.'

'So why not use the front door like a normal police fellah?' The pipe waggled erratically in the corner of the fellow's mouth, belching tobacco smoke up into Lavender's face.

For a moment, Lavender was speechless. Then the builder threw back his head and burst out laughing. He slapped Lavender playfully on the shoulder and the two grinning builders joined in the merriment. Even their slack-jawed companion managed a weak smile.

Lavender smiled; the foreman's laugh was infectious.

'I had yous vexed there for a moment, didn't I?'

'You did, indeed.'

The builder held out a filthy hand. 'I'm Macca: master stonemason – and the gaffer of this gang of cork-brains.' His right hand waved in the direction of the labourers, then pointed to the nearest group. 'That's Frank,' he said, indicating the scarred man, 'and 'is mate, Bonner. The dozy bugger beside them is Windy.'

'I'm pleased to meet you, Mr Macca – gentlemen.' Lavender nodded to the workmen. 'Now if you'll excuse me, Magistrate Read waits for me.'

Mindless of the damage to his boots, Lavender took the direct route to the rear door of the building. Behind him, the three workmen broke out into a ribald Scottish ditty popular at the music halls. They were surprisingly tuneful.

> *I wish, my dear Nelly, thou wert an oat cake,*
> *Then on thee like butter I'd spread,*
> *Or wert thou a floweret most sweet, for thy sake,*
> *Like a bee, would I suck till I'm dead . . .*

Their song carried into the hallway of Bow Street. Oswald Grey, the Chief Clerk, glanced up from his high desk and frowned. Lavender closed the door behind him: Grey didn't approve of bawdy songs.

The Chief Clerk's name was peculiarly apt. A tall, pallid, greying man of sixty with pale, humourless eyes and a preference for drab clothes, Grey had some responsibility for allocating workload, and the Bow Street officers did their best not to upset him.

'Good morning, Grey.' Lavender dropped a purse full of coins onto the high wooden desk. 'This is payment from the Duke of Gainsborough's estate.'

'Good afternoon, more likely,' snapped the clerk. 'You're late to work today, Lavender – and we're short of men.'

'Magistrate Read knows I didn't arrive back from Bristol until late last night; he isn't expecting me until noon.'

Grey opened the purse, poured out the money and counted it.

Lavender glanced around the empty hallway. Normally, the gloomy, wood-panelled passage heaved with the shackled dregs of London, waiting for their details to be recorded before they were locked in the cells. 'It's quiet in here today. Where is everyone?'

'It wasn't quiet earlier.' Grey pointed to a large sheaf of papers on the edge of his desk. 'There were two more burglaries reported this morning, an assault – and the Earl of Yarmouth sent his manservant to let us know he was robbed by highwaymen on the Edgware Road last night. We've had more victims today than felons.'

'Were none of the horse patrol out on the Edgware Road?'

'No; there's a lot of trouble from footpads up on Blackheath and the patrols tend to go there. North-west London was vulnerable last night. To be honest, Lavender, I'm pleased to see you back; we're short of men and there's been an increase in crime.'

'Where are the other Principal Officers?'

'Old Townsend is working for the Bank of England this week; the rest are out of town.'

'What? All of them?'

Grey nodded. 'Vickery and Adkins are expected back soon, but Magistrate Read already has new cases lined up for them in the provinces – and for you too, I shouldn't wonder.'

Lavender's heart sank. He'd barely been at home since Christmas. His wife, Magdalena, would be upset if he were to go away again so soon.

Grey jerked his quill and pointed it in the direction of the back yard. 'That's the problem, I think. The building work is expensive.'

Lavender glanced thoughtfully towards the stable yard. Bow Street received a stipend of six hundred pounds a year from Parliament to pay for the premises, horse patrols and services of the Principal Officers, but it was never enough. Fortunately, the Principal Officers had an excellent reputation for solving difficult crimes and Read supplemented Bow Street's income by hiring them out to provincial magistrates and wealthy landowners who needed help with baffling cases. This private detective work was a lucrative business; Lavender received a guinea a day in expenses every time he went out of town on a case.

'Has Magistrate Read finished his morning court session?' Grey nodded and Lavender strode off towards the staircase.

'Ask him to send you to the Earl of Yarmouth,' Grey shouted after him.

James Read sat behind his cluttered desk in his court robes, his wig discarded amongst the inkstands, broken quills and piles of paper. The only magistrate in London to refuse the mandatory knighthood that went with his position, Read's office was as unadorned as his wigless self. Dark, towering bookcases lined almost every wall, bulging with legal tomes and a dusty collection of rolled maps, giving the room a cheerless appearance along with the bare floorboards and tall drapeless windows overlooking the bustle of Covent Garden.

Gesturing for Lavender to sit on the hard-backed chair opposite his desk, Read said, 'Good afternoon, Stephen. Did you catch the Duke's arsonist?'

'I did, sir. It wasn't a difficult case. The Duke's steward already had his suspicions about the identity of the culprit and wanted an objective opinion about the evidence that had come to light.'

Read nodded and laid down his quill. 'Well done, Lavender. Did the steward pay our invoice?'

'Yes, I've deposited the money with Grey downstairs.'

A visible wave of relief passed over Read's features. 'Good.'

Lavender smiled. 'Are the renovations costly, sir?'

'Yes. We need every penny we can get. This job becomes more and more expensive by the day.'

'It's always the way.' Lavender nodded sympathetically. 'You begin one project and the job expands into several others.'

'Apparently, the clay is also heavier than the foreman, Macca, expected and it's taking longer to dig out the foundations. What with this – and the persistent rain – the work is already behind schedule.'

'Is the man's name really Macca?' Lavender asked.

Read sighed and rolled up the architect's plans. 'I don't know. Macca must be an abbreviation for something Scottish or Irish? None of his builders seem to have proper names either. They're from Liverpool,' he added, as if this explained the anomaly.

Lavender smiled. 'I'd worked that out from his accent.'

'You've met him?'

'Yes, he accused me of stealing a wheelbarrow.'

Read laughed. 'The fellow has a way of making you feel guilty. He virtually accused me of being responsible for the atrocious weather.'

'I've heard of the terrible unemployment in Liverpool. Is this why these builders are here?'

The smile fell away from Read's face and he sighed. 'Liverpool has been gripped with economic misery since the abolition of the slave trade.' He opened a drawer and put the plans away. 'Macca and his crew came to London to find work, and I applaud them for it.'

The corners of Lavender's mouth twitched cynically. 'And I suppose they're cheaper to hire than our native London builders?'

'Well, yes – but that's not the point, is it, Lavender? We must play our part in supporting those less fortunate than ourselves.' Read became animated as he warmed to his theme. 'There's an economic crisis that threatens to engulf us all. Our naval blockade on France – and their retaliatory blockade on us – has slowed world trade to a trickle as neutral ships are searched and their cargos impounded. The Americans are the worst hit and are threatening war against us. Meanwhile, there are millions of pounds' worth of imports and exports tied up in warehouses in Manchester and Leeds. Spencer Perceval leads the most unpopular British government for years.'

Lavender nodded. 'I'd heard there'd been an upsurge in Luddite activity in the Midlands, and the Irish are furious about the lack of progress in the emancipation of the Catholics.'

'Ah yes, speaking of the Irish' – Read pulled out a sheet of paper from one of the stacks on his desk – 'I have your next assignment here. The Home Department in Dublin need help. Two of their operatives have been murdered, probably by Catholic rebels.'

'Ireland!' Lavender's heart sank; he desperately wanted to spend some time at home in London.

'Yes, Stephen. The *Shona Adare* leaves Rotherhithe docks for Dublin next Monday evening. Book yourself a passage. They intend to pay us well to solve this crime – and you know more about Catholics than the rest of us.'

Lavender ignored Read's last comment. Like most of the English, his employer was prejudiced against the Catholics and hadn't forgiven Lavender for marrying Magdalena. Lavender's main concern right now was to delay his departure. 'Surely there are more pressing matters for the Bow Street officers in London?' he suggested. 'Grey's concerned about the highway robbery of the Earl of Yarmouth.'

'Oh yes – you can deal with that today.'

'Today?'

'Yes. I'm sure you'll have the case wound up by the time you set sail. The Earl will be pleased I've sent along one of my most experienced and famous detectives.'

'And if the investigation should prove lengthy?'

'It won't.'

'Can I have Ned Woods to help me?'

'I'm afraid not. I can't spare him from the horse patrol at the moment.'

There was a sudden sharp smell of pipe tobacco. 'Yous fellahs 'ave a right nerve.'

Lavender turned around. Puce with anger, Macca stood in the open doorway of the office, puffing away furiously on his pipe.

Read frowned and gave the builder the hard, unblinking stare he usually reserved for prisoners in the dock. 'Is something wrong, Mr Macca?'

'Something wrong?' A vein protruded and throbbed in Macca's neck. 'Yer damn right there's somethin' wrong in this 'ere place!'

'What?'

'We've found yer dustmen, that's what!'

'Dustmen?'

'Stiffs!'

'Stiffs? Lavender, what on earth is he talking about?'

'I don't know. I think you'd better show us the problem, Mr Macca.'

Macca spun on his heel and headed back down the staircase. 'Come 'ed with yous!'

The two men rose to follow him. Read threw Lavender a baffled glance. 'How did he get into the room without us hearing him?' Lavender shrugged.

Macca led them out into the cold back yard. The labourers stood solemnly around the trench where Frank, Bonner and Windy had been digging. The silent crowd parted as Macca led Read and Lavender to the edge of the hole. Frank and Bonner looked grim; Windy looked more terrified than ever.

At their feet, on the rim of the trench, lay three human skulls. Their gaping eye sockets stared forlornly back across the muddy hole in the ground at the horrified magistrate and his officer.

'Good grief!' Read was aghast. 'What is this?'

A large pile of grey, tangled, skeletal remains lay half buried in the rubble at the bottom of the trench. The passage of centuries had left the bones entwined in a grisly embrace amongst broken bricks and pale clumps of mortar. Thigh bones, clavicles and more skulls were jumbled together along with the jagged arch of a broken ribcage and the flaring curve of an ear-shaped pelvis.

For a second, Lavender was stunned – then he cleared his throat and suppressed his smile.

'Oh dear, Magistrate Read. It looks like Mr Macca and his men have discovered where we hide the bodies.'

Chapter Three

Magdalena Lavender and her good friend Lady Caroline Clare climbed down from the hired carriage in the shadow of the creamy neoclassical arches of Somerset House on the Strand. While Lady Caroline paid the driver, Magdalena shook the creases out of her fur-trimmed, black velvet cloak, wrinkled her nose and tried to ignore the overpowering stench of the river. She pushed a rogue curl back inside her stylish bonnet as she glanced up at the colonnaded upper storeys of the magnificent building.

When Lady Caroline had proposed this mystery outing, Magdalena suspected it would be to the Exhibition Room of the Royal Academy of Arts in Somerset House. As a respected and successful portrait artist, Lady Caroline was a frequent visitor to the Royal Academy.

'This way, my dear.'

To Magdalena's surprise, Lady Caroline took her arm and steered her across the Strand through a gap in the rumbling traffic towards the opposite side of the road. This wasn't an easy manoeuvre for Lady Caroline, who walked with a silver-topped cane, and they were forced to sidestep several piles of horse dung.

Lady Caroline paused in front of a narrow shop-front dwarfed between a coffee house and the overhanging gabled windows of a tavern. A freshly painted sign hung over the door of the establishment, which read: 'The Gallery of Women Artists'.

Magdalena smiled in delight. A colourful selection of watercolours and oils was displayed in the window. Lady Caroline had brought her to an art gallery after all.

'Every one of them is painted by a woman,' Lady Caroline said with pride. 'This gallery is financed and run by my fellow artists, Lady Mary Gordon and Lady Susan Percy. It's organised by women for women. The Royal Academy has ignored the female artists of Britain for too long.'

Magdalena glanced back over her shoulder at the towering facade of Somerset House and laughed. 'So this is a protest against the London art establishment – right opposite the Royal Academy? How very modern!'

Lady Caroline shrugged. 'A number of curious visitors have already crossed over the street after visiting the Royal Academy. The artists benefit from the location. But both Lady Mary and Lady Susan have been snubbed by society because of this venture. Lady Jersey told Lady Mary it was a shocking and scandalous idea and refused an invitation to her ball.'

'They are brave women,' Magdalena said thoughtfully.

'And stubborn.' Lady Caroline smiled. 'When the gallery opened, one gentleman wrote a letter of complaint about the sauciness of blue-stockinged artists to the editor of *The Times* and they printed it alongside a satirical cartoon of both Lady Percy and Lady Gordon.'

'Have they regretted their decision?'

Lady Caroline's auburn ringlets wobbled as she shook her head and smiled. 'No. The quality of the artwork on display speaks for itself, and even the bad publicity has been beneficial. Come – let's go inside.'

A bell jangled above their heads when they entered the low doorway, narrowly missing the peacock feathers in Lady Caroline's pearl-studded silk turban. The gallery was long, cramped and poorly lit compared to the magnificent Exhibition Room across the road with its high ceiling and glazed atrium. But despite the poor light from the oil lamps, the interior had a cosy and informal atmosphere.

Groups of curious visitors talked in hushed tones in front of the paintings. Several of them nodded politely and greeted Lady Caroline by name as she led Magdalena to the back of the gallery. However, one pair of richly dressed, stout, middle-aged women turned their backs when they approached. Magdalena heard them whispering about her friend and her cheeks burned. Lady Caroline either didn't hear or didn't care about the slight. The younger daughter of the impoverished Earl of Kirkleven, she'd first scandalised the high society of London when she'd eloped with Victor Meyer Rothschild, a member of the wealthy Jewish banking family. After Victor's death, she'd married again, this time to a minor baronet, and lived quietly in the country until he too died. Her second husband had left her penniless and she was forced to earn an income from her painting. This, plus her unconventional lifestyle and penchant for younger men, added to the notoriety surrounding Caroline Clare.

Portraits, landscapes and cameos covered every inch of the walls. Magdalena walked leisurely down the gallery, marvelling at the talent of the artists, before stopping abruptly in front of an oil painting of a beautiful waterfall tumbling out of a cave into a pool. An ancient chapel dedicated to the Virgin Mary was built in the cave; she recognised the location and gasped. 'The Holy Cave of Covadonga!' she exclaimed in surprise. The signature in the corner of the painting was indistinguishable, though a 'Sold' sign sat next to it.

'Do you like my painting, my dear?' Lady Caroline asked.

'You're the artist?'

Lady Caroline nodded. 'As you know, I've always considered your part of Spain to be one of the most striking with its spectacular landscapes. It has wonderful light.'

'It's beautiful,' Magdalena said softly. 'I love the wisps of low-lying mist around the milky pool and the opaque appearance of the water.'

'I painted it from a sketch of the cave and chapel I made twenty years ago when I visited the region with Victor. I'm so glad you like it.'

Magdalena was enthralled by the landscape. She and Stephen already owned one of Lady Caroline's paintings, a watercolour of the Cantabrian Mountains, which she had given them as a wedding present two years ago. It took pride of place in their dining room and Magdalena never passed it without a pang of homesickness. 'It's lovely. You're so talented, Lady Caroline – but I knew this already. You should paint more landscapes and fewer portraits.'

Lady Caroline gave a little laugh. 'Unfortunately, my dear, the commissions for portraits keep the wolves and the bailiffs from my door. However, I have received payment for this landscape and my new patroness has requested a companion piece.'

'How wonderful! Who is she?'

'Ah, you can meet her at my soirée tomorrow night. I trust you and Stephen will still be joining us?'

'Oh yes, he returned last night. We're looking forward to it.'

'Good. Is he well?'

'Oh yes. Tired – as usual – but in good health.' She sighed heavily.

Lady Caroline missed nothing. 'Is Detective Lavender's exhaustion a problem?'

Magdalena raised her hands in a gesture of helplessness but her words came out in a frustrated torrent. 'I've barely seen him this year, and when he's at home he's always so exhausted. Last night, he fell asleep straight after dinner.'

'Dear me, that makes conceiving a child rather difficult.'

'Lady Caroline!'

'Now don't look so shocked, my dear, I know it's your dearest wish.' She opened her reticule and pulled out a small card. 'I may have no children of my own, but I do know something about attracting the attention of exhausted men.'

Magdalena took the card, which advertised the establishment of Mrs Pearce, a maker of fine corsets and other items of ladies' lingerie.

'Mrs Pearce and her staff make exquisite corsets, petticoats and chemises, but she also provides a more risqué line of underwear and accessories especially designed to reignite the passion in tired husbands.' Magdalena's cheeks flushed, but Lady Caroline continued unabashed: 'You should pay her establishment on Regent Street a visit.'

Magdalena's fingers toyed with the card; then she placed it inside her reticule.

They spent a pleasant half-hour enjoying the artwork before they left. No sooner did they step outside into the busy street than a drunken man lunged at them. He fell towards Lady Caroline, who screamed and stumbled backwards against the brick wall of the shop. Her cane clattered to the ground. Instinctively, Magdalena reached out to catch her. The man lurched and began to run away with Lady Caroline's pearl-encrusted silk reticule in his hand.

'Stop, thief!' shrieked Lady Caroline. 'Oh, stop him, someone!'

'*Dios mío! El cerdo!* Stop him!' Magdalena desperately wanted to give chase but was struggling to hold up Lady Caroline.

Further down the street, a tall man of about thirty heard the women's cries and leapt out at the silk-snatcher. He wrestled him to the ground, but the thief spun around and aimed a blow at his head. The man dodged the blow but it dislodged his hat. The thief scrambled to his feet and scarpered.

Magdalena's view was suddenly obscured by a crowd of shocked pedestrians, who had moved forward to assist the two women. Gentle hands helped Lady Caroline back to her feet and Magdalena retrieved the cane from the ground. Lady Caroline quivered with shock and was close to tears; Magdalena shook with anger.

The crowd parted and the man who'd grappled with the silk-snatcher appeared, brushing the dirt off his coat with one hand. In the other hand, he held Lady Caroline's reticule. 'This is yours, I believe, ma'am?'

Lady Caroline almost fell on him with relief. 'Oh, thank you, sir! Thank you so much!'

'I'm sorry I didn't apprehend the cove, ma'am. Damned fellow slipped from my grasp and disappeared into the crowd.'

Their rescuer was a handsome man, Magdalena decided, if a little dusty from his roll on the pavement. Thick, fair hair flopped forward over his broad forehead. His eyes were an unusual and distinctive shade of green and his long lashes swept down onto the most prominent cheekbones she'd ever seen.

'Never mind, never mind,' Lady Caroline enthused. 'At least you've recovered my reticule. I cannot thank you enough for your assistance, sir.'

'My pleasure, ma'am.'

The crowd of concerned shoppers dispersed, leaving them alone with their rescuer.

'Are you hurt from your encounter with the ruffian?' Lady Caroline asked.

The man gave a pleasant laugh and shook his head. 'I've taken worse tumbles. I trust you're not injured?'

'No, no. Only a little shaken.' Lady Caroline opened the reticule. 'Please let me reward you for your help.'

He laughed again. 'Heavens no, ma'am. Money is the last thing I need these days. It's reward enough for me to see the light return to your eyes.' To the women's surprise, he reached out, took Lady Caroline's gloved hand in his own and raised it to his lips. 'If you're not hurt, I shall bid you good day and be on my way.'

Flustered, Lady Caroline pulled back her hand. 'Well, at least let me know the name of my saviour!'

'Captain Leon, ma'am. James Leon. Lately from Manchester and formerly of His Majesty's merchant navy. I've just arrived in London.'

'I'm Lady Caroline Clare – and this is my friend, Mrs Lavender.'

Captain Leon's laughing green eyes turned to Magdalena. 'I'm delighted to meet you, ma'am.' His attention switched back to Lady Caroline almost immediately. 'Perhaps I should escort you home? You may be more shaken than you suppose by your ordeal.'

'That's kind of you, Captain Leon,' Lady Caroline said, 'but unnecessary. Thanks to you, there is no harm done, and Mrs Lavender and I are both resilient in times of distress.' Magdalena smiled at her friend's use of understatement; this habit of the English amused her. She imagined that Captain Leon's unusual eyes would widen with surprise if he learned how she'd shot her way out of Spain and, a year later, helped her husband and Ned Woods overcome a gang of highwaymen.

'However, can I prevail upon you to hail us a cab, Captain Leon?' Lady Caroline continued. 'I would be most grateful.'

'Certainly, ma'am.' He stepped out into the road to flag down a hackney carriage.

'What a charming young man! And how heroic!' Lady Caroline whispered.

The cab pulled up and Captain Leon reached up to open the door of the vehicle. He offered his hand to help Magdalena climb inside, but Lady Caroline lingered on the pavement. 'You said you've recently arrived in town, Captain Leon. Do you have many acquaintances here, in London?'

'Not yet,' Leon replied. 'To be honest, your ladyship, I only arrived this week. I came into my inheritance last month and thought to treat myself to a spell in the capital. Although I never thought it would be quite as eventful and momentous as this!'

'Yes, unfortunately crime is rife in this city – despite the dedication of the Bow Street officers. Please tell me, do you appreciate the arts and the theatre, Captain?'

'I do, ma'am. I plan to expose myself to all manner of culture during my stay. In fact, I'm on my way to Drury Lane Theatre to purchase a ticket for the performance tonight.'

Lady Caroline clapped her hands in delight. 'How wonderful! Although I would always recommend the Sans Pareil Theatre over Drury Lane – my stepdaughter, Miss April Divine, is in the cast.'

'Miss April Divine? By Jove! I've heard great things of the lady. I'll alter my course and steer windward towards the Sans Pareil.'

'Of course, I'm prejudiced in her favour . . .'

'Naturally, ma'am. I would expect nothing less.'

'In this case, Captain Leon, you must attend my soirée tomorrow night in Lincoln's Inn Fields. Many of my fellow artists and my friends and acquaintances from the Sans Pareil Theatre, including my stepdaughter, will be present. I insist you join us.'

'You paint, ma'am?'

'Yes, some of my work is featured here.' She made an elegant gesture with her hand towards the gallery behind them. 'If you won't take any monetary reward for saving my reticule, you must at least let me introduce you to a few people here in London.' She pulled out a visiting card from her purse and gave it to him.

'It'll be my pleasure, ma'am.'

'Then I bid you good day, sir.'

Captain Leon handed Lady Caroline into the cab and glanced up at Magdalena, his eyes still full of warmth. 'Will Mrs Lavender also be present at this soirée?'

'Yes, she will. Please come at seven, Captain Leon.' Lady Caroline sank back into her seat in a ruffle of green velvet and peacock feathers. 'I look forward to seeing you there – please don't disappoint me.'

The smile flashed across Captain Leon's handsome face once more before he closed the cab door. 'It's my mission in life never to disappoint a lady, ma'am.'

'Oh, such a charming young man!' Lady Caroline's cheeks flushed. 'He has a fair countenance, don't you think?'

Magdalena smiled. 'Yes, he has pretty eyes.'

Lady Caroline smoothed the curls below her turban. 'This young man clearly intends to better himself with his new-found windfall. I do hope he attends my soirée, I would so like to get better acquainted with him.' The cab jolted forward and picked up speed.

'I'm not sure Duddles would approve,' Magdalena teased. Henry Duddles had been Lady Caroline's consort and lover for several years.

Lady Caroline waved a dismissive hand, shook her head and paused thoughtfully for a moment. 'Alas, poor Duddles may not be in my life for much longer to care what I do.'

Magdalena frowned. 'Why?'

Lady Caroline sighed. 'His uncle, Baron Lannister, wants Henry to return to the family estate. He demands that Henry marry a suitable young woman and produce a son and heir.'

'No!'

'Oh yes, he has threatened to stop his allowance unless the poor boy does his duty, and already has a suitable match in mind, I believe: the daughter of a neighbouring aristocrat.'

'Oh, Caroline – I'm so sorry. Stephen and I have . . . well, we've got used to Duddles over the last few years. We like him. You must be devastated.' Although awkward and foppish, Henry Duddles was a sweet young man and the thought of Lady Caroline without him by her side distressed Magdalena. 'Why don't you marry him? You are the daughter of an earl; surely Baron Lannister can't object to that?'

Pain flitted across Lady Caroline's features; then she sighed. 'It's all about begetting an heir to the Lannister fortune, Magdalena. I never bore a child for either of my first two husbands. I don't think I'm considered a suitable match. Then there's the age difference between Henry and myself, of course . . .'

Magdalena grimaced inwardly at her own lack of sensitivity, but Lady Caroline shrugged. 'Henry and I knew this day would come sooner or later. Loveless, political marriages are the fate of the aristocracy, are they not? You must understand; you told me your first marriage in Spain was arranged by your father – as was my second marriage to Baron Clare.'

'Yes,' Magdalena said, 'but I wasn't in love with someone else at the time. It's horrible to think of you and Duddles wrenched apart like this. You're so natural together.'

Lady Caroline gave another nonchalant and helpless gesture with her hands. 'Never mind, my dear, it's the nature of things and I'm sure I won't be alone for long.' She smiled happily. 'Not while there are young men like Captain Leon sailing upon the seven seas. My, what a gallant and intriguing gentleman!'

Chapter Four

A deep growl of horror emanated from the throats of the shocked men standing in the stable yard at Bow Street Police Office.

Macca spluttered at Lavender's casual comment about hiding the bodies. His pipe fell out of his mouth but he managed to catch it before it joined the remains in the trench. 'What? Yous kills yer prisoners?'

Lavender winked. 'Only the ones who won't confess.'

The scar-faced labourer called Frank suddenly burst out laughing. 'I can see yer a wag,' he said.

'This is no time for jesting, Detective!' Magistrate Read's voice was shrill. His muddied court robes flapped irritably in the wind. 'Where have these skeletons come from?'

Lavender smiled. 'It's the old plague pit, sir. Don't you remember? Bow Street is built over the site of a medieval plague pit.'

If Lavender expected the workmen to be comforted by the fact these weren't the remains of Bow Street's murdered prisoners, he was mistaken. They looked even more aghast.

'The old plague pit?' Read frowned, then heaved a huge sigh of relief and straightened his tense shoulders. 'Of course! Well done, Lavender.' He turned back to the foreman. 'There you go, Mr Macca, there's always a simple explanation for everything. I'm sure you have old plague pits in Liverpool, don't you?'

It was the builder's turn to be wrong-footed. For a moment, Macca seemed lost for words; then he shrugged. 'I can't say as I knows about that. But what the devil do yous want me to do with these dustmen?'

Read pointed to the far wall of the compound. 'Stack the bones against the wall for now. Lavender, do you think the glue factory would purchase them?'

Another audible gasp of horror went around the crowd and several of the workmen crossed themselves.

'We can't send 'uman bones to the glue factories!' Macca exclaimed indignantly. 'These poor souls deserve a church burial.'

'Burial?' Read snapped. 'What a ridiculous notion! That costs far too much money.'

'May I make a suggestion?' Lavender said. 'I think Sir Richard Allison would be interested in this find.' He turned to Macca. 'Sir Richard is a surgeon at Guy's Hospital and he would treat these remains with respect.'

This wasn't strictly true. Sir Richard revelled in the mysteries of dead bodies; he kept a gruesome collection of human remains at Guy's Hospital for the Incurables and used them for teaching and dissection purposes. But Macca wasn't to know this.

'It'll 'old up the job,' Macca said. 'And it'll add to the cost.'

'It might not hold up your work,' Lavender said. 'Well, no longer than a church burial would.'

'This extra werk will cost yous.'

'I'm sure it will,' Read snapped.

Macca grunted. 'I suppose that'll have to do.' He gestured towards his workmen. 'Come on now, yer slackers. Back to werk – get these remains over by that damned wall.'

'Good, that's settled. Come on, Lavender – back to work for us too—' Read's jaw dropped and his eyes widened in shock.

Lavender followed his stare to the arched entrance of the stable yard.

Constable Barnaby was leading two patrol horses into the yard. He wore a ridiculous pair of shabby blue flannel trousers that barely reached the top of his riding boots and exposed a section of his hairy and well-muscled young calves. Ned Woods and a lank-haired, manacled prisoner followed. Woods was in his red waistcoat and shirtsleeves; his coat was tied tightly around the waist of their prisoner by its sleeves.

Macca and his men burst out laughing at the sight of Barnaby, but their laughter turned to jeers and whistles when they saw Woods' prisoner. The wild-eyed man was bare from the waist up, his stick-thin white legs with mud-blackened and bloodied feet protruding from beneath Woods' coat.

'I thought you went to catch those footpads up on Blackheath, Constable?' said the exasperated magistrate. 'Please God, don't tell me they committed their robberies stark naked?'

'This ain't a footpad,' Woods replied calmly. 'We came upon this strange fish cavortin' in the river at Greenwich. Constable Barnaby dragged him out of the Thames and soaked his trousers. We thought it best to bring the fellah back here – he's Rabbie Waverley, an escaped Bedlamite.'

Suddenly, Waverley threw back his head and cried out in a thick Scottish accent: 'My servant Isaiah has walked naked and barefoot for three years!'

Woods yanked on the chain and jolted the man to silence. 'Enough of that.'

'Did you drag him all the way back from Greenwich dressed like that?' There was a note of desperation in the magistrate's voice.

'Gawd's teeth! No! I bundled him into a hired carriage. You owe me for the fare. Oh, and I brought something for Detective Lavender too.' Woods handed Waverley's chains to Barnaby and pulled an object wrapped in a rag out from his saddlebag. 'I found this washed up on the beach. It's a bit of a mystery, like, and I thought Detective Lavender would like to see it, knowin' how he likes his mysteries.'

He unwrapped the rag and revealed the severed foot in its boot. Read, Macca and the workmen recoiled from the sight and the smell of the festering remains.

Woods caught sight of the pile of human remains in the bottom of the trench. 'Oh.' His face fell with disappointment. 'I see you already have some old bones of your own.'

Lavender grinned. 'Yes, but there's no mystery here, Ned. The workmen have dug up part of the old plague pit.'

'For God's sake, Constable Woods!' Read snapped. 'What on earth do you expect Detective Lavender to do with this thing?'

'Find the rest of him?' Woods suggested hopefully.

Read's face contorted with anger. 'Lavender. Woods. Get inside – now! No – not you, Barnaby. You take the lunatic to the cells and change your trousers – you look like a clown from the Vauxhall Gardens.'

Woods caught Lavender's eye as they fell into step behind Read and entered the building. Lavender winked at him, and Woods grinned back. 'Is the magistrate havin' a bad day?' he whispered.

Read stopped in the privacy of the quiet hallway and turned to face his officers. His cheeks were still red with fury. 'Right, firstly, Woods, throw that – that thing – back in the river where it came from. Don't look so shocked. A ship's surgeon has obviously carried out an amputation and tossed the unwanted limb overboard. There's no mystery to it and we don't need to bother ourselves with it. Then retrieve your coat, return to Blackheath with Barnaby, and catch those footpads.'

'Yes, sir.'

'Lavender? I want you to go to Lord Yarmouth's immediately. On no account are you to start looking for body parts on Greenwich Beach. Do I make myself clear?'

'Yes, sir.'

For a moment, Read's eyes flicked suspiciously between the impassive faces of his two officers, then he grunted and set off back up to his office. He stopped almost immediately and turned back, frowning.

'Lavender, when those workmen made the sign of the cross back there in the yard . . . you don't suppose, do you, that they're Catholics?'

Lavender kept his own face expressionless. 'Mmm . . . a crew of workmen from Liverpool? Probably all of Scottish or Irish descent? I suppose it's possible.'

'Humph!' Read scowled and continued up the stairs.

'What was that about?' Woods asked.

Lavender grinned. 'I'll explain later. Tell me more about this severed foot. I'm intrigued.'

Woods' broad face beamed with joy and he quickly related the story of how he had found the boot and its grisly contents on the shoreline at Greenwich.

Lavender unwrapped the severed foot and examined it at length. 'I'll give this mystery some thought while I travel to Lord Yarmouth's,' he said. 'In the meantime, put it in the morgue. Sir Richard Allison will be here soon to examine the skeletal remains in the yard. I'll ask him for his thoughts on our mysterious foot too.'

Woods smiled, delighted.

'On your way to Blackheath,' Lavender continued quietly, 'stop by Greenwich Beach and see if there are any more bones lying around. Have a good look – but don't tell Magistrate Read about your detour.'

The grin widened across Woods' broad face. 'It's good to have you back, sir.'

Chapter Five

The crime in this city is a disgrace!' Betsy Woods exclaimed angrily. 'You could have been hurt!'

Magdalena and Betsy were drinking tea by the fire in the former's drawing room. Despite the weak afternoon sunlight falling softly through the tall windows overlooking the central garden in Westcastle Square, a small fire was still necessary to ward off the chill. Betsy's youngest daughter, three-year-old Tabitha, played with her doll at the other side of the room.

Betsy's glance flitted nervously between the child and Magdalena's lovely collection of porcelain figurines and vases. Magdalena knew Betsy would prefer to take her tea in the kitchen, away from so many fragile objects. But the housekeeper, Mrs Hobart, and her maid, Teresa, were there and Magdalena wanted to talk to Betsy alone.

She replaced her china cup in her saucer. 'I don't think we were ever in great danger – and besides, Captain Leon came to our rescue quickly. However, there was a moment when I wished I still carried my pistol.'

Betsy humphed at that; she didn't approve of women, especially ladies like Magdalena, secreting pistols in their petticoats. But Betsy was English and had never had to flee from a war-torn country.

'It's still a shockin' state of affairs – to be robbed in broad day-light in a respectable street.' The mass of grey curls peeping out from beneath Betsy's white cap wobbled with indignation when she spoke. 'You should tell Stephen and get him to make Magistrate Read recall the Principal Officers from the provinces. They need to send out a search party to track down that silk-snatcher. Thank goodness Captain Leon were passin'!'

Magdalena lowered her head to hide her smile at the thought of Bow Street's finest officers racing around London to avenge this harmless affront. 'Oh, I suspect the villain has crawled back into the gutter of the Seven Dials by now. He'll need to lick his wounds; Captain Leon gave him a shock, I think. But what did you mean, "recall the Principal Officers"?'

Betsy put down her own cup and leaned forward, conspiratorially. 'Accordin' to Ned, they're all out of town on commissions; there's only the horse patrol left to police the city. He says it's on account of the building work at Bow Street. The only way Magistrate Read can afford it is to send the Principal Officers out of town on these lucrative cases in the provinces.'

Magdalena's high forehead creased into a frown. 'I didn't think the situation was so bad. Stephen only returned late last night and he said very little. He fell asleep by the fire once he'd eaten his supper.'

Betsy nodded. 'He must be exhausted, poor man. Ned says Magistrate Read is workin' the officers like dogs.'

Magdalena sighed. 'Stephen has barely been home since Christmas. He did not see Sebastián at Easter when he came home from boarding school. Sebastián was disappointed and quite lost without him.'

Betsy nodded. 'Stephen is a good stepfather; he's always been very good with our four rascals – especially the boys.'

Magdalena's face lit up. 'Yes, Sebastián adores him. Stephen becomes – how do you say it? – like a boy himself when he is with Sebastián or your sons.'

'Boyish?' suggested Betsy.

'Yes, he's boyish.'

'You and Sebastián are the best thing that ever happened to Stephen,' Betsy declared firmly. 'When his first love, poor Vivienne, died, we all thought he'd lost his chance of family life – and I think he thought it too. He buried himself in those books of his.'

Magdalena's heart warmed with this unsolicited praise, but when her eyes turned back to little Tabitha a wave of sadness washed over her. The child had tired of her doll and was now watching the light glinting through the crystal brandy decanter and glasses on the elegant rosewood console table beneath one of the windows. 'I'd hoped . . .' she whispered. 'I'd hoped to have given Stephen a child of his own by now.'

'Oh, there's plenty of time for that,' Betsy said lightly. 'Tabby, come here my dear and leave Aunt Magdalena's pretty glasses alone.'

'She's fine, Betsy. I think she likes the light.' But Tabitha turned and ran across the room into her mother's arms with a little squeal of delight. Betsy scooped up her daughter and pulled her onto her lap. Tabitha nestled her head into her mother's ample bosom and stuck her thumb in her mouth.

Magdalena watched mother and child with an aching heart. 'I'm thirty-one now, Betsy,' she said. 'Stephen and I have been married for two years – and there's still no sign of a child.'

'It doesn't help if your husband is never at home.'

'No,' Magdalena agreed, 'but I'm concerned there may be something wrong with me.'

Betsy frowned. 'How can that be? You've got Sebastián.'

'Yes, but I was married to Antonio for eight years. I had Sebastián in the first year of our marriage, and there were no more children after that.'

'Huh! From what you've told me, your first husband were another one who were never at home, leavin' you alone in the countryside while he waltzed around the Spanish court and went swannin' off to war.'

Magdalena smiled. Betsy was an outspoken but good-hearted friend. She always cheered her up. 'When Stephen is at home he's always so tired. All he wants to do is read or sleep. Do you have this problem with Ned?'

Shock passed over Betsy's face. 'Ned has never read a book in his life.'

The two women sat silently for a moment, then Betsy said: 'Did you know that Ned and I lost three babies before I had Eddie?'

'No.'

'Well, we did. It broke our hearts when they died. We thought we'd never have a healthy child. Then, whoosh! Not only was Eddie born, all lusty and bawlin', but a year later he was followed by Dan. I went from no babies to two healthy infants within twelve months – and I were about your age when they were born.'

'And then you had your little girls . . . ?'

'That's right.' Betsy paused, then inched forward with the child on her lap to the edge of the blue velvet sofa and leaned towards Magdalena. Her kind face was etched with concern but full of hope. 'I think you're worryin' yourself too much, Magdalena,' she said. 'When it's the right time, a baby will come along for you and Stephen. It's always struck me that Mother Nature is a Contrary Mary, anyway; she'll give you a houseful of nippers when you're least expectin' it.'

Magdalena felt reassured. 'I hope you're right.'

'I know I am, my dear.' Betsy sat back, her job done. 'Before you know it, your baby will be thirteen and threatenin' to run away to sea, like my Eddie.'

When Lavender arrived at the Earl of Yarmouth's elegant home in Berkeley Square to investigate the highway robbery, he was shown into his lordship's library to meet the Earl and his secretary. Towering bookcases, containing hundreds of leather-bound volumes, gave the spacious room a dark and sombre atmosphere.

Middle-aged and overweight, Yarmouth had a florid complexion and was sprawled in a leather chair behind a Chippendale desk. A smart, dark-suited man sat in a chair beside him. The desk between the two men and Lavender gleamed with inlaid brass ornaments and the glossy veneer of rosewood.

Yarmouth looked grim and was sombrely attired in a chestnut-brown coat, buff-coloured breeches and a cream silk waistcoat that stretched over his expansive stomach. Only the diamond pin securing his cravat and the exquisite tailoring of his coat hinted at his considerable wealth. He waved a hand at the chair opposite his desk, inviting Lavender to sit. 'I'm glad you're here, Detective. This is a bad business, a bad business. I told my man to fetch a good officer from Bow Street. I hoped for either you or Vickery. This is my secretary, Clayton.'

Lavender bowed to the Earl and nodded politely to Clayton. 'I'm pleased to be of assistance, your lordship, and I'm sorry to hear about the robbery. What happened, exactly?'

'We were robbed, that's what. Held up on the Edgware Road at Kilburn by a gang of masked scoundrels. They appeared out of nowhere from the fog. My coachman never even had time to raise his blunderbuss before he had the cold steel of a pistol barrel sticking in his neck.'

'Was anyone hurt?'

Yarmouth shook his head. 'No, no. I suppose we should be grateful for that. Lady Yarmouth is upset – she's resting today in her chamber. They took her jewellery and her reticule. She's particularly distressed at the loss of her favourite necklace and earrings: an unusual set made of rose-coloured gold and set with pink seed pearls and pink-hued diamonds.'

'I'm not surprised Lady Yarmouth is upset,' Lavender said gently. 'It's an audacious crime.'

'To be honest with you, Lavender, I was rather shaken myself.'

'What else was stolen?'

'My pocket watch and ring, and a box of money. Clayton has drawn up a list in case any of our valuables come to light; it should help you identify them. My wife's jewellery has great sentimental value for her and considerable worth.'

Lavender took the list with a grateful nod to the silent secretary and scanned the description of the stolen items. This should save time. It was routine procedure to visit the capital's known fences and pawnbrokers after such a high-profile robbery.

'Would it be possible to advertise a reward for the safe return of these items?' he asked.

'Do you think it'll do any good?' Yarmouth asked.

'There's a slim chance some of the articles may be recovered,' Lavender admitted, 'but it's a very slim chance. Your wife's necklace and earrings sound unusual, but experienced criminals break up such distinctive pieces of jewellery, extract the stones and melt down the gold.'

Yarmouth nodded. 'I see.'

'However, inexperienced and foolish thieves sometimes try to sell or pawn their haul. The offer of a reward may help.'

Yarmouth gave a short, cynical laugh. 'So whether or not my wife regains her precious jewels depends on the proficiency of those coves?'

'I'm afraid so, your lordship. And unless the money stolen was in traceable notes, I'm afraid there's no hope we'll recover your stolen cash; coins are untraceable.'

Yarmouth sighed and nodded again.

'How much money was stolen, exactly?'

'About two hundred guineas – mostly in coins.'

Lavender started. 'I'm sorry to hear that, your lordship. That's a considerable sum. Do you normally travel with such a large amount of coins in the carriage?'

'No.' Yarmouth shook his head. 'I had some expenses at our estate in St Albans. We went to Lady Alderney's party at her home in Brook Street last night, but we left early to travel to St Albans. It's a trip we've done many times. It's just devilish bad luck that on this occasion we were robbed.'

'Yes,' Lavender replied, thoughtfully. 'Can you describe the toby-men – sorry, the highwaymen? Did they have any distinguishing features?'

Yarmouth shook his head. 'It was a dark night. They wore masks, black hats and black cloaks. I never saw any of their damned faces.'

'What about their horses? Was there anything unusual about them?'

'Not that I noticed – but like I said, Lavender, I was rather shaken and it all happened so fast.'

'Their voices? How did they sound?'

Yarmouth thought for a moment, a frown creased along his fleshy forehead. 'To be honest, they didn't say much. Only one of them spoke; he sounded educated – he had a sickening laugh. The bugger was obviously enjoying himself, but he spoke politely enough when he asked for the box of coins.'

Lavender grimaced inwardly at this information. Another gentleman highway robber was the last thing they needed in London. They inspired the romantic imagination of the ballad sheet writers. It was impossible to have a quiet tankard of ale in a Covent Garden tavern these days without some drunk singing the praises of James MacLaine.

'Where did you hide the money – I mean, I assume the money was hidden . . . ?'

'It was.' Yarmouth paused and frowned. 'Now you mention it, Lavender, that's a bit strange – by Jove, it is.'

'What's strange, my lord?'

'Well, when he'd stripped us of our valuables, the cove just said: "Now for the rest. Where's the cash?" It was almost as though he expected us to have a box full of money.'

'Was it visible?'

'No, it was damned dark out there and I had the box beneath my legs under the seat.'

Lavender paused, his mind racing. He chose his next words carefully. 'Do you think it's possible someone in your household worked in league with the highwaymen? Could they have been forewarned about your trip to St Albans?'

'By Jove! I hope not!' Yarmouth's horrified face turned purple with anger. 'Most of our servants have been with us for years. I'd flay the hide off anyone who betrayed us!'

'Yes, yes,' Lavender said hastily. 'Unfortunately, this happens sometimes and it's a line of inquiry I need to follow up, no matter how unpleasant the thought.'

Yarmouth grunted and remained silent.

His secretary leaned forward across the desk. 'I'll arrange for you to speak to the coachmen, Lavender – and any other member of staff who might have known about the box of money in the coach. And I'll notify the news-sheets about a fifty-pound reward for information pertaining to the robbery and the safe return of the stolen items.'

'Thank you.'

Lavender spent the next few hours interviewing the Earl's coachmen and other servants. The coachmen's account of the robbery matched the one he'd received from Yarmouth, and they seemed genuinely distressed.

The servants were wary of the Bow Street officer. He didn't take their protestations of innocence at face value, but none struck Lavender as particularly suspicious and most of them seemed fiercely loyal to the Earl and Countess. His lordship was a stern man but fair, he learned, and her ladyship was a benevolent mistress and a great patron of the arts. Both were good Christians and contributed generously to charitable causes.

Lavender left Berkeley Square and visited two pawnbrokers and a jewellers' shop on the way back to Bow Street. He found no trace of the missing jewellery but made sure he told the scowling shop owners about the Earl's reward. Trying to find the missing jewellery singlehandedly in a city the size of London would be like looking for a needle in the proverbial haystack. The reward was his best hope of bringing forward information about the robbery. He also decided to ask Oswald Grey to send some members of the horse patrol up to Kilburn to see if the coves had left any clues on the roadside and to question the residents of the scattered hamlets lining the road.

His thoughts turned back to Woods. He wondered if Ned had returned yet and how he had fared in his search for the rest of the mysterious skeleton.

If he hurried, he might still catch Sir Richard Allison. The thought quickened his step. Chasing highwaymen and tracking down stolen goods were routine parts of his job, but nothing fired his imagination more than an unusual mystery. He was keen to find out more about the severed foot washed up on Greenwich Beach.

Chapter Six

The Romney Road was virtually empty of traffic and it didn't take Woods and Barnaby long to canter back to Greenwich. When the magnificent twin domes of the Royal Hospital for Seamen came into sight, the two officers reined in their sweating horses to let them walk for a while and cool down in the breeze. The sky was overcast and threatened rain. They rode side by side, past scattered thatched cottages, a blacksmith's and a dilapidated tavern whose ancient timber frame sagged and leaned.

Barnaby was unusually quiet.

'Are you feelin' unwell, son?' Woods asked.

For a second Barnaby hesitated, then his words poured out in a torrent. 'Do you think Bow Street Police Office is 'aunted?'

'Haunted? By whom?'

'By the souls of them poor wretches buried in the yard?'

Woods laughed. 'What? The plague victims?'

'It's not funny, sir. I 'eard them builders talkin' about it by the stables when we left. They reckon the place must be cursed and crawlin' with the spirits of those dustmen. They were threatenin' to put down their tools and walk away from their job. They said Bow Street were grim and eerie.'

Woods' mouth twitched with amusement. 'All police offices are grim. They're supposed to be. That's how we frighten the coves. Did they know you were listenin' to their talk?'

'No.'

'If they did, I think it might be a bit of banter to unsettle you, son. It strikes me they would enjoy a good jape. Some of them have a wicked twinkle in their eyes.'

'They were serious; sullen and grumblin',' Barnaby insisted. 'They said they'd 'eard the rattlin' of bones while they'd been at work.'

'Ah, that'll be old Detective Townsend; they'll have heard him walk past.'

Barnaby grinned at the joke. 'So you don't think there's anythin' to fret about?'

'No more than there were yesterday, before they uncovered those old bones.'

This wasn't good news about the mutinous builders, Woods realised. The building work was troublesome enough for the magistrate and the officers without dissent amongst the workforce. 'There's no such thing as ghosts,' he said, trying to sound confident. 'The only thing hauntin' Bow Street is a bad-tempered magistrate and his overworked officers. Labourers tend to be a superstitious lot, especially those from the north. They've some weird folklores and traditions up there.'

Barnaby sat straighter in his saddle and glanced across expectantly. 'Like what?'

'They reckon there's wild dogs roamin' the moors, howlin' at the moon, and witches who come out at night to steal children to eat them.' Barnaby grimaced. Woods lowered his voice for effect. 'In the murky depths of northern bogs live creatures called grindylows who'll grab hold of you with their long fingers and drag you down to your death.'

Barnaby shuddered. 'I'll make sure to avoid them moors and bogs when I'm in the north.'

'Plannin' a trip, are you?'

'I'll go in a few years, when I'm a Principal Officer like Lavender and Vickery.'

Woods smiled. He liked Barnaby and had no doubt the lad would realise his ambition; the young constable was keen, sharp-eyed and enthusiastic about his job. Woods wished his own son, Eddie, had half as much enthusiasm and ambition.

'There's another thing, sir,' Barnaby said. 'Them northern builders workin' at the police office – what do we know about them?'

Woods' bushy grey eyebrows rose on his broad forehead. 'They're builders, son – from Liverpool. What else is there to know?'

Barnaby leaned in his saddle towards Woods. 'I've 'eard from one of my acquaintances – an informer in St Giles – that there's a new gang of criminals abroad in London now, a gang from the north.'

The frown on Woods' forehead deepened. 'Who are they?'

''E didn't know but 'e said our local villains weren't 'appy about their arrival.'

'Aye, they won't be.' This was a grim thought. The Bow Street officers had enough to do without policing gang warfare in the rookery of St Giles as well.

'You don't suppose it's our builders, do you?'

Woods shook his head. 'I doubt our builders are the coves he means, son. How long have you had an informant in St Giles?'

Barnaby bristled with pride. 'A while,' he said. 'I've got several now. I slip them a coin now and then.'

'You'll soon be like old Detective Townsend, with his notebook full of villains' names.'

Barnaby's eyes brightened at the thought.

Woods smiled, pulled on the reins and turned off the road into the central square of the Royal Hospital. 'Come on, son. Let's get back on the beach and find Detective Lavender some more bones.'

◆　◆　◆

They tied the horses to the railings on the promenade and slithered down the shingle to the spot where they'd uncovered the severed foot. The tide had turned and the black river was reclaiming the beach. The light was poorer now.

'We'll have to work fast,' Woods said. 'Best if we split up. You follow the river and I'll head upstream. Don't forget, son – the rest of the skeleton may be buried in the mud.'

Barnaby nodded and the two men parted.

Low-lying mist still hovered silently over the marshes of the Isle of Dogs on the opposite bank. Woods tried to avoid looking in that direction but, as if on cue, the distant, anguished howl of a dog drifted across on the breeze. The hairs stood up on the back of his neck.

'Gawd's teeth!' he muttered. 'Pull yourself together, man!'

He saw plenty of old bones amongst the stones, river-rounded bricks and lumps of coal littering the beach. But they were burnt animal bones, distinguished by the cut-marks of butchery. Some would have come from the glue factories upstream, but he'd heard that most of the old bones on Greenwich Beach had been thrown out of the palace kitchen during the reign of Old King Henry. For hundreds of years, the King's discarded lamb cutlets had floated on and off the beach with the ebb and flow of the tide. Now that was a fanciful thought, he decided. And a good one to distract himself from silly superstitions.

Apart from the old bones, his boots slithered and crunched over discarded oyster and nut shells, peach and plum stones and pottery shards. A rocky outcrop with half a dozen pools blocked his way. Using a long piece of driftwood, he poked around in the dark water and rotten weeds. But there was nothing there.

When he reached the curved edge of the rockfall, he sighed with frustration and disappointment. The estuary of Deptford Creek blocked his way. To his left a narrow sweep of beach ran beside the slow-moving river, the ivy-clad ruins of an old church rising amongst the reeds. At least he assumed it was a church: it had a jagged, tumbledown stone tower.

It was an isolated spot. Hidden around a bend of the meandering creek was the busy town of Deptford, with its docks and boatyards. Only a smudge of smoke on the horizon from the town's coal fires hinted at its presence. Tall ships and seagull-encircled fishing boats continued to glide seamlessly up and down the Thames behind him, but nothing sailed out of Deptford Creek to join them today.

Child-sized footprints pock-marked the dark sand beside the creek. In the distance, he saw the pack of barefoot young beach-scavengers who'd watched Barnaby drag Waverley out of the Thames. The tall lad with the distinctive red hair was amongst them. The youngsters dragged something out of the shallows. Woods narrowed his eyes and stared hard. Was it the dead body he sought? He chided himself: most nippers would run screaming in the opposite direction if they found a corpse in the Thames.

Then he remembered something. Earlier in the day, the tall red-haired boy had called him 'Constable Woods'. How did the lad know his name? Had they met before?

Woods grinned as the memory came to him. It was Nathanial Higgin. Of all the boys in London, he definitely wouldn't be afraid of a dead body. He'd fetched the Bow Street officers to that dead actress a few years ago. He decided to enlist the help of the children.

The children's prize turned out to be a section of rotten tree trunk and they were absorbed in some sort of game with the timber. They didn't see Woods coming until his shadow fell across the sand. They leapt up like startled rats and raced away, shrieking.

'Nathanial!' Woods yelled. 'Nathanial Higgin! Come back here, lad – or I'll tell your ma.'

The tall boy stopped in his tracks and turned around. The other grubby little urchins paused and watched Nathanial walk back to Woods.

'What d'you want?' The lad's freckled face scowled as he spoke.

'Good afternoon, Nathanial,' Woods replied cheerfully. 'I remember the help you gave us at Bow Street two years ago, when that gal were found at Raleigh Close.'

'What of it?'

Woods paused for a moment and wondered why cheerful young children like this lad and his Eddie turned into such surly brutes when they got older. 'Well, I'm hopin' you'll help me find another body.'

The boy's eyes widened but he said nothing.

'I found a severed foot back there on Greenwich Beach. It's nothin' more than a skeleton, but I need to find the rest of the poor fellow's bones.' The other urchins crept forward and listened curiously. They were a grimy bunch, dressed mostly in rags and aged between six and eleven, although it wasn't always easy to tell the age of a nipper when they had such undernourished bodies. Nathanial must be about the same age as Eddie. He was the best dressed and best fed of them all. He wondered why the lad was spending his time with such young children.

'A skeleton, you said?' Nathanial asked.

'Yes. It'll be somewhere around here. Will you look out for it and send me word at Bow Street if you find it?'

'What's in it fer us?'

'A three-penny bit?'

'Sixpence,' piped up a high-pitched female voice. 'There's six of us, yer see. It'll 'ave to be sixpence; a penny each.' The little girl wore ragged trousers and had short matted hair that looked like it had been hacked off with a kitchen knife. If it hadn't been for her voice and the tattered woollen shawl pinned over her filthy jacket, Woods would have taken her for a lad.

'Very well,' he said. 'Sixpence it shall be.' He turned back to Nathanial. 'How's your ma?' Jacquetta Higgin had been running a bakery in Covent Garden when he'd met her and her son.

'She married a darkie!' yelled one of the urchins.

Nathanial reddened and lunged towards the boy, but the smaller child was quick on his feet. Soon the two of them were splashing through the shallow water, hotly pursued by the rest of the shrieking gang.

Woods turned, trudged back along the beach and returned to his horse, where Barnaby was waiting.

'Anythin'?' Woods asked.

Barnaby shook his head. 'I went all the way along the beach but found nothin'.'

'Never mind.' Woods swung up into the saddle. 'Let's go and catch us some footpads.'

Chapter Seven

H is Highness is outside with the bones.' Oswald Grey scowled. 'He's got the men digging up half the yard.'

Lavender grinned, thanked the clerk and went out to join Sir Richard in the chilly stable yard.

Sir Richard Allison expected to be treated like royalty whenever he deigned to assist the officers at Bow Street, and his condescending arrogance made him unpopular. Even the genial Ned Woods disliked him. Lavender tried to remain professional in the surgeon's presence, but Allison also had a vigorous enthusiasm for carving up dead bodies, which Lavender couldn't help but find repulsive. A short, loud man with a brisk walk, jowly chin and bulbous nose, the surgeon was also vain and fashion-conscious. He wore his thick mop of curly grey hair brushed forward and piled up on top of his head in the latest Brutus style favoured by Beau Brummell.

Three young men from the hospital stood ankle-deep in the mud, lifting out the human remains and using a variety of small hand tools and brushes to clean off the sludge. Sir Richard stood beside the trench, supervising. The builders were at the far side of the yard, though there was no sign of Macca. The stack of tangled bones was alarming and gruesome in its size.

Allison pointed to something in the trench and barked out an instruction. His beige kid gloves matched the cut-away coat he wore over a brilliant green waistcoat. The gloves were spotless; obviously Allison had no intention of getting his hands dirty. He caught sight of Lavender across the yard and waved cheerfully. 'Lavender! Lavender, my man! How good to see you.'

Lavender grimaced at the appellation 'my man', but smiled politely and walked across to shake hands with the surgeon. 'How does your work progress?' he asked.

'Excellent, my dear fellow, excellent. These skeletons will be very useful for anatomy and osteology classes.'

'It'll be hard to reassemble them.'

'True, true – but that's what medical students are for. Although no doubt, many of the fools will place a female pelvis above a pair of male thigh bones. I shall enjoy correcting their errors.'

'How many bodies are down there, do you think?' Lavender asked.

'It's difficult to tell until we widen the trench further, but they seem to have been stacked up to four deep. We'll pull out as many as we can. It's better this way, of course – we don't have to hack through coffins with spades and pickaxes!'

One of the students suddenly raised a ribcage into the air. It was still attached to a section of its sternum and was entwined with another ribcage. The second set of bones dangled grotesquely in the breeze like a shattered birdcage.

Lavender glanced across at the surly crowd of superstitious builders. Fortunately they were too far away to hear Allison's words and tone. The surgeon's casual – almost flippant – attitude to the dead never ceased to amaze him.

'We'll discard some of them but I imagine we'll be able to sell several sets on to St Thomas' Hospital,' Sir Richard continued.

Lavender nodded but he barely heard the words. An unusual sight had distracted him. One of the builders, at the back of the crowd, appeared to have pulled a small sack over his head. A pair of eye holes had been cut out of the front of the material. Lavender blinked to clear his vision. Was it a trick of the fading light? The strange apparition disappeared.

He turned back to the ebullient surgeon. 'Can you help me with another matter, Sir Richard? We recovered the remains of a severed foot from the beach at Greenwich this morning. Would you examine it?'

'A severed foot? Are you sure it's severed? The hands and feet often detach themselves from a skeleton disintegrating in, or near, a watercourse and drift away.'

'Yes, I'm sure. It appears to have been cut off through the fibula and tibia, just above the ankle.'

Sir Richard grinned. 'Ah, there's no fooling an educated man like yourself, is there, Detective? I'm intrigued. Lead the way.'

Lavender lifted a lantern from its hook on the stable wall and led Sir Richard into the Bow Street morgue, a dark, airless room in a shed next to the cells. The smell alerted him to the location of the grisly package. He lifted it off the shelf where Woods had left it and laid it on the stone slab in the centre of the small room.

With brisk efficiency, Sir Richard removed his kid gloves and donned a bloodied apron kept for autopsies. He picked up a knife and expertly slit open the boot's sides. The remains fell apart and landed on the table with a thud. Lavender lit a candle and moved it closer. Sir Richard leaned over the foot, carefully fingering the two jutting bones of the ankle.

'Mm, so what is it you think you have here, Lavender?'

This was always Sir Richard's way. He would encourage the officers to state their theories, then take great delight in proving them wrong and showing off his superior medical knowledge.

'I suspect it's the right foot of a man,' Lavender replied, cautiously.

'You're correct, so far.'

'Magistrate Read thinks it's the amputated foot of a sailor which was tossed into the river – or the sea – after the ship's surgeon had removed it.'

'But you think this fellow was murdered?'

'I have no notion either way.'

'Yet something intrigues you about it, doesn't it?'

'Yes.'

Sir Richard stroked the protruding bones tenderly and grinned. 'Ah, Detective, your love of mystery must lead you along so many false paths. You said it was found on Greenwich Beach?'

'Yes.'

'Well, Magistrate Read is wrong on two counts with his suppositions,' Allison said with glee. 'Most of the detritus in the Thames eventually washes up on Greenwich Beach. That bend in the river catches nearly everything – but flotsam and jetsam from the sea doesn't usually reach this far inland. Mark my words, this foot went into the Thames, not the sea. And it was definitely not removed from the rest of the leg by a surgeon, so Read is wrong about that too.'

'It wasn't?'

'No. Surgeons use saws for amputations, which always leave what we call false starts, or hesitation marks on the bones when the blades skip across the surface. These striations left after an amputation are always square-shaped from the blade of the saw. Can you see anything of that nature on the bone here, Lavender?'

Reluctantly, Lavender leaned closer and resisted the urge to gag at the sickly-sweet smell of rotting flesh. 'I don't see any cuts or notches on the bone.'

'Exactly. This ankle was severed in one sweeping blow: possibly from a sword blade, or a scythe.'

'A scythe?' This was a new development. Much of the Thames embankment was still farmland; there were fields right up to the high-tide line.

'Yes, your victim may have been a bankside farmer or agricultural labourer who caused his own injury through the careless use of a scythe. While he lay bleeding to death on the shoreline, those who came to his aid probably forgot to retrieve the foot.'

'Would he have died from this injury?'

'Most certainly – unless the bleeding was stemmed immediately and the wound cauterised.'

'Can you tell me any more about him?'

Allison stepped back, poured water into a metal bowl, picked up the soap and washed his hands. 'Not without the rest of the skeleton, I can't. I suggest you hunt for it.'

'Constable Woods is scouring the banks of the Thames while we speak.'

'If the skull has become separated from the spine, it'll travel the furthest because it will float or roll along the river bed.'

'Thank you, you've been very helpful. A final question, if I may: how long do you think this man has been dead?'

Sir Richard narrowed his eyes and glanced back at the mouldering remains on the slab. He leaned forward and sniffed them. 'The presence of a small amount of flesh suggests less than two years. However, water-logged soil keeps bodies intact for longer. Decomposition is slower. Do you still think him murdered, Detective?'

'I didn't say I did; I don't know what happened to him at this point.'

Sir Richard stepped back and smiled. 'You've a naturally suspicious mind, Lavender. Very well, keep your cards close to your chest if you will, but I'd recommend you consider the possibility that this fellow has already been given a decent Christian burial and recent flooding in the churchyard may have washed his corpse out of its grave.'

'That's possible,' Lavender said cautiously.

'The weather has been atrocious this year,' Allison continued. 'The river is high and flooding has been common across London.'

'I can see this is a line of inquiry to explore. You've been very helpful, Sir Richard.'

The surgeon reached for his coat. 'Don't forget to tell Magistrate Read he was wrong with his theory that the limb had been amputated,' he called over his shoulder.

'I won't.' Lavender followed him outside, leaned back against the brick wall, closed his eyes and inhaled the familiar smells of horses and coal smoke, desperate to remove the stench of the foot from his nostrils. It was late afternoon and already growing dark.

When he opened his eyes, he saw the strange apparition that had haunted him before. One of the builders was digging at the far side of the yard with his back to him. The man definitely had a sack over his head. A few yards away, Frank and Bonner poked at the ground with their pickaxes. Lavender walked across to them. 'Who's that fellow with the sack?'

'It's our marra, Windy.'

'Why's he wearing a sack?'

'It's the plague, yer see,' Bonner said.

'I'm afraid I don't.'

''E thinks 'e may gerrit from these bony dustmen,' Frank explained.

Lavender bit back his laugh. 'Who put that ridiculous notion into his mind, I wonder?'

The lined, wind-burnt faces of the two workmen expressed injured innocence.

'Gawd's strewth! Windy, fer Christ's sake, yous saphead! Get that ruddy sack off yer noggin!' Macca was back. The short, bald foreman stomped angrily across the muddy cobbles towards Windy.

Lavender left them and went inside up to Read's office.

The magistrate looked tired and more strained than ever. He listened to Lavender's report about the Yarmouth robbery, nodded curtly, then reached across his desk for a pile of crumpled papers. 'I need you to deal with this case as well as the highway robbery.'

Lavender's heart sank at the thought of another case being added to his workload.

'The Home Department asked me a few weeks ago to set officers to watch this man, John Bellingham,' Read continued. 'Vickery spent some time trailing him before he left for Hampshire.'

Lavender frowned. 'Why? What has this Bellingham done?'

'He hasn't broken the law but he's a serious concern to some prominent people. The fellow has a lot of grievances against the government and our ambassador to Russia, Lord Granville Leveson-Gower, who is currently at home in London. Bellingham has badgered the government for compensation following some ill-treatment he endured in Russia – but to no avail. The man has pestered everyone in authority in London. I myself received this letter from him two weeks ago and, when you read some of the content, you'll see why I sought advice from the Home Department.'

Lavender took the crumpled letter and scanned it. Bellingham had written expansively about his dissatisfaction that his right to petition for compensation had been denied by government ministers. Lavender's eyes were drawn to a section underlined in red ink, presumably by another hand: '. . . *Should this reasonable request be finally denied, I shall then feel justified in executing justice myself . . .*'

It was a threat. 'Whom does he threaten?'

Read shrugged. 'We assume it's Leveson-Gower. Bellingham was imprisoned for several years in Archangel in Russia after a trade dispute. He claims the Ambassador ignored his pleas for assistance. In fact, on one occasion Bellingham escaped from prison and went to the embassy for assistance – but Leveson-Gower saw fit to return him to his captors.'

Lavender grimaced. 'No wonder the man has a grievance.'

Read rummaged amongst the unstable pile of documents on his desk and pulled out a small pamphlet and a thin file. Lavender recognised the cramped, neat handwriting of his fellow officer, John Vickery, on the paper.

'This is Vickery's report. Peruse it at your leisure.'

'What's the pamphlet?'

'Bellingham recorded his sorry saga in this pamphlet and printed it about a month ago. He gave one to every Member of Parliament in support of his petition for compensation.'

Lavender raised an eyebrow as he slipped the pamphlet into the file. 'Clearly the man is not short of funds. What line of work is he in?'

'That's part of the mystery. Bellingham is a bankrupt merchant and shipping insurance broker. However, he's been in London for the last four months pursuing his claim against the government and he seems to have plenty of money.'

'Where are Bellingham's lodgings and how shall I recognise him?'

'He resides at number nine, New Millman Street, between Lincoln's Inn and Gray's Inn Road. He's a tall fellow – Vickery has put a description in his report. Just keep an eye on him and the company he keeps. The man is clearly obsessed with these perceived injustices, but hopefully this threat is hollow and mere bluster.'

Lavender stood up, buttoned his coat and nodded. 'So you want me to deal with both cases at once: the highway robbery of Lord Yarmouth and the surveillance of Bellingham?'

'I'm sure an officer of your experience can manage, Stephen.' Read picked up his quill and bent his head over his papers. Lavender had been dismissed.

'I'll need assistance. Ned Woods . . . ?'

'I've already told you, he's busy with the horse patrol.'

Lavender bit back his frustration and left the office. Read was being unreasonable. He couldn't catch the highwaymen and trail John Bellingham at the same time. However, there was a consolation. This heavy workload would probably delay him and put off his trip to Dublin. Anything that kept him in London with Magdalena was welcome. The thought of the beautiful woman waiting at home quickened Lavender's step.

Chapter Eight

A silvery mist had descended over the sloping, dark-coloured scrubland of Blackheath by the time Woods and Barnaby arrived. It muted the brilliance of the vivid yellow gorse and the chattering of the natterjack toad. The birds sat silently amidst the dripping leaves of the trees, while invisible sheep called balefully to their lambs.

'How are we supposed to find anyone in a jerry this thick?' Barnaby asked in frustration.

'Patience, son. Don't forget, if we can't see them, they can't see us either. 'Tis perfect weather to go out upon the pad; those coves'll be around here somewhere.' They turned their horses off the gravel path onto the spongy moss to muffle the sound of their hooves.

Their quiet patience paid off. Within a few minutes they heard shouting and screaming from the other side of a copse. They urged their horses forward, circled the trees and reined in sharply beside two distraught women who clutched each other in terror. Their baskets lay upturned on the ground, the contents scattered upon the gorse.

'They robbed us!' screeched one of the women. 'Snatched our purses, they did, and – Meggie's ham!'

'Which way did they go?'

The women pointed south. Woods and Barnaby set off in pursuit. It didn't take them long to catch up with the footpads – or to identify them. Overconfident in the mist after their vicious robbery of a couple of helpless women, the idiots had sat down by the side of a pond to gnaw on Meggie's ham. The sight of the approaching officers and the silver glint of Woods' pistol made one of them choke on the meat. Neither made any attempt to escape from the mounted officers when Woods raised his weapon.

It was dark as well as foggy when Woods and Barnaby finally returned to Bow Street with their prisoners walking behind in chains. The fog cast Covent Garden into gloom and muffled the usual sounds from the river and the ceaseless rumble of cart-wheels over the cobbles. Night lanterns glimmered on the dripping walls of the tavern opposite the police office and a warm pool of light emanated from the interior when two drunks staggered down the steps onto the street.

Woods frowned as they entered the narrow alleyway at the rear of the building. Something shimmered pearly-white on top of the arched entrance to the stable yard. The mist cleared for a moment and he saw a row of three skulls backlit by guttering candles.

'Gawd's teeth!'

One of the skulls had the top of its head missing. A candle flickered inside the cranial cavity, giving an eerie yellow glow to the eye sockets and the gaps between its teeth.

The superstitious young Barnaby swore loudly.

'Easy, son, someone's been havin' a lark, that's all.'

Behind them, one of their prisoners whimpered and stopped. The chain between him and Woods' horse went taut but the steady pace of the beast yanked him forward again. Woods grinned and half turned his head to address them over his shoulder: 'You fellahs had better behave yourselves while you're here – or you'll have the same fate.' He turned and winked at the pale-faced Barnaby.

The stable yard was a hive of noisy activity. Bustling with officers, snorting horses and jangling harnesses, it reeked of wet horse and male body odour. The night horse patrol had arrived for work as the day shift slid wearily out of their saddles.

Woods carefully steered his horse alongside the edge of the cavernous hole and rode towards a group of laughing men. Someone had attempted to reconstruct a full skeleton with bones from the plague pit and had propped it up into a sitting position against the wall of the morgue. It was a crude attempt at anatomical reconstruction but gained a little realism from the old pipe shoved into the gaping hole where the mouth had once been. A jaunty hat flopped on the skeleton's pearly dome and a red horse-patrol waistcoat was draped over its angular shoulders and half-crushed ribcage. On the wall by its side some wag had chalked: *Constable Napoleon Bone-Apart*.

Woods burst out laughing and dismounted.

Barnaby slithered out of his own saddle, frowning, and landed beside him. 'This don't seem right.'

'It's humour, son. Macabre, yes. But still humour.'

The Chief Clerk, Oswald Grey, walked towards them. 'Good evening, Woods – Barnaby. Who've you got there?'

'They're the footpads from Blackheath.' Woods and Barnaby handed over the reins of their sweating horses to one of the ostlers.

Grey gave a visible sigh of relief. 'Well done, Woods – and you too, Barnaby. You've done well to catch those coves – it's one less job for the night patrol.'

Woods and Barnaby acknowledged the clerk's praise with a nod.

'Detective Lavender left a message for you, Woods,' Grey continued. 'He wants you and Barnaby to go up to Kilburn tomorrow to find out if the residents know anything about the highwaymen who robbed Lord and Lady Yarmouth.'

'Yes, sir.'

'He also wants you to join him in The Nag's Head tomorrow at one o'clock for a bite to eat.'

The talk of food reminded Woods of the great rumble in his belly. He handed over the chains of their prisoners to Barnaby. 'Get these two villains to the cells, will you, son? I've got an appointment with one of Betsy's meat and potato pies.'

Woods heard Betsy shouting as soon as he entered the front door of his home. He didn't wait to remove his coat but strode straight down the narrow hallway into the back kitchen.

Red with fury, Betsy was chasing their eldest son around the wooden kitchen table with her broom, trying to rain blows down on his head. Eddie was laughing and dodging the blows like an expert.

'You idle skelpie-limmer!' Betsy shrieked. 'You only came home because you smelt the food!'

The other three children had retreated to a safe distance. Dan leaned against the scullery door, grinning with his arms crossed, but eight-year-old Rachel looked frightened. In her arms, little Tabitha was crying.

'Heaven and hell!' Woods roared. 'Whatever's amiss?'

'Him! That's what!' Betsy made another lunge, which the boy neatly sidestepped. The broom swung wildly by Woods' head. He grasped the handle and pulled it out of Betsy's hands. She didn't give it up without a struggle. Woods placed a comforting hand on her shoulder, but she shook him off.

'The cocky rascal has been missin' all day and refused to fetch some water from the standpipe when he came back.'

'Oh, that's not good, son.' Woods shook his head sadly.

'And he's been cussing!'

'You must always respect and help your ma.'

An ugly scowl spread across Eddie's large round face. 'That's a job for one of the nippers; not a man's job – and all men cuss.'

'Not in my kitchen they don't!' Betsy yelled.

'It's a man's first job to pay heed to his ma,' Woods said. 'Always.'

Eddie's face contorted again and flushed at his father's criticism. 'She's a bleedin' scold!'

Woods growled with anger and Betsy shrieked again. 'See! See, Ned, how he treats me! Put him out! Put him out.'

'Aye, I will.' Woods moved fast. Eddie was tall and strong for his age, but years of grappling with London's rag-tag and scum had served Woods well. He grabbed his startled son by his shirt collar and frog-marched him up the hallway to the front door. Before the boy knew what had happened, Woods had wrenched the door open and heaved him out onto the cold step in the foggy street.

Breathing heavily with the exertion, father and son glared into each other's eyes. Woods tried to stare him out, but found it hard. Eddie looked too much like a younger version of his mother. Betsy's round brown eyes glared back at him from beneath a curly mop of brown hair.

What was wrong with the lad? Woods barely remembered his father and had been raised by his hard-working mother, whom he'd adored. Eddie's rudeness to Betsy was incomprehensible to him. 'Your ma says to put you out,' he said awkwardly.

'No. I'll put you out.'

To Woods' surprise, Eddie grabbed him by his coat lapels, yanked him out onto the doorstep and walked quickly back over the threshold into the house. Woods regained his senses just in time to stop Eddie slamming the door of his own house in his face. He didn't know whether to burst out laughing at the lad's audacity or to punch him on the nose.

'You've got this the wrong way round, son. Your ma said I'm to put *you* out.'

'No! I'm putting *you* out!' For several minutes, father and son grappled and tussled with each other on the doorstep. Each tried to inch back into the house and leave the other out in the cold. The ridiculousness of the situation eventually dawned on Woods. He stopped pushing

Eddie out and concentrated on holding the squirming lad firm. 'We've got to stop this, son. Let's talk.'

'Talk about what?'

Woods grabbed the handle and shut the door, leaving them both out on the step.

A neighbour suddenly loomed out of the shadows, treading his well-worn path towards the tavern. 'Evenin', Ned, takin' the air with yer lad, are you?'

Woods nodded and waited while the man's footsteps faded away down the street. 'We need to do this more often, son,' he said. 'Leave the women and the nippers inside and spend some time talkin' together like men.'

'We'd be more comfy in the tavern,' Eddie said hopefully.

Woods laughed. 'You're a cheeky rascal, no mistake. Now tell me what's amiss.'

'There's nothing amiss.'

'I don't believe you. You're upset about somethin' and your blamin' your mother. What's amiss?'

Eddie sighed and began to grumble about his mother. Woods listened patiently and didn't interrupt. The boy's accusations and comments about Betsy were unjust, but he let the lad unburden himself, knowing they'd get to the real reason for his unhappiness soon.

'It seems to me you've lost your way a little. You spend too much time in the house. Now you've parted company with that school and become a man, we need to find you a worthwhile occupation – a man's job.'

'I want to go to sea,' Eddie said. 'I want to see the world and sail to foreign lands – but Ma won't let me.'

He was right there. Betsy had been vocal in her refusal to entertain the idea of a seafaring career for Eddie, and he'd quietly agreed with her. He remembered the two old salts with their missing limbs and toothless grins he'd met in Greenwich that morning and shuddered. They'd saved up to pay for apprenticeships for both their sons, but Betsy refused to pay the fee and sign the papers for a position on a ship. 'It's a dangerous life out at sea,' he said. 'And you're too young. Let's get you settled with a land-based trade for now and discuss seafarin' another time.'

'I need to get away,' Eddie blurted out.

'Why, lad? Are you on the run from the constables?'

'You shouldn't even jest about such things!'

Woods eyes narrowed. 'Why?'

'Have you any notion of how many scraps I've had to fight because of you and your job with the horse patrol?'

Woods swallowed hard.

'Do you know how many times I've had to fight fer your honour, when others have called you foul names – or spat in the mud at the sound of your name?'

'No, son, I haven't. Tell me about it.'

And Eddie did. It was as if a wooden lock had breached down in the dry docks; a torrent of misery poured out of his son's mouth.

Woods' heart sank. He'd grown up in Southwark, just like his boys. Fighting with the other lads was part of the way of life. A good brawl now and then was a rite of passage for them all but, according to Eddie, he and Dan had been mercilessly picked out by the older lads for years – simply because of their father's job. Woods was saddened but he wasn't surprised. Law-keepers weren't popular in this crime-ridden city, and the Bow Street officers were the most distrusted of them all. No one had ever been charged with the crime but accusations of corruption against the officers were common.

'I guess you won't be joinin' me at Bow Street in the horse patrol, then,' he said quietly when Eddie had finished.

'No, I won't!'

Woods sighed and bit back his disappointment; he'd often dreamed of his son working beside him. 'Well, the horse patrol is not the only job in the world – but runnin' away from your problems is never the right answer. It would break your ma's heart for a start and leave Dan alone in these brawls. If things are as bad as you say they are, then Dan will need you by his side for another year or so yet.'

Eddie shuffled uncomfortably on the step, clutching his arms to ward off the cold. 'I hadn't thought about Dan bein' left alone.'

Woods let him think about that for a moment longer.

'I also feel bad about what I said about Ma.'

Woods ruffled his hair. 'I knew you would sooner or later. You're a good lad despite your temper. Anyhow, I hear the Barclay and Perkins brewery is takin' on apprentice dockhands. Shall we pay them a visit in the mornin' before I go out to work and speak to the foreman? That would get you off the streets of Southwark for a while.'

'Their wharf's only half a mile away.'

'Yes, I know – but it's a start and you'll make new friends there amongst the other dockhands. A lad of your size and strength should fit in well.'

Eddie nodded. His teeth were chattering now.

Woods reached for the door handle. 'We'll go first thing – and next time we have one of these chats we'll go up to the tavern. It's too ruddy cold out here.'

'If I get the apprenticeship, will you take me to the tavern for a tankard of ale anyway?'

Woods laughed. 'Yes, I will. And when you get your first wages you can buy your old da a glass of brandy in return.'

Eddie grinned, then stopped in the hallway, his face anxious. 'What about Ma?' he whispered.

'Leave your ma to me, son – just apologise for your rudeness.'

The other children were sitting at the table in the kitchen. Betsy was dishing out portions of pie, her eyes red-rimmed with crying. Woods smelt burning, but the pastry was its usual glorious golden-brown.

Woods and Eddie slid into their seats, and the two little girls rushed to their father for a cuddle. Woods pulled them up onto his lap, squeezed their warm bodies and smiled at their chatter. After a few minutes, he kissed the girls on the top of their heads and sent them back to their seats.

'I put Eddie out, Betsy,' Woods said, 'but he came back in again.'

Dan snorted but shut up promptly when his father raised a stern, greying eyebrow in his direction. Betsy's lips tightened. She sniffed, said nothing and concentrated on the gravy.

'So Eddie and I have been talkin'.'

'You were gone a long time, Da,' said Rachel.

'Yes, treacle, it were a long talk. First of all, Eddie wishes to say something to his ma.'

'I'm sorry, Ma.'

Betsy said nothing. She took off her apron and sat down at the table.

'I'm sorry, Ma,' Eddie repeated.

Betsy still said nothing, so Woods hurriedly continued: 'We're going to the Barclay and Perkins brewery tomorrow. We'll see if we can get Eddie an apprenticeship there. With any luck, we'll have another breadwinner in the house soon – and he won't be under your feet so much, Betsy.'

'Ooh, Eddie, will you buy me a new ribbon when you're workin'?' Rachel asked.

Eddie smiled. 'Of course I will.' He turned to his mother. 'And I'll buy you somethin' nice too, Ma.'

Betsy nodded stiffly, sniffed again and said: 'I let the water boil dry in the carrots. They're burnt.'

'Never mind,' Woods said. 'Serve them up anyway and we'll build castles with them after we've eaten.' He reached into his pocket and pulled out a halfpenny. 'I'll give this halfpenny to whoever makes the best model of the Tower of London.'

Rachel squealed with delight, and the boys laughed.

A smile flickered at the edges of Betsy's lips. 'You're addle-pated, Ned Woods. They shouldn't play with their food.'

'Oh, you must play too, Ma!' Rachel said. 'Don't you want to win the ha'penny?'

'Of course she does!' Woods announced. 'Now serve up those burnt carrots, Mrs Woods, and let's play our game.'

There was trouble a few moments later when Dan stole a spoonful of diced, blackened carrot from Rachel's plate, but the rest of the meal was spent in laughter and contentment.

Normally Woods felt a huge surge of satisfaction while he watched his family around the table, but tonight his pleasure was tainted with sadness.

They grow up too fast.

Eddie was already kicking at the traces. How long did they have before Dan would want to follow his brother and leave home? Before he knew it, young men would be knocking at the door wanting to marry his daughters. An involuntary groan rose in Woods' throat at this thought and he choked on a piece of meat. Betsy heard his stifled cough and glanced at him curiously.

Eddie leaned over Dan's plate and frowned at his carrot structure. 'What's that supposed to be?'

'It's a man o' war,' Dan replied proudly.

Eddie prodded it with his knife and the charred carrots slithered down into a pool of gravy. 'Not now, it ain't. I've just scuttled it.'

'Oi!'

Everyone laughed.

Woods banished his sadness, sat back and tried to imprint this image of his family on his mind's eye.

Hold onto this moment, fellah, he told himself sternly. *Never forget you're the luckiest man in the world.*

Chapter Nine

Across town, in a warm dining room in Marylebone, Magdalena was admiring the profile of her husband's handsome face and his strong jaw line, darkened with a day's growth of stubble. Tonight, he wore his dark blue coat and a matching silk waistcoat. His spotless cravat gleamed like cream in the soft candlelight. When he turned to look at her, warmth and love shone in his dark brown eyes and a smile lit up his face. He looked far younger than his thirty-three years when he smiled. She loved to see him smile.

He told her about his new cases and she listened in fascination to his account of his day, although she did grimace and ban discussion of the mysterious severed foot.

Before she'd met Stephen, she had never paid much attention to men who worked for a living: it wasn't the social class she was born into. But Stephen had changed her. Sometimes, when she thought back to her life with her first husband, Antonio, whose conversation revolved around the latest gossip and intrigue of the Spanish court, she was embarrassed. She'd been brought up to dismiss men who worked as not worthy of her attention. But there was something noble about Stephen's tireless pursuit of justice.

She shook her head sadly when she heard of the suffering of Lord and Lady Yarmouth. 'Perhaps it wasn't a servant who told the highwaymen about Lord Yarmouth's journey,' she suggested. 'Maybe you need to widen your inquiries to their wider circle of friends and acquaintances.'

Stephen reached for the Madeira and refilled their glasses. 'Lord and Lady Yarmouth move in the upper echelons of society. Are you suggesting, my darling, that someone amongst *le bon ton* has turned highwayman?'

'Hah!' she exclaimed. 'Aristocratic society is full of villains; half of them are bushed and spend their time evading their creditors.'

'Bushed? Where on earth did you learn that expression for bankruptcy?'

'From Teresa. Isn't it a suitable word for a lady?'

Stephen laughed. 'Not really. How did Teresa come by such a word?'

Magdalena sighed. 'I believe it was from her young coachman, Alfie Tummins.'

'Is he still hanging around the house like a moon-struck calf?' Alfie and Teresa had met around the time of their wedding, and the young man had become an ardent admirer of Magdalena's maid.

'Yes, he's as besotted as ever. Teresa's English has improved considerably since he began to woo her; however, I have noticed one or two strange expressions in her vocabulary.'

Lavender smiled. Alfie Tummins' cab was frequently left abandoned in Westcastle Square while its driver loitered around their basement servants' entrance, hoping for a few words with Teresa. 'How does Teresa feel about Tummins? Does she care for him as much as he cares for her?'

Magdalena patted her mouth with her napkin and smiled. 'I don't think I'll lose my maid to matrimony just yet. She finds Alfie amusing, I think. To be honest, I suspect Teresa is still a little sweet on you.'

Stephen laughed. 'Tell me about your day. How was your "mystery outing" with Lady Caroline?'

But before Magdalena could reply, Teresa appeared to clear away their plates and bring them their dessert of hot-house peaches and syllabub. Her frizzy hair was pulled back into a neat bun at the nape of her neck. Her dark eyes narrowed slightly as she concentrated on pouring their coffee.

Stephen smiled. 'Good evening, Teresa. Are you well?'

She nodded her head vigorously. '*Sí, sí*, Señor the Detective. I'm a fubsey wench.'

'Really?' The corners of Stephen's mouth twitched. 'Who told you that you were a fubsey wench, Teresa?'

The coffee pot paused in mid-flow above his cup. 'Mr Alfie Tummins tells me this. It's good, yes?'

'Yes, I suppose so. It means you're a plump but healthy young woman.'

'Plump!' The coffee pot banged down on the table. Teresa's hands flew onto her hips and her freckled face flushed in anger. 'He call me fat?'

'You're not plump, Teresa.' Magdalena's shoulders shook with laughter.

'I think it's meant to be a term of endearment,' Stephen suggested.

Teresa turned on her heel and marched towards the door. 'You pour own coffee,' she shouted over her shoulder. 'I need speak with Mr Alfie Tummins about how he talk of me!' She slammed the door behind her.

They burst out laughing. Magdalena shook her head. She knew she was overindulgent with Teresa, but her little maid had shared in her terrifying flight from Spain and had been her only companion during her first difficult year in London.

Still smiling, Stephen reached into his coat pocket, pulled out his penknife and began to cut the fruit, an old habit he refused to abandon.

He held out a piece towards her and placed it between her lips. She enjoyed the intimacy of the act as he fed the slices to her, piece by piece. His warm, brown eyes met hers over the fruit and they exchanged a silent promise about the night ahead. But it was too early to retire yet.

She told him about the gallery and Lady Caroline's beautiful painting of the Holy Cave of Covadonga. When she told him about the attempted robbery of Lady Caroline's reticule, his spoon clattered down into his dish.

'Good God – you could have been hurt!'

'We were unharmed.' She smiled at his solicitude. 'Thanks to the assistance of Captain Leon, Lady Caroline safely retrieved her reticule and her pride.'

'Thank goodness he was passing. Lady Caroline is indebted to him – as are we. I would like to shake his hand.'

'She's invited him to her soirée tomorrow night. You can meet him there.' Her eyes glanced across to the gilt-edged invitation propped up against the mirror over the fireplace. 'It starts at seven o'clock – you'll remember, won't you, Stephen? And make every effort to come home at a reasonable hour?'

'I will, *querida*,' he promised. 'I wouldn't dare be late for one of Caroline Clare's soirées.'

She smiled at the Spanish term of endearment.

Teresa reappeared to clear away the dirty crockery. She still looked cross. A cab rumbled down the street outside and Magdalena wondered if it signified the hasty departure of Teresa's scorned lover.

'Please leave the coffee, Teresa.' Stephen stifled a yawn. 'I need something to keep me awake tonight.' He rose and pulled back Magdalena's chair. 'I'm afraid I have some reading to do, Magdalena. Magistrate Read has given me a file of papers about a man called John Bellingham. Shall I join you in the drawing room or take myself off to my study?'

She stood up gracefully and – despite her disappointment – gave him her most brilliant smile. 'Join me, please. I have seen so little of you recently. I need to remind myself what my husband looks like – even if his head is bent over a pamphlet.'

Lavender fetched himself an oil lamp, placed it on the small rosewood table next to his fireside chair and sank wearily back into the cushions. Magdalena picked up her embroidery basket and lowered herself elegantly across the dark blue velvet sofa on the opposite side of the hearth rug. She threaded her needle with silk thread, inclined her head and turned her attention to her work. Only the crackle of the fire in the grate and the rumble of carriage wheels in the square outside disturbed the peace and quiet in the room.

Lavender watched Magdalena sewing and admired the deftness of her elegant fingers. The candlelight enhanced the gleam of the ebony ringlets framing the flawless skin of her face. With her head lowered, it seemed as if her long eyelashes were resting on her cheeks. His eyes drifted downwards to the soft movement of her breasts beneath her muslin gown as they rose and fell with the rhythm of her breathing. It still astounded him that he had been able to woo and win such a beautiful, educated and cultured woman for his wife. He longed for a lifetime of Magdalena by his side at this fireplace.

But even now, after such a charming evening, self-doubt crept into his mind.

Was Magdalena really contented, he wondered? Something frustrated her, he knew. He'd seen a dark shadow settle on her brow several times since his return. Did she still hanker after her old life in Spain, the luxury and wealth she had known? He knew their frequent separations, caused by his job, were lonely for her, especially when Sebastián was away at school. Wellington's advance across the Iberian Peninsula was relentless. Would the role of a police officer's wife still be enough when it was safe for her – and Sebastián – to return to their estates in Asturias?

Already this year, there were reports that Wellington had opened up a northern invasion corridor from Portugal into Spain. They were only a few miles away from Asturias. The besieged French army were too busy defending their supply lines from Spanish guerrilla attacks to mount an effective offensive against the British. It was only a matter of time before Madrid fell to Wellington's forces. Then King Joseph Bonaparte would flee back to his brother in Paris with his tail between his legs and his usurper's crown clattering in the road behind him. Victory in Spain would be a blessing for Britain, Lavender realised – but what would it mean for his wife and stepson?

Stifling another yawn, Lavender opened up the file of papers on his lap. Thankfully, the correspondence between Read and the Home Department regarding John Bellingham and his threat to the Ambassador, Lord Leveson-Gower, was short and succinct. It told him nothing that Read hadn't already mentioned. He picked up a single sheet of paper containing the report of his fellow officer, John Vickery, who'd trailed Bellingham the previous week. Vickery hadn't written much: Bellingham spent a lot of time in the public gallery at the House of Commons and liked to drink in a tavern called The Porcupine, where he would moan to anyone who'd listen to his sorry story or buy him a brandy.

Finally, Lavender picked up Bellingham's pamphlet and immersed himself in the bankrupt merchant's account of his grievance against the government. The bitterness of the tone struck Lavender immediately.

Originally from St Neots, Bellingham moved to Liverpool ten years ago. In 1804 he made an ill-fated business trip to northern Russia. He chartered a ship from Hull to Archangel to fetch back a cargo of timber and iron but soon fell into disagreement with his Russian trading partners, who accused him of welching on his debts. He was arrested and imprisoned in the city gaol.

Lavender grimaced at the thought of anyone spending time in a prison so close to the Arctic Circle. The man must have been desperate for his freedom. But Bellingham stubbornly insisted on his innocence, refused to compromise with the Russians and became obsessed with the injustice meted out to him.

The British Embassy refused to help him because it was a matter of civil debt, and he started to blame the government. At one point

Bellingham escaped from prison, raced into the British Embassy and became violent and abusive when the Ambassador ordered his return to gaol.

He wasn't released until December 1809, and returned to England financially ruined and a bitter and broken man.

Now, two years later, Bellingham was back in London and still in the grip of his obsession. His pamphlet made it plain he felt he deserved compensation from the British government.

The warmth of the fire made Lavender sleepy. His eyes drooped and he sank lower into the cushions of his chair. He fell asleep.

The drawing room door banged shut and he jerked awake. Magdalena had left the room – hurriedly, it seemed. Her needlework basket and its contents lay strewn across the carpet.

Weary beyond belief, and worried that he'd offended his wife, Lavender dampened down the fire, extinguished the lamp and candles, and cautiously followed Magdalena up the stairs.

Chapter Ten

Thursday 7th May, 1812
Marylebone, London

Dawn was breaking over the smoking chimneys of the capital when Lavender left home. He pulled up the collar of his coat against the cold and damp of the fog. Heavily laden farm carts lumbered towards the city's markets, but few pedestrians were out on the streets. Warm pools of diffused light spilled out from ground-floor windows and helped him carefully pick his way around the puddles and piles of refuse.

Vickery's report had mentioned that Bellingham wasn't an early riser; the man rarely left New Millman Street before ten o'clock. This gave Lavender a few hours to track down some of his contacts and make further enquiries about Lord Yarmouth's stolen jewellery.

Something Magdalena had said last night had been bothering him. Lord Yarmouth was an intelligent and sensible man; if Yarmouth's instincts told him the highwaymen already knew about the vast quantity of money he carried in the coach that night, then this was probably the case. Yesterday's interrogation of the household servants had proved fruitless. What if the thieves' informant did lurk in the wider circle of the Yarmouths' acquaintances? Magdalena was right: refined manners and diamond cravat pins were no indication of a man's moral integrity; he'd come across many fraudsters and unscrupulous villains amongst the British elite during his time as a Principal Officer. He needed to talk to Lord Yarmouth and his wife about this as soon as possible.

His mind drifted back to Magdalena. He'd left her sleeping peacefully, with her tousled hair strewn across the pillow and one arm thrown above her head. He'd been tempted to scoop her up into his arms and make love to her while she was so relaxed and sleepy. But the urgency of the calls he had to make this morning stopped him.

He'd neglected Magdalena lately and he knew it, although the specific nature of his offence last night eluded him. By the time he'd reached their bedroom she'd turned her back on him and was feigning sleep. Wary of prompting an argument and exhausted beyond measure, he lay quietly until her rigid body relaxed and her breathing assumed the slow, gentle rhythm of deep sleep before he drifted off himself. It sometimes took them a few days to adjust and regain the intimacy of their relationship when he returned from one of his work trips.

He quickened his step as he approached the dangerous slum known as the rookery of St Giles. A maze of gin shops, hovels and secret alleyways divided by open sewers, it was the most notorious part of London and the stench always made him recoil. He pulled out his scented handkerchief to cover his nose and rested the other hand on the loaded pistol in his pocket. Cut-throats lurked around every dark corner in St Giles. Bow Street officers were often attacked, especially if they ventured here alone in the dark.

Lavender turned down a dark alleyway between a disreputable tavern and a flesh-shop. He ignored the curious stare of a blowsy harlot leaning out of a window and the outstretched hand of a beggar slumped in the doorway of the tavern. The walls of the buildings above him bulged out with age and dripped with slime, while the overhanging upper casement windows blocked out most of the light. He picked his way through the stinking refuse towards a short flight of steps leading down to a basement cellar. It wasn't unusual to find whole families of starving paupers and immigrants crammed in the squalor of these single-roomed, damp cellars. But Lavender's informant and his woman had this cellar to themselves.

'What you doing 'ere?' Fletcher had a pronounced cast of one eye, which sometimes meant it was hard to gauge his mood. But his tone of voice left Lavender in no doubt that he was unwelcome here. Fletcher glanced nervously over Lavender's shoulder. There was sleep crusted in the corners of both his eyes and his filthy shirt had been hastily dragged over his matted head, judging by the state of his hair.

'I need to speak to you.'

Reluctantly, Fletcher let Lavender enter the dark room.

Fletcher's mousy little woman was frying ham over the fire and scratching at the lice beneath her armpit. She offered Lavender a dish of tea.

'No, thank you. I won't keep you long, Fletcher, but I'm desperate for some information.'

The woman shrugged and gave Fletcher a cracked plate of greasy ham and eggs. The two of them sat down on the battered old chairs in front of the fire to eat, watching Lavender warily out of their three good eyes. They didn't invite him to sit, and he wouldn't have done so anyway. God only knows what was crawling through their furniture.

'There's been a vicious hold-up on the Edgware Road,' he said. 'A lot of jewellery was stolen.'

Fletcher nodded but never looked up from his food. 'I've 'eard about it.'

'Do you know who did it?'

Fletcher shook his shaggy head; his long, matted hair nearly swung into his food. 'No. They were talkin' about it in Annie's Gin Palace the other night.'

'Who were?'

'Just folks.'

Lavender pulled out a shilling from his pocket and let it glint in the weak light from the fire.

Fletcher wiped his greasy stubble with his shirtsleeve. 'I may 'ave somethin' fer you.'

'I thought you might.'

'There's a new gang of coves causin' trouble around here.'

'Oh? Who are they?'

'I don't know; they're from out of town. Furriners.'

'Foreigners? Where on earth are they from, man?'

'They jabber in a furrin tongue; that's what I've 'eard sed anyway.'

'You've not heard them yourself?'

'No.'

Lavender hesitated. Here in St Giles, a 'foreigner' could be anyone from the Baltic to Dulwich Village on the other side of the Thames. He struggled to see a connection between this vague information about jabbering foreigners and Lord Yarmouth's description of an eloquent gentleman highwayman. 'Who's their arch-rogue?' he asked. 'Who leads them?'

Fletcher shook his shaggy head. 'They keeps themselves to themselves and I don't ken where they drink, but the local crews seem to think they're after their patch. There's talk of trouble. Micky Sullivan 'as 'ad his nose put out.'

Lavender frowned. Micky Sullivan was well known to Bow Street Police Office. Sullivan claimed he was a respectable moneylender but he ran several criminal gangs both here and in Seven Dials. According to rumour, many of the men in his crews were once honest folk whom Sullivan had forced into a life of crime after they became heavily indebted to him. The rogue had no qualms about snitching on his own gang members or sending them to the gallows if it suited him. This threat meant his crew were forced to stay loyal.

No evidence had ever been found to incriminate Sullivan himself of breaking the law; the man was as slippery as a Thames eel.

Lavender tossed the coin across to Fletcher and described the Yarmouths' stolen jewellery. Fletcher's eyes widened. 'There's some pretty plate and sparklers amongst that lot.'

'There'll be a handsome reward if any of it is found.'

''Ow much?'

'Fifty pounds.'

Fletcher's jaw dropped. He nodded, and Lavender left.

When Woods walked into the kitchen that morning he was surprised but pleased to find Eddie already up and energetically blacking his boots. The boy's Sunday-best shirt was spread out on the kitchen table, waiting for the flat iron to heat in the fire. Betsy was cooking their breakfast, a shawl thrown over her nightgown.

'I thought I should look smart,' Eddie said.

Woods took a dish of tea from Betsy and sat down at the kitchen table. 'That's good thinkin', son. The foreman will be impressed with the shine on them boots.'

'Da.' Eddie paused. 'I think I'd like to go on my own. You know, because of them things I told you last night.'

Woods nodded. 'I understand.'

'Well, I've no notion what the two of yer are jabberin' on about,' Betsy said, 'but one thing's for sure – no foreman will employ you unless you run a comb through that hair of yours.'

'Oh yes.' Eddie dropped his boots on the newspaper and left in search of a hair comb.

'What were all that about, Ned?' she asked.

'Our boy's makin' his choices and his way in the world now, Betsy.'

The night patrol officers were already returning, bleary-eyed and splattered with mud, when Woods and Barnaby arrived at Bow Street.

According to Constable Upton, there had been no sign of the gang of highwaymen on the Edgware Road. Everything was peaceful in Kilburn and the night-watchman had been surprised to hear of the highway robbery the previous night.

Woods thanked Upton and turned to Barnaby. 'These tobymen will be in some tavern, drinking away their ill-gotten gains. Never mind, let's see what the daylight brings.'

The skulls still sat on top of the stable yard wall and three sets of empty eye sockets gazed forlornly at the two officers when they rode out through the archway. There was no sign of the skeletal Constable Bone-Apart.

It was a bright dawn, though the red sky and ominous black clouds in the distance promised rain later.

Woods and Barnaby were soon out into open countryside. Spring had come later this year and there were still primroses sprouting at the base of the hedgerows. Lambs gambolled in the fields of lush grass and cowslips, while penned animals at the roadside farms lowed softly for their feed. Woods' heart lifted and he began to hum again.

'You're in a good mood today, Constable Woods,' Barnaby said.

Woods grinned. 'Oh, it won't last, son. It won't last.'

When they neared Kilburn, they left the meandering road and made enquiries at the scattered farmhouses. No one knew about the highway robbery; nor had there been any other incidents in, or around, the pretty village with its leafy lanes, gardens and beneficial wells.

They rode out to the wooded area of the road where the theft had taken place. A soggy carpet of old leaves muffled the sound of their horses' hooves. An ancient copse of oaks towered overhead and cast them into shade. Weak sunlight filtered through the canopy of fresh green leaves, creating a soft, mottled effect on the glossy necks and flanks of their horses. The leaves above whispered in the breeze and Woods wondered what secrets they shared. He grimaced; he'd never liked the spooky way trees arched over you, groaning and blocking out the light. You never knew who or what hid behind them.

He dismounted quickly. 'Come on, lad. Let's see if those coves have left us any clues.' They scoured the area but apart from a lot of trampled grass they found nothing.

'It's as if those thievin' rogues just rode out of a moonbeam and then rode back into it again,' Woods exclaimed in frustration.

Barnaby's eyes widened. 'Are you suggestin' they're phantoms?'

'Now don't start that superstitious malarkey again, son.' Woods glanced up at the dappled green canopy overhead and tried to make out the position of the sun. He raised his foot to the stirrup and remounted his horse. 'Come on. There's nothin' to see here. Let's get back to Bow Street. I've got to meet Lavender in The Nag's Head.'

Chapter Eleven

Lavender paid a quick visit to an unscrupulous pawnbroker he knew in Hatton Garden, then walked to John Bellingham's lodgings. The pavements of Guilford Road were crowded with shoppers and hawkers; Lavender tugged his hat further down his head and pushed his way slowly through the crowds towards the corner of New Millman Street, surveying the situation with a critical eye.

It would be difficult to loiter inconspicuously outside Bellingham's lodgings. Blocked off at the southern end, it was a short street of neat, yellow-brick terraced houses, all four storeys high. It was treeless and narrow; the kind of quiet, respectable little cul-de-sac where the neighbours would know each other by sight. Lavender decided to wait outside the grocer's at the junction with Guilford Road, where he would easily be able to see anyone leaving and entering the house.

A tall man eventually emerged in a black coat with a bulky parcel beneath his arm. Thanks to Vickery's description, Lavender recognised John Bellingham immediately. He led Lavender to a tailor's shop. When Bellingham emerged from the shop, the bankrupt merchant no longer had the parcel. Lavender assumed he'd taken something in to the tailor for repair.

Bellingham came within a few feet of him. Lavender stepped back into the shadows of a shop doorway and regarded him curiously. Bellingham's long face was impassive; there was nothing in the man's unremarkable features and dull brown eyes that hinted at the suffering he'd endured or the obsessive madness lurking in his tortured mind.

Bellingham went south towards Westminster and the river. The pale, gothic stone towers of the Abbey dominated the skyline ahead. Through the gap in the high buildings lining the busy street, Lavender saw the masts and spars of the tall ships reaching up towards the grey sky. Sunlight forced its way through the clouds over the south bank of the river and made the tips of the choppy waves on the Thames sparkle.

When the two men neared Henry VIII's old palace of Whitehall, the tide of pedestrians slowed to a virtual halt. New government offices were being constructed and the pavements were obstructed with scaffolding and building rubble. A steady stream of horse-drawn vehicles rumbled towards Westminster Bridge and prevented the pedestrians from overflowing into the road. Lavender lost sight of Bellingham in the crush but he wasn't too concerned. He knew where his quarry was headed; Vickery's report mentioned that Bellingham often spent time in the public galleries above the House of Commons.

The crumbling, smoke-stained facade of the ancient Palace of Westminster rose above Lavender's head as he entered Parliament Square. He strode across Palace Yard and climbed the steps of St Stephen's entrance into the lobby of the House of Commons. Parliament was already in session and the large double doors of the debating chamber were closed.

A large crowd of politicians, lobbyists, clerks, errand boys and petitioners were engrossed in animated discussion.

Nearby, a lanky man with long, greasy hair framing his pock-marked face leaned against one of the marble pillars, scribbling in his notebook while he eavesdropped on the conversations around him. It was Vincent Dowling, the parliamentary reporter for *The Day*. Lavender knew him from his previous work as a spy for the Home Department.

Lavender avoided Dowling and made for one of the dark-oak staircases leading up to the public galleries.

Bellingham was sitting on the front row of benches, leaning forward over the wooden bannister. A small notebook lay open at his side. Lavender sank down into a seat in the shadowy back corner of the gallery. The muffled voices of the politicians rose from the floor below as they debated their response to a petition from the ship owners in the port of Scarborough. The ship owners were disturbed and upset with the present system of granting licences to foreign vessels to import timber, deals and staves into the country. It was extremely dull, but Bellingham seemed entranced.

After an hour, Lavender pulled out his pocket watch to check the time and decided he'd had enough. He was about to rise to leave when the door opened and Dowling entered the public gallery. He moved towards the front and stopped next to Bellingham, spotting Lavender as he sat down. Surprise flitted across Dowling's face but he was distracted by Bellingham, who pointed below and asked the journalist to identify several of the speakers.

Seizing the chance to escape, Lavender rose and left the gallery, but no sooner had he stepped out onto the black-and-white tiled floor of the lobby than he heard hasty footsteps on the stairs behind him.

It was Dowling. 'Lavender, wait! Why are you here?'

Lavender shrugged. 'I'm exercising my civil right to listen to parliamentary debates. These are momentous times.'

One side of Dowling's thin lips curled cynically. The movement emphasised the disfigurement of his skin caused by the smallpox; the scarring was worse down that side of his face. 'You think the belligerent moaning of a group of Yorkshiremen is momentous? Don't lie to me,

Lavender. You're following John Bellingham – just like Vickery did last week. Why?'

Lavender hesitated.

'What's Bow Street's interest in the man?' Dowling licked his pencil and lifted his notebook.

'You know I can't divulge Bow Street's business, Dowling.'

'Come on, Lavender, for old times' sake, give me an inkling. What's the story here? Will it interest our readers at *The Day*?'

Lavender's mind raced. He needed to distract Dowling from John Bellingham. Perhaps taking him back to Bow Street might be the answer? 'No, there's no story for you and your readers here, Dowling, but I do have something that may interest you.'

'What?'

'The builders at Bow Street have uncovered the medieval plague pit; we're up to the top of our boots in skeletons.'

Dowling narrowed his eyes. 'I don't believe you. You're trying to palm me off with a lesser tale.'

'It's all I have for you. I'm returning to Bow Street right now. Come with me if you want and see it for yourself; I'll show you the excavation. Sir Richard Allison from Guy's Hospital is assisting us with the removal and identification of the bones. I'm sure your readers will be fascinated with a grisly find like this.'

Dowling hesitated, then grinned and pocketed his pencil and notebook. 'You understand the ghoulish nature of our readers very well, Lavender. Lead the way to the Bow Street plague pit.'

Vincent Dowling swore under his breath at the hellish sight that greeted them when he and Lavender stepped through the arch into the remains of the cobbled stable yard. 'God's strewth! It's a charnel house!'

Under Sir Richard's direction, the recovery of the bones had become a major excavation. The long trench was now a huge square pit. The greyish bones and skulls stacked against the far wall had grown into a massive pile. Huge mounds of earth and rubble blocked part of the yard, making access to and from the stables dangerous for both man and beast.

Read was yelling at Macca at the far side of the yard. His magisterial robes flapped demonically in the breeze. Both men were livid and red in the face. Sir Richard Allison and his interns watched them, grinning.

Dowling glanced at the altercation between the magistrate and the builder, but Lavender steered him towards Sir Richard. He introduced them and politely asked the surgeon to explain about the skeletons for the benefit of *The Day*'s readers. Fortunately, Sir Richard was in an excellent mood and was happy to show off to the journalist.

Lavender left them to it and joined the gaoler, who was standing grinning outside the cell block. 'Did Ned Woods and young Barnaby catch those footpads last night?'

'Aye, they're both under the 'atches in our cell block and waitin' fer their meetin' with the beak.' He grinned.

Lavender thanked him and picked his way through the devastated remains of the stable yard towards Magistrate Read.

'For heaven's sake, Detective! Please tell me that isn't Vincent Dowling from *The Day* talking with Sir Richard. What in God's name is he doing here?'

'I had to bring him here to distract him,' Lavender said quietly. 'He saw Vickery following Bellingham last week, and when I arrived three paces behind the man this morning, Dowling put two and two together and realised Bow Street has an interest in the man.'

'Ah.' Read nodded.

'So I thought I'd distract him – and throw him a bone, so to speak.' The corners of Read's mouth twitched but he didn't smile. 'But I, er, didn't realise we had quite so many. What's happening here, sir?'

'Sir Richard has taken leave of his senses,' Read snapped. 'He's trying to recover as many bones as possible and has made the builders dig up half the yard. Heaven knows what he plans to do with them. I suspect he's simply doing this to distress me. Macca has done nothing but moan about how this will hold up the job. It wasn't one of your better notions to involve Sir Richard, Lavender.' Lavender glanced around at the devastation in the stable yard and silently agreed with him.

Suddenly, Ned Woods and Barnaby rode into the stable yard. Lavender beckoned to Woods to join them. Woods nodded and swung out of his saddle. He gave the reins to the ostler and strode towards them, brushing the dust off his coat.

'How is your investigation into the theft of Lord Yarmouth's money and jewels progressing?' Read asked.

'A fifty-pound reward for information has been offered,' Lavender said. 'I've visited a few second-hand jewellers and pawnbrokers but haven't found any stolen goods or clues. Woods and Barnaby have been back to the scene of the robbery. Did you find anything, Ned?'

'Sorry, sir. Nothin',' Woods said. 'Those coves seem to have appeared out of nowhere and vanished again into the night like wood sprites.'

Read frowned. 'I thought I sent you out to catch the footpads on Blackheath, Constable?'

'It's done, sir. We caught the coves last night. They're below hatches in the cells. I'm surprised Mr Grey didn't tell you.'

'I haven't checked my list for this afternoon's court session – but well done, Woods – and Barnaby.'

Lavender saw his chance. 'I've made enquiries about the Yarmouth robbery but I need help from Woods and Barnaby. I can't manage this case on my own, sir – not with the Bellingham issue you want me to deal with as well.'

'I know you've always worked well together but I told you yesterday you would have to manage on your own this week.'

'Lord Yarmouth suspects the robbers had prior knowledge of his travel plans,' Lavender persisted. 'I need to speak to both him and Lady Yarmouth and try to get to the bottom of this. Meanwhile, someone else needs to visit the rest of the known fences, pawnbrokers and second-hand jewellers to describe the stolen items and spread the word about the reward. I need Woods and Barnaby for that.'

Oswald Grey suddenly appeared at Woods' shoulder. 'Constable Woods? You'd better come with me to the clerk's desk. You've had a delivery.'

'A delivery?'

'Yes – and you owe me sixpence.'

Woods shrugged and fell into step behind him.

'So what is your decision, sir?' Lavender asked.

Across the yard, Dowling was interviewing Macca. The builder gesticulated wildly and jabbed an angry finger towards the piles of bones. For a moment Read said nothing. He pulled out his pocket watch and checked the time. 'Very well, you can have help from Woods and Barnaby until one of the other Principal Officers arrives back in London. In the meantime, please ask Mr Dowling to pay me a short visit in my office. There's still half an hour until court begins again. Dowling is a former government spy. He may be of use rather than a hindrance with the Bellingham case. Oh, and you should give him the particulars of Lord Yarmouth's reward too.'

Relief swept through Lavender. 'Thank you, sir. I told Dowling about the robbery and the reward on the journey here.'

Read nodded and turned to go back inside the building.

Inside the dimly lit and grim interior of the main hallway, the usual crowd of shackled miscreants waited morosely with their arresting officers. The two young clerks working behind the desk glanced up curiously when Woods and Grey approached. A long, irregularly shaped parcel lay slumped against the grimy wall, wrapped in a filthy blanket.

'What is it?' Woods asked.

Grey simply pointed at the object and said nothing.

Woods bent down and untied the crude knots at one end of the parcel. A mass of pale bones slithered and clattered onto the wooden floor and a skull rolled towards the desk.

One of the women prisoners screamed and the clerks hastily stepped back. A murmur of concern rippled around the hallway.

'Gawd's teeth! Where have these come from?'

'A group of children, young mudlarks by the state of them, brought these in first thing this morning,' Oswald Grey said. 'They told me you'd asked for them and that you owed them sixpence. I paid them off to get rid of them, the smelly little urchins.'

Woods' heart sank. This wasn't what he'd expected when he'd struck his deal with Nathanial Higgin and his little friends. And something wasn't right about these bones; there were too many of them.

'What on earth!' Magistrate Read stood behind him. Woods groaned silently to himself.

'More bones, Constable? Don't you think we already have enough?' One of the shackled prisoners laughed. The young desk clerks grinned at Woods' discomfort.

'You'd better have a good explanation for this!' Even the scalp below Read's close-cropped grey hair was scarlet.

'Yes, sir,' Woods said, though for the life of him he couldn't think of a damned thing to say right at that moment. Playing for time, he turned to Oswald Grey. 'How did those nippers carry this pile all the way from Greenwich to here?'

'Greenwich!' Magistrate Read turned a darker shade of puce. 'What did I say to you and Lavender about Greenwich?'

'They said they'd hitched a ride on a farm cart bound for Covent Garden,' Grey continued.

'Never mind how they were transported in here, Constable – get them out!' Read shrieked.

'Yes, sir. I'll take them to Sir Richard right now and let him stick them with the rest.' He stooped, retied the corners of the blanket and heaved the bag of dry bones up from the floor onto his broad shoulder. It gave a sickening jangle.

'You were going to explain?' Read blocked Woods' escape, his face dark with anger.

Woods' addled brain finally came up with an answer. 'When I found that severed foot on the beach, sir, I asked a group of nippers to keep an eye open for the rest of the fellah. It looks like they've found him.' This was the truth after all, of a sort. Read didn't need to know that he and Barnaby had been back to the beach.

Read's eyes narrowed. 'I doubt they're anything to do with your severed foot, Constable. But don't let me delay you.' He stepped aside and gestured towards the rear door. 'Take them to Sir Richard for his expert opinion. I shall open my window so I can hear his laughter up in my office.'

'Yes, sir, very good, sir.'

'And if you – or Lavender – go anywhere near Greenwich Beach again, I'll dock you both a day's pay!' Read yelled after him. 'Do you hear me?'

'Yes, sir.' Woods lunged forward towards the door with his awkward cargo.

'Did you hear me, Constable?' Read yelled after him.

'Yes, sir.'

'Oi! You owe me sixpence!' shouted the Chief Clerk.

Sir Richard Allison glanced up as Woods staggered towards him with his gruesome parcel. 'What on earth do you have in there, Constable?'

Lavender had disappeared into the stables. With a strong sense of foreboding that he'd been duped by a gang of children, Woods dropped the bones in a muddy puddle at the surgeon's feet. He'd never liked the arrogant sawbones, but with Read at his back and Lavender so keen on the case, he needed Sir Richard's opinion. He stepped back and braced himself for bad news. 'It might be the rest of that fellah with the severed foot . . .' His voice died away.

Sir Richard reached down and untied the corners of the blanket. 'My, my, what have we here?' When he stood upright he had a lower leg bone in his hand. 'Gracious me! This fellow has grown back his right foot! This is truly a miracle!'

Woods' heart sank, but Sir Richard hadn't finished with his humiliation yet. The surgeon stooped and pulled out a pair of gleaming ivory skulls and a long, knobbly object with a row of blackened teeth. 'Two heads? One of them female? Good grief! By Jove! He also had a sheep's jawbone!'

'Thank you, Sir Richard.' Woods clamped shut his jaw and backed away towards the stable block.

'What do you want me to do with these, Constable?' Sir Richard called after him, laughing.

'Stick them between your blind cheeks!' Woods muttered between gritted teeth. He entered the stable, hurled a blanket over the back of a fresh horse and reached up amongst the tack hanging on the stable wall for a saddle.

'What's amiss, Ned?' Lavender stepped out of the shadows at the far end of the long building with Barnaby at his side.

'We'll have to cancel our trip to The Nag's Head, sir. I've a gang of young scamps to thrash and I'm goin' to enjoy every ruddy minute of it.' He told Lavender about the trick the children had played on him.

Lavender grinned and reached out for a saddle. 'This I must see. We'll go together; you and Barnaby are working for me now. I've just set Barnaby some tasks.'

'No, you can't come. Read said he'll stop our money if we set foot in Greenwich again. But it'll be worth it for me – I want to put the fear of God in those nippers.'

Lavender shrugged, pulled the girth tight and gave Woods a wink. 'Someone has to make sure you don't go too far and commit infanticide.'

'I don't rightly know what that means, sir.' Woods swung himself up into the saddle. 'But if it involves a big stick and their bare backsides, then you may have some trouble stoppin' me.'

Chapter Twelve

The weather chose that moment to deliver the long-threatened rain, and thunder rumbled in the distance. Huge raindrops obscured their vision as they battled their way through the carriages and drays congesting the roads of Covent Garden. Skittish horses shied and reared with each thunderclap; pedestrians and shoppers scurried for cover. Lavender and Woods were drenched by the time they crossed Westminster Bridge, but the downpour stopped as suddenly as it had started and the clouds cleared. After the stench of the river, they welcomed the delicious scent of wet vegetation from the fields and dripping trees. Leaning forward, they spurred their horses forward and cantered through the open countryside.

Deptford soon came into view and, behind it, the twin domes of the Royal Hospital in Greenwich reached up towards a vivid double rainbow.

The stone bridge over Deptford Creek marked the boundary with Greenwich. Woods reined his horse into a slow walk when they reached the bridge and turned to Lavender, frowning. 'I've just remembered – I don't know where that damned Higgin boy lives.'

'He used to live above a bakery in Covent Garden with his widowed mother, didn't he?'

'Yes, but they live here now and I think she's wed again.' Then he remembered something and his face brightened. 'One of them nippers said yesterday she'd "married a darkie". That might be a good clue, sir, don't you think? There won't be many white women married to darkies in Greenwich.'

Lavender shrugged. 'I don't know, Ned. I read somewhere that one out of every hundred people who live in the London area are men and women of colour. There are about ten thousand of them in the city now.'

Woods' forehead creased and he nodded slowly. 'My brother, Alby, worked with a few darkies down at the Rotherhithe docks – and several families live near us in Southwark. Pretty chocolate-coloured little nippers they have. But every man who works on the docks soon ends up with coal dust smeared in the lines of their faces and skin like weathered old leather. Sometimes it weren't possible to tell apart a swarthy man born in Rotherhithe from a 'Gyptian or an Ethiope.'

Lavender smiled. 'It's not just the sailors and dock workers; many foreign traders have moved here or sent their sons to be educated in Britain. We also have many freed slaves and their descendants.'

Woods grimaced. 'I never liked that business, sir – usin' folks as slaves; it never seemed decent to me.'

Lavender nodded. 'The American slaves who fought for us against their former masters in the colonial rebellion thirty years ago were offered repatriation in England, and many of them are still here.'

A small boat-building yard stood just below the bridge next to the swirling black water of Deptford Creek. Several men were working on the upturned hull of a fishing coble in the sawdust-strewn yard. Lavender turned his horse off the road and rode towards them, gesturing for Woods to follow him. The workmen's saws, hammers and planes fell silent when they recognised Woods' uniform. Lavender reined in next to a leather-skinned older man whom he suspected was their foreman.

'Can we 'elp, you, sir?'

'I'm looking for a woman called Jacquetta Higgin. She's a baker and may be married to a man of colour.'

The older man spat a wad of tobacco into the mud at his feet. 'Aye. It's Mistress Cugoan. They 'ave their bakery on Church Street.'

The Cugoans' bakery was in the centre of Greenwich. The smell of freshly baked bread and pastries wafted down the narrow cobbled street, guiding them to their destination. Lavender heard Woods' stomach rumble as he dismounted and tied his horse to a post. 'Let's buy something to eat before you grab her son and thrash him,' he suggested.

Jacquetta Cugoan was kneading dough at the shop counter when they entered. She didn't look up at first and continued to thrust her hands into the soggy mass, lifting it and slapping it back down on the counter in a steady rhythm. 'Mornin', gentlemen, 'ow can I 'elp yer?'

Lavender recognised her instantly. She had a few more lines beside her eyes and across her brow and the faded ginger tendrils trailing down beneath her cap were tinged with grey, but her features looked softer and more content than those of the woman he'd met two years ago.

She glanced up when they didn't reply and her broad face flushed with a smile of recognition. 'Why, if it ain't Constable Woods! And his clever detective pal too! Don't tell me ye've come all this way from London just to buy one of me raisin tartlets?' She raised a fat, floury arm and pointed towards a tray of fresh pastries.

'Yes, madam,' said Woods. 'I've a great need for one of your raisin tartlets. In fact, we'll take six.'

She smiled and fetched them the confectionery. Another customer came into the shop, so they handed over payment, stepped to one side and enjoyed the warm tarts. The pastry melted in Lavender's mouth, while his tongue flicked the sugar from his lips.

By the time the other shopper had left, Lavender had eaten two of the tartlets, while Woods had devoured the rest.

Lavender cleared his throat. 'Actually, madam, we need to speak to your son, Nathanial. Is he here or at school?'

She took a sharp intake of breath and disappointment soured her features. 'What's 'e done now? The ruddy little scoundrel!'

'Is he at home?' Lavender persisted.

'Yes, 'e is. 'E were supposed to be at school today but came back an 'our or so ago sayin' 'ow 'e felt bad. I don't know why I still pay fer 'im to go. Two shillings and sixpence a week I spend on 'is schooling!' She banged the knife down onto the counter and stepped back to a curtain doorway at the rear of the shop. 'Nathanial! Nathanial – get yourself out 'ere right now – and you too, Mr Cugoan!' She marched to the shop door, locking it and turning the small, dangling sign to read 'Closed' from the outside.

They heard movement in the rear of the premises. The curtain was pulled aside and a tall, scowling boy with vivid red hair entered the shop.

Behind him walked a small, wiry black man of indeterminate age. Slightly stooped, his soft brown eyes squinted behind a pair of wire spectacles. He held a sheaf of papers in his ink-stained fingers. 'Is there something the matter, my dear?' His diction was clear, his tone calm but his accent foreign.

'Is there somethin' awry, Mr Cugoan?' said the angry woman. 'There most definitely is. These gentlemen are runners from Bow Street and they want to talk to our Nat.'

'Good afternoon, gentlemen. I'm Ignatius Cugoan. How can we assist you?'

'Detective Lavender and Constable Woods.' Lavender reached out and shook his hand, but Ned was in no mood for pleasantries. He stepped towards Nathanial.

'Right, lad, where did you find them bones you brought to us at Bow Street?'

'Bones!' Jacquetta Cugoan shrieked. 'Dear Lord! Don't tell me ye've been body-snatchin' now!' She stepped forward and gave the lad a sharp cuff around the ear. It left a smear of flour in his vivid hair.

'Ouch!' Nathanial squealed and backed away from his mother, rubbing his sore ear. 'Lay off me, Ma. We found them lyin' around in that ruined old church by the creek.'

'St Alphege's?' Lavender asked.

Nathanial nodded and pointed an accusing finger at Woods. ''E asked us to fetch him some old bones.'

'So ye've not been to school today? Ye've lied about that, as well?' Jacquetta stepped forward again with her hand raised.

Her husband quickly placed himself between the angry woman and her sulking son. 'Let's hear the full story, my dear, before we decide how to deal with Nathanial. I'm curious to know why Constable Woods asked the children to fetch him a pile of old bones.' Lavender heard the soft drawl of an American in his strange accent.

Woods cleared his throat and explained how he had sought out the assistance of Nathanial and the other children the previous day after discovering the skeletal remains of the foot on Greenwich Beach. 'I told 'em to send me word if they found anythin' – I didn't expect them to turn up at the police office with a blanket full of bones.'

Cugoan nodded and lowered his eyes to hide his smile. 'It's well known that there are ancient bones scattered around in the crypt of the ruined Saxon church. It seems the children thought you wouldn't notice if they brought you those instead of the ones you sought.' His full lips twitched. 'Do you want Nathanial to take you there?'

Lavender shook his head. He knew the location of the old church of St Alphege. Built on the site where an early Archbishop of Canterbury called Alphege had been murdered by the Danes, it became prone to flooding as the Thames shifted its course. Finally, the good burghers and aldermen of Greenwich had abandoned their battle with the rising flood water of Deptford Creek, built a new church in the centre of the town and dedicated it to the memory of their sainted martyr.

'In that case, Nathanial,' Cugoan continued quietly, 'all that remains for you to do is apologise for wasting the constable's time – and repay his sixpence.'

This was too much for the boy. 'But I've only got one penny – the others have the rest!'

'I'll just take back the penny,' Woods growled. 'I'll deal with the other nippers later.'

Nathanial's lower lip trembled. He fumbled in his breeches pocket, pulled out a penny and handed it over to Woods. His eyes stared down at his boots, mumbling an apology.

'Now go back into the house. Your mother and I will deal with you later.' The youth turned and disappeared through the curtain.

'I'm so sorry for yer inconvenience, Constable Woods.' Anguish flooded across Jacquetta's face. 'We've done our best with the boy and I thought movin' 'ere, away from the gin palaces, lewd women and villains in Covent Garden, would 'elp him settle down – especially after I married Mr Cugoan. But 'e gives us nothin' but grief these days and barely attends school.'

Woods nodded. 'I understand, Mrs Cugoan. Nathanial's the same age as my Eddie – and we gave up coaxin' him to his own school recently and he's started work. Perhaps we shouldn't be too hard on the lads?'

Lavender smiled at Woods' sudden change in attitude; a full belly always restored his constable's good humour.

'They're such a worry, aren't they?' Jacquetta sighed.

'It's all part of their growin' up, ma'am,' Woods said. 'Your Nathanial will come right in the end; you see if he don't.'

'I don't know if this will help you, Detective,' Cugoan said quietly, 'but there are human remains amongst the reeds on the far bank of Deptford Creek. I heard some of the water-taxi men discussing it a few days ago.'

'Good God! Why didn't they tell the local constables?' Lavender asked.

'From what I heard, none of them will go near them. They're too superstitious.'

'Why are they wary? Every lighterman I've ever known has hauled at least one dead body out of the Thames.'

'Apparently, the skeleton doesn't have a head,' Cugoan continued. His wife gave an involuntary shiver. 'They call him "Headless Ted".'

'On the far bank of the estuary, you say?' Woods asked. Cugoan nodded.

Woods turned to Lavender. 'I never got that far yesterday, sir.'

Lavender nodded and pulled on his gloves. 'You've both been very helpful, thank you.'

'It's our pleasure, sir,' Cugoan said. 'After Nathanial's little prank, it's the least we can do. If you'll excuse me, gentlemen.' He quietly disappeared through the curtain into the accommodation behind the bakery.

Jacquetta's eyes shone with warmth as she watched him disappear. ''E's such a good father to Nat,' she said proudly, 'and a scholar too. 'E were a slave in the Americas and 'e's suffered terrible. But 'e were freed and educated by a gentleman. 'E's writing his memoirs now – and there's many that wants to read 'em.'

'I'm sure there are.' Lavender fished in his pocket for some money. 'Please add my name to the list of people who wish to subscribe to his book.'

Jacquetta flushed to the roots of her faded red hair with pride. She told Lavender the price of the subscription and took his money. 'Mr Cugoan will be so pleased!'

'We'll leave you now, ma'am. The tide is rising and I want to find these remains. Thank you again.'

'Wait a moment.' She popped a couple of raisin tartlets into a small paper bag and pressed them into Woods' hand. 'For your journey, Constable – and your inconvenience.'

Chapter Thirteen

Lavender and Woods cantered back onto the Romney Road. They crossed the bridge spanning the creek and passed through the bustling town of Deptford with its docks and boatyards. Once they reached the shoreline, they tied their horses to an old post and went on foot across the shingle. Deptford Creek was on their right now, the ivy-clad tower of the old Saxon church just visible on the far bank.

The Thames heaved with boats and ships of every size and type. Coal barges rose and fell in the wake of the tall ships and the East Indiamen, all low in the water from the weight of their cargo.

They picked their way carefully along the line of driftwood and rotting vegetation that delineated the high-water mark on what was left of the beach. The tide inched across the land. At some points, the river had already breached the sand bar and flowed into the low-lying marshes. Tiny waves rippled down through the reeds. Damp seeped into Lavender's boots as they trudged through shallow water and squelching mud. Startled waterfowl squawked and scurried out of the reeds.

'He's got to be in the reeds along the high-tide line,' Lavender called over his shoulder. 'Keep your eyes open, Ned.'

A fluttering fragment of muddy brown cloth in a dense clump of reeds caught his eye. It was the torn trouser leg of a thin, bent and raised human leg. Lavender braced himself. He'd seen many dead bodies in his life but it was never easy to walk up to them.

A sudden flash of silver and black caught their eyes as they squelched towards the corpse. The four-foot-long body of a river eel undulated languidly just below the surface of the shallow water. 'Urgh,' Woods said. 'Them buggers taste much better than they look.'

Lying parallel to the waterline, the skeleton's left leg was the highest point of the carcass. The boot had jammed against a rock, raising the knee. The flesh on the bones had been stripped away by scavengers. The right leg lay submerged in the shallow water, truncated by its missing foot. A good section of the ribcage, backbone and pelvis was half buried in the mud. Shoots of fresh reeds already sprouted between the bones. The right hand had detached from the wrist and lay a few inches away, semi-clawed, with its bony index finger raised accusingly. It pointed back at the smoke-wreathed spires and chimneys of London. Mr Cugoan was right; there was no sign of the skull.

Lavender felt a huge surge of satisfaction. They'd found the skeleton to match the severed foot. He and Woods bent low and gave the surrounding area a cursory examination. Lavender didn't expect to find anything important here. The man had been dead for two years, according to Sir Richard. It was unlikely he'd died here, and the constant ebb and flow of the tide would have sucked away any remaining clues if he had.

'We need a cart to take his body back to Bow Street. Hopefully Sir Richard will still be there.'

'Shall we keep lookin' for the skull, sir?'

'Yes, I'll do it while you return to Deptford, hire a carter and get this poor chap dug up and loaded.' Something in the wary expression on Woods' face made him stop and smile. 'Don't worry, Ned. I'll not let you face the wrath of Magistrate Read alone. Whereabouts did you find the severed foot?'

'Near the first set of stone steps leading up to the esplanade in front of the Seamen's Hospital.'

What had Sir Richard said? *'If the skull has become separated from the spine, it'll travel the furthest because it will float or roll along the river bed . . .'*

'These bones are washing downstream,' he said. 'I'll go back to Greenwich Beach and look for it. When I return, we'll go back to Bow Street together.'

Woods nodded and Lavender sensed his relief. They set off back to their tethered horses.

'Everything now depends on finding the skull,' Lavender said. 'Without it, Sir Richard will be restricted in the help he can give us. I've also a notion that Read won't allow us to investigate this mystery any further without a full set of bones.'

'Young Barnaby searched that part of the beach,' Woods said. 'He didn't find nothin', and the lad has the eyes of a hawk.'

Lavender nodded. 'It can't hurt to try again.'

Lavender tied his horse to the railings on the esplanade in front of the Royal Hospital for Seamen, climbed down the stone steps and crunched his way through the shingle towards the waterline, following in Woods' footsteps of the previous day. There wasn't much of the beach left now thanks to the high tide. The skull, if it was still intact, would be larger and more rounded than the multitude of ancient animal bones littering the beach.

He walked slowly, turning over the detritus with the toe of his boot and occasionally stooping to examine an object more closely. His persistence paid off. Half an hour later, some distance downstream, he found a large, greyish dome half buried amongst the shingle and mud. He knelt down, scraped away the sand and broken shells, and carefully dug it out. Apart from a small hole in the top, the skull was intact; even the jawbone was still attached.

He brushed off the slime with his gloved hand and stared into the empty eye sockets of his mysterious victim. A wave of sympathy went through him. 'Who are you?' he asked quietly. 'And what in God's name happened to you? How did you end up here?'

There was something unusual about the slope of the forehead and the nasal aperture. *That's a mystery for Sir Richard*, Lavender decided, wrapping the skull in the cloth he'd brought from his saddlebag and tucking it beneath his arm.

Glancing at the mastless prison hulk anchored in the middle of the river, a new thought crossed his mind. Maybe their victim had been a convict?

When convicts died on board the hulks, their corpses were usually given to their family for burial. If they had no family to claim them, they were stripped of their clothes and possessions and rowed over for a shallow burial on a bleak and gruesome piece of waste ground known as the 'Rat's Castle'. The clothing of the dead convicts was sold to rag merchants and the money divided up between the gaolers. According to rumour, sometimes the corpses never reached the Rat's Castle and were sold to gangs of body-snatchers who took them to surgeons like Sir Richard for dissection.

With all this demand for flesh and clothing, it seemed highly unlikely that a fully clothed dead convict would wash up on the river-bank after two years.

Lavender shrugged and turned to walk back to his horse. He'd send Woods to make enquiries at the convict ship. They also needed to follow up Sir Richard's suggestion and visit the bankside church graveyards in case any of them were disgorging their grisly contents into the Thames. It was better to leave no stone unturned, and now he had help from Woods and Barnaby, he'd be able to quietly pursue some answers to this mystery.

With the skull safely stowed in his saddlebag, Lavender decided to pay a brief visit to the church of St Alphege while he was on this side of Deptford Creek. He was curious to see what the children had discovered. He strode along the beach and climbed over the rockfall. Because of the high tide he had to cling to the rocky face of the low cliff, inching his way towards the ruins of the old church. He made a mental note to return to his horse through the fields at the back.

The old Saxon church had been ravaged by time, the weather and the local population, who'd helped themselves to the rough-hewn stones for their own building projects. What remained of the walls had crumbled or been scattered across the uneven, cracked and weathered flagstones of the nave. In a couple of places these jagged walls reached higher than his head, but not much higher. A startled ewe with twin lambs scurried out of the tumbledown tower when he approached.

Weeds sprouted everywhere, jostling for space on the lower, boggy sections with river reeds. The mossy flagstones of the nave were littered with piles of sheep dung and the whole place smelt of damp, stagnant water and wet masonry. Deptford Creek licked at the edges of the ruins, only inches away from the walls. A high spring tide was due in a few days and would swamp the entire building.

Lavender glanced around for the entrance to the crypt, which would take him below the uneven floor of the transept. There was nothing to see inside the ruins, so he waded through the shallow water to the outer walls, where he found a low, arched doorway. He lit his pocket lantern, stooped below the lintel and held it out before him. A dangerous flight of worn, slimy stairs descended into the stinking black bowels of the old church. He took a few cautious steps down, the foul stench of rat urine combined with rotting vegetation almost overpowering him.

The floor was ankle-deep in black water. Lavender paused halfway down the stairs, stooping below the low vaulted ceiling, and held out his lantern. Around the edges of the small room, the Saxons had hewn into the walls to make the final resting places of their bishops and lords.

The stone ledges were empty now. Anything of value had been robbed centuries ago and the invading river had swept everything else onto the floor. Below the dark water, Lavender saw the pearly glimmer of scattered human bones and skulls.

He laughed quietly at the courage and stupidity of the children who had entered this death trap to rob it of its bones. His laughter echoed eerily around the cramped chamber. Lavender climbed back outside, blinked at the strength of the daylight and went back across the fields towards his horse, scattering sheep as he walked.

Chapter Fourteen

Woods and a sullen-faced carter were heaving the wrapped remains of Headless Ted into the back of a wagon when Lavender returned.

'Phew!' Woods wiped the sweat off his brow with the back of his sleeve and turned to face Lavender. 'Did you find the skull, sir?'

Lavender reached down and tapped his saddlebag. 'I did.' He nodded towards the tarpaulin in the back of the wagon. 'He looks heavy.'

'It were a bit hard to get this bony fellow to part with the river mud,' Woods said, 'so we brought most of it with him.'

'Never mind, we'll be able to wash it off him back at the morgue in Bow Street.'

The carter swung himself up into the driving seat of the wagon and picked up the reins. He was a hairy fellow with a full set of whiskers and a bushy, grey beard below his pock-marked face. 'Let's get goin', shall we?' he said sharply.

'This is Charlie Harris,' Woods said with a wink. 'He were a bit unhappy about helpin' us at first. But then he remembered that we'd met before back in London and he owed me a favour or two from the old days.'

Lavender smiled and didn't ask. His resourceful constable had been a Bow Street patrolman for over twenty years and had a good memory for faces. No doubt Charlie Harris had once been a small-time crook.

'I'll ride back to Covent Garden with Mr Harris and take the body straight to Sir Richard. Meanwhile, I need you to make a few calls for me, Ned.'

'Oh, yes?'

'Firstly, I want you to ride over to the prison barracks opposite the convict ship and ask if they lost a footless convict two years ago. Next, go to St Mary's church in Rotherhithe. It's right next to the river and has always been prone to flooding. Make sure the graves are secure and nothing has washed down into the river. Seek out the sexton if necessary and ask him. After that, make your way back along the south bank of the river to St Olave's and afterwards to St Saviour's in Southwark. Do the same there.'

Woods grinned and pointed to the skeleton in the back of the cart. 'If he's come from one of them graveyards, then our mystery will be solved, won't it, sir?'

'Yes. We'll just have to find ourselves another one.'

Woods laughed. 'I'll see you back at Bow Street later.' He swung himself up into the saddle and cantered off in the direction of Rotherhithe.

It was a slow journey for Lavender and the cart. After his initial reluctance to help the officers retrieve the remains, Charlie Harris now developed a stubborn determination to treat the unusual cargo in the back of his wagon with reverential respect. He refused to travel at anything more than a funereal pace. It was two hours before they joined the stream of traffic rumbling over Westminster Bridge into the capital and another twenty minutes before they'd navigated their way back into Covent Garden.

They were held up at the rear of the building while another cart, covered with a thick tarpaulin, came out of the stable yard along the narrow alleyway. The bones from the plague pit were finally making their way to Guy's Hospital for the Incurables. The excavation was over.

To Lavender's relief, Sir Richard Allison was still there, talking with some of his students at the far side of the yard. There was no sign of Lavender's own irascible employer, but the windows of the ground-floor courthouse glimmered with light. The afternoon court session must be running late; Read was still on the premises.

Lavender hastily dismounted, retrieved the skull from his saddlebag and handed over the reins of his horse to the ostler.

Sir Richard's eyes widened with surprise when he asked him to examine the skeletal remains in the back of the cart. 'You've found the rest of that skeleton – and the skull? My goodness, Lavender, you never give up, do you, man?' The surgeon turned to two of his students and instructed them to carry the remains into the morgue and clean the bones.

Lavender gave them the skull to reunite with the rest of the bones. 'Excuse me for a moment,' he said. 'I need to locate Constable Barnaby.'

Barnaby was lolling on the clerk's desk in the hallway. He straightened up when Lavender approached. 'I'm afraid I don't have anything for you, sir,' he said sheepishly. 'I visited all the pawn shops and jewellers you mentioned, but they've heard nothin' about Lord Yarmouth's stolen jewellery. The word is out on the street about the handsome reward the Earl is offerin' for their recovery, though.'

Lavender bit back his disappointment. 'Never mind, Constable. What about my interview with Lord and Lady Yarmouth? Did you call at Berkeley Square?'

'Yes, sir – but they won't be able to receive you until the day after tomorrow at the earliest.'

'Saturday? Why not?'

'Lady Yarmouth has recovered from the shock of the robbery and they continued their journey to St Albans; they're not due back until Saturday.'

This was a blow and would drag things out, but that wasn't necessarily bad. Read had threatened to pack Lavender off to Dublin as soon as he'd solved the case; anything that delayed his trip to Ireland was welcome. It also meant that once he'd finished with Sir Richard he would be able to leave for home and enjoy a full evening with his wife for once. He thanked Barnaby and sent him home to his supper.

Woods had arrived when Lavender stepped back out into the chilly yard, and was enjoying a chat with Frank and Bonner. Something the Liverpool men said made Woods throw back his head and laugh. They were watching the dopey fellow called Windy shovelling rubble back into the trench.

Lavender joined them. 'Good evening, gentlemen. I'm pleased to see your nervous friend has recovered from his fear of contracting the plague from the old bones.'

'Aye, but that were just a ruse all along,' said Frank. He shook his head sadly, his face a mask of innocent concern.

'What do you mean?' Lavender asked, cautiously.

''E didn't want anyone to recognise 'im, yous see?'

Lavender frowned. 'Why?'

'He weren't afraid of the plague.' Bonner had lowered his voice to a whisper. ''E's an escaped convict from Botany Bay. 'E were sent there on a seven-year ticket but sneaked back as a stowaway afore 'is time were up.'

For a moment there was a stunned silence, then Woods threw back his head and laughed again. 'That were a nice try, fellahs,' he said. 'A nice try.'

Smiling, Lavender turned towards the morgue. 'Come on, Ned.' Woods fell into step beside him, but Lavender paused before they entered. 'Did your enquiries at the convict ship and the graveyards help us?'

Woods shook his head. 'No. None of them remember losing a body to the Thames in the last two years.'

Lavender nodded, secretly pleased that the mystery hadn't been solved so easily.

The cramped morgue was well lit with lanterns and candles. Headless Ted was laid out on the central table in the airless room; the flickering light gave an iridescent quality to the skeleton's bones, which had been stripped of their ragged clothing and cleaned.

'Good timing, Lavender,' Sir Richard said. 'We've just about finished our examination. Oh! And Constable Woods is here too. You haven't brought me another sheep's jaw to identify, have you, Constable?'

Woods stiffened. 'No, Sir Richard, I haven't.'

'Shame,' teased the surgeon. 'There's nothing like a few animal bones thrown into the mix to sharpen our understanding of human anatomy, is there, Kingsley?'

The young man he addressed glanced up nervously from beneath his fringe. 'No, Sir Richard, there isn't.'

'Now, Lavender, what do you want young Kingsley here to tell you about this fellow?'

'As much as possible, please.'

The surgeon leaned back against the shelves on the wall, removing his gloves and pulling out a thin-bladed pocketknife to clean his fingernails. 'Continue, Kingsley.'

The student cleared his throat. 'Here we have the robust bones of a healthy male of about thirty years of age. The length of the femur suggests he was quite a big fellow, possibly close to six foot in height.'

'But he's hardly healthy, is he, Kingsley?' Sir Richard interrupted. 'The poor chap has had his right foot chopped off!' The other student stifled a laugh.

'I was just coming to that, Sir Richard. Apart from the severed foot, there appear to be no other injuries to any of the bones apart from an old fracture, long since healed, on the thumb of the left hand – possibly a childhood injury.'

'What about the hole in the skull?' Lavender asked.

'That happened post-mortem, sir – after he died. The skull probably got bashed by a rock when it bounced along the river bed.'

Sir Richard continued to examine his fingernails. 'How did you determine his age, Kingsley?'

'From the shape of the fourth rib, sir, and the cranial suture closure.'

Sir Richard nodded. 'And what else can you tell us about him?'

The young man hesitated. 'I don't think . . .'

'Oh come on, man! It's staring you in the face!'

Kingsley flushed red with embarrassment and stared down at the skeleton in confusion.

Woods squirmed uncomfortably beside Lavender. Even the other student had stopped laughing now. He ran a finger around the edge of his cravat to loosen it; he was sweating.

'I have to say, I thought there was something unusual about the slope of the forehead and the nasal aperture when I first found the skull this afternoon,' Lavender said quietly.

'Did you?' Sir Richard glanced up sharply. 'Do you hear that, Kingsley? Perhaps I should dismiss you and employ Lavender as a student of anatomy instead?' There was another awkward silence.

'And what was Constable Woods doing while you found the skull, Lavender?' Allison asked.

The strain in Woods' voice told Lavender that Ned was struggling to remain civil. 'I were investigating the graveyards along the south bank of the river to see if the flood water had breached any of the walls and washed any bodies away.'

Sir Richard burst out laughing. 'Well, that was a waste of time.'

'I believe it was your suggestion, Sir Richard,' Lavender said coldly.

'Well, maybe it was, but as things turned out, perhaps I was premature – that word means a bit early, Constable Woods.'

'I know what it means.' Woods' voice was a growl.

'This fellow has never had a Christian burial,' Sir Richard continued. 'You were wasting your time, Woods. There you go, Kingsley. That's another clue for you. How do I know these remains don't belong to a Christian? What is it I'm seeing that you're not? It's staring you in the face, man. The face.'

The young doctor shook his head in confusion and peered down at the skull.

Lavender had had enough. 'Please enlighten us yourself, Sir Richard.'

'I wondered when it would come to that.' Sir Richard stepped forward into the space hurriedly vacated by his student. Using the blade of his pocketknife, he pointed towards the different parts of the skull. 'Take note, gentlemen, of the long cranial shape of the skull, its sloping forehead, the projecting jaws and the wide inter-orbital distance . . .'

'Of course!' Kingsley suddenly exclaimed. 'I see it now! This fellow doesn't have the prominent nose and chin we would normally expect. By Jove, we don't see this every day!'

'Exactly,' said Sir Richard. 'And I suppose we should be grateful to Detective Lavender. Skeletal finds like this are rare.'

'Why?' Lavender snapped. 'What do you see?'

'It's simple, Lavender.' Sir Richard's eyes gleamed with excitement. 'You've brought us a rare find. It's the skeleton of a negro; a man of African descent.'

Chapter Fifteen

Woods downed his first tankard of ale in one and gave a satisfied belch. 'What I don't understand is how everyone else gets things wrong but that sly old sawbones is only ever "premature"?'

Lavender smiled. They were slumped on a settle in a quiet corner of The Nag's Head. Lavender knew he had to get home early tonight but he was a bit dazed, if truth be told, and talking things through with Ned usually helped. Sir Richard's latest revelation had taken the wind out of his sails. *Their mysterious skeleton belonged to a black man?*

Was he a foreign sailor who'd fallen overboard after losing his foot in a bizarre accident? How long had the corpse been bobbing around the Thames? And where had it been for the last two years since the man died?

'He were wrong about that Christian thing.' Woods gestured to the barmaid to refill his tankard. 'Sometimes them darkies are Christians. I've seen them in church in Southwark – and Ignatius Cugoan in Greenwich wore a crucifix below his shirt. I saw it.'

Shirt? What had happened to the ragged clothing they'd dug up with the bones? Lavender remembered the pile of muddy rags discarded in the corner of the morgue. Maybe they would offer up a clue to the black man's identity?

'You saw a crucifix around Cugoan's neck?'

'Yes.'

Lavender nodded, thoughtfully. 'You're right, Ned; there's no reason to suppose that our victim wasn't a Christian. Sir Richard has a tendency to jump to conclusions. He understands human bones and dead people but he's not an expert on the fully fleshed, living kind.'

'He should leave the detectin' to us – or rather to you. That's what you do best. So, what's to do now about this poor fellah? Shall we investigate the churchyards on the north bank of the Thames for a breach?'

'That might be a good way to proceed. I still think our victim has been buried close to the river for the last two years, but I need more time to think.' He pulled his pocket watch out and grimaced. 'I need to get home soon or Magdalena will be annoyed. We've a social engagement tonight and I'm already in trouble after falling asleep last night in my chair.'

'You'd best gather a bunch of hot-house flowers from the market before you go home tonight.'

'Well, yes – thank you, Ned. That's a good thought.'

'And if that doesn't make Doña Magdalena happy, try rubbin' her back.'

'Why? And why do you still call her Doña Magdalena? She wants you to simply call her Magdalena.'

'I'm a man of old habits.'

'Stubborn habits, more like.'

Woods took another sip of his drink. 'Backrubs work a treat with Betsy. They always calm her right down.'

'Thank you again, Ned. As usual, Constable Woods, you're full of good advice about the ladies.'

'Glad to help, sir.' Woods grinned and downed his ale.

Lavender finished his own drink and reached for his gloves. 'To be honest, Ned, I think we'll keep today's discovery a secret from Magistrate Read for a while.'

'Why so?'

'Well, he's not likely to notice the arrival of one more skeleton amongst so many others and, unfortunately, Read has less regard for our coloured brethren than he does for Catholics – and that's saying something. He won't consider this case a priority.'

'That's a shame. The fellah deserves the same justice as any other poor blighter we drag out of the Thames.'

It was more of a shame than Ned realised. Apart from Lavender's burning urge to get to the bottom of this mystery, he'd also hoped this case would be another excuse to postpone his looming trip to Dublin.

'I need to ponder this development for a while.' He stood up and pulled on his hat. 'At least Headless Ted has regained his head and severed foot and is safe at Bow Street.'

Woods rose with him. 'Ah, but he's not Headless Ted any more, is he? He's "Ted-with-a-Head" now.'

'Quite,' said Lavender. They parted at the door of the tavern.

'Don't forget to rub her back!' Woods called after him.

It was nearly half past six when Lavender finally reached his home, armed with a large bunch of flowers. Hopefully, there would just be time to wash and change before they needed to leave for Lady Caroline's. A bite to eat wouldn't go amiss either. The house was warm, well lit and smelt of roast beef. But there was no sign of Magdalena in the drawing room.

'The mistress is upstairs with young Teresa,' their housekeeper informed him.

'Thank you.' Feeling suddenly invigorated, he leapt up the stairs two at a time. He burst through their bedchamber door. 'Magdalena! I've brought you these . . .' He stopped short, surprised by the alarm his sudden appearance had caused.

Magdalena and Teresa were standing in front of the long, rose-wood-framed mirror, but they shrieked when he entered the room.

Lavender just caught a glimpse of a flash of red silk before Teresa threw a long shawl over her mistress's shoulder.

'What in God's name . . . ?'

'Ah, Stephen . . . the flowers are lovely, thank you.' Magdalena was flustered.

Teresa glared at him with her hands on her hips, half shielding Magdalena with her own body.

'What on earth are you doing?'

Mistress and servant exchanged a furtive glance, and Teresa whispered something in Spanish that Lavender didn't hear.

Magdalena sighed. 'No, Teresa. We can't send Detective Lavender away to find a vase to arrange the flowers. Honesty is always the best policy in marriage.'

'Magdalena?'

'I have a little problem, Stephen.'

'Oh?'

'Yes. Today I went shopping – on Lady Caroline's recommendation, I hasten to add – and purchased some new lingerie. It wasn't the best notion. I was just about to take it off and return it to the shop . . . but I can't. It's not the best quality and the clasps appear to be stuck.'

Lingerie? He smiled and stepped forward, his face full of solicitude. This was a problem he would enjoy solving. 'Let me see.'

Magdalena stared innocently up at the ceiling and let the shawl slither from her shoulders. It pooled gracefully by her stockinged feet on the rug. Her curvaceous body was strapped into a scarlet bone corset, the garish kind favoured by the harlots on Hart Street.

'Caroline Clare recommended that you purchase this?'

'Yes. It was a terrible mistake, wasn't it?'

Lavender didn't know how to reply. Magdalena continued to gaze at the ceiling and he wondered if this was a game. Had she been waiting for him to return home and find her like this? A wave of anticipation swept through him.

'You can leave us now, Teresa,' he said. 'I'll release Mrs Lavender from the offending article.'

Their maid humphed, picked up the discarded flowers and walked stiffly to the door. 'You be kind, Señor the Detective.' She threw the words over her shoulder as she left. 'You be plummy and kind.'

'I always am,' he murmured, more to himself than Teresa. 'Plummy is my middle name.' He couldn't take his eyes off his wife. 'Let down your hair, *querida*. I want to see the full effect.'

Magdalena's forehead wrinkled into a small frown. 'But Teresa has just spent ages . . .' She stopped; something in his gaze silenced her protest. Smiling, she reached up and pulled out the hair pins. Her glossy black hair cascaded in waves over her bare shoulders, framing her beautiful face.

'Stand still.' He circled her slowly, taking in the view from all angles. The tightness of the corset had the same enhancing effect on her behind as it did on her bosom. His wife's curvaceous flesh had taken on a new and decidedly interesting appearance.

'It's the hooks at the back,' she said. 'Teresa can't get them undone. Please hurry, Stephen. I can hardly breathe.'

But he wasn't to be hurried. He stopped in front of her, hooked his forefinger through the top laces of the corset and pulled her towards him, their mouths meeting in a long and lingering kiss. Afterwards, he lowered his head to kiss her neck and gently sucked on her earlobes. The softness and scent of her warm skin and the faint perfume of her hair intoxicated him all over again.

'I've neglected you recently, haven't I, *querida*?' he murmured when they finally broke apart for air.

'Yes, you have, Stephen,' she replied simply. Her violet-black eyes smouldered with desire and happiness.

'And now for this damned contraption.' He broke away, pulled out his pocketknife and flicked open the blade.

She started in surprise at the sight of the knife. 'It's the back, Stephen, the hooks at the back . . .'

He smiled and raised the blade to the tight ribbons lacing up the front of the corset. Twang! The smooth flesh of her bosoms quivered when he sliced through a ribbon. He continued slowly down the line of ribbon laces, enjoying the sight. The corset slithered to the floor. Magdalena melted into his arms.

He scooped her up and carried her to the bed.

On the other side of the river in Southwark, Woods sat back in his chair and rubbed his full stomach in satisfaction. Betsy had excelled herself tonight; the stew and dumplings had been superb and they'd finished off their meal with plum pie. There was also an atmosphere of celebration which made the meal even more enjoyable.

Eddie's trip to the Barclay and Perkins brewery had been a success. They'd employed him immediately and set him to work on the wharf. Flushed with excitement, Eddie spent the entire meal regaling them with the details of who he'd met, what he'd done and seen and who had said what at his first day down at the wharf.

'I'll have to go to bed early, Ma,' Eddie said. 'I'm jaded. I'm needed back at the wharf at six tomorrow mornin'. You'll have to keep the youngsters quiet so I can get a good night's sleep.'

'I'll keep them quiet,' Betsy said, struggling to hide her amusement. 'And Dan and Rachel can help clear up the kitchen tonight. You're a workin' man now, Eddie. There'll be no more household chores for you.'

Young Dan opened his mouth to protest, but Betsy silenced him with a frown.

'You'll have to come down to the wharf to sign the papers and pay my indenture, Da.'

'I'll do that tomorrow. I'm glad it's worked out well for you, son.'
Woods smiled.

'Yes, but there's so much to do and learn. The foreman, Mr Irish,
is stern but seems a fair man; he had me runnin' a lot of errands today
and cleanin' out barrels. Captain Johnson were nice too.'

'Who's he?'

'It were his ship, the *Aurora*, they were unloadin'. He pointed out
the different ships tied up at the wharf and told me their names, what
cargo they carried and where they sailed.'

'He sounds kind,' Betsy said.

'He also explained about the terrible stench of the *Georgia Grange*.'

'What's the *Georgia Grange*?' Woods asked.

'She were also berthed at the wharf. You can smell her hulls from
yards away. Captain Johnson said she were a slave ship. He said the
owners can't never get rid of the smell once it's seeped into the timber.'

Betsy gasped, but Eddie continued regardless. 'There's some cargoes
these slave ships can't carry because they just end up stinkin' so bad . . .'

'Eddie! I'll not have that kind of talk in the house, do you hear me?'

'Your ma's right, son,' Woods said. 'It's not a nice thing to talk about
with women.'

'Sorry, Ma.' Eddie grinned his apology to his mother, then turned
to answer a question from little Rachel.

Woods sat quietly for a moment. *Slavery*. Was it possible that Ted-
with-a-Head had been a slave? Slave trading had been abolished years
ago – and Lavender said their mysterious victim had only been dead for
two years. His broad forehead crinkled as he struggled to make sense of
the notion. This was a conundrum for Lavender to sort out.

Chapter Sixteen

L avender and Magdalena were late, but both of them were smiling
when their cab drew to a halt outside Lady Caroline's ground-floor
apartment in Lincoln's Inn Fields.

Magdalena looked stunning tonight. Her long black curls trailed
over her shoulders beneath her bonnet, with short ringlets framing her
oval face in the Grecian fashion. Beneath her velvet cloak she wore a
midnight-blue, high-waisted silk gown, decorated with seed pearls and
a few glistening stones at the neckline. Teresa had recreated the theme in
her mistress's hair, which was adorned with jewelled and pearl hair pins.
None of the stones were real, of course, but the effect was still striking.

Lady Caroline's apartment was warm and beautifully furnished.
Exquisite oil paintings of landscapes and gilt-framed lithographs jostled
for space on the walls of the hallway, interspersed with tiny cameo portraits suspended on brass chains from the picture rail. The maid took
their coats and hats and led them to the noisy drawing room.

The soirée was well attended. Despite her parentage, Lady Caroline
had been barred from the salons of her aristocratic peers years ago, following her scandalous elopement with Victor Rothschild. Unperturbed,
she'd made her own circle of friends. She counted a few minor nobles
amongst her acquaintance but mostly surrounded herself with fellow

artists, musicians and the actor friends of her stepdaughter, April. Her soirées were always an eclectic mix of London society.

The tall dividing doors between the two reception rooms had been pulled back to create one long space. It heaved with vibrantly attired guests, most of whom clutched china plates of food. The majority of the female guests favoured white muslin, and the vivid hues of their feathered headdresses, wafting fans and fine shawls clashed delightfully with the patterned silk waistcoats of the men and the vivid scarlet of officers' uniforms. The brilliant candlelight reflected the glittering jewellery of the women, making the scene sparkle. A mixture of perfume and the scent of dozens of beeswax candles burning in the chandeliers above flavoured the stifling air. Lavender felt as if he had just walked into the colourful sunbeams slanting down from the stained-glass windows of a cathedral. A very hot cathedral.

A hired butler, resplendent in green livery, announced their arrival. 'Detective Lavender, Mrs Lavender.' But hardly anyone heard the announcement.

A footman in the same livery stepped forward with a tray of champagne; they took a glass each and glanced around for their hostess. Lavender craned his neck to see over the regimental hats, turbans and waving ostrich feathers of the women's headdresses. In the noisiest part of the long room, the actors and actresses of the Sans Pareil Theatre had gathered around the pianoforte while William Broadhurst, the company's leading man, played a popular love ballad.

Lady Caroline's stepdaughter, April, and her ladyship's nephew from her first marriage, Solomon Rothschild, were at the centre of the group. Rothschild's eyes already gleamed with too much champagne. The black velvet yarmulke on his dark head had fallen to a lopsided, almost rakish angle.

The theatre's Italian actress, Helena Bologna, slid onto the wooden stool beside Broadhurst and patted his thigh affectionately. Lavender sensed, rather than saw, a glowering, middle-aged man on the edge of their crowd stiffen with anger at her action.

Was the fellow her latest lover? he wondered. Miss Bologna's love-conquests filled columns of tittle-tattle in the daily news-sheets and the stage door of the theatre was often besieged with infatuated men. Her latest conquest, if that is indeed what he was, was obviously a man of some breeding: his dark-green coat had been exquisitely tailored, gold rings flashed on his meaty fingers and an emerald pin secured his silk cravat. But he was a glowering brute nonetheless.

Magdalena tapped Lavender on his arm with her fan. 'I can see Lady Caroline.' He followed her gaze and saw a familiar pearl-studded turban topped with yellow ostrich feathers in the orangery at the far end of the room.

Lavender fell into step behind her. The crowd seemed to part before his wife as she glided gracefully towards the bobbing feathers. Lavender smiled as he followed. Magdalena was in her element; this was her world and her aristocratic breeding glowed like a halo around her. He knew Magdalena had married beneath her when she'd wed a common police officer, but the status of the Principal Officers was unusual. Famous throughout London, the aristocracy loved and feted the officers; invitations to soirées and parties were common. Lavender had never been comfortable with being shown off in a drawing room like a pet poodle and he tended to avoid these occasions; if he was honest, he'd rather be home tonight by his fireside with a good book and a glass of brandy in his hand. But marriage had meant they'd both had to compromise.

Lady Caroline's face lit up with smiles. 'Magdalena! Detective Lavender! You've arrived!' She greeted Magdalena with a kiss on her cheek but raised a quizzical eyebrow to him. 'Has naughty James Read been overworking you again at Bow Street, Detective? Is that why you're so late?'

Lavender and Magdalena exchanged a furtive glance. He bowed low to their hostess. 'You're quite right, Lady Caroline,' he said. 'I was late home again tonight; please accept my apologies for our tardiness.'

'How could I not forgive such a beautiful couple?' Lady Caroline said. 'My goodness, you must be the most striking pair in the room tonight. Magdalena, you look radiant, my dear; you're glowing.' A faint flush crept up Magdalena's neck and she murmured her thanks.

Lavender took Lady Caroline's gloved hand in his and raised it to his lips. 'But no one, absolutely no one, can outshine our hostess tonight. You look ravishing, Lady Caroline.' This wasn't a lie. Tall and willowy, with an excellent complexion and vivid auburn curls peeping below her turban, Caroline Clare always turned heads whenever she walked into a room, and it wasn't because she needed the help of a walking cane.

Lady Caroline paused just a tiny bit longer than necessary with her hand in his, and smiled. 'I'd forgotten how charming you can be when you want to be, Detective,' she said.

'Alas, I spend too much time growling at villains. I worry sometimes I'm out of practice when it comes to polite company.'

She lifted her hand and gestured to the company around them. 'Well, there are no villains here tonight – apart from the usual crowd, of course. So, you should have plenty of opportunity to practise your charm with the ladies. And talking of ladies . . .' She turned to the woman who stood beside her. 'Detective Lavender? Magdalena? Please let me introduce you to my fellow artist, Lady Mary Gordon. You'll remember, Magdalena, that I told you Lady Gordon was one of the women behind the women's gallery on the Strand?' She gestured to the lanky young man hovering at the edge of the group. 'Come, Duddles, greet our friends.'

More introductions followed. Lavender bowed to Lady Gordon and Magdalena sank into a deep and beautiful curtsey. Henry Duddles, a fresh-faced young man with a huge shock of baby-blond curls, stepped forward and bowed to Magdalena before vigorously shaking Lavender's hand. 'How now, Lavender? How goes the world of crime?'

Lavender smiled and answered him politely. Although still awkward, at least Duddles spoke to him these days; the young man had barely said a word for the first few years of their acquaintance.

'I'm delighted to meet you, Mrs Lavender.' Lady Gordon smiled warmly as she spoke. 'Lady Caroline told me of your fascinating background in Spain and your desperate flight to safety here in London. I'm intrigued to know more about the Spanish court.' She wore a simple white muslin dress with an ornamental gold brooch pinned to her bosom and a long red Kashmir shawl draped over the top of her arms. The edges of the shawl reached the ground and were exquisitely embroidered with gold silk. A small pair of ruby earrings was the only other jewellery she wore besides her rings.

'I'm delighted to meet you too, Lady Gordon – I would love to know more about your gallery and how you turned the idea into reality.'

'My goodness, your English is excellent.' Lady Gordon barely hid her surprise. 'I'd always assumed you conversed with Caroline in Spanish.'

Lady Caroline frowned. 'They do have schools in Spain, you know, Mary.'

Magdalena smiled. 'Actually, I was taught English by my governess. Is your new patroness here – the lady who purchased your painting? You promised to introduce me to her.'

Lady Caroline shook her head. 'I'm afraid she was called away to her estate in the country unexpectedly.'

'Oh, what a shame. Has Captain Leon arrived yet? Stephen wants to meet him.'

Lady Caroline shook her head again, then turned back to Lady Gordon. 'My goodness, Mary! I forgot to tell you about the shocking experience Magdalena and I endured yesterday at the hands of a devilish silk-snatcher.'

'Good grief! Were you hurt?'

The three women began an animated conversation about the attempted robbery of Lady Caroline's reticule, leaving Lavender and Duddles in companionable silence. A welcome breeze drifted gently through the open glass windows behind them.

Lady Caroline's studio had been tidied up and the furniture pushed back against the walls. There was no sign of her great easel, and the table, normally littered with discarded paintbrushes, tubs of mixed oil paint and greasy rags, had been transformed into a supper table. It groaned under the weight of partridge, pheasant and ham, larded oysters, small savoury pastries and a large selection of desserts, including a quivering blancmange, sweetmeats, marzipans and a bowl of spiced pears.

A familiar portly figure stood in the far corner of the orangery, a vivid yellow-and-black checked waistcoat stretched over his rotund belly. It was William Turner, the renowned and eccentric maritime and landscape artist. He was deep in conversation with another man in front of one of Lady Caroline's oil paintings.

'I see Turner's here,' Lavender said to Duddles.

'Yes – and that's Joshua Reynolds he's with. Neither of them are sociable fellows. Not like you and I, Lavender. But Caro is pleased they came. You'll have to lock up your wife once Turner gets a whiff of her scent. Damned fellow always makes a beeline for her.'

Lavender smiled. 'Oh, Magdalena can take care of herself.'

Duddles frowned and pushed his shock of blond curls out of his eyes. 'I don't see why fellows should always be going at the women of other men. Seems damned uncivilised to me.'

Lavender heard the jealousy in his voice and wondered if there was friction between Duddles and Lady Caroline. The fellow seemed less jovial than usual. Magdalena had told him about Duddles' impending nuptials and he wondered how this was affecting them. Was Lady Caroline already casting around for his replacement?

'A little flirtation generally does no harm if it is in a chivalrous spirit,' he said softly. 'You'll discover this yourself once you're married: you'll flirt with other married women while their husbands flirt with your wife.'

'Ha! I'll be damned if I do! There's too much flirting in the world already.'

Lavender decided to change the subject. 'That reminds me, who's the fellow over there – and the woman behind him?' He pointed to the glowering man behind the actress, Helena Bologna.

Duddles stiffened and frowned. 'That's Baron Danvers from Southerly Park in Middlesex – Helena Bologna is his latest mistress.'

Lavender grimaced. Danvers' reputation preceded him and it wasn't pleasant. 'Didn't you and Lady Caroline once tell me that Danvers—?'

'Beats his wife worse than he beats his dogs?' Duddles interrupted sharply. 'Yes, that's the cad. His first wife drowned herself to get away from him. That's his second wife, Lady Eliza, behind him.'

'What? He's brought his poor wife along to watch him ogle his mistress?'

Lavender's gaze turned sympathetically to the pale woman standing behind Baron Danvers, fiddling nervously with her wedding band. Despite the heat of the room and the high neck and long sleeves of her plum-coloured taffeta gown, Lady Danvers appeared to be shivering. He remembered Lady Caroline's comments about the baroness's preference for long-sleeved gowns . . . *They hide the bruises and lacerations on her skin.*

'Why on earth is such a man here?'

Duddles shrugged. 'Miss Bologna and April are friends. April persuaded Caro to give the Danvers an invitation. Caro's not happy about it, but she didn't want to make a fuss and refuse April's request.'

Danvers' lascivious eyes followed every gesture and movement of the glamorous actress. Lavender felt another stab of sympathy for his poor, humiliated wife. Lady Danvers was probably about the same age as Magdalena and may once have been quite pretty in a mousy kind of way, but she looked haggard and pained now, despite the elegance and richness of her clothing and jewellery.

'He's a cad,' Duddles said simply.

Lavender nodded. 'And that, Duddles, is why we should sometimes flirt with married women. A few kind words and a compliment here and there can brighten their entire day. I'm sure Lady Danvers, for one, would relish a bit of harmless attention. Although it could also be cruel to make someone believe you admire them or have feelings for them when you don't.'

Through a gap in the crowd, he caught sight of another familiar face. Josef Rothschild was Lady Caroline's brother-in-law from her first marriage and had employed Lavender for security work at the Rothschild Bank. He stood with an austere-looking woman whom Lavender assumed to be his wife. They kept glancing at their son, Solomon, over at the pianoforte with the actors. The Rothschilds looked out of place.

'Excuse me, Duddles. I've just seen someone I know.' He began to walk towards the couple but stopped short in alarm.

A wild-haired man with a large hooked nose and cold emotionless eyes had joined the Rothschilds and engaged them in conversation. While he talked, the man's eyes roamed brazenly up and down Mrs Rothschild's flat, board-like chest, following the long double rope of black pearls entwined around her throat. Lavender's hackles rose. The man was appraising their value.

Where had he seen that wild, sandy-coloured hair and those bushy sideburns before? His memory jolted and he turned sharply back to Duddles. 'Is that Micky Sullivan talking with the Rothschilds?'

Micky Sullivan. The notorious moneylender and vicious gang leader from the rookery of St Giles. *What the devil was he doing here?*

Duddles shrugged. 'Can't say, Lavender. All I know is the fellow has been a nuisance. Always at the damned house.' He could barely conceal his jealousy as he added, 'The devil knows what Caro sees in him.'

Lavender groaned inwardly. Caroline Clare was a renowned spendthrift who'd never adjusted to her straitened financial circumstances following the death of her second husband. No doubt she'd borrowed money from Sullivan.

One thing was for sure: the Rothschilds needed rescuing from the villain immediately.

Chapter Seventeen

Sullivan glanced up when Lavender strode towards him, recognition and annoyance flashing across his features in equal measure. By the time Lavender reached Mr and Mrs Rothschild the wretch had vanished.

'Lavender!' Josef Rothschild shook Lavender's hand and introduced him to his wife. Almost bald beneath his black velvet yarmulke, Josef was unusually fair-skinned for his race and had a permanently startled expression in his soft, brown eyes.

They exchanged pleasantries and chatted about the work Lavender had done for Josef the previous year, then Lavender asked them about their acquaintance with Micky Sullivan.

'Oh, is that what he's called?' Mrs Rothschild said tartly. 'The fellow didn't introduce himself properly.' Both the Rothschilds had strong German accents, but Mrs Rothschild was as fluent in the English language as her husband.

'He claimed he was in banking,' Rothschild said. 'Do you know of a Sullivan's Bank, Detective?'

'No, I don't. Would you like to come over and meet my wife, Mrs Rothschild? I'm sure she would be delighted to make your acquaintance.'

Her sour expression lightened immediately. 'I'd be delighted to! Solomon has told us much about your charming and accomplished wife.' Lavender smiled. Solomon Rothschild was another of Magdalena's conquests. The young man had been infatuated with her since they first met.

They returned to the group below the vaulted glass ceiling of the orangery. The ladies had taken a plate of supper and Magdalena was nibbling on a piece of iced orange, while Lady Gordon chased syllabub around her dish with a spoon. After more introductions, Magdalena and Mrs Rothschild were soon chatting about their sons' education, a topic on which the latter had plenty of advice. Lavender helped himself to another glass of champagne and tried to relax.

A tall, smartly dressed man with thick fair hair flopping over his forehead walked towards the group, smiling.

'Captain Leon!' Lady Caroline's face lit up with delight.

'My apologies for my lateness, dear lady.' Captain Leon bent over his hostess's hand. 'I've only just this moment escaped from a dreadful performance of *Macbeth* at the Drury Lane Theatre.'

'Oh?' Lady Gordon said. 'Did the divine Sarah Siddons fail to move you with her famous portrayal of Lady Macbeth?'

'On the contrary ma'am,' Captain Leon replied. 'I was so moved by her performance I found myself blubbing like a seasick cabin boy missing his mother. I went through both of my lawn handkerchiefs and scrambled to be the first to leave the theatre in case some fellow recognised me. I've not felt so dreadfully wretched for years.'

Everyone laughed, Lady Caroline the loudest. Lavender wondered how many glasses of champagne she'd had. She seemed to be leaning more heavily on her walking cane than normal.

'Well, shame on you, Captain Leon,' she said, 'for not heeding my advice! I did suggest that you visit the Sans Pareil Theatre instead.'

'Ah, but I did, ma'am. I went to the Sans Pareil last night and saw your delightful stepdaughter play Cupid in *The Magic Pipe*.' His narrow, green eyes wandered over to April at the piano. 'This is how I know the two performances didn't compare favourably and that *Macbeth* was the inferior play.'

Lady Caroline's neck flushed and her eyes gleamed with delight. 'Let me introduce you to some of my guests, Captain Leon. This is Lady Gordon, a dear friend. See? Didn't I tell you, Mary, that our Captain Leon has the prettiest eyes?'

'Humph!' Duddles exclaimed.

'You've already met Mrs Lavender,' Lady Caroline continued. 'This is her husband, Detective Stephen Lavender from Bow Street.'

'A pleasure to meet you again, ma'am.' Leon raised Magdalena's hand to his lips and his eyes slid sideways to glance curiously at Lavender. 'You never mentioned your husband was one of Bow Street's finest officers.' He straightened and turned to Lavender. 'We've heard of you and your successes even up in Manchester, sir; our news-sheets are full of your exploits.'

'Then there must be nothing else to write about.' Lavender shook Leon's hand. 'I believe I owe you a debt of gratitude for the assistance you offered Lady Caroline and my wife yesterday. Thank you.'

Leon was about his own age and had unusual features. His prominent cheekbones gave him a Slavic appearance but Leon was a name of Spanish origin, rather than Russian. Lavender wondered briefly about the man's ancestry, then dismissed his curiosity as idle; Leon probably didn't know himself.

Thanks to its extensive trade, England had been a melting pot for people from many different races and nationalities for centuries. London, in particular, welcomed everyone, from a Hanoverian king to an African man like Ignatius Cugoan.

'It was the least I could do, sir,' Leon said. 'Any man would have done the same.'

'Are you staying long in London, Captain Leon?' asked Lady Gordon. 'We need more gallant young men like you.'

'I'm not sure, my lady. Until recently I was an honest working man like Detective Lavender here; a captain of the merchant navy.'

He didn't look or sound like an ordinary working man, Lavender thought. The tailoring of his buff-coloured coat was excellent. Apart from the occasional seafaring expression, Leon's accent was educated.

'So what changed, sir?' Lady Caroline asked.

'Well! A wealthy great-uncle, whom I'd never met, went and died and left me his entire fortune. I'm worth four thousand a year now.'

'How unfortunate for your uncle,' Lady Mary murmured.

'Yes, but fortunate for me,' Leon replied, grinning. 'I'm down in London for a while looking at a few investments and enjoying the best of the distractions the city can offer.'

Lavender smiled when he caught the look of excitement in Caroline Clare's eyes. 'Do take care, Leon,' he said. 'London is full of villains – you'll meet plenty of coves who'll be more than happy to divest you of your fortune.' *And women*, he nearly added.

Leon had no time to respond. A loud, chesty cough announced the arrival of the shuffling and portly artist, William Turner.

Lady Gordon gave a wicked smile. 'Ooh, here comes one of your villains, Detective.'

'Felicitations of the evening, ladies and gentlemen.' Turner's voice was deep and gravelly. 'You find yourself well, Lady Caroline?'

'In excellent health, thank you, Mr Turner.'

Turner gave Lady Gordon a brief nod. 'And our blue-stockinged belle?'

Lady Gordon bristled. 'I assume you're referring to me, Mr Turner? Yes, I'm in good health, thank you.'

'Good venture that – the women's gallery.'

For a moment, it looked like Lady Gordon's frosty attitude might soften. 'Have you visited our humble establishment, Mr Turner?'

'No, but it's a good venture – you gals need somewhere to display your work.'

Lady Gordon bristled. 'It would be better if the Royal Academy gave greater recognition to our endeavours and let a few more of us "gals" through the portals of its hallowed halls.'

Lady Caroline stepped forward to intervene. 'Mr Turner, you haven't greeted Mrs Lavender or Mrs Rothschild yet.'

Turner grunted, nodded at Mrs Rothschild, then bent low over Magdalena's hand. 'As usual, ma'am, you're a vision of profound beauty. Aphrodite herself must quiver with jealousy when she gazes down on your form from the dizzying heights of Olympus.'

Magdalena gave a slight curtsey and bowed her head to hide her smile. 'Thank you, Mr Turner. You're too kind.'

'Not kind at all, not kind,' Turner continued. 'An artist must venerate his muse; all other emotion is spent. I shall paint you as Aphrodite once I have finished with Dido building Carthage.'

'Be careful, Magdalena,' warned Lady Caroline with a smile. 'Aphrodite is usually depicted unclothed.'

'I say!' Duddles exclaimed.

'Of course she's naked.' Turner reached for his silver snuffbox. 'Aphrodite's body is expressive of her nature. She's the embodiment of physical beauty, forever associated with the power to rivet attention, stir admiration and arouse sensual feeling.'

'Josef! I wish to go home,' Mrs Rothschild said.

'Just a moment, my dear,' her husband replied.

'Oh, it's all very well espousing the classics, Mr Turner,' Lady Gordon interrupted, 'but you're primarily a maritime and landscape artist. Where would a naked Aphrodite fit in amongst "Dutch sailing vessels in a storm"?'

Turner took his snuff and gave Lady Gordon a heavy wink. 'Figureheads, milady,' he growled. 'The wooden figurehead of a great ship. All prodigious seagoing vessels need a bare-chested female figurehead. 'Tis the way of things. Mrs Lavender shall pose for me naked from the waist up as Aphrodite, the carved goddess of the sea.'

'We'll think about that for a while, Turner, if you don't mind,' Lavender said hastily.

Turner shrugged and snapped shut his snuffbox. 'As you wish. I merely offer immortality in oil.' He gave Magdalena a leering grin. 'All goddesses should be immortalised on canvas.' With that, he turned and shuffled away.

'That man gets more insufferable each time I meet him,' Lady Gordon announced.

Mrs Rothschild clearly agreed with her. 'It's time we left, Josef. We've an early start tomorrow morning.'

'Yes, my dear.' Josef Rothschild turned to face Lavender. 'I meant to ask you about the state of the roads around Blackheath, Detective. Leah and I will be travelling to Rochester tomorrow morning and I'd heard there was a dangerous gang of footpads on the heath.'

'They were captured by Constable Woods of the horse patrol yesterday,' Lavender said with some relief. 'The roads should be clear of trouble now.'

'Thank you, Detective.' The Rothschilds said goodbye to everyone and left.

Lavender realised that Micky Sullivan was lurking behind them again. Once more the cove caught Lavender's eye, turned and drifted away.

Irritated, Lavender left the group and followed the moneylender towards the buffet table. A liveried footman watched Sullivan closely, his eyes flickering protectively over the silver cutlery as if he half expected Sullivan to pocket it.

'What in hell are you doing here, Sullivan?' Lavender hissed.

The shoulders of Sullivan's dun-coloured coat shrugged. He stacked a pile of larded oysters onto his plate. 'I'm enjoyin' a little light supper, Detective.'

'But why are you here? You must realise you don't belong at a gathering like this.'

Sullivan turned his pale, cold eyes towards Lavender. 'And you do, Lavender? That grammar schoolin' of yours and a year at Cambridge University qualifies you to 'ob and nob with the toffs, does it?'

Lavender was surprised that Sullivan knew so much about his past but he kept his face fixed. 'I was invited here tonight. My wife and Lady Caroline are good friends.'

'And so were I.' The smug satisfaction in Sullivan's voice grated on Lavender. 'And you can 'ardly blame a fellow fer a little curiosity, can you? I've allus wondered 'ow the other 'alf lives, so ter speak. Besides which' – Sullivan paused to put a handful of hot-house strawberries next to his pile of oysters – 'I paid fer most of this spread, so I'm damned well goin' to enjoy it.'

Lavender groaned inwardly and wondered how much money Lady Caroline owed to this odious man. 'So you extracted the invitation from Lady Caroline under duress?'

'Yer 'ave a poor opinion of me, Lavender. I'm an 'onest business-man.' Sullivan picked up a savoury pastry and held it up to the light to examine it before popping it into his mouth. 'It were 'er ladyship 'erself who suggested I came 'ere to 'ob and nob wi' 'er fancy pals.' He spoke with his mouth open, strings of saliva glistening in the candlelight. 'The invitation were in lieu of a small portion of interest on 'er loan. Mind you, the jilt drives an 'ard bargain. The foxy wench said this would be an excitin' party of pleasure wi' dancin', card tables, pretty women and the rest, but I've 'ad more fun at a song-and-supper evenin' at The Dog and Duck.'

This was a small consolation. If Sullivan wasn't enjoying himself, he would probably leave soon, Lavender supposed. He heard Captain Leon laugh loudly in the group surrounding Magdalena. He certainly was a cheerful fellow.

'Well, as you're here, perhaps you can help me out with something.'

A half-smile flicked across the moneylender's face. It didn't reach his eyes. 'And what would that be, Detective?'

'I understand there's a new gang of villains in the rookery. Who are they and who's their arch-rogue?'

The corner of Sullivan's thin lips curled sardonically. 'And 'ow would an 'onest businessman like me know anythin' about such villains and rogues? No, yer best off askin' around. There's a fellah called Fletcher – lives down the alley off Carrier Street – 'e might be able to 'elp yer.'

Lavender's guts lurched. *Sullivan knew about his informer?*

Sullivan's deadpan eyes suddenly lit up at the sight of something over Lavender's shoulder. ''Old up! It's startin' to liven up at last!'

Raised voices made Lavender turn and follow Sullivan's gaze. Lady Caroline, flushed from the champagne, was in the middle of a public spat with Duddles. 'But Henry!' she exclaimed. 'You're far too young to have conversations with the dead; you barely know anyone who's died.'

A hush descended over the room. Heads turned in their direction. William Broadhurst's fingers paused mid-air over the pianoforte keyboard.

'You treat me like a child, Caro!' Duddles replied, angrily. 'But I know what you're up to. I'm a man – and a hot-blooded buck too. You see if I'm not!'

He turned sharply on his heel and strode over towards the wide-eyed Lady Danvers. Lifting her hand in his, he kissed it and bowed elaborately. 'You've the prettiest eyes, m'lady,' he exclaimed hotly. 'But you spend too much time conversing with villains. Let me take you away from here and paint you naked from the waist upwards.'

Lady Caroline's loud shriek rose above the gasp of shock that filled the room. 'Good God! Duddles has gone stark raving mad!'

Lavender stepped forward quickly, but Lord Danvers reached Duddles first. In one smooth and vicious movement, he raised his large hand and slapped Duddles across his face.

Duddles blinked and rocked on the heels of his boots. The force of the blow left a flaming pink mark on his cheek.

The furious baron leaned forward into Duddles' face. 'I demand satisfaction, sir!' Spittle sprayed everywhere. 'You've insulted my wife and impugned my own honour. Tomorrow at dawn in the copse in Hyde Park. Choose your second and bring your own pistols.'

'Gentlemen!'

'Oh, Lavender, here you are,' Duddles said with obvious relief. 'Will you be my second?'

'No, I won't,' he said forcefully. 'May I remind both you gentlemen that duelling is against the law?'

'Don't be such a killjoy, Lavender!' Micky Sullivan yelled.

'Duddles, you need to apologise to Baron Danvers for the offence caused.'

'I won't.'

'Yes, you will. This is a misunderstanding – but you've insulted Baron Danvers. Apologise.'

'Oh, all right. Sorry there, Danvers. A chap meant no harm.'

'I refuse to accept your apology,' Danvers snarled. 'I can't imagine anything better than shooting you through your stupid head. I'll see you in Hyde Park at dawn.' He turned sharply. 'Eliza! We're leaving.'

The brute stormed towards the door, but his wife seemed rooted to the spot. She gazed at Duddles in awe, seeming neither shocked nor insulted.

'Eliza!'

Finally, Lady Danvers gave Duddles a sweet smile, turned and followed her bad-tempered husband. She stopped when she reached the door, turned back and raised her hand to give Duddles a little wave. Unbelievably, he waved back.

The room exploded the moment the door was closed. Everyone had an opinion about the incident and the prospect of a duel.

'Duddles apologised,' Lavender said over and over again. 'There is no need for a duel; Danvers should accept the apology with good grace and back down.'

His reasoning fell on deaf ears. Too much champagne had fired up the emotions of the guests. Every one of Duddles' unusual choices of words was remembered, reiterated and discussed. The marksmanship skills of Duddles and Danvers were compared. A book was opened and money changed hands. Someone declared the event more dramatic than a night at the theatre. Captain Leon laughed at this and declared that that depended on which theatre you attended.

Lady Caroline had an attack of the vapours and had to be led to a sofa to sit down. 'I couldn't bear it if anything should happen to poor Duddles!' she wailed. Magdalena crouched at her side and wafted *sal volatile* beneath her nose.

'Nothing will happen to him, if you don't let him out of your sight tomorrow morning,' Lavender hissed in Lady Caroline's ear. 'Keep him close.' But she barely seemed to hear him.

Meanwhile, Duddles stood in the centre of the room as if mesmerised, seemingly oblivious to the slap mark still burning on his cheek.

Exhaustion washed over Lavender and a sharp pain stabbed at his temple as he cursed himself for encouraging the young fool to try to flirt with Lady Danvers. He pulled Magdalena aside and suggested they went home.

Lavender relished the fresh air and relative quiet of the dark street when they left. It was never silent in London, of course, even late in the evening: there was always the distant rumble of wagon wheels grinding over the cobbles, feral dogs fighting over a rat and noisy drunks staggering home from the taverns. An empty hackney carriage waited on the other side of the street and he hailed the driver, helping Magdalena into the vehicle.

Captain Leon and Micky Sullivan came out of the house together, laughing. Leon was the worse for drink and stumbled down the last three steps. 'Aren't you walking home tonight, Detective?' he yelled. ''Tis a pleasant evening for a stroll.'

'We've found a cab. Mrs Lavender is tired. I wish you a good night.'

'Well, I shall walk back to my lodgings on Jermyn Street with my new friend, Mr Sullivan.' He reached out, patted the moneylender's shoulders and began to weave down the street with Sullivan.

Lavender hesitated. His instinct was to warn Leon about the company he was keeping. If anyone were to fleece the captain of his new-found fortune, it would be the devious Sullivan. But he thought better of it and climbed up into the cab after Magdalena. He'd already warned Leon to be careful earlier in the night; that would have to suffice.

He slumped back into his seat and took Magdalena's gloved hand in his own. The cab lurched forward and the pressure in his temple subsided. 'What on earth happened, *querida*?' he asked. 'What was the argument about between Duddles and Lady Caroline?'

Magdalena sighed. 'Lady Caroline was flirting outrageously with Captain Leon. Duddles became angry and jealous, but I have no explanation for why he suddenly took off and made those outrageous comments to Lady Danvers. What possessed him, do you think?'

Lavender shuffled uncomfortably on his cold leather seat. 'Well, part of what Duddles said was a condensed version of William Turner's flattery of you.'

'Yes, I can see that – and you had earlier said to Lady Caroline that you spend too much time conversing with villains. Duddles seems to have combined both conversations and made them into his own awkward attempt at flattery. But what I don't understand was why he approached Lady Danvers. You talked to him earlier; did he give you any indication he had a fondness for the poor woman?'

'No, none.' He grimaced, thankful for the weak lamplight in the cab, which prevented Magdalena from reading his guilty expression. 'Why were Lady Caroline and Duddles arguing? What was all that talk about dead people?'

Magdalena sighed again. 'Captain Leon has heard of an amazing woman who lives in Clerkenwell. Her name's Peggy Dunne and she's . . . well, she earns a living by communing with the spirits of the dead.'

Lavender smiled in the darkness. 'You don't believe any of that, do you, *querida*? She's just another charlatan, determined to fleece the gullible of their hard-earned money.'

'Well, it doesn't matter what I believe now, does it? I'll never meet her. Captain Leon proposed to escort us to the woman's home tomorrow afternoon. Lady Mary declared she was unavailable and Lady Caroline told Duddles he couldn't come along – I think she wanted Captain Leon to herself. They argued and now there will be no outing for anyone.'

'You sound a little disappointed.'

'Perhaps I am.' She paused. 'What do you think will happen tomorrow morning, Stephen?'

'With any luck, Duddles and Danvers will both calm down, sober up and agree to fire their pistols in the air and go home to breakfast. Failing that, we must hope Caroline chains Duddles to her bedpost and doesn't let him out.'

Magdalena giggled and slapped him lightly on his leg again. The cab swung into Westcastle Square and slowed when it approached their house.

'Who do you want to speak to?' he asked quietly. 'Is it Antonio, your first husband?'

'Good heavens, no!' She turned towards him and he saw the genuine surprise on her face. 'No, I thought . . . I would like to speak to my father once more.'

Relieved, he kissed her cheek affectionately, reached for the handle of the cab and opened the door.

Chapter Eighteen

It was still dark when Lavender arrived at Bow Street. Low cloud and drizzle delayed the arrival of daylight and cast the building into shadow. A lamp burned in Read's upstairs office. The yawning and bleary-eyed clerk in the hallway told him Magistrate Read was keen to speak with him, but Lavender decided to first pay a quick visit to the morgue to try to examine Ted-with-a-Head's clothing.

The back yard was deserted. The night patrol had yet to return and there was no sign of the builders. The ostler snored peacefully on a pile of hay in the stable.

Lavender opened the door of the morgue and recoiled slightly at the smell of death lingering in the dismal room. His eyes strained against the gloom and it took him a moment to realise Ted-with-a-Head had disappeared from the slab. No doubt the negro's skeleton and skull now had pride of place in a display cabinet at Guy's Hospital for the Incurables.

The poor fellow's stinking clothing still lay discarded in a heap in the corner. He fetched a pail of water from the pump outside and doused the rags to remove the river mud before spreading them out on the central slab. Thin, torn and made of the cheapest material, they consisted of a long shirt and a ragged pair of trousers, which Lavender suspected would barely have reached down the calves of the tall negro. There were no underclothes and no stockings.

'Mornin', sir.' Woods appeared by his side. For a big man, Woods could move quietly when he wanted to. 'Are those our Ted's clothes?'

'Yes, I hoped they might give us a clue to the man's origin or trade, but the only conclusion I've reached is that the poor wretch must have been frozen and barely decent in this outfit.'

'I were wondering last night . . .'

'If he was a slave?'

Woods' eyes widened in his round face. 'Well, yes! Were you thinkin' along the same lines, sir? Is it possible? Seein' as we no longer trade in slaves?'

'I honestly don't know, Ned. The slave trade was abolished five years ago but the royal navy still deploys several vessels off the west coast of Africa to try to disrupt the slavers, so someone must still be involved in the vile practice.'

'Are they British ships, these slavers?'

Lavender shrugged. 'Allegedly, many slave owners sidestepped the abolition and simply registered their ships under foreign flags – though proving this is difficult.'

'I know what we can do,' Woods said. 'Let's take these rags over to Mr Cugoan in Greenwich and ask him for his opinion. If this is the kind of garb worn by slaves, he might know.'

'That's a good thought, Ned.'

'Shall we ride out today?'

'No, not today. I daren't risk the wrath of Magistrate Read any further with this case.'

Woods' face fell with disappointment.

'But we'll go on Sunday, after church, if you so wish. Read doesn't dictate how we spend our Sunday afternoons.'

'I'll be there,' Woods grinned. 'Sunday afternoons are always good for a jaunt south of the river.'

They left the morgue and made their way up to Magistrate Read's office.

As usual, Read was wigless and dwarfed behind the huge pile of papers awaiting his attention on his untidy desk. 'Ah, Lavender – Woods. Glad you're here early.' He gestured for them to sit down. 'There's been a development in the Bellingham case, Lavender.'

'What?'

'The Ambassador, Lord Granville Leveson-Gower, sent me a note this morning with one of his servants. He's sure he saw John Bellingham lurking in the square outside his home last night.'

Lavender frowned. If true, then this was a disturbing development. But nervous men were often tricked by shadows in the fading light. 'I've read Bellingham's pamphlet, sir. I found it worrying, but so far I've seen no indication that the man is a danger to Lord Leveson-Gower – or anyone else.'

'Well, I need you to stay close to him today – and tonight. If he goes anywhere near the Ambassador's residence on Hanover Square, I want you to arrest him immediately for harassment.'

'Yes, sir.'

'How goes the investigation into the robbery of Lord and Lady Yarmouth?'

'Woods and Barnaby have continued to make enquiries with known fences, jewellers and pawnbrokers, but we've no leads yet. Meanwhile, the Earl and Countess have left town for St Albans and aren't due to return until tomorrow. I'll visit them then. The Earl was convinced the thieves knew about his money-chest and that the robbers had information from an inside source. I've questioned their servants at length and I now want to question Lord and Lady Yarmouth about who in their acquaintance knew of their travel plans.'

Read raised a grey eyebrow and observed Lavender silently for a moment. 'That won't please them,' he finally said.

'I know, sir, but I need to ask. In addition to this, I need your help.'

'My help?'

'Yes. The Yarmouths were at a social event at Lady Alderney's the night of the robbery. I need you to write to Lady Alderney and discreetly request a copy of her guest list for that night.'

Read gave a strangled laugh. 'That's the first time I've heard the word "discreet" used in the same sentence with Sarah Alderney's name.'

'It's possible the Yarmouths, or their servants, mentioned their plans at the party. I can leave no stone unturned.'

'Very well, Lavender, I shall do this today. In the meantime, stick close to John Bellingham – and, Woods, you continue to make enquiries about the stolen jewellery. I need Barnaby back in the horse patrol, I'm afraid; we're under-manned again.'

There was a sudden familiar smell of pipe tobacco.

'Yous fellahs 'ave a right bloody nerve!'

Macca stood in the open doorway of the office, puffing away furiously on his pipe.

Read sighed wearily. 'What's wrong now, Mr Macca?'

'We've found another one of yer dustmen, that's what!'

Read threw up his hands in frustration. 'Another skeleton? Oh, for God's sake, man, this is hardly worth getting upset about. Put it with the rest.'

'I would, except this stiff still 'as 'is flesh on 'im.'

'What?'

'He's fresh.'

'Fresh? Lavender, what on earth is he talking about now?'

Lavender frowned, pushed back his chair and stood up. The builder's anger wasn't just caused by frustration; there was genuine distress in his eyes. 'I think we'd better go and see.'

For the second time that week, Macca led them down the stairs and out into the rear courtyard. 'This fellah can move quiet like,' Woods observed. 'I never heard him enter the room.'

'I know.'

The yard had been transformed by the arrival of daylight and the builders. Several of the night horse patrol were dismounting and brushing dust off their uniforms, but most had joined the silent group of grim-faced workmen staring down into the trench at the far wall. The clerks had also left their desk in the hallway and joined the crowd. These thin and slightly hunched men were dwarfed by the burly, mud-splattered patrol officers and Macca's strapping gang of swarthy, heavily tattooed builders.

Lavender, Read and Woods pushed their way to the front of the crowd.

'Heaven and hell!'

At the bottom of the trench, half submerged in the watery mud and rubble, lay the lifeless body of a well-dressed man.

'Don't just stand there!' Read yelled at his officers. 'Get him out!'

Three of the patrol officers leapt down into the mud and hauled the corpse out of the hole. They laid him on his back.

Lavender froze with the shock of recognition. It was Baron Danvers.

A neat pistol hole, blackened at the edges, sat in the middle of the dead man's lined forehead. His cruel face was contorted in the agony of his death throes, eyes glaring and thick lips curled in a last blood-curdling yell.

Woods dropped down beside the corpse and made a futile attempt to find a pulse. Everyone watched in shocked silence. 'He's dead, sir.'

'Who the devil is this?' Read demanded. 'And what is he doing in a trench in the middle of my courtyard?' The voluminous folds of his black court robes slapped angrily in the wind.

Lavender opened his mouth but his dry throat strangled his words and he swallowed painfully. He cleared his throat. 'He's Baron Lionel

Danvers from Southerly Park in Middlesex. He intended to fight a duel at dawn this morning in Hyde Park. I don't understand what's happened or how his body ended up here.'

'A duel?' Read's jaw tightened with anger. 'And who was the other party in this illegal activity?'

Lavender swallowed. 'Duddles – Henry Duddles.'

'What? That saphead English nephew of Baron Lannister, the Glaswegian shipping magnate?'

'Yes.'

'Good. So at least we know who to arrest. But what I want to know is how Danvers' corpse arrived here, in the police office stable yard, without anyone noticing?' His voice rose with his fury and he glowered at everyone in the vicinity. 'My magistrates' court will be the laughing stock of London! How can we call ourselves the finest police office in the country when villains can turn up and drop dead bodies on our doorstep?' His officers shuffled uneasily, and the builders grinned at their discomfort.

Read paused for a moment to make sure he had the undivided attention of the crowd of men. 'Nobody – I repeat, nobody – is to breathe a word about Baron Danvers until we've got to the bottom of this mystery, do you hear me?' He lowered his voice menacingly. 'If I find out anyone has disobeyed my instructions, I'll clap the fool in irons and send him to Newgate for a month in contempt of court. Do you understand?' His glowering eyes swung from face to face. Even the builders stopped grinning.

'Well, don't just stand there!' Read pointed to the officers who'd lifted Danvers out of the trench. 'You officers carry Baron Danvers into the morgue and get him out of sight.'

'Yes, sir!'

Read turned to his Chief Clerk. 'Grey, send for Sir Richard Allison to examine the body. Lavender? You and Woods will go and notify poor

Lady Danvers about her husband's untimely demise and then arrest this Duddles for murder. Constable Barnaby?'

'Yes, sir!'

'I'm giving you the job of finding out how the devil someone was able to dump a corpse in the yard of our police office without anyone noticing.'

'Yes, sir!'

Inspired by Read's assertive leadership, everybody sprang into action. Lavender reached out his hand and grabbed the magistrate's shoulder as he started to walk back to his office. 'Sir, I've got to speak to you.'

'What is it, Detective?'

'Henry Duddles couldn't have committed this atrocity. He's just not capable.'

'Do you have an alternative theory, Lavender? Another suggestion about how Baron Danvers ended up with a pistol hole between his eyes on the morning he was supposed to take part in a duel?'

'Not at the moment.'

'Well, it seems cut and dried to me.'

'Micky Sullivan was also present when the duel was arranged. This chaos is his modus operandi. He always plays men off against each other. Let me interrogate Sullivan before I arrest Duddles – please.'

'Micky Sullivan?' A slow smile spread across Read's face but it didn't reach his eyes. 'Micky Sullivan wouldn't be so stupid as to dump a corpse in the back yard of Bow Street Police Office. This is the work of an idiot of the first measure – an appellation frequently attached to young Duddles, I believe.'

'Strikes me more as an act of provocation, sir,' Woods said thoughtfully.

Read turned sharply. 'Explain yourself, Constable.'

Woods held up a hand. 'Let me ponder on it for a while, sir.'

Read turned back to Lavender. 'In addition to this, I happen to know Sullivan has the perfect alibi.' It was Lavender's turn to look shocked.

'Sullivan couldn't have had anything to do with the murder of Baron Danvers,' Read continued. 'But be my guest, Lavender. Interrogate him. You won't have far to go.'

'What do you mean?'

'Sullivan's locked up in our own cells – and has been since the early hours of this morning. He was arrested by the night watch for fighting. His name is on my list for this afternoon's court session. Even the wily Micky Sullivan couldn't kill a man and dump his body here while incarcerated.'

'Fighting?'

'Yes. I have to confess I thought it was a bit odd. The night-watchmen brought him and another fellow in here about midnight. He's over there in the prison block. Interview him by all means – and if you think the case against him won't stand up in court, do me a favour and release him. The less I have to deal with today, the better.'

Read turned and picked his way back through the rubble towards the building. Lavender stood in despair.

But he wasn't alone. Ned Woods slapped his shoulder and whispered in his ear: 'There's somethin' not right here, sir, I can smell it. But don't you worry – we'll get to the bottom of it.'

Chapter Nineteen

The men's prison cells consisted of one long, dark block divided by metal cages, which enabled the prisoners to talk to each other if they wished. Water dripped down the bare walls in winter; in summer, the stench of the human faeces in the fly-infested buckets was overpowering. Half a dozen prisoners sat or lay languidly on the piles of mouldy straw in the cells. In one of them, Rabbie Waverley squatted on the floor, quietly rocking himself back and forth on his heels. The shuffling gaoler led Lavender and Woods towards Micky Sullivan at the far end of the cell block. The low murmur of dispirited conversation ceased. Heads turned and curious eyes followed their progress.

Sullivan leaned nonchalantly against the back wall of his cage. He smiled coldly when they approached. 'Ah, Lavender. At last – someone in this place wi' some sense.'

Lavender glanced around, half expecting to see Captain Leon in the next cell. 'Where's the other fellow they arrested with him?' he asked the gaoler.

''E were dragged off to the Marshalsea debtors' gaol by the bailiffs who arrested 'im. They were more bothered about gettin' their money back than seein' 'im charged for affray.' The gaoler lifted his heavy ring of jangling iron keys and unlocked the padlock on the door of Sullivan's cage. The moneylender shuffled forward and gestured to the rattling chains on his legs. 'These?'

Lavender hesitated. There were benefits to having Micky Sullivan at his mercy. 'Let's leave them for the moment, shall we?' He waved the shuffling Sullivan out of the cell and towards a dark room with a high barred window which they used to interview the prisoners. They sat down around a scuffed wooden table.

'So what happened, Sullivan? How did you end up here?'

Sullivan scowled. 'I 'ave yer friend to thank fer this. That Leon.' His lace cuff was torn. He had a bruise on his cheekbone, some dirty scuffs on his breeches and a few missing buttons on his plain, dun-coloured coat.

'Captain Leon isn't my friend,' Lavender said.

'Well, 'e ain't no gentleman either, for all his fine clothes and servants.'

'He has a servant?'

'Yes, 'is man were waitin' fer 'im in the kitchens but 'e sent 'im on 'is way. "Walk wi' me, Sullivan," 'e said. "We should become better acquainted." I knew 'e were in his cups but "Aye," I sez. "I will."'

'What happened next?' Woods asked.

'So we walks up Piccadilly – straight into the arms of a gang of bum bailiffs and creditors, brayin' fer 'is blood and money. Turns out the fellah's dipped.'

'That must have been a shock for you, Sullivan.' Lavender smiled. 'I assume he'd told you the same story he'd told Lady Caroline about a recent inheritance?'

Sullivan glanced down at his feet and shuffled on the hard wooden seat. 'Aye, 'e may 'ave mentioned it. The next thing I knew, all 'ell broke loose. Leon starts to fight them, doesn't 'e? Like a bloody demon, 'e was. Knows 'ow to 'andle 'is fists, does that one. One against four, too. Next thin' I knew, the devils had set upon me an' all. Then the beadles arrived and rounded us both up.'

'Dear me,' Lavender drawled. 'What an awful experience for you, Sullivan.'

'It were. I'm a man of peace, I am.'

'Did you meet anyone else during your late-night walk with Captain Leon?'

'No. Look, be a good fellah, Lavender, and release me. I 'ad no part in this; I'm a wronged man, I am.'

'I'm afraid I can't do that, Sullivan. You're up in the dock before Magistrate Read this afternoon.'

Sullivan's face fell and his pallid complexion turned a shade paler. 'This afternoon? Goddamn it, man! I've got a respectable business to run.'

Lavender sighed. 'Yes, it must be a real problem for you.'

'Come on, man! You can get me out of 'ere. Everyone knows yer the Chief Constable at Bow Street.'

'You flatter me, Sullivan, but alas, my hands are tied.'

'But what about me business? Me good name will be ruined if I spend much more time under these 'atches.'

'Yes, you don't want anyone else encroaching on your patch while you're clapped in irons, do you? Not with a new gang of villains in the rookery of St Giles.'

'I'm an 'onest businessman, I am!'

'So you said last night when I asked you about the arch-rogue running this new crew.'

There was a short, strained silence, broken only by the familiar sounds of the horse patrol and their animals outside in the yard. Sullivan glared at Lavender across the table, his eyeballs bulging like those of a codfish.

'So that's 'ow it is, is it, Lavender?'

'Would it hurt you to give up a name?' Woods asked.

Sullivan slumped back angrily in his chair. His irons rattled. ''E's called Nidar.'

'Nidar? Where's he from?' Lavender frowned. He recognised the name but couldn't place it.

'I don't rightly know. Just sounds foreign to me.'

'Where does he live and operate? How can I find him?'

'Don't know. His crew are the Packet Knucklers.'

Woods gave a short laugh. 'Well, there ain't nothin' foreign about *them.*'

Lavender frowned. *Packet?* Packet ships took emigrants to Boston and New York.

His fist slammed down on the table and his voice rose. 'What do you mean, you don't know? Stop fooling about, Sullivan – give me some proper information!'

Sullivan glanced nervously over his shoulder at the open door leading back to the cells. 'Keep yer voice down, Detective. I've already told yer too much. I know nothin' more about them – and God knows, it ain't fer lack of tryin'. They first arrived and started causin' trouble in St Giles a couple of years ago, but I were onto them back then and they skulked off to their rat 'ole. But they're back now.'

'You're lying.'

'I'm not. I swear on the life of me old mother that I'm not lyin' to you, Detective.'

Lavender watched him silently for a moment, then stood up. Sullivan glanced up at him hopefully.

'Ned? I need you to ride over to Marshalsea debtors' gaol in Southwark.' Woods nodded.

'What about me?' Sullivan wailed.

Lavender turned back and placed both hands firmly on the table. He leaned forward into Sullivan's face. 'If Captain Leon is still incarcerated at Marshalsea and confirms your story, you'll be released without charge. If he's not, you can rot in here and face the wrath of Magistrate Read this afternoon – he's in a foul mood today.'

Sullivan swallowed heavily.

'In addition to this' – Lavender lowered his voice to a hiss and inched closer until he could smell the moneylender's rank breath – 'if anything should ever happen to my informer, Fletcher, I'll hold you personally responsible and haul your bony arse back in here on every charge I can find – and dozens I'll invent. Do I make myself clear?'

Sullivan said nothing. Lavender and Woods left him with the gaoler and went outside.

Leaning back against the rough stone wall of the cell block, Lavender paused for a moment to let his eyes and nose adjust to the brilliant daylight and sweeter smells of the stable yard.

'Do you believe him, sir?' Woods asked. 'About this Nidar fellah?'

Lavender frowned. 'I don't know.'

'Constable Barnaby told me the other day he'd heard about this new crew. His informant said they were northerners.'

Lavender raised an eyebrow. 'That might explain the rumour that they're foreigners. Some northern accents can be indecipherable to Londoners.'

'What we goin' to do, sir?'

'Let's see what Captain Leon has to say.'

'This captain sounds like a slyboots to me.'

Lavender smiled for the first time that morning. 'We'll see. If he's a con man, he's a very good one. If they've already released him when you get to Marshalsea, ask for his address at Jermyn Street and we'll pay him a visit later.'

'What are you goin' to do?'

'I'm going to give poor Baroness Danvers the news that her husband is dead – and try to find out what the devil happened in Hyde Park this morning.' He grimaced. 'I don't think the Danvers were happily married but I'm sure she'll be distressed. Come and meet me in Westcastle Square after your trip to Marshalsea.'

'You goin' home afterwards?'

'Yes. If I've got to arrest Henry Duddles, the kindest thing I can do is take Magdalena with me to comfort Lady Caroline. She'll be distraught.'

Woods frowned. 'Do you think he did it, sir, this Duddles fellah?'

'No, Ned. I'm sure he didn't. Of all the men in London, Henry Duddles is the least capable of committing an atrocity like this. There are other forces at play here, forces I can't quite fathom.'

'It's odd the body ended up here. Someone wanted us to find it – and fast.'

'Yes – and you were right when you said it was provocative. It's almost as if someone is sending us a message.'

'We've made a lot of enemies over the years between us all.' Woods sighed sadly. 'There's lads beatin' up my sons on the streets of Southwark because of it. Just think of all the coves we've sent to Newgate, Botany Bay and the gallows.'

Lavender stood up and brushed down his coat. His face was grim. 'Yes. Come on, Ned. We've got work to do. Danvers was a miserable brute of a man but he deserves justice; let's go and catch his killer.'

Giving relatives the dreadful news about the death of their loved ones was the worst part of Lavender's job, and in this case his own connection with the chief suspect made it even more difficult. His chest tightened with tension when he mounted the steps of the Danvers' Mayfair home. He coughed to clear his throat, steeling himself for the encounter.

Fortunately, Lady Danvers wasn't alone when the maid showed him into a pretty yellow morning room. Her brother, Lord Rothbury, had arrived a few minutes previously. Rothbury paced up and down in front of the tall windows overlooking the street below. Lavender wondered if Lady Danvers had sent for him or if Rothbury had already heard rumours about the impending duel and had come quickly to his sister's side. News travelled fast in London.

'Unfortunately, Lady Danvers, I'm the bearer of some terrible news. This morning we recovered the body of your husband. He had been shot.'

Lady Danvers screamed and crumpled, burying her face in her hands and bursting into tears.

Her brother rushed to her side and placed his arms around her. 'Dear God! What happened?'

'He was shot, sir,' Lavender repeated.

'What am I going to tell the boys?' Lady Danvers wailed, over and over again. 'What will I tell little Lionel?'

Lavender stood uncomfortably before the sobbing widow and waited for the first shock to subside.

'Who did this?' Her voice cracked with distress. 'Was it Duddles?'

'Of course it was Henry Duddles!' snapped her brother. 'Who else? He'll hang for this, damn him!'

This brought forth another flood of tears from the distraught widow.

'Have you arrested him, Lavender?'

'We're on our way to arrest him now, Lord Rothbury. Obviously, I needed to tell Lady Danvers the news first.' He paused until he thought it was appropriate to ask a question. 'I appreciate this is distressing for you, Lady Danvers, but I need to ask you what happened this morning. What time did your husband leave the house?'

She dabbed her red-rimmed eyes, sniffed and lifted her puffy face up to him. 'He rode out well before dawn.'

'Alone?'

'Yes.'

'To Hyde Park?'

She nodded and swallowed hard. 'He said he couldn't wait to teach Duddles a lesson . . .'

'Who was his second and when did he meet him?'

'He . . . he said . . . he didn't need a second, that it would only take him a few minutes to kill Duddles and there was no point in disturbing anyone's breakfast.'

She started crying again, and Lavender waited patiently. Taking a second might have saved Baron Danvers' life. On the other hand, it might also have meant that Lavender had a second widow to visit this morning.

Lady Danvers turned to her brother. 'Oh, Alphonse! I pleaded with him not to go – you must believe me!'

'I do, Eliza,' Lord Rothbury said softly. 'I know what a stubborn fool Lionel was.' He turned to face Lavender. 'I think that's enough, Detective; my sister is too distressed to answer more questions. Go and arrest the murderer. You can return another time if you need to.'

Lavender bowed and offered his condolences once more before turning to leave. 'We have Baron Danvers' body at Bow Street,' he added.

Rothbury acknowledged the information with a curt nod, his attention firmly fixed on his sister. Lavender left them, thankful he hadn't had to tell them how the corpse had mysteriously appeared in the stable yard at Bow Street.

They'd enough to come to terms with at the moment. That was a shock for later.

Bright sunshine flooded the street outside. It was only just after nine o'clock but already surprisingly warm. Lavender retrieved the reins of his horse from the small boy in whose care he'd left them and stood by the animal for a moment, stroking its neck and scratching its ears.

Relieved that the worst part of his job was now over, he turned his full attention to the mystery of Baron Danvers' death and tried to sort out the facts in a logical manner.

Danvers had been shot between the eyes in the manner reminiscent of a pistol duel – but that didn't mean a duel had taken place.

His body had been found in the stable yard at Bow Street, but he hadn't been killed there. The sound of a shot in the centre of Covent Garden would have brought the night clerk, the ostlers and half of the neighbours running.

All he knew for a fact was that Baron Danvers had ridden from this building before dawn in the direction of Hyde Park and had met his death.

Ridden. Where the devil was Danvers' horse? Lady Danvers and Rothbury hadn't mentioned the animal returning home. They probably assumed Bow Street had it. And where were the duelling pistols Danvers must have taken with him?

Lavender swung up into the saddle, dug his heels into his horse's flanks and set off at a brisk trot in the direction of Hyde Park.

The park was quiet this morning. A group of uniformed nurse-maids, young mothers and children strolled around the pretty ornamental lake in the distance, and a few liveried grooms on thoroughbreds thundered up and down the loose gravel bridle path known as Rotten Row. But it was still too early in the day for the promenading gentry in their gleaming carriages and elegant finery.

Lavender knew the quieter part of the park favoured by duellists. He left the manicured lawns and cantered over the vast swathes of rougher grass, towards a distant wooded area.

It didn't take him long to find what he was looking for. A solitary horse, quietly chomping grass near a secluded copse at the far side of the park. He was a well-bred hunter standing about eighteen hands high. He approached the animal cautiously, but the horse showed no alarm and allowed Lavender to grab its broken reins and lead it to a short but sturdy stretch of wooden fencing beside the ring of trees. He tethered both horses to the fence before turning his attention to Danvers' saddlebag.

It was empty. He frowned. Most men travelled with a few personal possessions in their saddlebags, but there was nothing, not even a hip flask of brandy. Where were the duelling pistols? Had Danvers been robbed as well as murdered? This was an area frequented by footpads. But if Danvers had been the victim of a robbery, why had the thief left his valuable horse behind? The saddle alone must be worth thirty guineas.

He picked up the broken reins, frowning. There was dried white sweat under the stallion's neck and around his flanks. At some point this morning, he had either been ridden hard or had bolted and broken his reins. Possibly both. Lavender didn't have Woods' vast experience and knowledge but he knew that a horse left on its own would often gallop straight for home in a panic. Was this what had happened? Had the creature set off for home but, unsure of the way, finally returned to the spot where he last saw his master?

Lavender moved into the copse and examined the knee-high vegetation on the ground beneath the trees. It didn't take him long to find a large patch of freshly trampled grass and ferns. The greenery was mottled with a dark brown stain. He dropped to his haunches, took off his glove and ran his hand over the stain: congealing blood, some of it still sticky to the touch.

He'd found the spot where Baron Danvers had been shot.

But how did the murderer move the body to Covent Garden? And why?

On the far side of the copse, just outside the line of encircling trees, Lavender's sharp eyes spotted another area of trampled ground and churned-up mud, this one bigger and more disturbed than the first. Amongst the fresh hoof prints there were deep ruts from wagon wheels. He had his answer. A gang of men had waited for Danvers before robbing and murdering him. Then they'd transported the body back to Covent Garden in a wagon. He remembered the sleeping ostler he'd seen in the stable and sighed. It would have been easy for them to dump Baron Danvers in the plague pit and leave undetected.

This murder must have been planned down to the last detail. It was no duel or opportunistic attack.

But why leave a valuable thoroughbred horse and an expensive saddle behind? He glanced at the tethered animal and wondered about its temperament. He took his pistol out of his pocket, pulled back the hammer and loaded it with shot and powder before aiming at the cloudless sky and firing. The single shot cracked through the air with its customary blue flash. Dozens of roosting birds rose out of the treetops squawking, and circled noisily above.

Danvers' horse whinnied with fear and half reared. Nostrils flaring, it kicked, stamped and jerked at the reins tethering it to the fence. Meanwhile, his own well-trained patrol horse remained calmly on the other side of the trees. Finally, the snorting stallion settled himself.

Here was his answer: the animal had bolted when the murderer fired the shot that killed Danvers and, in the course of the ensuing hours, had returned to the spot where it had last seen its master. The only strange thing was that the saddlebag had been emptied before the horse bolted. It looked like the murderers had robbed Danvers before killing him.

Lavender tried to imagine the scene. Danvers arriving by starlight at the designated area, expecting to find Henry Duddles and his second. Instead, a gang of murderers lurked in the shadow of the dripping trees, waiting to pounce, rob and kill.

He had solved the mystery of how Baron Danvers had been murdered.

Now all he had to do was work out by whom.

Chapter Twenty

Lavender took Danvers' horse back to the mews behind the baron's Mayfair house and handed it over to a stable boy with minimal explanation. He then returned home, but the detour had delayed him. Woods' horse was already tied to the railings on Westcastle Square when he arrived.

Lavender was relieved to see that Alfie Tummins and his cab were also waiting outside his house. He'd hire the vehicle to take Magdalena to Lady Caroline's. Lavender had a quick word with the young man and asked him to wait for a few minutes while he persuaded Magdalena to come with him.

Then he braced himself for Magdalena's anger. Ned would have already told her about the death of Baron Danvers and his need to arrest Duddles. He knew she wouldn't like it. He was right.

Everyone was in the basement kitchen waiting for him. Magdalena paced the flagstone floor in fury, while Woods sat on a chair eating a plate of fried eggs and ham. Teresa hovered nervously in the background with Mrs Hobart, their housekeeper. The kindly woman handed Lavender a welcome cup of tea when he entered, and he managed to take one gulp before Magdalena exploded.

'This is ridiculous, Stephen! Duddles isn't a murderer!'

He put down the cup and reached out to console her, but she shrugged him off angrily. 'Magdalena . . .'

'And Lady Caroline promised me she would keep him close this morning. How did he kill Baron Danvers if he never left the house?'

'I don't believe for one moment Duddles is responsible.'

'So why do you have to arrest him? Why are you doing this to our friend?'

'Because he's the main suspect. Half of London – including the poor widow and her family – think there was a duel this morning between the two men, and we have to hold Duddles until I can prove otherwise.' He stepped forward and tried to take hold of Magdalena's arm. She shook him off again.

Woods shuffled uncomfortably in his seat. The other women looked distressed.

'Magdalena – listen to me. I have already found evidence that suggests Danvers was killed by a gang of thieving murderers.'

Her mouth snapped shut but her dark eyes continued to blaze with fury.

'But I need more time to prove Duddles is innocent and to track down these killers. In the meantime, I have to arrest him. And I need your help. For the love you bear Caroline Clare, please get your cloak and come with Ned and me.'

She swallowed hard, her face softened and her lower lip trembled.

'It will be a kindness,' he added.

'Why does anyone care if Danvers is dead?' Magdalena snapped. 'The man was a monster; his wife will dance on his grave once she gets over the shock.'

Behind him, Mrs Hobart spluttered something incomprehensible. Teresa crossed herself.

'Magdalena . . .'

For a moment, he thought she would burst into tears; then she shook her head. 'Very well. I'll fetch my cloak. Teresa, come with me!' She turned and left, Teresa following after her mistress.

Lavender sank down into the chair opposite Woods and picked up his cup again, grateful to rest for a moment.

Mrs Hobart pushed a small plate of ham, cheese and bread in front of him. 'Eat this,' she said. 'Sounds to me like you'll need to keep up yer strength today, what with catchin' murderers and all that. I've already fed yer constable.'

Lavender thanked her, wrapped the ham and cheese in the bread and took a few bites. Mrs Hobart disappeared into the scullery.

'Captain Leon had already gone when I got to Marshalsea,' Woods said. 'His man turned up at first light with the money for the creditors and they released him. Them wardens had heard from the bailiffs about the arrest and it sounds like that cove, Sullivan, were tellin' the truth fer once.'

Lavender swallowed his mouthful of food. 'We still need to speak to Captain Leon. Did you get his address at Jermyn Street?'

'Yes. Number fifty-seven. How could Sullivan be involved in Danvers' death? We had him under the hatches all night. He's got one of them Ali Baba things.'

A small smile flickered at the corner of Lavender's mouth but it quickly vanished. 'I think you mean "alibi". Micky Sullivan is wily enough to get himself arrested in order to have an alibi while his henchmen murdered Danvers. And from what I've uncovered this morning, Danvers' murder has Sullivan's filthy paw prints all over it.' Quickly, Lavender explained what he'd learned from Baroness Danvers and discovered in Hyde Park.

Woods rubbed his stubble and frowned. 'You know, sir, if that fellah, Danvers, were as unpopular as everyone says he was, then there may have been quite a few folks lined up under those trees waitin' to take a shot at him. Maybe we ought to take a look at who else might want him dead?'

'I agree – but it still doesn't explain why his body was brought to us. Last night I slighted Micky Sullivan at Lady Caroline's soirée; I made it plain he wasn't welcome there.'

Woods' eyes widened. 'You think he's tauntin' you?'

Lavender shrugged and finished off his tea. 'Unfortunately, knowing Caroline Clare, she may also have inadvertently offended Sullivan. I wouldn't put it past him to want revenge on the pair of us.'

Magdalena was calmer when she climbed up onto the cracked leather seats in Alfie Tummins' cab. Lavender sat with her, while Woods trotted behind the cab on his horse, leading Lavender's mare. Magdalena listened quietly to Lavender's explanation as they wound their way through the traffic towards Lincoln's Inn Fields.

'I want you to tell all of this to Lady Caroline after we've taken Duddles away. She's an intelligent woman and will recognise that someone has contrived the situation to make it look like Duddles shot Danvers.'

'But why are you still arresting him? Can't you just explain to Magistrate Read what you've discovered? He usually trusts your judgement.'

He frowned. 'I hope that once I arrive at Bow Street and explain, Read will agree with me and let Duddles go before he's charged – but I have to follow his instructions, Magdalena. Read will be angry and less open to persuasion if I arrive without Duddles in tow.'

She turned and stared out of the window. The weather had turned again and soft rivulets of rain ran down the window, obscuring their view of the jostling crowds on the pavement.

'So taking Duddles to Bow Street should be . . . how do you say it? A formality?'

'I sincerely hope so. I need you to do something else for me, Magdalena. I need you to find out how indebted Lady Caroline is to a moneylender called Sullivan.'

'A moneylender?' Magdalena was visibly shocked.

He nodded. 'I need to know if she's ever reneged on her debt or done anything to offend the man that may have prompted him to take revenge on her and Duddles.'

She gasped – then nodded. 'I'll do my best. It'll be unpleasant, Stephen,' she said quietly. 'So different from our journey to Lady Caroline's last night.'

He took her gloved hand in his own and squeezed it. 'As Betsy Woods often reminds us: our lives spin on a sixpence and we can fall within seconds.'

Lady Caroline and Duddles were in the glass-vaulted orangery when Lavender, Magdalena and Woods were shown through by the maid. All signs of the previous night's party had been cleared away and Lady Caroline's paint-splattered easel and the furniture had been returned to the room. The supper table had lost its fine linen and crystal and was again scattered with paintbrushes, paints, rags and a clean glass of water.

Duddles and Lady Caroline were sipping coffee and lounging on a mismatched daybed and chaise longue. Duddles had taken off his boots and his waistcoat was undone. Lady Caroline wore a dark-print, elbow-length day dress with a floaty embroidered fichu around her neck and tucked into her bodice. For once, her trademark turban was absent and her thick auburn hair contrasted vividly with the pale, faded cotton of the chaise longue on which she reclined.

'Magdalena!' Lady Caroline smiled in delight when they entered. 'What a pleasure to see you again so soon! You too, Detective – and Constable Woods.'

Lavender bowed his head politely but didn't take her extended hand. 'Lady Caroline. Duddles. Unfortunately, today I'm the bearer of some terrible news. This morning Baron Danvers was found shot dead.'

'Good grief!' Their faces registered genuine shock.

'How unfortunate,' Lady Caroline said, once she had recovered a little. 'But I'm not surprised. He was an odious man. I'm sure his poor wife is delighted. Did she shoot him?'

'I don't think you understand, Lady Caroline . . .' Magdalena said gently.

'I'm afraid I need to take Duddles to Bow Street for questioning,' Lavender interrupted, more harshly than he intended.

'What?'

Duddles paled, then nodded calmly. He leaned forward and reached for his discarded footwear. 'I'd better put on my boots.'

Lady Caroline sat upright and grabbed Duddles' arm to stop him. 'What on earth for, Detective?'

Lavender paused.

Shocked realisation flashed across Lady Caroline's face. 'Oh, for heaven's sake, Lavender! You don't think it's anything to do with that silly duel, do you? No, Duddles – leave your boots alone!' The young man hesitated, his face white as milk beneath his foppish fringe.

'A room full of people heard Danvers challenge Duddles to an illegal duel,' Lavender said quietly, 'and now the man is dead. I'm sorry, Lady Caroline, I have instructions to take Duddles to the office for questioning.'

Lady Caroline was on her feet now, her balance unsteady without her walking cane. Magdalena rushed to her side and supported her. Duddles remained seated and calmly tugged his boots up his leg. 'But this is ridiculous! The duel never took place. Duddles couldn't shoot a man dead in cold blood. Besides which, he was here all night with me.'

'Would you be prepared to stand up in court and say that, Lady Caroline?' Lavender asked.

'What? In a packed courtroom?' Horror flashed across her face. 'With reporters present? Of course I wouldn't – the scandal would be horrendous!'

Duddles stood up and buttoned his waistcoat. 'Has a chap got time to fetch his coat?' His voice cracked.

'No!' Lady Caroline shook off Magdalena and grabbed hold of him. 'You're not going anywhere, Henry! You can't do this, Lavender!'

Magdalena tried to pull her away. 'You must trust Stephen, Lady Caroline.'

'Yes, Caro – trust Lavender,' Duddles said. 'Fine chap. Never let us down yet.'

'I'm afraid I must take him, Lady Caroline, but rest assured I believe you both. I have already begun a thorough investigation into Danvers' murder and will have Duddles released soon. Magdalena will explain.'

'Released?' Lady Caroline's eyes widened. 'Do you intend to detain him in your dreadful little police cells?'

Woods stepped forward. 'Come on, sir,' he said to Duddles, 'let's get your coat and get this over and done with.'

'Oh, my God! Surely you don't intend to clap him in irons and parade him through the streets like a common criminal?' Lady Caroline threw herself on Duddles' chest with her arms wrapped around his neck. 'I can't bear it!'

'That won't be necessary, I'm sure, ma'am,' Woods said. 'Detective Lavender has a cab waitin' outside.'

It took a few minutes for Magdalena to persuade Lady Caroline to let go of her young lover. She sank, sobbing, onto the sofa, with Magdalena at her side.

Duddles walked unsteadily across the room to Woods.

'May I look at your hands, please, sir?' the constable asked. Duddles held up his hands, and Woods examined them and the cuffs of his sleeves carefully. 'Nothing.' Woods spoke over his shoulder to Lavender. 'Cleanest pair of daddles I've seen for years – even his fingernails are clean.'

'What are you looking for?' Lady Caroline demanded.

'Gunpowder residue, ma'am,' Woods replied cheerfully. 'There isn't any.'

'Well, of course there won't be any!' She burst into a fresh flood of tears.

'Examine his gloves and coat,' Lavender whispered to Woods. 'We have to conduct a thorough investigation.'

Ned nodded and led Duddles out of the room to retrieve his hat and coat.

Lavender waited awkwardly with the women. He felt like a complete cad. When Woods put his head around the door to indicate they were ready to leave, Lady Caroline let out another hysterical wail.

Magdalena held her tighter. 'Go now, Stephen,' she said. 'I will take care of Lady Caroline.'

Chapter Twenty-One

S hall we charge him?' Woods asked, when they arrived back at Bow Street.

'No,' Lavender replied. 'Wait in the hallway. I'll go and try to talk some sense into Magistrate Read. I hope when I tell him what I've discovered in Hyde Park, he'll send Duddles straight home.'

He took the stairs up to Read's office two at a time and was relieved to find the magistrate behind his cluttered desk. 'I must talk to you, sir.'

'Have you arrested that Duddles fellow?'

'Yes, sir – he's downstairs with Woods.'

Read waved at the chair opposite his desk. 'Well, close the door and sit down. I've got a few minutes before my afternoon court session.' He looked and sounded in a better mood.

Lavender sat down and explained, starting with the challenge Danvers had made at the party the night before and ending with his discoveries in Hyde Park. Read listened impassively. Occasionally, he nodded and asked for clarification.

'So you see, sir, for the reasons I've mentioned, I don't believe Henry Duddles murdered Danvers. The Baron was murdered by persons unknown, who transported his body back here in a cart to confound us. I need to interrogate Sullivan further; I suspect he's behind this.'

Read gave a little smile and shook his head sadly. 'Duddles had both the motive and the opportunity to shoot Baron Danvers. The lawyers for the prosecution would rip your evidence to shreds in the courtroom. So you found blood in a park full of wild animals – and a cart track? Neither of those things are unusual. There's nothing to link that site to the murder of Danvers and I don't have the men to make a full search of an area as vast as Hyde Park. In fact, I need Woods back with the horse patrol today.'

Lavender felt his hope sinking. 'There was Danvers' horse, sir . . .'

'Yes, an animal that bolted and wandered alone for hours.'

'It had returned to the scene of the crime, where it last saw its master.'

Read laughed. 'That suggestion won't stand up in court, Stephen. Your loyalty to your friend does you credit but I think you're too close to this case to be objective.'

Lavender opened his mouth to argue his case further, but Read waved him to silence. 'As for Micky Sullivan, he must be released immediately. I have more important things to deal with in court today than a scuffle between a couple of gentlemen and the bailiffs.'

'I've yet to track down Captain Leon and hear his side of the events of last night.'

Read stood up and reached for his wig, discarded amongst the inkpots and files on his desk. 'No, you need to track down John Bellingham and continue your surveillance of the fellow. Lord Granville Leveson-Gower is an impatient man. The sooner we have that odd fish arrested and in custody, the better. And don't forget, Lavender, you've a boat to Dublin to catch on Monday.'

Lavender's heart sank. Read was dismissing him.

Read smoothed out the creases from his black gown and stood up to his full height, which was only an inch or so shorter than Lavender's. 'Put Henry Duddles in the gentleman's cell – the one with the fireplace and bed – and send for his lawyer. It'll be the lawyer's job to prove his client's innocence from now on, not yours.'

'He was with Lady Caroline Clare all night,' Lavender said helplessly.

Read laughed again. 'Will she say that in court?' Lavender's hesitation gave the magistrate the answer he needed. 'No? I didn't think so. Duddles has no alibi he can use. He should have returned home to his own bed and let his servants vouch for him this morning. And as for that silly woman, Caroline Clare, you should advise her to steer well clear of Sullivan. Heaven knows what possessed the woman to get involved with the likes of him.'

'I believe the loan was temporary,' Lavender said.

Read shook his head and moved towards the door. 'And don't forget,' he called over his shoulder, 'I need Constable Woods back with the horse patrol this afternoon. There's been drunken brawling up on the Holborn Road again. He can deal with that after he's taken Rabbie Waverley back to the Bethlehem Hospital.'

Lavender felt wretched when he descended the stairs back to the hallway, where Duddles and Woods awaited his arrival. 'I'm afraid we must take Duddles to the desk and charge him with the murder of Baron Danvers.'

Woods looked shocked. Alarm replaced the hope in Duddles' clear blue eyes. 'Will it be the noose for me, Lavender?'

Lavender tried to put on a brave face. 'No, Duddles – this is just a temporary setback, but you must notify your family lawyer of your predicament.' The young man nodded.

Fortunately, the hallway was empty for once and although awkward, charging Duddles and booking him into the cells was a quick, if solemn, affair.

Lavender asked Woods to take Duddles to Bow Street's most comfortable cell and told him Read wanted him to return Rabbie Waverley to the asylum and rejoin the horse patrol that afternoon.

Woods nodded grimly but spoke cheerfully to the downcast Duddles. 'Don't you worry, sir. Detective Lavender will find the real murderer and get you out of here before you know it.'

Lavender squirmed at Woods' optimism and stomped out to the main cell block in a foul mood. He instructed the gaoler to release Micky Sullivan.

The moneylender grinned when the shackles fell away from his wrists. 'I sees ye've come to yer senses, Lavender. Captain Leon came through fer me, did 'e? 'E's a rum fellah.'

'Just get out, Sullivan,' Lavender snarled.

Sullivan needed no second bidding. Lavender followed him out of the door and watched him hurry through the rubble and scurry out onto the street.

Beside Lavender, the gaoler sniffed loudly. 'The place already smells better without 'im on the premises.'

Lavender didn't agree but said nothing.

'Ye've 'eard about old Wilson, the ostler, I suppose?' the gaoler continued, as he turned to go back inside. Lavender shook his head. 'Magistrate Read's sent 'im packin'. Turns out 'e were asleep most o' the night in the stables when the body were dumped in the plague pit.'

Lavender sighed sadly; to lose his job would be devastating for a man as elderly as Wilson. It all seemed so unfair. The ostlers weren't supposed to sleep when working, but most of them did take a nap on quiet nights and it'd never caused a problem before.

There'd been many criminals over the last sixty-odd years who had tried to sneak out of Bow Street – but no one ever expected criminals to try to sneak in. His jaw set in anger. He'd get to the bottom of this mystery and someone would pay for the trouble they'd caused.

Vincent Dowling walked through the archway into the yard. He saw Lavender and headed towards him. 'Good afternoon, Lavender. I've heard rumours that a duel took place this morning. Two gentlemen, I believe, one of them titled. Can you confirm this?' He slid his notebook and pencil out of his coat pocket.

Lavender's lips tightened. He kept his face impassive, his eyes averted. 'I don't know anything about this.'

'Really? I understand there was a fatality and Baron Danvers from Southerly Park in Middlesex was shot dead.'

Lavender ground his teeth together and said nothing. *Could this morning get any worse?*

'I would have thought that as the only Principal Officer left in London, you'd know all about it, Lavender.'

This damned reporter knew too much. If Dowling wrote about the scarcity of officers in the capital, there'd be anger in Parliament and repercussions for Magistrate Read and Bow Street's funding. The provincial cases they undertook were a profitable sideline for Bow Street but they were never supposed to be at the expense of policing in London.

'Perhaps that's why you don't know about the duel, Lavender,' Dowling continued. 'Been too busy doing the job of six Principal Officers, have you?'

Lavender's mind raced. Duddles was in custody and the events of last night and the circumstances, the *imagined* circumstances, of Baron Danvers' death would soon become common knowledge anyway.

'It's a pity you can't tell me anything, Lavender, because I happen to know where our mutual friend is lurking at the moment.'

Lavender's head snapped around. 'John Bellingham?'

A slow smile crept across Dowling's pock-marked face. 'Yes, Bellingham.'

Lavender cleared his throat. 'Don't mention my name. An illegal duel was arranged between Baron Danvers and Mr Henry Duddles, to take place in Hyde Park this morning at dawn. Baron Danvers was later discovered dead. Mr Duddles is being held for questioning here at Bow Street.'

Dowling licked his pencil and grinned. 'That's more like it, Lavender.'

'And Bellingham?'

'Drowning his sorrows in The Feathers, on Great Wild Street . . . Hey! Lavender – wait! I need to ask you more questions . . .'

But Lavender was already halfway across the yard.

Great Wild Street was an ancient and squalid thoroughfare of irregular and dilapidated buildings that ran through the heart of the rookery of St Giles. Rife with poverty, the smoke-stained facades and filthy windows of the overhanging properties were centuries old. It housed a noisy, ragged and immoral population in its cramped rooms, most of whom were out on the street today, basking in the miserable glimmer of sunlight filtering down through the narrow gap between the high buildings. Above their heads, poles of drying laundry poked out from the upper casement windows.

Desperate to avoid attention, Lavender pulled up his coat collar and yanked his hat low over his eyes, pushing his way through the crowds and almost gagging at the sickening odour of tan, tallow, rotting fish and vegetables.

The gutters spilled over with garbage. Beside them, filthy barefoot children crouched and searched through the refuse for playthings, and emaciated dogs scrapped with each other for morsels.

He stepped around a group of laughing Irish women sitting greasing the walls with their backs. In a nearby doorway, their children nursed bundles of dirty rags containing wailing infants. All the children were drowning in their parents' cast-off rags: small, filthy faces swamped by unravelling bonnets. Their baggy breeches were held up by string.

Even the fowls pecking amongst the detritus had a beggared appearance and seemed to be perpetually moulting.

Lavender approached The Feathers with caution and sidestepped a group of young lads of about twenty who blocked his entrance. Hands deep in their dog-eared pockets, they leered and catcalled across the road to a pair of drunk and garishly dressed prostitutes, lounging beside the dank alley where they did their business. The whores gave back as good as they got and the air was filled with vile profanities and laughter.

The stench of unwashed bodies and the noise of rowdy drunks were both amplified beneath the low-beamed ceiling of the tavern. A favourite haunt of costermongers, navvies, dockers, out-of-work actors from the theatres and jobbing men from the nearby Covent Garden market, The Feathers had a notorious reputation. Lavender wondered about Bellingham's decision to drink here and came to the conclusion that a man who'd spent five years in a Russian gaol probably wasn't too fussy about the company he kept. It took him a few minutes to locate the former merchant in a far corner of the smoky tavern.

Hunched low over a small tankard, Bellingham looked wretched. But it didn't seem to be ale that bedevilled him. Every time the blowsy barmaid approached the merchant and offered to refill his tankard from her jug, he waved her away. Dowling had been wrong about him drowning his sorrows: Bellingham was sober.

Lavender sank down onto a stool against the splintered wood-panelled wall, accepted a small tankard of ale from the barmaid and watched Bellingham repeatedly take out his pocket watch to check the time. Lavender sipped his ale and smiled to himself. Bellingham was waiting for someone.

A noisy quarrel broke out amongst a nearby crowd of drunken navvies. They pushed and shoved each other across his line of vision. Coat sleeves strained over taut muscles; large, grimy fists were clenched and waved in each other's faces.

A dark-coated man, swathed in scarves and with his hat pulled low over his eyes, forced his way through the heaving, yelling crowd of men. Lavender couldn't glimpse his face and had to rise to his feet to see over the shoulders of the scuffling men.

The mysterious new arrival approached Bellingham's table. The merchant's features lit up with pleasure and he held out his hand towards the stranger.

'Lavender?'

Lavender swung around. His informer, Fletcher, stood awkwardly at his shoulder. 'For the love of God, don't call me that in here!' he hissed. 'Do you want half the tavern to turn on us?'

'I've got somethin' fer you; it's important.' Fletcher's one good eye blinked in confusion below a battered low-brimmed hat.

Lavender glanced around, hoping he and Fletcher had escaped noticed. His instincts told him otherwise. He sensed lowered eyes in scowling faces. It was time to leave.

'Go outside. I'll meet you in the side alley.'

Fletcher slid away towards the door. Lavender cast a final glance back towards Bellingham. The stranger had sat down with his back to Lavender, and the smiling merchant now held a plain brown money-bag. He beckoned the barmaid to approach. It looked like the two men were about to have a drink together. He had time to step outside for a moment.

He found Fletcher in the alley, leaning against the dripping wall of the tavern. The place stank of urine and was ankle-deep in foul garbage.

'What is it?'

'I've got the name of the arch-rogue of that new gang. 'E's a rum cove, this one; he ain't afraid of being stretched on the gallows at Newgate.'

Lavender fished out a coin and passed it across. 'Who is he?'

''E's called Nidar.'

Damn Sullivan. The man must have been telling the truth. *Where had he heard the name 'Nidar' before?*

'Where can I find him?'

'You can't.' Fletcher's misaligned eyes widened with fear. ''E's a shape-shifter, a man of different forms: animal, 'uman – no one knows.'

Lavender frowned, irritated by the superstition. 'No man can transform himself into an animal, Fletcher. If he uses disguises, a little perseverance will soon unmask him. I don't pay you to bring me fairy stories.'

'No one knows what 'e looks like,' Fletcher said sulkily. Then he added: 'They're plannin' somethin' big in the city.'

'What? When?'

'I don't know, but word on the street is it'll be soon and it'll shake the nobs in their boots.'

Nobs. Street slang for the moneyed elite. This was bragging; nothing new for criminals – especially new gangs who wanted to establish themselves and create a climate of fear. And the 'word on the street' meant late-night drunken speculation in Annie's Gin Palace.

But Fletcher's next words made the hairs on the back of Lavender's neck stand up: 'You've been mentioned.'

'Me?'

'Yes, 'e ain't afraid of you nor the other runners. Some saphead warned Nidar that Lavender was back in town, and 'e laughed. Said 'e'd already sent a message to Detective Lavender.'

'He'd sent me a message?' *Good God! Was Nidar behind the death of Baron Danvers?* No. That wasn't possible. Was it? He felt like he'd just been kicked in the gut. 'What message was this?'

For the first time, Fletcher looked confused. 'Or it might 'ave been that 'e were *about to* send yer a message. I ain't sure . . .'

'Anything else?'

'No.'

'Did you know we had Micky Sullivan under the hatches at Bow Street this morning?'

For the first time, Fletcher's face relaxed and a small smile curled his mouth. 'All of the rookery knew that; there's been celebrations in The Porcupine and The Angel.'

Lavender fished in his pocket for another coin. 'Take care of yourself,' he said. 'Sullivan is back out on the streets now and he knows you're giving me information – but I've warned him off.'

Fletcher's face paled beneath the grime. 'Me and the missus'll take ourselves out of town fer a while. 'Er folks are Romany; we'll join 'em on the road.' He turned and soon disappeared into the heaving crowd.

Lavender remained in the alley, trying to make sense of what he'd just heard. Fletcher's information disturbed him.

Nidar *laughed* when he heard he was back in town? Just like the well-spoken highwayman *laughed* when he robbed the Earl and Countess of Yarmouth? Was there a connection between this elusive Nidar and that crime? And what the devil was this message?

Magistrate Read needed to get the other Principal Officers back as soon as possible and abandon this ridiculous notion of sending him to Dublin. Something new and evil was writhing in the seedy underbelly of the city and they needed to expose it.

He shook his head to dispel the sense of foreboding that had formed like a dark cloud in his mind and walked back into the tavern. He needed to think, and a few mind-numbing hours trailing Bellingham would be the best time to do it.

His fingers reached into his pocket, around the handle of his pistol. If anyone wanted to make any trouble, he was ready for them. But no one accosted him when he returned to the rear of the tavern; even the truculent navvies had calmed down.

He stopped dead in his tracks and cursed when he realised John Bellingham's companion had disappeared. The bankrupt merchant was alone in his corner and drinking heavily.

Lavender hurried back out into the seething street, glancing around frantically for the dark-coated man swathed in scarves. It was hopeless. His quarry had vanished into a sea of bobbing heads and hats. He'd missed the opportunity to discover the identity of Bellingham's financier.

Chapter Twenty-Two

Magdalena stayed with Lady Caroline all afternoon, trying to calm her worst fears about what lay ahead for Duddles. Her presence, plus copious cups of sugared tea and the warm sunlight streaming down through the high glass ceiling, seemed to soothe Lady Caroline. She also took comfort from the news of Stephen's discoveries in Hyde Park.

'I'm pleased Lavender is on the case,' Lady Caroline said. 'Duddles is right; your husband has never let us down. He was ruthless in his pursuit of those fiends who kidnapped my poor stepdaughter Harriet and left her to die in that dreadful place.'

Magdalena sat back in her chair, relieved Lady Caroline didn't blame Stephen for arresting Duddles. Small motes of dust floated in the sunbeams above the paraphernalia scattered on the table. She watched them for a moment and wondered what Stephen was doing now.

'Did you say Baron Danvers' body was dumped ignominiously in the Bow Street plague pit?'

Magdalena's attention snapped back to her friend. 'Yes, but this isn't common knowledge. You must be very discreet about everything I have told you. Lady Danvers and her brother don't know about it yet.' She reached for her teacup.

A half-smile twitched at the corner of Lady Caroline's lips. 'What a fitting end for the odious man,' she declared.

Magdalena spluttered slightly in her cup.

Lady Caroline reached for the milk jug. Her hand had stopped trembling now. 'This will be the best thing to happen to poor Eliza Danvers; the man made her life a misery.'

Magdalena was pleased to see some colour return to her friend's cheeks. The distress had made her look haggard and closer to her real age of forty-five. Her eyelids were still swollen from crying but a gleam of light had returned to her eyes.

'It's a comfort to know Lavender believes Duddles is innocent and that the ridiculous situation has been contrived, although I can't imagine by whom.'

'What about that moneylender, Sullivan?' Magdalena asked cautiously. 'Stephen thinks Sullivan might have wanted to hurt you and Duddles.'

Lady Caroline's auburn ringlets wobbled when she shook her head. 'No, my debt was paid on time and in full – and I even gave the dreadful little man an invitation to my soirée. He had nothing to complain about.'

Magdalena's eyes narrowed. 'How were you able to repay him so promptly?'

Lady Caroline smiled. 'With the money I made from the sale of my painting to Lady Yarmouth, of course.' She patted Magdalena's hand. 'And don't worry, my dear, the promise she made of future patronage will ensure I'll never need the services of a man like Sullivan again.'

'Lady Yarmouth is your new patroness?' Magdalena frowned. *Wasn't this the countess who'd been a victim of highway robbery a few days ago?*

'Yes – oh, I forgot. I'd intended to introduce you to her last night. Yes, Georgina Yarmouth is my new patroness.'

Magdalena's throat was dry and she struggled to respond. 'The Yarmouths were held up by highway robbers earlier this week.'

'Good grief!' Lady Caroline's hand flew to her mouth in shock.

'Stephen's been asked to investigate this robbery in addition to his other cases.'

'Oh my goodness! The poor woman! Were they hurt?'

'No one was hurt, thankfully, but Lord Yarmouth lost a lot of money and Lady Yarmouth lost her jewellery.'

'This is dreadful! She's such a lovely woman; she didn't deserve that.'

Magdalena's mind struggled to make sense of this new development. Was it just a coincidence that Lady Yarmouth and Lady Caroline knew each other? Stephen's cases were colliding. Was there some unknown connection between them?

'Georgina Yarmouth has always been a great patron of the arts,' Lady Caroline continued. 'She's an ardent supporter of The Gallery of Women Artists, and has been since its inception. I'm flattered she singled out my landscape amongst so much talent.'

'The painting is beautiful.' Magdalena suddenly remembered the silk-snatcher who'd attempted to steal Lady Caroline's reticule on the Strand and her stomach lurched. In addition to their acquaintance, both Lady Caroline and Lady Yarmouth had been the victims of crime this week. Another coincidence?

'Are you all right, my dear? You look a little strange. I can always send for April to sit with me until we've more news of Duddles.'

'No, no, I'm fine.' Magdalena regretted the words immediately; she needed to go home and send a message to Stephen at Bow Street. This coincidence was surely too big to be ignored. Raindrops pattered down on the glass roof of the orangery. She would take a cab, and if she hurried she might get home before the shower became a downpour.

'Lady Yarmouth was due to attend my soirée but she sent her apologies – she told me something distressing had occurred and she needed to return to the family estate in St Albans immediately. I imagine this must have been the robbery. I must write to her with my condolences as soon as possible.'

'Lady Caroline, I'm sorry but I need to go home now.'

'Of course, my dear.' Lady Caroline reached for the bell pull. 'I shall write a note for April and ask her to call on me. No doubt she's already heard about poor Duddles' trouble.' She sighed. 'Half of London is probably talking about that wretched duel by now. It'll be a terrible scandal. I dread to think what his uncle will make of it all.'

'He might not hear about it,' Magdalena said hopefully. 'Didn't you tell me he lived near Glasgow?'

'Yes, but he's down in London at the moment. Oh dear, what a terrible mess!'

Lady Caroline's maid appeared with a message. 'There's a gentleman here to see you, ma'am. It's Captain Leon. He says you've an appointment with him.'

Lady Caroline's hands fluttered in confusion. 'Oh, good grief! I'd forgotten all about it. It's the outing we discussed last night to see that Peggy Dunne woman who speaks with the dead. I can't possibly go now!' She sank back against her chaise longue in distress.

'Shall we send him away?'

'No, no. That would be discourteous – even in these circumstances. We need to explain what has happened. Ethel, please show in Captain Leon.'

'And please fetch my cloak and bonnet,' Magdalena added. The servant dropped a polite curtsey and left. Magdalena picked up her friend's hand again. 'Don't worry. I'm sure once we explain the situation, Captain Leon will understand.'

Lady Caroline sat up, patted her curls and smoothed out her gown. 'Do I look presentable? Are my eyes still red?'

Magdalena smiled. 'You look fine. I'll help you explain to Captain Leon, but then unfortunately I must go.'

Captain Leon strode confidently across the room towards them, cutting a handsome figure in a dove-grey velvet topcoat over a powder-blue silk waistcoat and dark breeches. His face was full of concern as he bowed over Lady Caroline's hand. 'I cannot tell you, ma'am, how grateful I am you can see me at such a distressing time.'

'You already know about poor Duddles?'

'Yes, ma'am, I'm afraid the town is agog with the news of the death of Baron Danvers in the duel. The tongues of the gossips in the coffee shops on the Strand can't work fast enough.'

Lady Caroline withdrew her hand and let out a short wail. 'But he didn't do it! He wasn't even there!'

Leon straightened up. 'I did my best to stem the tide of gossip, ma'am. I explained to everyone who would listen that Duddles apologised last night for any offence caused and I doubted any such duel had taken place.'

Lady Caroline was visibly relieved. 'Well, thank goodness for your support, Captain Leon. It's at times like this we learn who our true friends are.'

'And talking of friends' – Leon turned to face Magdalena and gave her a little bow – 'I see the loyal Mrs Lavender is already at your side.'

'Yes, Mrs Lavender and her husband don't believe Duddles murdered Baron Danvers either.'

'He doesn't?' Magdalena saw the slight flash of surprise on Leon's handsome face. It was only a slight twitch of a muscle below his prominent cheekbones, but it was there all the same. 'Then all is not lost, Lady Caroline, especially if the eminent Detective Lavender is on the case.'

'Yes, he's already found evidence—'

Magdalena leaned forward to interrupt: 'The nature of which he hasn't told us.'

Lady Caroline caught her warning glance and gave a slight nod. 'Yes, naturally, we wouldn't expect him to do that. It would be inappropriate to discuss the details of a police inquiry at this time. Please take a seat, Captain Leon.'

Leon sat down on the daybed opposite the two women on the sofa, his breeches pulled taut over his muscular thighs. 'Of course, it's excellent news Lavender has already found evidence for Duddles' defence, but—'

Fortunately, Ethel returned at that moment with Magdalena's cloak and bonnet. She rose and reached for her cloak. 'If you'll both excuse me, I must return home.'

Leon scrambled back onto his feet. 'What, so soon? I'd half hoped to persuade you ladies to accompany me to Clerkenwell, to the house of Mistress Peggy Dunne. It's all nonsense, of course, this talking to the dead, but I thought it might be a welcome distraction from your current distress.' He looked hopefully at each of the two women.

Magdalena put on her bonnet and tied the ribbons. 'I'm afraid not, Captain Leon – and I'm sure Lady Caroline is too distressed to leave the house. She's waiting for news of Duddles.'

'Of course, of course; it was foolish of me to suggest it.'

Lady Caroline smiled. 'You're forgiven.'

'Well, at least let me be of assistance to you, Mrs Lavender. I've hired a carriage and it's waiting outside. I'd hoped to use it to drive us to Clerkenwell. Let me take you home instead.'

'Thank you, that's kind but unnecessary; I can make my own way home. Please stay and keep Lady Caroline company until her step-daughter arrives.'

'No, no, Magdalena,' Lady Caroline said. 'You must let Captain Leon escort you safely home. I'll send for April.'

Captain Leon bowed to them both. 'It'll be my pleasure, ma'am, to do this small service for you on such a difficult day.'

Magdalena frowned. She was uncomfortable with the thought of travelling unaccompanied by Teresa with a man she barely knew, but they had given her no choice but to agree. Anything else would be dis-courteous. She kissed Lady Caroline on her cheek, squeezed her hand one last time and reluctantly followed Captain Leon outside to the coach. It was raining more heavily now and Magdalena felt a pang of relief that she hadn't had to traipse around the streets searching for a cab. It was only a short journey from Lincoln's Inn Fields to Marylebone, so her discomfort would be short-lived and she would soon be able to send a message to Stephen.

The smart vehicle smelt of wood varnish and new leather. Captain Leon gallantly helped her up the steps but to her annoyance he threw himself down on the seat beside her rather than taking the one opposite. His thighs pressed against her own through the material of their clothes as the coach lurched forward.

'This is a rum business,' he said. 'I did my best to keep a cheerful countenance for Lady Caroline, but Duddles is headed for the long drop. Lavender's talk of "evidence" is just to keep poor Lady Caroline happy, isn't it?'

Magdalena turned her head to look out of the rain-spattered window. 'I wouldn't know,' she said irritably. 'It's not my business to know.' They were travelling down one of the seedier stretches of Long Acre: a narrow, grimy street made even narrower by the proliferation of street stalls at the side of the road. Their carriage slowed as the driver struggled to avoid a collision with the crowds of shoppers and drunks milling around the stalls. Street hawkers screamed about their wares only a few feet from the window.

'Lavender keeps you in the dark about his work, does he?' She didn't reply and kept her head averted. How many rebuffs would it take for this man to finally understand she wouldn't discuss her husband's work with him?

He gave a short laugh. 'I'll wager he keeps you close too, doesn't he? A beautiful woman like you.'

She didn't know whether to thank him for the compliment or slap him for the impertinence.

'You're definitely the prettiest gal I've seen since I arrived in town. I'll wager Lavender's the jealous type—'

She swung around to face him. His grinning features were only inches from her own. 'I'll thank you, sir, to keep your opinions to yourself.'

But his grin widened and his hand slid onto her leg. She recoiled with shock at the caress and shoved his hand away. 'Keep your hands to yourself, sir! Stop this carriage immediately.'

His broad shoulders shook when he laughed. 'Now, now, Magdalena, Magda. I knew from the start you were the kind of wench who'd not be averse to a little rumble. I saw the way you looked at me the first time we met.' He replaced his hand on her thigh and she felt his fingers bruising her flesh. Fresh anger flared at his gross insinuation.

'*Cerdo asqueroso!*' She tried to stand up in the swaying vehicle, but he pushed her back down in the seat and clamped his arm over her shoulders, pulling her close.

'Do you whisper saucy Spanish words into Lavender's ear while he's docking with you?'

'Captain Leon! Get off me! Stop this coach!'

'Oh, come on, Magda.' Lust burned in his eyes – along with something else that disturbed her, something she couldn't quite fathom.

He forced his mouth over her lips. His hand began to explore the contours of her body through her gown. His grip was brutal. She struggled and writhed in his grasp. He bit her lip. She squealed with pain and she tasted blood. He tugged at the ribbons tying her cloak. It fell away and his hand roamed over her breasts, hard, insistent and demanding.

He relaxed his guard for a second. That was all she needed. In one quick smooth movement, she reached down her legs, hitched up her gown and whipped her loaded pearl-handled pistol out from the top of her boot. Pressing it to his temple, she pulled back the hammer. 'Now get out of this carriage.'

Shock flashed across Leon's face. 'You wouldn't shoot me, Magda . . .'

'Wouldn't I?' She almost laughed. The idiot knew nothing.

Slowly, he rose to his feet and banged on the wooden partition between them and the driver. He sat down on the opposite seat and eyed her warily. 'I never took you for the kind of wench who secretes a pistol in her petticoats.'

She didn't take her eyes from him for a second. Her forefinger itched to pull the trigger. She pushed her gown back over her legs and straightened her bodice with her free hand. It seemed like an age before the coach finally slowed and pulled in to the side of the road.

'Now get out!'

'But I'm miles from home!'

'Get out!' she screamed.

'All right, all right . . .'

He threw open the door, climbed out and slammed it shut behind him. She reached for the protective bolt and rammed it home. She sank back in her seat, breathing heavily, and watched Leon's back disappear into the crowds. He'd gone.

She pulled down the sash window and shouted up to the driver to continue to Westcastle Square. Only when the vehicle pulled out into the traffic again did she finally feel safe. She collapsed back into her seat again, dabbing at her bleeding lip with her handkerchief. She felt filthy, defiled. She'd ask Teresa to draw her a bath when she got home. She wanted to scream and cry at the same time, but she was too angry to cry and too shocked to scream.

Misery filled her as the implications of Leon's behaviour dawned on her. She must send a note to Lady Caroline immediately to warn her of the true, bestial nature of Captain Leon, but she must never, ever mention the incident to Stephen.

There would be no honourable gentlemen's duel.

Stephen would just kill him.

Chapter Twenty-Three

Woods took Rabbie Waverley back to Bedlam, then spent several long, frustrating hours patrolling Holborn Road, where the reports of drunken brawling on the street had been exaggerated. His forced separation from Lavender when there was so much to investigate irked him. It was unfair of Magistrate Read to leave Lavender alone to deal with so many different cases, and there was something fishy about the body turning up at Bow Street. Now he'd met young Duddles, he knew the fellah didn't have the gall to commit such an audacious crime. Lavender was right; the whole thing smelt of the deviousness of Micky Sullivan.

It began to rain again. Woods cursed and decided to go home early for once; he'd put in enough hours this week and there was nothing happening on the Holborn Road.

Eddie was already home when he got back. The boy was sitting in the chair by the kitchen range, with Betsy standing before him. She jumped at the sudden appearance of her husband and he saw the bloodied rag in her hand.

It took Woods a second to take in the shocking state of his son's cut and battered face, the throbbing black eye and swollen mouth.

'Gawd's teeth, son! What the devil happened to you?'

Mother and son glanced at each other.

'I got into a fight, Da.' Eddie's voice came out thick from his puffy lips.

'I've sent our Dan to the Temperance Hotel to buy some ice for his eye,' Betsy said.

Woods ignored her, his attention fixed on his son. 'At work? You got into a fight on your second day at your new job at the brewery?'

Eddie shuffled uncomfortably in his seat. He held his left arm as if it pained him. His curly fringe was flattened back, wet and smeared with blood. 'I were picked on.'

'It's all right, Ned,' Betsy said hastily. 'He's left that job now.'

'What?' Woods couldn't believe his ears.

'That Captain Johnson, you know – the one who befriended him yesterday – has told him there's work to be had downstream in the Port of London.'

Woods' jaw dropped further in shock and confusion.

'I've got to get further away, Da. Too many folks know you round 'ere.'

Eddie's words were like a kick in the gut. Eddie had been beaten up again because of his damned job. Anger flared into a burning rage. 'Who did this to you, son?'

Eddie looked at the floor while his mother continued to dab at his bleeding eyebrow.

'I said: who did it?'

'It were Ellis and Simonside,' Eddie yelled back. Blood and saliva showered his mother's apron. 'You arrested Simonside's brother two years ago for pilferin' down at the wharf! And Ellis is their bloody cousin.'

'Two of them?' Woods slammed his fist down on the kitchen table. The crockery jumped and rattled.

'Ned . . .' Betsy put down the rag and moved towards him.

He remembered the arrest of Simonside. The pilfering had been going on for months and the wharf manager had enlisted the help of

Bow Street to track down the thieves. After a long night spent hiding in the timber yard, Simonside and the other coves were captured red-handed.

Betsy reached out a comforting hand towards him, but he shook her off.

'So the cowards rounded on you, two against one?' The rage inside him was ice cold now. He'd never felt more deadly. He picked up his hat from the kitchen table and turned sharply on his heel.

Betsy blocked his exit from the kitchen, standing between him and the door. 'Sit down, Ned, and calm down.'

'I won't sit down, woman!' he roared. 'I'm going to find this Simonside and knock the livin' daylights out of him!'

'That's why you've got to calm down, Ned, because if you hit him – or this Ellis – they'll never get up again.'

'For God's sake, Betsy! This isn't a scrap between young lads on the street. These are grown men who've attacked our boy!'

'I know, Ned – and that's why you need to calm down.'

'Damned cowards beatin' up a lad of thirteen! They need to find out what it's like to be on the wrong end of the fist of a real man!'

'But you'll kill them, Ned. One blow from your fist in this mood and you'll crush their skulls.'

'Good!'

'Then you'll end up inside your own police cells. And what use are you to me and the nippers imprisoned – or worse – for assault and battery? I know you, Ned Woods, when the rage comes upon you.'

'I swear, Betsy, I've never laid a hand on you before, woman – but if you don't move out of my way, I'll swipe you aside like a fly.'

Betsy pulled her rolling pin out from behind her back and pointed it menacingly in his direction. 'Don't you even try, Ned Woods! Now sit down. Sit down – NOW!'

Woods glared into the determined eyes of his wife.

'It's all right, Da,' Eddie mumbled behind him. 'I hit back and broke Simonside's nose. There were blood everywhere.'

Woods gulped and unmanly tears of rage and frustration sprang unbidden to his eyes. He was torn between his desire to beat the hell out of Simonside and the urge to pick up his son and cradle him in his arms like he did when he was a baby.

Betsy saw his weakness, prodded him in the ribcage with her rolling pin and forced him backwards onto one of the chairs at the kitchen table.

He groaned. 'What's the use of a man who can't protect his family?'

She glided to his side, put down her weapon and gently stroked his head. 'There's protectin' him and there's fightin' his battles for him, Ned, and they're different. Eddie will recover in a few days. This is the price we pay for you havin' a regular and respected job, food in our bellies and a warm roof over our heads.'

'Respected?' Woods asked incredulously. He'd never felt so wretched and useless.

'Yes, you're respected. I see it and hear it every day in the faces and voices of our neighbours and friends when they ask after you.'

'Seems to me half our neighbours are lurkin' in the shadows waitin' to pounce on our nippers!'

'Nonsense! Why, only today Mrs Adams from church stopped me in the street to tell me how she'd heard about you catchin' them footpads on Blackheath. There'll always be villains – and London needs you to catch them, Ned. You've done so well, and the decent folks know it. I'm not havin' you damagin' the respect you've earned over a lifetime of hard work by murderin' Simonside.'

Woods growled, but Betsy's soft words and gentle caressing soothed him.

'And as for Eddie, well, he's makin' his own choices now – and there'll be more opportunities for a bright lad like him in the Port of

London than at the brewery. You've got to stop fightin' his battles, Ned, and let the lad make his own way in the world – whatever it takes.'

'Ooh, I'm a bright lad, am I, Ma?' Eddie mumbled cheerfully from the other side of the room.

'You be quiet a minute, son,' Betsy said, 'while I talk to your da.'

'I can't stand the thought that those bastards will get away with this,' Woods said.

'They won't,' Betsy replied. 'They're bad 'uns, Ned, from a family of bad villains; they'll slip up soon enough and fall to the wrong side of the law. A quiet word in Stephen Lavender's ear – or Magistrate Read's – and they'll soon be sailin' away to join their precious relative in Botany Bay. Revenge is always a dish best served cold, Ned. You'll see.'

She pulled his head into her bosom and held him tight for a minute, swamping him with her delicious smell of pastry and soap. Despite his misery, he savoured her unusual display of public affection; it weakened him. She finally released him and returned to dab at Eddie's face again.

Woods sat there for a moment watching his beloved wife and precious firstborn son. Betsy said something funny and made Eddie laugh. But he choked on his laughter and clutched at his swollen face. 'Don't, Ma! Don't make me laugh – it hurts.'

Woods' murderous anger subsided, but it left behind a painful ache in his gut and heart. Betsy was right; Betsy was always right when it came to the family.

But Woods still ached for his boy.

John Bellingham was drunk when he staggered out of The Feathers onto Great Wild Street. He headed north, weaving his way out of the dark and dismal thoroughfares of St Giles towards the broader, leafier streets surrounding the British Museum, with Lavender trailing in his wake.

It started to rain again and Lavender pulled up his coat collar, cursing the damned weather, as he followed Bellingham.

Bellingham turned into Fitzroy Square and stumbled up the steps of a house on the east side, number fifteen. A maid answered the door and he disappeared inside.

Lavender found refuge from the rain beneath a dripping tree on the opposite side of the small park and settled down for a long wait.

The rain had driven everyone off the streets, apart from an elderly flower seller who sat in her voluminous black skirts below a battered umbrella at the corner of the square with Grafton Street.

She could be useful, he realised, but he hesitated a moment before he approached the woman. Normally, he would have sent Woods across to make her laugh and glean information about the owner of the house which Bellingham had entered; Woods had the common touch, a quality he often lacked.

Lady Caroline's words from the previous night came back to him: *'I'd forgotten how charming you can be when you want to be, Detective . . .'*

His confidence buoyed by the memory, he strolled across to the woman and examined her wilting collection of posies.

Her rheumy eyes lit up in delight. 'You want a nice nosegay, sir? Or perhaps a posy for your lady?'

He forced himself to smile jovially. 'How much are the posies? They're pretty. I think my wife would like one.'

'Oh, she's a lucky lady to 'ave an 'andsome, kind fellah like you. That'll be tuppence, sir.'

'You're too kind yourself, ma'am.' It was daylight robbery, of course, but Lavender just smiled and fished about in his pocket for the coins. He deliberately took his time. He wanted to drag out the conversation. A few moments later, he walked back to his spot beneath the tree, clutching the limp posy in his hand. The woman had told him that number fifteen was the residence of General Isaac Gascoyne, the Member of Parliament for Liverpool – Bellingham's home town.

A vociferous Tory and a huge critic of the Prime Minister, Spencer Perceval, Gascoyne was strongly against Catholic emancipation and had deplored the abolition of the slave trade, which had decimated his constituency. If Lavender remembered rightly, the unpleasant man had once declared that slavery was such a wonderful invention, if it hadn't already been invented, he would have had to invent it himself.

He wasn't surprised Bellingham was visiting Gascoyne. It was only natural the merchant would seek help from his Member of Parliament.

Lavender sighed with frustration and wondered again if they were wasting their time. He'd an inkling where he might have heard the name Nidar before and needed to go home and check his books. Then he thought of poor Duddles languishing in the cells of Bow Street and winced. He needed to solve the mystery of that murder quickly.

Thankfully, Bellingham soon left General Gascoyne's house. His long features were as dour and impassive as ever. He turned east, in the direction of his home. When Bellingham finally turned down New Millman Street and disappeared into his lodgings, Lavender sighed with relief and hailed a cab to take him home. He was tired, soaking wet and had had enough. He'd return tonight to make sure there were no more nocturnal visits to the Ambassador's residence.

Magdalena was upstairs, warming herself in front of the fire blazing in the hearth of their bedchamber. She'd just climbed out of the large tin bath they used in the anteroom and had wrapped herself in a loose gown. Teresa stood behind her chair, towelling Magdalena's long wet hair. It gleamed like ebony in the firelight and her cheeks were pink with the heat and steam of her bath water.

'Stephen!' Her initial look of delight turned into concern. 'But you're soaking! Come and warm yourself by the fire.'

He kissed her and stood shivering for a moment by the hearth. 'Teresa, is the bath water still warm?'

Teresa picked up Magdalena's silver-backed hairbrush and began to tease out the knots in her mistress's wet hair. 'Yes, 'tis nice and peppery,' she said.

Peppery. Lavender smiled, pulled off his wet shirt and headed for the anteroom. Someone must have a word with young Master Alfie Tummins about his influence on their maid's English.

The bath water was as peppery as Teresa had promised. He sank below the surface and let the hot water soothe his aching muscles. It had been a long and upsetting day.

When he surfaced, Magdalena was sitting on a chair beside his bath. Her loose gown fell slightly open at the neckline. She had a familiar gleam in her dark eyes and smiled when she passed him the soap. 'It's wonderful to have you home early for once, Stephen. But Mrs Hobart said it'll be at least another hour until dinner.'

He smiled back and winked. 'I'm afraid I'll have to go out again later – after dinner – but there is a lot we can do in an hour, *querida.*'

She smiled again. 'Lean forward; let me wash your back.'

When she'd finished, he took her face in his hands and gently kissed her mouth. There was a small cut on her lip and she flinched slightly.

'What's that?'

'It's nothing; a small accident, that's all.'

When he climbed out of the bath, he barely had time to dry himself before she took his hand and led him to their bed.

The heavy rain had slowed to a light drizzle when Lavender arrived back at the entrance to New Millman Street around half past seven. Most of the established traders had closed up shop for the night. A steady stream of traffic, pulled by steaming wet horses, still rumbled along the street, spraying up water onto the few unwary pedestrians who loitered on their way home to supper. The grey clouds made it darker than normal for the time of day, but Lavender was glad of the shadows.

He beckoned to a small boy on the street and offered him a half-penny to deliver a message on a scrap of paper to a 'Mr Wilkins' at Bellingham's address. 'You're to give it to no one else, do you understand? You must only put it into the hands of Mr Wilkins.'

It wasn't long before the boy returned to his side with a large frown across his grubby little face. 'There ain't no Mr Wilkins lives there, mister,' he complained.

'Are you sure?'

'Yes. The lady said that only a Mr Bellingham lodged wi' 'er.'

'Did you see him?'

'No. 'E were upstairs, she said.'

Lavender breathed a silent sigh of relief and gave the child his coin. Good. His quarry was still at home, probably sleeping off the ale he'd imbibed earlier in the day. Lavender took shelter in a damp and shadowy alleyway opposite the street and waited for Bellingham to emerge. He desperately hoped that the merchant would make a beeline for the residence of Lord Granville Leveson-Gower. Then he could arrest the man, wind up this case and turn his attention to more pressing matters.

Over dinner, Magdalena had told him about the connection between Lady Yarmouth and Lady Caroline. Like her, he found it strange that the two friends had both been the victims of crime in the space of a few days. The coincidence bothered him. He needed to talk to both women urgently, but Lady Yarmouth wasn't back in town until tomorrow and Lady Caroline wouldn't be pleased to see him while Duddles was still incarcerated in the cells at Bow Street.

Then there was the murder of Baron Danvers and the blatant attempt of someone unknown to contrive the situation so Duddles took the blame. On top of that, Fletcher's news about Nidar bothered him. Nidar: the new criminal force in the city. A man from the north.

For a brief second, Captain James Leon jumped into Lavender's mind, but he dismissed the notion immediately. Leon may be new to London and from the north, but that was where the coincidence ended.

Yes, the man had exaggerated the state of his finances, but many men did that; it didn't make them criminals and Leon was languishing in the debtors' gaol at the time of Danvers' murder. Besides which, this was Leon's first visit to the capital and, according to Sullivan, Nidar had been coming and going for some years.

This was the problem, he realised. All he had to work with was speculation and rumour. He needed hard evidence to track down this shape-shifting Nidar. The superstition annoyed him. He remembered a case back in Northumberland when a gypsy girl had warned him that Magdalena was the shape-shifting Queen of Elphame. What rot that had been.

Nidar claimed he'd sent him a personal message. Was this message Baron Danvers' dead body dumped in a muddy plague pit? Was Nidar behind Danvers' contrived death? If so, how? How had he known about the duel? Lavender remembered the cream gilt-edged invitation Magdalena had kept on the dining room mantelpiece. He made a mental note to ask Lady Caroline for a full guest list for her soirée. Perhaps there were more villains than just Micky Sullivan lurking in her drawing room last night. What was it she'd joked? *'There are no villains here tonight – apart from the usual crowd . . .'* Those words might come back to haunt her.

Lavender pulled a slim volume of northern folk tales from his coat pocket. He'd grabbed it from his study just before he left the house. He walked out of the shelter of the alley onto Guilford Road and stopped beneath the weak glimmer of a wall light. Flicking through the well-thumbed volume, he soon found what he was looking for.

Nidar: the Old Norse serpent who gnaws at the roots of Yggdrasil, the Nordic tree of life. Nidar the serpent. Nidar the wise. Nidar the knowledgeable.

Wise and knowledgeable? Mm, we'll see about that. Lavender slid the book back into his pocket and pulled up his collar against the chill and the drizzle. The cove may be educated, but that didn't always go hand in hand with wisdom and knowledge. The filthy snake had slithered onto Detective Lavender's territory now.

John Bellingham didn't leave his house. At half past nine, Lavender returned home to Magdalena.

Chapter Twenty-Four

Saturday 9th May, 1812
Bow Street Magistrates' Court and Police Office

Yet again a light was burning in Read's upstairs office window when Lavender arrived at Bow Street, signifying that the magistrate was already at his desk. Despite Read's faults, Lavender felt a surge of respect for the man. The other magistrates came and went depending on their need to be in court, but Read worked long hours just like his officers. He took his responsibilities as their most senior magistrate seriously and was one of the best they had ever known.

It wasn't until he entered the building that Lavender remembered poor Duddles was languishing in a cell on the ground floor. 'How's the prisoner in cell number seven?' he asked the bleary-eyed night clerk at the desk. 'Has he been well fed?'

'Oh, 'e were released yesterday evenin'.'

'What?'

'Yes, 'is uncle, Baron Lannister, turned up with their lawyer. Magistrate Read sent 'im 'ome.'

Lavender didn't know whether to be pleased or annoyed about Duddles' surprise release. Had new evidence come to light? Or had Read simply capitulated to pressure from the wealthy peer after ignoring his own concerns about Duddles' innocence? Either way, it was excellent news for Duddles and Lady Caroline. He hurried up the stairs to Read's office.

Read wasn't alone when Lavender knocked and entered the room. All thoughts of Duddles left Lavender's mind when he recognised the dark-coated man in a black velvet yarmulke sitting opposite Read. It was Josef Rothschild. The banker's gentle features looked drawn and strained in the soft glow of the lamp.

'Ah, Lavender, thank goodness you're early.' Read gestured to him to sit down next to Rothschild. 'I've some bad news, I'm afraid. There's been another highway robbery; Mr Rothschild and his wife were held up by tobymen on the Rochester Road yesterday.'

Rothschild held out his hand. 'Glad to see you, Lavender. We need your help.'

'I can't believe it!' Lavender exclaimed. 'Constable Woods has only just cleared that area of footpads.'

'These weren't footpads,' Read said. 'They were mounted highwaymen – just like the coves who robbed Lord and Lady Yarmouth.'

Rothschild nodded, sadly. 'I read about their robbery in *The Day*.'

'How is Mrs Rothschild?' Lavender sank down onto a chair next to him. 'She must be very distressed.'

'Leah is made of stern stuff, as you English say,' Josef replied. 'My wife is angry rather than upset. They took her ring and her jewellery as well as my pocketbook and watch. I have a list here of everything that was stolen.' He placed a sheet of paper on Read's desk.

'Tell me what happened,' Lavender said.

Rothschild carefully recounted the incident. They were at an isolated spot on the far side of Blackheath. The carriage jolted and stopped sharply. The villains fired a warning shot into the air to show they meant business. The carriage door was forced open and the snarling, masked faces of the tobymen appeared at the door. They hauled the terrified Rothschilds out onto the road and stripped them of their valuables.

Lavender's jaw clenched with anger as he listened. 'How did they speak? Lord Yarmouth reported that one of them sounded educated and laughed a lot.'

Rothschild shook his head. 'There was no laughter. Leah and I were scared.'

'Did they harm you?' Read asked.

'No, no. They just took the valuables, checked the coach for anything we may have hidden, and left. I'm afraid I wouldn't be able to tell if they spoke with an educated accent – or any accent, Lavender. British accents all sound the same to me.'

Lavender frowned. 'Did they seem surprised to find out you were Jewish when they opened the carriage door? Did they make any comment about your race?'

'No, they spoke mostly in grunts and they used a lot of gestures.'

Lavender's frown deepened. Prejudice against the Jews swirled like a bad taste through every stratum of British society – but especially in the lower orders. Rothschild's yarmulke and his strong accent marked out his religion and race. It was almost unbelievable some comment hadn't been made. Unless the coves were expecting the Jewish couple to travel on that road and this attack on the Rothschilds was planned . . .

'Is there anything else you can tell me about the thieves?'

'Yes, but it's a trifle.' Rothschild reached into his coat pocket and pulled out a piece of paper. 'Mrs Rothschild saw this tattoo on the wrist of one of the robbers who'd taken off his glove for some reason. It was only a fleeting glance, but she felt it was distinctive enough to reproduce it.'

He handed over the paper. Excitement flooded through Lavender. It was a drawing of a clenched fist with the knuckles foremost: *The Packet Knucklers.*

His chair scraped across the floor as he hastily rose to his feet. 'Please thank Mrs Rothschild and let her know her clever observation has given me a significant clue about the identity of those highway robbers.'

Rothschild looked delighted.

'Where are you going, Lavender?' Read asked.

'To follow this lead. It's the best piece of evidence we've uncovered so far in this damned investigation.'

Woods had arrived and was waiting for him in the hallway. 'I didn't know whether I were with you or back on the horse patrol today . . . ?'

'You're with me,' Lavender said firmly. He pulled Woods aside, told him everything he'd learned about Nidar from Fletcher the previous afternoon, and showed him Leah Rothschild's drawing.

'So Sullivan were tellin' the truth after all?'

'It looks that way.'

'I suppose there's a first time for everythin'.' Woods gave a short laugh but then his face fell and he gave an involuntary shudder. 'I don't like the sound of this shape-shiftin' Nidar. Do you remember the time that gypsy girl told you Doña Magdalena were a shape-shifter and would break your heart?'

'Yes, Ned, I do, but . . .'

'She told me to beware of a hairy beast with a ring through its nose.' Woods gave a little laugh. 'Ever since then, whenever there's trouble down at Smithfield meat market with an escaped bull, I always send Barnaby to deal with it instead.'

'Yes, yes, she also told me to beware of a man with a scarred face. Ned, you need to concentrate. This tattoo . . .'

'I've seen it before.'

'So have I.' Lavender pointed to the rear door to the yard. 'Out there.'

The builders were gathered around their short, bald foreman in the yard. Some leaned on their spades, others had pickaxes slung over their broad shoulders.

'Mr Macca?' Lavender said. 'Would you come with me, please? I need to talk with you.'

Macca frowned. 'Can't it wait? I'm busy.'

'No, I'm afraid not.'

'This'll 'old up yer job!'

'I'm sure it will – but I urgently need to talk with you.'

'Ooh, the detective's arrestin' Macca!' Frank said. The rest of the builders laughed.

'Clap 'im in irons, mister!' shouted Bonner.

Lavender led the grumbling foreman inside the building to a small ground-floor interview room. The three men sat down on the hard wooden chairs.

'What's this about?' Macca asked.

'This.' Lavender laid the piece of paper on the table between them.

Macca's ruddy complexion paled when he saw the drawing of the clenched fist and the knuckles.

'I can see you recognise it,' Lavender said, 'and I know you've got the exact same tattoo on the inside of your right wrist. I've seen it when you've had your shirtsleeves rolled back.'

'They all sed yous were a sharp one,' Macca said quietly.

Lavender leaned back in his chair and folded his arms. 'So, tell me about the Packet Knucklers, Mr Macca.'

'Why? Why do yous want to know? I've had nothin' to do wi' 'em for years!'

'I'm sure you haven't. But we've reason to believe they're now operating in London. What are they? Some gang from the Port of Liverpool?'

The builder sighed and fished his pipe, tobacco and tinderbox out of his coat pocket. He looked strained as he stuffed the tobacco into the pipe. 'That were a long time ago.'

'How long ago?'

Macca struck a light, lit his pipe and inhaled deeply. 'When I were a scally – a young nipper – I got in with a bad crew back in the 'Pool.'

'The Packet Knucklers?'

Macca nodded. 'Me folks were dead and I ended up beggin' down the docks. The Knucklers took me in, so to speak; gave me scraps of scran, a blanket and a few pennies for doin' little jobs fer them.'

'Pickpocketing?'

Macca gave another curt nod. 'I were short, see? The Knucklers would stall up a crowd headin' for the packets – or those disembarkin' after a long voyage at sea – and in the hustle of the crush I'd slip in quiet like, empty their pockets and sometimes their baggage. They never knew I were below 'em.'

'Tell me more.'

Macca sucked noisily on his pipe. 'The Packet Knucklers weren't like an ordinary gang of crimps and coves. They'd gorra new arch-rogue, see, Captain Possy. 'E were ambitious, like.'

'That sounds like a false name. Who is he?'

'I never knew; he were allus just Captain Possy to us. 'E were a bad-tempered brute but clever with it. 'E'd lost a leg in the navy. 'E were bitter and 'eld a grudge after they pensioned 'im off wi' a pittance.' The pipe waggled up and down in the corner of Macca's mouth when he spoke.

'How was he ambitious?'

''E expanded the business and spread out into the city. It weren't long before we was runnin' stolen goods, slavers and brothels and doin' all sorts of other evil.'

'Including house-breaking?'

''Ow'd yous know about that?'

Lavender smiled for the first time that morning. 'For a man who stomps around a building site, you move very quietly inside a building and materialise silently in rooms. That's a useful skill for a burglar.'

'Aye, well, I did it for a while until I were caught – but that were the makin' of me.'

'How so?'

'Aye, I told the beak I were younger than my real age and got away wi' it because of me height. I were worried I'd get a winder to Botany Bay or be sent fer the long drop, but I gorra whippin' and ended up in an institution wi' a load of other young bad 'uns. It were a tough life in there but they taught me my letters and gave me a trade. I've never looked back since.'

'And the Packet Knucklers?' Woods asked.

'Oh, they're still around and givin' 'em 'ell up in the 'Pool.'

Perhaps not, Lavender thought. The evidence suggested the Packet Knucklers had followed the trend of others from that devastated northern city and moved to the wealthier capital to try their luck.

'Possy 'as died now and been followed by 'is son,' Macca continued. ''E's had learnin'. They say the young 'un is worse than the old fellah, but ordinary folks don't trust men wi' learnin'.' Macca glanced up at Lavender and grimaced. 'Beggin' yer pardon like, mister.'

'No offence taken. What's the new arch-rogue called?'

Macca frowned. 'It's a long while since I've 'ad dealings wi' 'em, but they say 'e's christened 'imself strangely: Protish, or Proteus, or some such gibberish.'

Lavender gave a short laugh.

Woods glanced at him curiously. 'Does this mean somethin' to you, sir?'

'I'll tell you later, Constable. What does this Proteus look like, Mr Macca?'

Macca shook his head. 'I don't know but I've 'eard 'e's a bad cove who thinks everythin' is funny. Look, I can't tell yous no more – I need to get back to me men. I've 'ad no dealin's wi' the Packet Knucklers for thirty years and I wish them all in 'ell.'

Lavender nodded. 'You've been very helpful, Mr Macca. One final question: are any of your workforce involved with the Packet Knucklers?'

Macca looked disgusted at the thought. 'Naw, they're decent fellahs. Daft sometimes – but all good lads.' He pushed back his chair, stood up and hesitated. 'Yous won't tell Magistrate Read I've been up before the beak, will yous? We need this job and things 'aven't gone right since we arrived.'

'I won't tell Magistrate Read anything that will bias him against you,' Lavender promised.

Macca nodded and left in a billow of smoke.

'What's so funny about this cove's name, sir?' Woods asked.

'Proteus was the son of the Greek sea god, Poseidon. I think Poseidon is where the nickname "Captain Possy" came from. The new arch-rogue of the Packet Knucklers is as delusional as his father was about their power. Proteus is just another one of Nidar's false names.'

Woods' eyes widened. 'And were this Proteus a shape-shifter too?'

'Do you know what, Ned? I believe he was. Come on, we need to speak to Magistrate Read immediately.'

Chapter Twenty-Five

R ead was alone in his office when Lavender and Woods entered. He put down his quill, gesturing to the two vacant chairs opposite the desk. 'That was quick. Did the lead from Mrs Rothschild prove useful?'

'Yes,' Lavender replied. 'Thanks to our builders we now know a lot more about the highwaymen who robbed the Rothschilds – and possibly Lord and Lady Yarmouth too.'

'Good grief! Our builders aren't involved with this rabble, are they?'

Lavender shook his head. 'No – but the tobymen are from Liverpool. Macca knows of their crew and he has been very helpful.'

'I suppose there's always a first time for everything,' Read said.

'I also think that there's a connection between both robberies; the villains seemed to know who was travelling and when. They lay in wait for them.'

Read frowned. 'Highway robbery is usually more opportunistic. How's it possible the coves knew about the travel plans of the Rothschilds and the Yarmouths?'

'I don't know yet – I urgently need to speak to Lord and Lady Yarmouth. And I also think the same gang – the Packet Knucklers – are connected to the murder of Baron Danvers.'

Read's eyebrows rose high with surprise. 'Good grief! Robbery *and* murder? You've been very busy this morning. But if you're right, then it's good news for us because we no longer have a suspect for Danvers' murder. I released your friend Henry Duddles yesterday evening.'

'Yes, the clerk told me,' Lavender said sharply. 'Did his wealthy uncle and the family lawyer force you to release him?'

Read frowned again. 'That jibe is unworthy of you, Lavender. No, I released him after Sir Richard Allison examined the body yesterday afternoon – the Baron died from a broken neck.'

'Heaven and hell!' Woods exclaimed. 'We thought . . .'

'Yes, we all assumed he'd been shot to death,' Read interrupted. 'Perhaps we should have looked a little closer. According to Allison, the murder was contrived to make it look like his death was the result of a duelling accident.'

'Thank goodness for Sir Richard,' Lavender said.

'I released Henry Duddles into the care of his uncle because no jury in the land is going to believe that such a skinny, nervous young man would have the strength – or the motivation – to overcome a powerful man like Danvers and break his neck – and then shoot him in the head.'

'This makes sense of something else that bothered me when I examined the saddlebag,' Lavender said. 'It'd been emptied by the villains before the horse bolted. Yet it was the pistol shot that caused the horse to run. They must have broken Danvers' neck first, taken his possessions and then fired that shot between his eyes.'

'Your explanation about the attack in Hyde Park looks a lot more credible today,' Read admitted. 'I apologise for dismissing the notion out of hand yesterday.'

Lavender nodded. 'It's been a difficult week for us all.'

'Tell me about this gang you suspect.'

Lavender told him, but the information left Read frowning.

'Let me get this straight, Detective. You've heard lots of rumours of a new crew in town – possibly from Liverpool – who are causing trouble in the rookery of St Giles and who wear this knuckle tattoo on their wrists. But we don't know where they are based or how to find them?'

'There's definitely a seafaring connection,' Lavender said. 'Macca told me the gang had moved into slavers. Perhaps they come in and out of the city on ships and are hiding in the Port of London?'

'The Port of London!' Read exclaimed. 'Have you any idea how many vessels sail up and down the Thames every day? It would take us weeks to search every ship on the river!'

'I appreciate it'll be difficult but it's the only lead we've got. We need to search the port records for ships registered under the names Possy, Proteus and Nidar.'

Read waved a dismissive hand. 'I doubt you'll be so lucky. Most of the Liverpool slave-ship owners have registered their ships under foreign flags and names since the abolition of the slave trade. No doubt Nidar has done the same.'

'It's somewhere to begin,' Woods said enthusiastically.

Read gave Woods a scathing glance. 'On top of this' – his voice rose with frustration – 'the only evidence we have for any of this is a tattoo? And your theory that this gang is also responsible for the murder of Danvers is based on the rumour that this Nidar planned to send you a message?'

Woods nodded. 'That body in the back yard were very provocative.'

'And the only things you know about this gang's leader are that he had a gentleman's education, goes by a variety of different names and has an obsession with ancient folklore and Greek myths?' Read snapped.

'Yes.' Lavender smiled. 'I need a copy of Homer's *Odyssey* as soon as possible.' He glanced around the large, dusty tomes stacked in the bookshelves of Read's study. 'You don't have one here, do you, sir?'

'No, I do not! Lavender, have you thought how fantastical this sounds? Have you forgotten that the British justice system works on facts and evidence?'

Lavender smiled. 'We've had stranger cases to deal with than this.'

Read shook his head in disbelief. 'I hardly dare ask, but what about you, Woods? What do you make of this nonsense?'

Woods pulled himself up straight, looked pensive, then said: 'To be honest, sir, it's all Greek to me.'

Read had no chance to respond as they were suddenly interrupted by a loud rap on the door. It flew open and two familiar broad figures strode into the room, their greatcoats and boots still mud-splattered from their journey: Vickery and Adkins had returned.

Lavender gave a huge sigh of relief, grinned and rose to greet his fellow Principal Officers. He shook Adkins' hand and thumped Vickery on the back in affection.

Read also rose to his feet and shook hands with his officers. 'Thank God you're here! We've been overwhelmed with crime this last week – and Lavender has gone quite mad in your absence!'

'Are you runnin' the shop on your own, Lavender?' young Adkins asked.

'Almost,' Lavender replied, smiling. 'I've had help from Ned.'

'We thought things had been difficult round here when we saw that poor constable sittin' in the privy just now,' Vickery said with a wink. 'Worn down to the bone, he were.'

'Who's that?' Read asked, frowning. 'Which constable?'

'He didn't say much, but the note beside him said he were "Constable Bone-Apart".'

Lavender and Woods laughed, but Read looked confused. 'I don't employ any constables with that name.'

'It's all right, sir,' Woods said. 'It's just those builders playin' tricks again.'

'You should have promoted Ned Woods to Principal Officer, sir, if you were stretched,' Adkins said, with another wink. 'He knows everything goin' on around here and it's long overdue.'

Woods laughed and shook the hand of the lively young fellow. 'No thank you, sir. There's too much thinkin' involved in your job for my old noddle.'

Adkins pulled his gilt-topped badge of office out of his coat pocket and tossed it to Woods. 'Here you go, Ned. Have my tipstaff. Wave it around a bit and see how it feels.' Lavender and Vickery laughed when Woods gave it a little wave.

Read sat back down and smoothed out his voluminous black court gown. 'When we've finished with the horseplay, gentlemen, we've business to discuss.'

Adkins and Vickery pulled up chairs and joined them at his desk.

'Our coach just pulled into The White Bear in Piccadilly,' Vickery said, stripping off his hat and gloves. 'We came straight here.'

'Did you track down those escaped French prisoners of war?' Read asked.

Adkins grinned. 'They hadn't gone far, and once word got out about the reward, the good folk of Hampshire helped us to track them down. The magistrates paid the bill in full and the money is already with Oswald Grey downstairs.'

'Good,' Read said. 'Well, I'm glad you're back as we've had a hideous week: one murder and two unsolved highway robberies. Lavender suspects the same gang is behind all the crimes, but his story is fantastical. I'll let him explain.'

Once more, Lavender outlined everything they had uncovered. Vickery and Adkins listened closely and showed no inclination to mock his theory.

'Constable Barnaby, Micky Sullivan and your other informers are right, Lavender,' Vickery said, nodding. 'Before we left for Hampshire, I'd heard rumours there was a new crew from the north causin' trouble.'

'Woods and I need to visit Lord and Lady Yarmouth again,' Lavender said. 'I'm sure there's a connection between these two robberies; on both occasions the villains seem to have known the occupants of the coach and exactly when and where they were travelling.'

When Lavender told them of the link to the Packet Knucklers of Liverpool, Adkins turned to Magistrate Read. 'I've a brother-in-law who works in the offices at the Port of London. It wouldn't hurt to make a few enquiries. I know it's unlikely they've used these names, but I think it's worth checkin' if there were any ships registered to Captain Possy – or to his queer, two-headed son.'

'Very well,' Read said. 'Take Constable Barnaby with you in case of any trouble. And I need you and Vickery to sound out your own informers to learn what they know about this gang over the next few hours. Someone, somewhere, must know where they hide in the city.' Vickery and Adkins nodded. 'Oh, and the clerks downstairs have copied out lists of the stolen goods,' Read added. 'Make sure you pick up a copy when you leave.'

'What do you want me to do now, sir?' Vickery asked.

'Lavender has been trailing John Bellingham since you left. You can share the surveillance, starting now. That'll release him to work on the other crimes.'

Vickery nodded and reached for his hat and gloves. 'Seen anything unusual, Lavender?'

Lavender shook his head. 'He's done nothing out of the ordinary, as far as I can see. But there's something in Bellingham's expression I don't like – a hint of madness.'

'Lord Leveson-Gower claims that Bellingham's stalking him,' Read said.

Lavender shook his head. 'I've seen no evidence of this.'

'Just keep an eye on him, Vickery. We've already got the murder of one peer to deal with this week,' Read said grimly. 'I don't want another.'

Vickery stood up. 'I'll set off now and be waiting for when he rises. Does he still stay in the house until about ten?'

Lavender nodded.

Adkins pushed back his own chair and stood up. 'You've been sorely stretched in our absence, Lavender. I'll take my leave now, sir, find Barnaby and head down to the Port of London.'

Lavender sighed, relieved that his burden of work was now shared.

'We'll have a speedy resolution of these cases now Adkins and Vickery are back with us,' Read said. 'By the way, have you purchased your ticket for your voyage on the *Shona Adare* on Monday night?'

Lavender grabbed his hat and gloves and stood up hastily. 'Not yet. Come on, Ned. We've work to do.'

'Well, make sure you buy your passage today. Now Vickery and Adkins are back, there's nothing to stop you departing for Dublin on Monday. And before you go to Lord Yarmouth's, you may need this.' Read pulled several sheets of paper from a pile on his desk. 'Lady Alderney responded to my request for a guest list for the party she hosted the night Lord and Lady Yarmouth were robbed. Tread carefully with the Yarmouths. They won't be pleased to hear that you suspect someone in their acquaintance of being involved in the robbery.'

Lavender's eyebrows rose at the size of the list. 'Good grief! How big is her drawing room?'

'Sarah Alderney is an incurable gossip.' Read looked embarrassed. 'She's an old friend of my wife – but Mrs Read was unable to attend the party on that evening. I simply asked for a guest list, but Lady Alderney knows of my role here and has taken this opportunity to give me a full briefing about those amongst her acquaintance whom she feels might be the most suspicious. The names of the guests are accompanied by her view of their financial stability, their morals, the type of carriage they ride in and the number of servants they brought with them.'

Lavender smiled, pocketed the sheaf of papers and stood up. 'It may prove helpful. We'll take a cab, Woods. I'll read this while we travel to the Yarmouths'.'

Chapter Twenty-Six

Magdalena was struggling to concentrate on her embroidery in the drawing room. When Mrs Hobart announced that Lady Caroline had arrived to see her, she pushed her sewing basket aside with relief and greeted her friend warmly. She couldn't stop thinking about her narrow escape in the coach with Leon. When Stephen had been with her last night, she'd managed to push it to the back of her mind, but the memory haunted her today and her mood fluctuated between fury and despair. A visit from Lady Caroline was the welcome distraction she needed.

'I bring great news!' Lady Caroline kissed Magdalena on the cheek, then sat down on the velvet sofa opposite Magdalena's chair, resting her walking cane beside it. 'Duddles is free!'

Magdalena clapped her hands together in delight. 'This is wonderful news! When? How was he released? Would you like some coffee?'

'No, no coffee this morning, thank you. I merely stopped by to see how you were and to give you the good news. Well, I *say* it's great news – but in truth Duddles is now in the clutches of his furious Scottish uncle at their town house.' She smoothed down the creases in her gown and leaned forward towards Magdalena. 'Duddles sent me a note yesterday evening. Apparently, Baron Danvers wasn't shot in a duel at all.'

'What?'

'Some brute broke his neck and – after he was dead – shot him between the eyes to make it look like he had been killed in a duel.' Magdalena gasped. 'Lavender was right,' Lady Caroline continued. 'The whole thing was contrived to make poor Duddles look guilty.'

'Oh, this is wonderful. Well, no, it's not – not for poor Lady Danvers. But I'm so pleased for Duddles – and for you.'

'Well, there may not be a "Duddles and me" for much longer.' Lady Caroline sighed. 'He also said in his note that his uncle is now determined to push ahead with this dreadful arranged marriage. He's furious about the scandal and the shame Duddles has brought to the family name. Did you see the headlines in *The Day* this morning?'

'No, I . . .'

'Well, Duddles' arrest was all over the front page of that dreadful news-sheet. Baron Lannister wants him to settle down and marry this country girl as soon as possible. He thinks it will keep him out of trouble.'

'Oh dear!'

'I know, I know, but this is a disappointment I'll have to bear.' Lady Caroline sighed again. 'At least poor Duddles is now out of those dreadful police cells and free of suspicion.'

'Yes, of course.' Magdalena didn't know what to say. Lady Caroline seemed surprisingly sanguine at the prospect of losing her young lover. She wondered if it was merely a brave face to hide her heartache.

'But never mind me.' Lady Caroline leaned forward again, her eyes full of concern. 'I received your note yesterday about Captain Leon's despicable behaviour. It must have been dreadful for you. What happened, my dear? Are you all right?'

Magdalena's face fell as the memory resurfaced. 'Yes, and much better now you're here, Lady Caroline. I feel wretched about keeping this assault from Stephen, but I don't know what else to do.'

'Tell me everything, my dear.'

Slowly, Magdalena recounted the painful details of the incident. It was hard to talk about it, but she felt better for unburdening herself.

Lady Caroline's features registered shock, anger and sadness in equal measure. She patted Magdalena's knee again once the story was told. 'You were a brave woman – and thank goodness for your pistol. Leon is obviously a monster. You'd be surprised how many aristocratic women I know who always travel with a loaded pistol in their muffs.'

'I keep wondering if I was in part to blame. Had I given him some indication I would welcome . . . ?'

Lady Caroline held up her hand to silence her. 'Nonsense. Most men – even gentlemen – simply can't be trusted. And if anyone was partially to blame, it was me. I was so distracted with poor Duddles yesterday, I encouraged you to travel with the dreadful man in his coach.'

'It's not your fault.'

Lady Caroline's auburn ringlets quivered when she shook her head. 'No, I must take some of the blame for putting you in danger. Captain Leon charmed us all, but I should have remembered we barely know him. It was inappropriate for you to travel alone with him. I should have sent my maid with you.'

'I feel dreadful keeping this a secret from Stephen.'

Again, Lady Caroline shook her head. 'No, you were right to keep this incident from him. I can see how burdened he is at the moment with his work. There's nothing to be gained by distressing him further.'

'I think he'll kill Leon if he ever finds out.'

'Yes, he probably would. Your husband adores you, my dear. You're very blessed.'

They both jumped when Mrs Hobart suddenly entered with a small parcel wrapped in brown paper. 'It's a delivery for you, Mrs Lavender,' she said.

'A parcel?' She wasn't expecting any deliveries. 'Thank you.' Mrs Hobart handed over the small box and left the room.

Magdalena frowned. It was addressed to *Mrs Stephen Lavender*. The handwriting was unfamiliar, sprawling, the 'p' falling down in an elaborate swirl.

'Well, open it, my dear.'

Magdalena untied the string, unwrapped the brown paper and pulled out a small black box and a note. She lifted the lid, and both women gasped at the sparkling brilliance of the jewels lying within. '*Dios mío!* What's this?'

It was a heavy gold necklace encrusted with seed pearls and diamonds in a delicate, swirling design. At the bottom of the box lay a pair of matching earrings.

'Oh, how pretty!' Lady Caroline murmured. She took the box and lifted up the necklace to examine it more closely while Magdalena opened the accompanying letter. Her hands trembled as she read the first three words:

> My dearest Magda,
>
> I humbly apologise for my ungentlemanly behaviour yesterday afternoon in the carriage. I was overcome with desire at the thought of possessing you but cannot think what made me behave so roughly. I can only surmise I was driven mad with your beauty and elegance.
>
> Please accept this small gift as a token of my sincerity and deepest regret. A woman like you deserves better than a common constable can afford.
>
> Yours etc.
>
> James Leon, gent.

The letter scorched her hand. She threw it to the floor and jerked to her feet. 'It's from him,' she wailed, before bursting into tears. 'He won't leave me alone.'

◆　◆　◆

'What were all that about Dublin?' Woods asked, once they'd climbed into the cab.

Lavender pulled Lady Alderney's guest list from his coat pocket and smoothed out the sheets. 'Read has another case lined up for me in Ireland. I'm supposed to leave on Monday.'

'Gawd's teeth! Doña Magdalena won't like that.'

Lavender continued reading and didn't look up. 'No, she won't. That's why I haven't told her yet. I've been so busy since I returned we've hardly seen each other. I know she'll be disappointed.'

'But have you given her a back rub, like I suggested?'

Lavender glanced sideways at him. 'I believe I may have. Ned, what's this obsession you have with back rubs?'

Woods sat back, satisfied. 'Well, that's good. One thing leads to another, as they say.'

Lavender shook his head and returned to the list. It wasn't long before both his eyebrows were raised in his high forehead.

'Is it a bit saucy?' Woods asked.

'Hah! Saucy! If the tattle sheets got hold of this information and published it, half of the *beau monde* would be ruined. Apparently, Lady Silvester has been having an illicit affair with her footman for the last two years and the Earl of Oban is so badly in debt he's sold off most of the family heirlooms.'

'Do you know him? Is he the type to turn into a gentleman highwayman?'

The cab jolted violently in a rut in the road. Lavender steadied himself before he replied. 'No, I don't know him, but Lady Alderney added that the Earl has been saved from bankruptcy by a generous loan from his mistress, the Marchioness of Coniston.'

Woods tutted.

'In fact,' Lavender continued, 'I know hardly any of the guests on this list.'

'Sounds to me like you wouldn't want to know them better!' Woods said. 'All this scandal would rattle me old noddle. Are there any men on that list without notes from Lady Alderney? They might be the ones she doesn't know so well.'

Lavender turned to the last page. 'Yes, there are six people here without notes, including two women – although it says Doctor Pardus brought his servant with him.'

'Who's he?'

'A doctor of divinity from Oxford. The other men are the Earl of Stamford, Count Romanov and a Mr Lancashire.'

'Isn't Liverpool in the county of Lancashire?' Woods asked.

Lavender nodded and wondered. The cab slowed and pulled over to the side of the road. He glanced out of the window at the busy street. 'This is my favourite bookshop; I asked the driver to stop here.' He pushed the list back into his pocket and reached for the door handle. 'I won't be a moment.'

'Why don't you leave that list here with me for a while . . .' Woods said hopefully.

Lavender grinned and ignored him. He stepped down onto the street and hurried into the shop. It didn't take him long to find what he needed in the low-beamed, dusty emporium. He climbed back into the cab with a second-hand copy of Homer's *Odyssey*. 'Hopefully Mr Homer can tell us some more about Proteus, son of Poseidon.'

Woods sat patiently while Lavender leafed through the book. It wasn't until the cab turned into Berkeley Square that Woods' curiosity got the better of him. 'Anything?' he asked.

Lavender smiled. 'You were right about the shape-shifter thing, Ned.'

'Course I were. I'm famous for me knowledge of Greek, I am.'

'Proteus took on various forms to escape capture by men who wanted to harness his powers – these included a snake, a panther, a lion and a pig.'

'A snake?' Woods' voice rose with excitement. 'That'll be that serpent, Nidar!'

Lavender snapped the book shut and grinned with satisfaction. 'Yes, it's a tenuous link, of course – and I'm not sure what a jury would think – but we've another clue that Proteus is the same man leading the new gang of rogues in the rookery of St Giles.'

Lady Yarmouth was taking coffee with her husband in the library when Lavender and Woods were shown into the room. The Earl sat behind his great Chippendale desk with his pale silk waistcoat straining over his large belly. His elegant, grey-haired wife sat gracefully on a chair beside the fireplace, her white gown, gentle expression and the sparkle from her glittering rings and bracelet lifting the gloom of the sombre room. Lavender and Woods remained standing.

'Right, Lavender, what's this all about?' Yarmouth asked. 'Have you tracked down those scoundrels who robbed us?'

'I need to ask you some more questions,' Lavender said. 'Unfortunately, there's been another hold-up on the Rochester Road and I think there might be a connection between the highwaymen responsible for this and the villains who robbed you.'

'Oh dear!' Lady Yarmouth looked distressed. 'I hope no one was hurt?'

'Thankfully, no, although Mr Josef Rothschild and his wife are badly shaken.'

'The Rothschilds?' Yarmouth asked. 'I know the family. Jews, of course, but decent people. I wouldn't wish what happened to us on any poor souls.'

'The thing is,' Lavender continued, 'they attended a soirée at the home of Lady Caroline Clare the evening before.'

'I was meant to attend that event,' Lady Yarmouth said.

'I know you were.'

'Well, that's a coincidence!' Yarmouth exclaimed.

'Yes, sir, I was struck by the same thought myself. I know the Rothschilds discussed their travel plans in public at Lady Caroline's soirée. The thieves seemed to be expecting them.'

'Were they, by Jove? There's another coincidence for you, Lavender – those scoundrels who robbed us seemed to know when and where we were travelling too.'

'That's exactly what I thought, sir.' Lavender cleared his throat. 'Then I remembered you attended a social event at Lady Alderney's the night you were robbed.' He paused slightly before uttering the next words. 'I wondered if you or Lady Yarmouth had told anyone else about your intention to travel to St Albans – especially at Lady Alderney's party?'

Yarmouth gave a short laugh. He didn't look pleased. 'Do you suspect our friends now, Detective?'

Lady Yarmouth put down her cup and frowned. 'That is a most unpleasant thought.'

'No, sir, ma'am, I don't suspect your friends – not your *true* friends at any rate. But it was a large gathering by all accounts, with many people milling around. You told me yourself that the thief who robbed you seemed an educated man. I have already dismissed the notion that any of your servants were involved in tittle-tattling about your affairs . . .'

'Well, that's a relief!' Lady Yarmouth said tartly.

'But I must investigate every possibility.'

'So you think there's a gentleman highwayman mingling with our aristocratic friends while planning to rob them?' Yarmouth laughed again. 'Really, Lavender, you'll have to do better than this!'

Lavender pulled himself up straighter. 'Perhaps I can. Lady Yarmouth, did Lady Caroline Clare send you a cream, gilt-edged invitation card inviting you to her soirée on Thursday night?'

'Why, yes, she did. How did you know that?'

'My wife and I have been friends of Lady Caroline for some years and also received one. Do you still have it?'

Lady Yarmouth looked confused. 'I may have . . . no, I don't believe I do. I think I left it in my reticule.'

'The same reticule that was stolen by the highwaymen?'

Her hand fluttered to her mouth and she gasped. 'Oh, my goodness – yes!'

Satisfaction welled up inside Lavender. 'This may be how the coves knew of Lady Caroline's soirée.'

Yarmouth's jaw dropped with shock.

'I think you'll agree, Lord Yarmouth, that the connection between the two robberies has just become stronger than mere coincidence.'

Lady Yarmouth had turned pale. 'Oh, please don't tell me they used my invitation to Lady Caroline's soirée to find their next victims?'

'I'm afraid they did,' Lavender said. 'But please don't distress yourself, Lady Yarmouth. None of this is your fault. There's a devious con man at large who's manipulating us all. But his days of liberty are numbered.'

If he had hoped his words would bring comfort, he had misjudged the situation. Both the Earl and the Countess looked wretched.

Woods stepped in to his rescue. His deep voice was calm and soothing. 'It would be helpful to us if you could both think back to this party. Did either of you tell anyone about your travel plans that night?'

Yarmouth shook his head. 'No, I spent most of the evening with Wigton and Belvedere discussing the racing, then we moved to the card tables.'

'I think I may have said something to Lady Alderney,' Lady Yarmouth said.

'Oh for heaven's sake, Georgina!' the Earl snapped. His florid complexion turned darker.

'It was a private conversation! I think I mentioned our trip to St Albans but added that I intended to return to London for Lady Caroline's soirée.'

Lavender stepped closer to the distressed Countess and spoke gently: 'As I said, it must have been a crowded event.'

'Yes, the crush was quite awful at times.'

'Can you remember if there was anyone standing nearby while you and Lady Alderney were talking?'

'Half of London,' Yarmouth muttered angrily.

'No, no,' Lady Yarmouth insisted. 'It was a private conversation between myself and Lady Alderney.'

Lord Yarmouth sat up straighter and the anger dropped from his face. 'Who were you speaking to before that, Georgina? They may have been loitering and eavesdropping. Come on, my dear, think!'

Fine lines creased her ladyship's forehead as she struggled to remember. 'It was a friend of Lady Alderney's, a man from Oxford. No – he wasn't her friend. He was her son's friend from Oxford. Perhaps one of his tutors?'

Oxford. Doctor Pardus?

'What did you talk about?' Lavender asked.

'I can't remember. Not much. He was a nice young man but he didn't seem to know much about art.'

'I remember him too,' Yarmouth said. 'He was hovering around the card tables. I remembered thinking he was too young to be an Oxford don.'

Lavender's mind jolted. *Pardus. Panthera pardus – the leopard.* It was another one of Nidar's false names.

'He had unusual eyes,' Lady Yarmouth added.

'Mmph, I don't recall that,' Yarmouth said, 'but he seemed a jovial fellow.'

'He laughed a lot?' Lavender asked. His voice sounded strangled even to himself.

'Why, yes, now you come to mention it . . . are you all right, Lavender? You look a bit funny.'

A snake, a panther, a lion and a pig. Nidar the snake. Pardus the panther – and Leon the lion. It was Captain James Leon. The damned man had played them for fools.

'Excuse me, your ladyship – sir. I think we may have just worked out who robbed you.'

'We have?' Woods said, startled.

Lavender didn't wait to be dismissed. He turned and strode out of the room, with Woods hurrying behind him.

Chapter Twenty-Seven

L ady Caroline took Magdalena into her arms and comforted her. 'Let it all out, my dear,' she said. 'You've had a dreadful experience.'

'And it's not over yet!' Magdalena sobbed and pointed at the letter on the carpet.

'I shall ring for some tea, then we'll resolve this. Everything is always clearer after a cup of sweet tea.' Lady Caroline limped to the bell pull by the fireplace. 'Obviously, you can't keep this jewellery; it must be returned to Captain Leon immediately – with a sharp retort.' Frowning, she picked up Leon's letter from the floor and scanned it.

Mrs Hobart arrived. Lady Caroline discreetly covered the box of jewellery with her hand and asked her to fetch some tea.

'I can't believe the blind cheek of the man!' Magdalena yelled after Mrs Hobart had gone. 'Does he want me to shoot him? Because I will!' She blew her nose on her handkerchief and dabbed furiously at her eyes, embarrassed by her own weakness.

Lady Caroline pulled the necklace out of the box and examined it closely. 'Captain Leon is goading you, my dear. The question is, why.' She frowned again, stood up and slowly walked over to one of the tall windows in the room. When she held the necklace up to the glass, the sunlight bounced off the sparkling diamonds and sent tiny pink spots of light in a frenzied dance around the walls and the furniture.

'I think I've seen this necklace before,' Lady Caroline said quietly. 'Did you tell me yesterday that Lady Yarmouth lost a diamond and seed pearl necklace when she was robbed on the highway? Or did I read it in *The Day* after you'd left?'

Magdalena joined her and took the necklace from her hands. She noticed the rosy tone of the gold, the pink hue of the pearls and the tiny, glittering diamonds. It was a highly unusual piece and an item of great beauty. It was also exactly how Stephen had described Lady Yarmouth's stolen necklace.

'It *is* Lady Yarmouth's necklace. *El cerdo* has sent me stolen jewellery! Why?' Every time she thought Captain Leon could do nothing more to shock her, he twisted the knife.

'There are two possibilities as to why we're holding Lady Yarmouth's necklace,' Lady Caroline said calmly. 'Either Captain Leon purchased the set from a disreputable jeweller who bought them from the thieves and this is a coincidence . . .'

'Or he's stolen it himself. Damn him! The man's a highwayman as well as a molester!'

'I suspect the latter is true. We need your husband to take them to Lady Yarmouth for identification.'

'But how? How will I explain how they came into my possession?' Tears welled up again in Magdalena's eyes. She brushed them away angrily. 'Stephen must never know what happened yesterday – or read this note.'

They heard the rattle of china cups outside in the corridor. Mrs Hobart approached with the tea tray.

'I agree, my dear.' Lady Caroline took her arm and led her back to the sofa. 'We'll take tea and ponder the matter. Captain Leon thinks he's a clever rogue and he's obviously determined to cause trouble between you and Stephen.'

Magdalena groaned.

'But we'll find a way,' Lady Caroline continued. 'There is no man alive who can outwit two determined women when they put their minds to a problem.'

'Jermyn Street – quickly!' Lavender barked out the order to their startled cab driver. They scrambled aboard.

'Captain Leon, Doctor Pardus and Nidar are all the same man.'

'What!'

'He's that cove, Proteus, from Liverpool,' Lavender continued. 'He charmed his way into Lady Alderney's party with some tale about being her son's tutor in Oxford. Then he overheard Lady Yarmouth talking about their plans to travel to St Albans and robbed them that night. He also heard her mention Lady Caroline's soirée. When he found the invitation card in the reticule he'd stolen, he had Lady Caroline's address and decided to steal again. He must have followed Lady Caroline when she left her house on Wednesday morning.'

Lavender grimaced at the thought of the villain stalking Magdalena and Lady Caroline. 'He struck lucky when Josef Rothschild mentioned his own travel plans and set up the second robbery.'

'Didn't you tell me he rescued Lady Caroline's reticule from a silk-snatcher? Isn't that how they met?'

'Yes, that robbery was faked. He used one of his henchmen to steal the purse, then acted like a hero to elicit Lady Caroline's gratitude. God, it angers me to think he may have been stalking Lady Caroline and Magdalena! He already knew about the forthcoming soirée, of course, thanks to the invitation he found in Lady Yarmouth's stolen reticule. All he had to do was get himself invited. The man's shameless – and dangerous. He likes to play games – and he's very clever.'

'I can see how he might be Nidar and have had a hand in these highway robberies – but he can't have murdered Baron Danvers. He were locked up in Marshalsea debtors' gaol when Baron Danvers were killed.'

'That's why I dismissed him as a suspect yesterday,' Lavender replied. 'But don't forget that his henchmen were still at large. Lady Alderney's list mentions the manservant who accompanied Dr Pardus, and Sullivan told us Leon took one to Lady Caroline's. He probably gave the information about the Rothschilds' travel arrangements – and the duel – to his man before he left Lady Caroline's home with Sullivan. Then he deliberately orchestrated his arrest and imprisonment to provide himself with an alibi. While he was incarcerated his men murdered Danvers and robbed the Rothschilds.'

'That's what you thought Micky Sullivan did.'

'Yes. I was blinded by my prejudice against Sullivan. It never crossed my mind Captain Leon was doing the same thing. I doubt Leon was even drunk. It was all a pretence. He's tricked me like a fool! Damn this traffic! Can't the driver go any faster?'

Woods glanced out of the window and shook his head. 'We're nose to tail with a dray cart. It sounds to me like this Nidar fellah has stung everyone, sir.'

'He's an expert trickster – and attending one social event often leads to an invitation to others.'

Woods frowned. 'But what I don't understand is, if robbery is his game, then why murder Baron Danvers?'

'That,' Lavender said grimly, 'was a message to me – and the rest of the Police Office at Bow Street. He wanted us to be distracted, embarrassed – and to know he'd arrived on the scene. The man's arrogance is unbelievable.'

The cab drew to a halt outside a tall house at the wealthier end of Jermyn Street. Lavender fished his gilt-topped badge of office out of his coat pocket, while Woods hammered on the door.

'Is your pistol primed, Ned?'

'Primed and ready, sir.'

The startled landlady told them that Captain Leon rented a room on the first floor of the building. They didn't wait for her to show them up. Barging past, they mounted the stairs two at a time and threw open the bedroom door.

It was empty, the bed neatly made with the coverlet smoothed. The closet and the drawers were bare. Nidar had gone.

On the bedside table, a folded note stood up against the candlestick. It was addressed to *Detective Lavender*. He opened it and his guts churned with anger.

There were only six words.

What kept you so long, Lavender?

Magdalena and Lady Caroline drank their tea in near silence. Magdalena preferred strong coffee, but Lady Caroline had insisted on sugary tea for the shock. Magdalena knew the British swore by this remedy but she grimaced and put down her half-full cup. She glared at the box of jewellery as though it was cursed, her mood swinging between anger and despair.

Lady Caroline tapped her elegant fingers against the curved wooden end of the sofa while she thought. 'Tell me everything you know about these highwaymen who robbed Lord and Lady Yarmouth, my dear.'

'Stephen said he suspected a man called Nidar was behind this spate of crime in London. He disguises himself and uses different names.'

'Ah, so James Leon may not have been the captain's name after all? My goodness, we are learning something today. I don't think I'll ever trust a man again until I've seen his baptismal record. What a fool I have been!'

'This Nidar bragged that he would send Stephen a "message".'

'Oh, he did, did he?'

'Yes, Stephen thought the message was the body of Baron Danvers in the plague pit at Bow Street.'

Lady Caroline grimaced. 'That certainly was a powerful message.'

'His informant was unclear about whether the message had already been sent, or was to come in the future.'

Lady Caroline gave a little laugh and her ringlets wobbled, but her eyes weren't smiling. 'Men like Leon – or Nidar, as we must now call him – bring about their downfall in the end with their foolish bragging and displays of arrogance. They open themselves up to quiet manipulation from others. Right, my dear, we're going to send Lavender another message – and return Lady Yarmouth's necklace to its rightful owner at the same time. Do you have pen and ink?'

Magdalena was shocked. 'We're sending the jewellery to Bow Street?'

'Yes.'

'But we can't let Stephen read the accompanying note.'

'We won't. You must destroy this note – but not before I have studied the handwriting.' She reached for her walking cane. 'Bring everything over to the writing desk, including the wrapping paper and string.'

Magdalena gathered up the components of the parcel and Leon's letter and followed Lady Caroline to the rosewood console below one of the tall windows. Lady Caroline seated herself, took out a quill and removed the top from the bottle of ink. Magdalena hovered at her shoulder.

'We'll adjust the address on the wrapping paper first.' Lady Caroline smoothed down the brown paper and studied the writing.

'But the package was addressed to me alone,' Magdalena said. 'Stephen is bound to think it's suspicious.'

'Have faith, my dear.' Lady Caroline dipped the quill in the ink and carefully wrote *Mr and* before the name *Mrs Stephen Lavender*. It now read *Mr and Mrs Stephen Lavender*. Magdalena was impressed. Lady Caroline's handwriting was a seamless copy of Leon's and the words were perfectly aligned. No one would ever suspect the addition.

'Now,' Lady Caroline said. 'We need to make sure Lavender knows where this package has come from.' She dipped the quill again and wrote on the wrapping paper: *From your dear friend, Captain James Leon*. Once again the handwriting was a perfect match with Leon's own flamboyant style. 'There. We shall wrap up the parcel again so it looks unopened and send it straight to Bow Street. Lavender will assume you opened the parcel, recognised Lady Yarmouth's necklace and sent it to him like a good little wife.'

Magdalena struggled to hold in her laughter. 'His *dear friend?*'

'Well, that should irritate your husband and send him post-haste to Jermyn Street to vigorously question the dreadful scoundrel. I suspect Captain Leon will be arrested before nightfall.'

Doubts still plagued Magdalena. 'What if he tells Stephen about what he tried to do to me – or worse, that he claims he succeeded? I couldn't bear it if Stephen doubted me.'

'Then you must lie to him, my dear – and so will I. Captain Leon never visited my house yesterday afternoon. You never climbed into the carriage with him. Leon is a liar and a crook who is out to cause trouble. That's what we'll say. The necklace will damn him. We'll not let him get away with this.'

'But what if Leon didn't rob Lady Yarmouth?' Magdalena asked. 'What if he did buy the necklace in all innocence from a jeweller?'

Lady Caroline turned her head askew and glanced up, her green eyes locking Magdalena's in a serious gaze. 'I doubt that. But it doesn't matter if he's innocent of *that* crime. We know he's guilty of attempted rape and harassment. For the sake of all women across London, the cad should be thrown into gaol; if we can't have him arrested for what he's done, let's make sure he's arrested for something else.'

Magdalena nodded. Lady Caroline's approach to solving her problem fascinated her with its subtlety. For the first time in two days, she relaxed a little. Her urge to track Leon down and shoot him between his nasty smiling eyes subsided.

This wasn't justice – it was revenge. She'd never get justice for what Leon had tried to do to her; a jury, society – and perhaps even Stephen – would damn her for climbing unchaperoned into the carriage. But with Leon locked up in gaol for stealing the necklace, perhaps she'd find peace again.

'You're a brilliant artist, Lady Caroline – and wonderful at forgery.'

'The two often go hand in hand, my dear. There have been many occasions when I've been short of money and I've contemplated coun-terfeiting some banknotes – but, shh, don't tell your husband.'

Chapter Twenty-Eight

T he damned cove is toying with me!'
Lavender thrust Nidar's note into Woods' hand. His next few words were uttered between gritted teeth. 'Question his landlady, Ned, then take the cab and meet me back at Bow Street.'

'Where are you going?'

'I need some fresh air.' He turned on his heel and stomped past the alarmed landlady hovering on the landing.

The warm sunshine outside was at odds with his foul mood and the streets were too crowded. The last thing he needed at the moment was human contact, and the traffic and street hawkers were too loud for him to think.

Turning down Haymarket, he headed for the river. The tide was out and a narrow, rocky strip of deserted mud wound like a stained brown ribbon below the wharf of the timber yard. Oblivious to the stench and the damage to his boots, he clambered down beneath the barnacle-encrusted wooden pilings. It was more peaceful here. He found comfort in the monotonous creak of the metal oarlocks of the river taxis and the cries of the seabirds wheeling above.

He picked up a handful of pebbles and hurled them into the water. The physical aggression of the childish act calmed his anger. The slap of the heaving water against the pilings soothed his frustration.

So close. They were so close.

Nidar had vanished like a rat back into its sewer. Lavender cursed himself for not following through on his decision to seek Leon out the previous day. But yesterday he'd been obsessed with Micky Sullivan's involvement in the murder of Danvers and distracted by John Bellingham. Yesterday, he'd thought Leon a foolish drunk arrested for bad debts, nothing more. If he'd interviewed Leon, as he'd intended, would he have suspected him of anything else? He doubted it and sighed.

The cove was a superb dissembler – and a dangerous one. He'd beguiled his way into Lady Caroline's gratitude with the staged rescue of her reticule, and charmed and amused everyone at her soirée with his story about how he was moved to tears by Sarah Siddons' performance at the theatre. That was a lie. This man was heartless, incapable of emotion. *How had this villain managed to fool them all?*

But at least now they knew what he looked like and the net was closing in. With help from Ned, Adkins and Vickery, he'd soon catch him and his murderous crew.

The thought cheered him a little and he turned back to Bow Street. He knew he must stay calm and deal with this rationally: losing his temper and letting the man rile him would only impair his ability to function logically. Nidar might be determined to make this a personal vendetta, but Lavender knew he shouldn't rise to the bait. He'd a crew of his own now, and by working together the Bow Street officers would win out in the end.

Woods was waiting for him in Magistrate Read's office when he arrived. Both men cast a surreptitious glance at his mud-splattered boots but neither asked him where he had been.

'I'm glad to see you back, Lavender. Woods has told me what's happened.'

'Have Adkins and Barnaby found the ship Nidar uses for a base?'

Read shook his head. 'No ships registered under those ridiculous names have been through the Port of London.'

Lavender scowled and took off his gloves. 'So Nidar still eludes us?'

'For the moment, yes,' Read said, 'but thanks to you and Woods, at least we know what the villain looks like now. He won't be able to evade capture for long once we circulate his description and raise a hue and cry. In fact, I think we'll put a price on his head and advertise a reward for his capture.'

'Did Ned tell you the rest?'

'Yes, I understand the scoundrel left you another "message". Woods also told me about your brilliant deduction this morning and the connection you've made between the crimes. I still find it all extraordinary but I'm more inclined to believe you're right. You've done well, Lavender.'

Lavender sat down, feeling a small glow of contentment. This was high praise from Read. 'I'm still disappointed he's fled.'

'The landlady said he left yesterday,' Woods said. 'He'd stayed there about two weeks. She thought him a charming young man.'

'Charming – but deadly.'

'One step at a time, Lavender,' Read said. 'Nidar will make another mistake and reveal himself eventually.'

'The man's arrogance is insufferable.'

'Yes, I can see that it irks you, but don't take this goading as a personal affront. We've another problem and I need you to keep a clear head.'

'What's that?'

'Despite your deductions, there's still a lack of hard evidence to tie Nidar to these crimes. We know he's behind them but evidence remains as elusive as the man himself. As you rightly deduced, he must have arranged for his incarceration in Marshalsea to provide an alibi for the murder of Baron Danvers, and he wasn't present at the robbery of Mr and Mrs Rothschild.'

'Lady Alderney and Lady Yarmouth will be able to identify him and confirm he masqueraded as Doctor Pardus at the party,' Lavender said.

'Yes, but we've got to catch him first and find evidence to link him to the robberies and Danvers' murder. Which brings me to this.' Read reached for a small, brown package on the corner of his cluttered desk and handed it to Lavender. 'Your wife's maid brought this into Bow Street half an hour ago. Since Woods told me that Nidar also uses the name "Leon", the message on the packet has piqued my interest. I hope there's something more interesting than a sandwich in there.'

Lavender froze when he saw the writing: *From your dear friend, Captain James Leon.* Anger and alarm welled up inside him. Nidar had his home address; it was a threat.

'Is it another one of those "messages", sir?' Woods asked.

'Probably.' Lavender steeled himself, ripped open the package and pulled out the glittering jewels. Woods gave a low whistle.

'It's Lady Yarmouth's stolen necklace.' For a moment Lavender was confused, then he laughed. 'He's just put a noose around his own neck!'

'What?' Read reached for the packaging.

'Why's he sent it back?' Woods asked.

'I don't know,' Lavender confessed.

Read looked flabbergasted. 'He's sent stolen goods to a Bow Street officer with a message in his own handwriting?'

'Yes.' Lavender felt jubilant. 'A jury won't be able to ignore this; once we capture him and get a sample of his writing, then he'll hang. He's damned himself with his own hand.'

Read and Woods passed the necklace and wrapping paper between them.

Woods scratched his close-cropped grey head and shook it. 'I can't believe the blind cheek of the cove. It's like he can't stop goadin' Lavender. Why send back these sparklers? They must be worth somethin'.'

Lavender tried to put himself in the villain's shoes. 'It's a very distinctive set of jewellery,' he said. 'He probably thought twice about trying to sell it because it was too easy to identify. Maybe he doesn't have the time – or the contacts – to have it split up and melted down. He and his crew have already pocketed a fortune in the coins they stole from Lord Yarmouth. Perhaps he simply didn't need the money and the temptation to taunt me was too great. Like I said, his arrogance is insufferable.'

'Why doesn't he have the time? Do you think he's left town?'

'No, I don't. Fletcher told me yesterday that Nidar and the Packet Knucklers planned something "big". He doesn't know what it is or when it'll occur.'

Read looked alarmed. 'What? Bigger than the murder of Baron Danvers?'

'I have no notion what his plans are, but the thought is ominous.' Read and Woods exchanged worried glances. 'Sir, I think we must abandon this notion of sending me to Dublin. You'll need me here.'

'Actually, Lavender, I was thinking the exact opposite. This cove clearly has an obsession with you. It's possible he plans some harm to your person – and an attack on a Bow Street officer would certainly be "big" enough to shock London.'

'It'd shock all of us!' Woods interjected.

'I think it might be sensible to get you out of town for a while for your own safety,' Read continued. 'Let Adkins and Vickery deal with this investigation from now on.'

'What? And leave my wife unprotected?' Lavender snapped. 'You forget, sir, this murderous bastard has my home address.'

There was a short silence while the two men stared at each other across the desk. Lavender felt a vein throbbing in his neck below his cravat and he saw Read swallowing hard.

'I need to give the matter more consideration,' Read said eventually. 'Woods, you take these items back to Lady Yarmouth. Lavender, you can relieve Vickery for a few hours in the surveillance of John Bellingham. Thank goodness it's the Sabbath tomorrow. I think we need some time for reflection and guidance from the Lord. I shall be in my office for a few hours tomorrow afternoon. If anything should occur that needs my assistance, I'll be here.'

Lavender nodded. He and Woods gathered up the jewellery from Read's desk and left.

'We're goin' to need more than guidance from the good Lord to catch this bugger,' Woods muttered.

Despite the tension he felt, Lavender managed a small smile as they descended the stairs.

Woods paused in the hall before they parted. 'What about the ride out to Greenwich we discussed yesterday, sir? Do you still want to go tomorrow? Or do you think you should spend the day with Magdalena in case Read has you on that boat on Monday?'

'We'll ride out to see Mr Cugoan. Nidar may have escaped justice for the moment but there's still a chance we might solve the mystery of our negro skeleton. Magdalena and I will go to my parents' tomorrow after church for our Sunday roast, but I'll meet you here at the stables at two o'clock.'

'But what about . . .'

'Don't worry, Ned. I'll have plenty of time with Magdalena next week and I'll leave her with my parents and sisters tomorrow afternoon. If Read thinks I'll abandon my wife and leave her alone in London while this madman's at large, he's mistaken. Hell will freeze over before I get on that boat to Dublin.'

Chapter Twenty-Nine

Young Eddie Woods was waiting with his father by the stables at Bow Street when Lavender arrived. He glanced up from below his fringe and gave him a crooked smile with his bruised mouth. 'Hello, Uncle Stephen.'

'I hope you don't mind, sir, but I've brought Eddie along for the ride to Greenwich. I thought the fresh air and exercise would do him some good.'

Lavender grinned and ruffled the lad's curly hair affectionately. 'Of course not. It's always good to see you, Eddie.' He decided not to comment on the lad's black eye and the other bruises. Woods had told him about the attack on his son by the thugs Simonside and Ellis. That was another matter he needed to put his mind to once Nidar was caught.

Woods pulled two large packets out of his coat pockets and showed them to Lavender, grinning. 'It's the remains of the Sunday roast in bread,' he announced. 'Betsy has given us a picnic in case we get peckish.'

The traffic on the roads was always quieter on a Sunday and the three of them were soon cantering through the open countryside to

Greenwich. Eddie was a good horseman and didn't hold them back much. By the time they clattered up the small town's cobbled streets, the boy's cheeks and eyes glowed.

Ignatius Cugoan was still chewing on a mouthful of his lunch when he answered the door of the bakery. His dark face lit up with surprise to see Lavender and Woods again. He'd taken off his necktie and his Sunday-best waistcoat flapped open across his narrow chest.

Young Eddie glanced around the bakery and sniffed hopefully. The oven was cold today but the smell of fresh-baked bread and sweet pastries still lingered in the air. Lavender smiled to himself. Eddie might look more like Betsy, but when it came to food he was definitely his father's son.

'We won't take up much of your time, Mr Cugoan,' Lavender said. 'We found the skeleton we sought earlier in the week and it belonged to a man of African descent.' Cugoan stopped chewing and his eyes widened with concern. 'The man was wearing inadequate clothing, nothing but rags,' Lavender continued. 'We've brought them here.'

'And you want me to tell you if they're the kind of clothes given to slaves?'

Lavender nodded, grateful for the man's astuteness. 'I appreciate this may be distressing for you . . .'

Cugoan shook his head. 'I'll do anything I can to help, Detective.'

Lavender unwrapped the parcel he'd brought from his saddlebag and spread out the rags on the shop counter. He'd done his best to clean them but a terrible smell emanated from the pathetic pile. Eddie stepped back in disgust.

Cugoan nodded sadly. 'Yes, that's the kind of thing they made us wear. There's no underclothes, I assume?'

'No.'

'Those half-trousers barely reached the knees, just like a child's. They're another symbol of the emasculation of men of colour.' Cugoan's tone was calm and his voice quiet, but his words made Lavender squirm with discomfort. He reached out and took back the rags.

'Thank you, sir,' he said. 'We won't bother you any more. Please return to your family and enjoy the rest of the Sabbath.'

Lavender, Woods and Eddie were solemn as they walked back to their horses.

'I dread to think what that poor man must have suffered in his life,' Woods said.

'Cugoan or our skeleton?' Lavender asked.

'Both.'

Lavender nodded. 'Slavery's a despicable practice.'

Woods glanced around at the peaceful and pretty little town with its neat red-brick houses, gleaming doorsteps and windows, and well-swept streets. 'But how did the body of an African slave end up on the riverbank at Greenwich?'

Lavender looked through the gaps in the houses to the river beyond while he considered Woods' question. It was warm and cloudy on this side of the Thames, but on the other bank the low-lying Isle of Dogs was shrouded in fog. Somewhere beyond that barren wasteland towered the newly built and heavily protected West India Docks. He'd heard their tall brick warehouses were bursting at the seams with barrels of rum. They also stored a year's worth of sugar for the entire country, all harvested from the scorching plantations of the West Indian islands.

Slaves. Plantations. The West Indies. The West India Docks. *Was it possible there was a connection between their negro skeleton and the West India Docks?*

'We may never know the truth about our dead slave,' he said, 'but there is one place we haven't looked for clues.' He pointed to the misty Isle of Dogs. Eddie and Woods followed his gaze. 'How do you feel about a boat trip across the river, Eddie?'

Eddie grinned. 'Yes please, Uncle Stephen.'

Lavender thought he saw a flicker of alarm in Woods' face, but his constable quickly rallied. 'You might not be so keen when we draw closer, son,' Woods said in a mock-serious tone. 'They say the Isle of Dogs is haunted by the ghosts of huge hounds that bay at the full moon. Great black beasts they are, with matted coats, droolin' fangs and glarin' red eyes. Sometimes if you listen carefully, you can hear their anguished howls in daylight too.'

'Ha! Give over, Da.' Eddie snorted with disbelief.

'Ah, but I've heard them . . .'

'That's a story to frighten our Rachel. You'll have me believe anythin'.'

Lavender smiled and wished his stepson, Sebastián, was here with them too. 'We'll be looking for breaches in the riverbank, Eddie. Our mysterious skeleton was probably washed into the river from a shallow grave. Your father has already investigated the graveyards on the south bank of the Thames, so it's time for us to investigate the north bank.'

'You think there might be others? More skeletons over there?' Excitement lifted Eddie's voice into an unmanly squeak. He coughed gruffly to cover it up.

'We don't know, son,' Woods said, 'but you'd better watch out in case they come back to life and grab you!' He lunged at his son, making the lad jump.

'Gerroff, Da!'

Lavender smiled as father and son tussled in the street.

They left their horses with the blacksmith at the forge and soon found a boatman with a large water taxi at the wharf.

'What do yer want to go to the Dogs for?' asked the boatman. 'There ain't nothin' there but bogs and scrawny cows.'

'We just want to examine the riverbanks down Limehouse Reach,' Lavender said. 'There's been a lot of rain recently and we want to see if there's been a breach.'

'Well, yer right enough about the ruddy rain.' The man pushed them away from the quay with his oar. 'I've never known the river so 'igh. With the authorities, are yer?'

'Sort of,' Lavender said.

The boatman dipped and hauled on the oars. They lifted out of the Thames draped with slimy weed. 'It's about time you lot inspected that Mill Wall; it's been crumblin' fer years.'

They crossed the broadest part of the river without encountering any other traffic and soon slid into the wispy mist. The temperature dipped and Eddie gave an involuntary shiver. Only the cry of an invisible seabird wheeling high above them in the fog and the slap of the heaving water against the side of their boat ruptured the eerie silence. They couldn't see more than ten yards ahead. Their ears strained for any sounds.

The anguished howl of a distant hound suddenly rent the air.

'There you go, son.' Woods' voice was low and grim. 'I told you the Isle were haunted by ghostly dogs.'

Eddie sat up straighter and made a brave effort to appear unconcerned.

The boatman laughed. 'Do yer know 'ow it got its name, this godforsaken strip of land?'

'No, but I'm sure you're going to tell us,' Lavender said lightly.

'It were Old King 'Arry,' the boatman continued, unabashed. 'When 'e lived at Greenwich Palace 'e'd send 'is kennel men to exercise 'is 'untin' dogs out here. Passin' sailors 'eard them barkin' and christened it the Isle of Dogs.' He dipped his oars again. A frightened duck splashed and flew up squawking into the mist.

'Maybe the name is just a corruption of the Isle of Ducks,' Lavender said to Eddie with a wink. The boy grinned back.

'Aye, it's corrupt, all right.' The boatman's shoulders heaved as he pulled on the oars. 'There's foul 'umours out there and treacherous bogs that can swallow a man or a beast whole. You'd better be careful if you go ashore. Some parts of it are seven feet below sea level.'

Suddenly the mist cleared. The low clay banks encircling the Isle of Dogs appeared before them. A crumbling wall, the Mill Wall, ran across the top of the bank. Frequently breached, it was a futile attempt to keep the Thames out of the low-lying peninsula.

'Follow the shoreline,' Lavender said. 'We're looking for a gap in the bank.' The boatman turned the vessel and slowly followed the western shoreline up Limehouse Reach.

'Stop here,' Lavender said. They floated before a shallow inlet where the bank and the Mill Wall had collapsed against the weight and thrust of the Thames. Jagged stones from the wall had slithered down the avalanche of mud towards the waterline. The river had encroached several yards inland and was still eating away at the earth.

'Can you see anything?' Lavender asked the others.

Woods shook his head, but Eddie raised his hand and pointed: 'Look! There's a bone.'

Lavender narrowed his eyes and peered at the bank. There was something there, jutting awkwardly out of the debris. It looked like a branch to him but he didn't have fresh, thirteen-year-old eyes. 'Pull in where you can. We'll go ashore and you can wait for us.'

The man steered them to a thin strip of shingle. The boat grated across the pebbles and shuddered to a halt. Lavender, Woods and Eddie leapt over into the shallows and squelched up the mud towards the inlet.

'It's a bone all right.' Woods bent down to examine the object protruding from the slime. 'Possibly a leg bone.'

'Animal or human?' Lavender asked.

'I can't tell.' Woods yanked it out of the ground and passed it across.

'I think it's human,' Lavender said. 'Let's try to find more bones and the skull.' Balancing precariously on the uneven ground, he bent down and began scraping away at the mud and detritus.

Woods joined him, then glanced over his shoulder to Eddie, who seemed to be rooted to the spot. The boy stared at the grisly scene like a rabbit caught in a hunter's lamp, his eyes round as the moon. 'Come on, son. Your ma won't mind if you get your hands a bit dirty.'

'I've never been this close to a dead person before. I don't want to stand on him.'

Lavender straightened up and smiled. 'Stop thinking about this as a person, Eddie. It's evidence. We need to examine it for clues. Sharp eyes like yours will help us.'

The boy came closer and began to scrape away at the ground like his father.

Lavender soon unearthed a human ribcage, but it had been separated from the rest of the skeleton – probably by the disturbance caused by the mud slide. 'There's definitely at least one other body buried here.'

The wet mud surged up Lavender's arms and slithered down inside his gloves. 'We need tools.'

'It's all right, Uncle Stephen – I think I've found it.' Eddie stood awkwardly by a pale, half-exposed dome in the ground.

'Well done, son.' Lavender and Woods squelched across towards him. Lavender bent down, gently prised the skull from the ground and wiped away the dirt from the face.

'What do you think, sir?' Woods asked.

Lavender stared at the jawline and the forehead but he couldn't be sure about its ethnicity. This skull had slightly differently shaped eye sockets than Ted-with-a-Head. *Was it the skull of a woman? Did women have different shaped eye sockets to men?*

'Is this some sort of graveyard, do you think, sir?' Woods asked.

'I think "graveyard" is too good a word for it,' Lavender said grimly. 'I think this is where someone has dumped the dead bodies of slaves.'

'How?' Woods asked, perplexed. 'How's this happening in England?'

'I don't know. Let's climb up the bank and have a look around the marshes.'

Some protective sixth sense made Lavender turn to the boy and say: 'Eddie, please go and tell the boatman to wait for us and stay with him. Leave your father and me to do the rest.'

Eddie's face fell but he nodded and slithered back to the boat.

Lavender and Woods turned and scrambled up the embankment to peer over the edge of the clumps of marsh grass and reeds.

Fifty yards away, the tumbledown chimney of a derelict stone farmhouse protruded out of a dip in the landscape. There was no smoke or any other sign of life. The mist came and went like a shifting silk veil over the desolate building.

'Prime your pistol, Ned,' Lavender said, 'and keep your head down. We're going in.'

Chapter Thirty

Silently, they approached the back of the farm and crouched down by the rough-hewn stone walls. Lavender raised himself slowly and made a futile attempt to see inside the grimy window. He sank back down beside Woods and shook his head. The marsh had reclaimed the ground around the derelict building. Rusty farm tools lay scattered on the uneven ground amongst the reeds.

A scythe caught Lavender's attention. He gestured for Woods to remain motionless, took a few steps and examined the ancient tool. He remembered Sir Richard Allison's suggestion that the severed foot had belonged to an agricultural labourer and been amputated by a scythe. Was it his imagination or was there a darker stain along the rusted blade? It was impossible to be sure.

He returned to Woods and, step by cautious step, they rounded the corners until they reached the front.

They stepped back with a shout of alarm.

A huge black mastiff woke from its sleep and leapt to its feet. It lunged furiously at the two men, barking loudly. Lavender's finger tightened on the trigger of his pistol, but the animal's lunge jerked to a halt with the rattle of chains. Someone had tethered it to an iron stake in the ground, just in front of the age-blackened double doors of the farm.

Fangs bared and drooling, the dog strained on its metal leash and gave a deep, throaty growl.

'Gawd's teeth!' Woods said. 'I never expected this!'

'There's your ghostly hound, Ned. What's it guarding, I wonder?' Lavender stepped sideways and cautiously circled the dog until he was opposite the doors of the building. The dog followed his arc, growling with every step. He expected to see padlocks on the door but it was secured with a large plank across two metal hasps.

Woods was at his shoulder. 'The dog stops anyone gettin' in,' he said.

'And the plank stops something getting out. We need to get inside that building and see what's there.'

Lavender raised his pistol, pulled back the hammer and took aim at the dog.

Woods held up a hand to stop him. 'Wait a minute, sir. If you fire your weapon, Lord knows who you'll bring runnin'.'

'Do you have a better idea?'

'I might do. Look at its ribs – it's half starved. Let's see if some of Betsy's roast beef might help.' Woods reached into his pocket and pulled out the brown paper packet.

The beast stopped barking and gave a pathetic whine at the smell of the food. Saliva dripped in long globules out of its open mouth. Carefully, Woods lowered the food to the ground. 'You circle that way and see if you can get near the metal stake while he's distracted,' Woods said. 'If you can yank it out of the ground, you can free him.'

'What? Free him to attack us?'

'I think he'll be more interested in the food, sir, but if we have to shoot him, then so be it.' Woods backed away about twenty yards and laid the second packet down on the ground.

Lavender muttered under his breath about Woods' sanity. He knew his friend would risk his own life to help an injured horse, but he'd never realised this compassion extended to ruddy dogs. Every instinct told him this was a foolish notion but he knew better than to argue when Woods had that look of determination on his face.

He inched slowly towards the metal stake, entering the radius of the dog's territory. He half expected the animal to double back and lunge towards him, but Woods was right; it continued to strain towards the food, its chain stretched taut.

'Release him now!' Woods yelled.

'Madness.' Lavender strode forward and hauled out the stake.

The dog hurtled towards the first of Betsy's roast beef sandwiches, then on to the second, devouring the food in two gulps.

Lavender tensed, but the animal showed no interest in either of them. It gave its great head a satisfied shake and rattled its chains before lowering its nose to the ground and disappearing into the mist, trailing its shackles behind him.

'That was lucky.' Woods joined Lavender in front of the door. 'Hopefully he'll be too busy chasin' rabbits to bother us any more.'

'That chain will slow him down.'

'Someone will catch him soon. An animal like that is too valuable to roam free for long.'

Lavender lifted the wooden bar. The doors swayed and creaked apart. A horrific stench wafted out of the gap.

Woods' nose wrinkled in disgust. 'Heaven and hell! What's that?'

Lavender pulled out his perfumed handkerchief and covered his nose. With his other hand, he pushed open one of the doors. It grated and scraped over the filthy stone floor.

It was impossible to see until their eyes adjusted to the low light. Cautiously, with their pistols raised, they stepped inside.

It was a single, large room, open up to the rafters of the roof. An upturned wooden chair, a bucket and a few scattered tin mugs lay on the dirty flagstones in front of an empty hearth at one end. The other half of the room had been divided into animal pens. The ancient wooden stalls were riddled with woodworm and filled with a thin layer of mouldy straw.

It took Lavender a moment to locate the source of the terrible smell. He expected to see a rotting animal in one of the stalls. What he saw took his breath away.

'Gawd's teeth!' Woods' customary curse caught in his throat.

A huddled, wretched mass of humanity cowered together in one of the stalls. Barely clothed, painfully thin and shackled by their bare ankles and wrists, six black men and women looked up at the two officers in terror. The whites of their eyes were the only luminous things in the appalling scene.

Lavender swallowed hard. For a moment, the two men remained silent, unable to comprehend the horror of what they'd just stumbled across.

One of the women clutched a bag of bones to her chest. It was a child.

'What are we goin' to do?' Woods whispered.

'I don't know.'

Embarrassed and awkward, they gestured to the slaves to stand. Slowly, with a jangle of metal, the group unravelled themselves and clambered stiffly to their feet. They arranged themselves into a line, the order of which was dictated by the leg irons chaining them together. The two women were at the front. One began to sob. The sound tore at Lavender's heart.

'They think we're their gaolers come to get them,' Woods said gruffly.

'I know.' Lavender struggled to keep the emotion out of his own voice. 'There's nothing we can do about that. They won't trust us until we can get them out of here and get them some help.'

'Do any of you speak English?' Woods asked loudly. The slaves stared back at him with impassive faces.

'We'll take them back to Greenwich – to Ignatius Cugoan.'

'Will he be able to talk with them?'

'I doubt it – but we can try.'

The slaves shuffled outside, blinking at the light and shivering in the cold damp of the mist. Skeletal and soiled with matted hair, they were a dreadful sight. Several had open and weeping sores on their limbs. Beneath the wrist and ankle restraints their skin was chafed and raw. The biggest man at the back of the line wore a loose shirt, ripped and soaked with dried blood. Angry weals caused by a lash burned on his back.

Slowly, Woods and Lavender took the sorry procession back to the riverbank. The only means of communication they had was to wave in the general direction they wanted them to take. It was almost impossible for the chained slaves to descend the muddy incline back down to the boat unaided, especially for the woman who clutched the child. If she slipped, there was a danger she would drag the whole line down into the river.

'Damn it.' Woods pocketed his pistol and forced the child from her arms so she could descend. She fought against him like a cat, screaming, scratching his face and beating her feeble fists against his broad chest. Lavender grimaced, stepped forward with the pistol and gestured for her to move.

The babe in Woods' arms was lethargic and emaciated. While the slaves stumbled and slithered down the slope, Lavender compared the child with Ned's plump and rosy-cheeked youngest daughter, Tabitha. He knew Ned would be thinking the same.

Once the slaves were down on the narrow ribbon of shingle bordering the river, Ned held out the babe and the mother snatched back her child, sobbing.

Eddie and the boatman were horror-struck as the stumbling procession wound its way towards them.

'What devil's business is this?' their boatman demanded.

'We've made an unexpected discovery,' Lavender said.

'You've got to be jestin' with me!' the oarsman exclaimed. 'Surely you don't expect me to . . . ?'

'Yes, I do,' Lavender snapped. 'We're taking these poor wretches back to Greenwich to get them food and help – and you're going to assist us.'

'These darkies stink! It'll take me months to clean the stench out of me boat! Can't yer take 'em by road?'

'For the love of God! What road?' Lavender shouted. The man fell silent.

Lavender lowered his voice and pulled his gilt-topped tipstaff out of his pocket. He resisted the urge to shove it up the boatman's nose. 'Today is the Sabbath and the day you're going to do the greatest act of Christian charity you've ever done in your life.'

'You're a Runner?'

'Yes, I'm Detective Stephen Lavender from Bow Street. If you won't cooperate, I've the power to take your damned boat from you and leave you stranded here – alone – until the slavers come back.'

The boatman sniffed and stepped protectively towards his vessel. 'Yer never said who yer were.'

'Well, I'm telling you now. Eddie? Can you help this fellow get these people into the stern of the boat while your father and I catch our breath for a minute?'

The lad nodded and moved forward to help.

'Sir,' Woods said. 'I think I should stay here in case their gaolers return. We need to catch these ruddy slavers red-handed and get them to lead us to their lair. They must come back here to feed them. I think I'll lie in wait in case they do.'

Lavender shook his head. 'No. There's no cover and it's too dangerous on your own.'

'I've got a plan, sir – and we both know we need to catch the scoundrels responsible for this horror. I don't expect them to arrive with loaded pistols; they won't get much trouble from this lot, poor wretches that they are.'

Lavender hesitated. He knew Woods was right. The only way to catch these inhuman bastards was for one of them to lie in wait for them until they appeared, but he didn't want to leave Woods here on his own. 'No. You go with the slaves – take them to Cugoan. He'll help us, I'm sure. I'll deal with the slavers.'

Woods shook his head firmly. 'You're the one with the authority, sir. Go and raise hell in Greenwich – and fetch me some more constables. Besides which,' Woods added cheerfully, 'I won't be alone. I'll have Eddie.'

'Very well – but be careful, Ned. And for God's sake take care of your boy.'

'I will.'

'I never thought this would happen. I never expected to find . . .'

'I know you didn't.'

Anger flashed through Lavender. 'Ha! So much for a pleasant jaunt out into the country on a Sunday afternoon. I've let you both down.'

Woods gave him a beaming smile. 'No, you haven't. That's why I like workin' with you, sir, because trouble always finds you out.'

Woods' support calmed Lavender and he gave a strangled laugh. 'I'd love to know what Eddie thinks about all this.'

'He's havin' the time of his life, sir. Don't you worry yourself about Eddie.'

Lavender tried to think rationally. 'There's only one thing that makes sense, Ned. And that's our proximity to the ships in the West India Docks.'

Woods' broad face creased in confusion. 'I thought procedures were strict at those fancy new docks.'

'They are – that's why the slaves are here. There's a high wall surrounded by a water-filled ditch around the complex. Entry and exit are restricted to guarded gates. All newly arrived vessels are vigorously searched by customs men for any undeclared goods.'

'So any unscrupulous captain dealin' in this here illegal slave trade would need to offload his cargo before enterin' the basin?'

'Yes – and pick it up again later, probably by rowing boat, before he left the Thames for the Americas.'

Woods nodded grimly. 'So that's why they've hidden the slaves here. Well, I reckon it's time to spoil the plans of these ungodly bastards.'

'Oy! Detective! I need yer 'elp with the oars.' Lavender glanced at the boat. The prisoners were now crammed into the stern but the unequal weight distribution made the bow rise up out of the shallow water.

Woods beckoned for Eddie to come back to his side. 'You go now, sir, and do whatever you have to do to get help for them poor wretches. I'll sort out the villains.'

Lavender thumped Woods on the shoulder, then handed over his own pistol. 'You need this more than me.'

'Is that one for me?' Eddie asked hopefully.

'Not while I've still got two workin' hands, son,' Woods replied, smiling.

Lavender waded out to the boat, clambered onto the shallow seat beside the oarsman and took up the second oar.

Woods pushed them off, stepped back onto the shingle beach and put his arm around his son's shoulders. Lavender and the boatman leaned, stretched out and hauled on the oars. At the other end of the boat, their silent captives remained cowed and motionless, watching them with wide eyes. Motionless was good. Lavender had just left his only weapon with Ned. If the chained slaves decided to stage a mutiny in the middle of the Thames, they'd all drown.

They slid into the silent mist. Lavender's guts lurched when the figures of Eddie and Ned Woods disappeared from sight.

Chapter Thirty-One

'Right, son,' Woods said. 'Come with me and I'll show you what we're going to do.'

They clambered up the muddy bank, and Woods took a few moments to check out the lie of the land. The farm stood with its back to the river in the east. In the south was nothing but uninhabited marshes and bogs. Lavender was right: the slavers would come from the West India Docks in the north. It was the only thing that made sense.

He glanced around, searching for a suitable place to hide Eddie. He walked over to examine a natural hollow in the terrain to the south of the building. It was deep enough to keep the lad out of sight. 'This is where you can hide until those scoundrels turn up – or until Lavender returns with the Greenwich constables. Go and try it for size.'

Eddie slithered down the mud into the hollow, landing with a splash in the stagnant pond at the bottom. His boots disappeared in the water. 'I've got wet feet,' he complained.

'There's worse things in life, son,' Woods said. His mind flashed back to the captives they'd just released and wondered what horrors they'd suffered. 'Right, can you see the entrance to the buildin' – and beyond to the north?'

'Yes, it's a bit misty, though.'

'That's why you'll have to use your ears, son. Let's hope they're as sharp as your eyes. When you hear the slavers comin' you hunker down and stay out of sight, do you hear?'

'Yes, Da, but where will you be?'

'I'll be in the building waitin' for them.'

'Won't they know something's wrong when they see the dog gone and the door bar removed?'

Woods bristled with pride. His lad was a natural. He already thought like a criminal.

'Exactly. That's why you're goin' to lock me inside the buildin' before you hide in here. Come on. I'll show you.'

Eddie began to gag at the smell when they reached the doorway.

'Wait a minute, son.' Woods held his breath and went inside. He picked up the buckets of excrement left by the slaves and carried them outside to the back of the farm.

When he returned inside, he used the barrel of his pistol to smash out the glass in the bottom of the window. The draught began to clear the smell. Finally, he took out his handcuffs and threaded them through a stout metal rail on the animal stalls at the rear of the room. That'd be enough to secure two prisoners.

'Right, we're ready for visitors,' he said. He lifted up the fallen chair, settled it opposite the door and sat down.

'You should have asked Uncle Stephen for his handcuffs too.' Eddie's sharp eyes missed nothing. 'What if there's more than two of them?'

'Let's stay hopeful, son, shall we?' Woods chided. 'How many men do you think it takes to feed and water six chained slaves? I'm not expectin' the full crew to turn up.'

He walked over to the door with Eddie behind him and glanced outside towards the pearly mist in the north. Nothing. The only sounds were the whispering of the reed beds and the haunting cry of a curlew.

Woods picked up the large plank of wood and handed it to his son. 'Now, Eddie, I want you to shut the doors and then bar them from the outside with this. We're goin' to give those coves a real fright. They'll expect to find those poor wretches in here.'

For the first time, alarm flashed across the boy's face. 'But you won't be able to get out if I shut you in.'

'That's why it's important for you to stay hidden, right? Your old da won't be able to do anythin' to help you if they find you first.' He ruffled the lad's hair to distract him from the catch in his voice. Eddie nodded and grinned.

Woods stepped back inside and the two of them pulled and pushed the doors shut. He stood in the dark and heard Eddie drop the plank across the metal hasps. It wasn't until he heard Eddie squelch away through the boggy ground to his hideout that the true danger of their situation hit him. His innards twisted with fear for his son.

He shook his head, said a silent prayer for the safety of his boy, then settled down with his pistols on the hard chair.

He didn't have to wait long. Muffled voices reached his ears from outside the door. Muffled voices with the nasal tone and unusual rise and fall of the Liverpool accent. It sounded like there were two of them.

'Where's the bloody dog?'

''Ow should I know? Open that feckin' door, will yous?'

Woods rose from his seat and slid into the deeper shadows beside the protruding chimney breast. The double doors groaned and grated open across the flagstones. He knew it would take a few seconds for their eyes to adjust to the low light. He counted to three before he stepped out of the shadows.

'Evenin', gentlemen.' He aimed both pistols at the chests of the men. 'Raise your arms and step forward.'

The shock on the faces of the two coves was a picture to behold. One of them carried two pails. He dropped both of them with a clatter and raised his arms. Water and sloppy gruel spilled over the filthy floor.

The second recovered more quickly. 'Who the devil are yous?'

'Arms up. Questions later,' Woods said. 'These pistols are both loaded, and after what I've seen today I'm more than happy to discharge them.'

Reluctantly, the second, bigger man raised his arms. His eyes scanned the stalls at the far end of the room. 'What the 'ell 'ave yous done wi' our cargo?'

'Freed it.' A wave of satisfaction flooded through Woods when he said those two words. 'Now, move over there.' He gestured towards the handcuffs dangling out of the end of the stall.

'Hold on.' The biggest man stood his ground. 'There's two of us – and only one of yous.'

'No, there ain't,' growled a deep voice from behind him. The cove jerked forward as if something sharp had been prodded into his back. 'There's dozens of us.'

Woods' heart froze. Eddie stood behind them armed with a stick. He prayed his son's voice wouldn't squeak.

The two villains moved towards the irons without looking back, oblivious to the fact that they were being prodded forward by a child with a stick.

'Snap them on,' Woods said.

One of the men cuffed himself immediately. Eddie stepped forward and snapped the other half of the irons around the second brute's wrist before he realised what was happening. Both men had familiar tattoos on their shackled wrists.

'He's just a nipper!' snapped the biggest fellow.

'Search them, son.' Woods never lowered the pistols or took his eyes off the men. One false move towards his boy and he would shoot.

Eddie searched their pockets and removed an ugly pair of knives of the sort favoured by street gangs.

'Who the devil are yous and what do yous want?' the big man growled.

Woods pulled his wooden chair closer, sat down and grinned with satisfaction. 'My son and I are Bow Street constables. More constables will arrive soon, along with Detective Stephen Lavender. While we wait, you're goin' to tell me all about your foul operation, your ship and that arch-villain who leads you.'

The big fellow spluttered and swore angrily. 'Why should we tell yous anything?' he yelled.

Woods smiled, then lowered his voice into a menacing growl. 'Because if you don't, I'll tell every lag who ever shares your gaol cell you was arrested by a thirteen-year-old boy with a stick. You'll be a laughin' stock from here to Botany Bay. Now start ruddy talkin'!'

Knowing that it would be impossible to get the shackled prisoners up the ladder onto the Greenwich wharf, Lavender's boatman steered the vessel to the beach in front of the Royal Hospital for Seamen. Crowds of people were taking a Sunday stroll on the promenade. They gathered at the railings and shrieked in shock and disgust as Lavender unloaded his wretched and hobbling charges onto the beach.

He told the boatman to wait for his return and led the slaves across the sharp stones up towards the road. He intended to take them to the blacksmith to remove their shackles, but after that his plans were hazy. He desperately needed to round up the constables and get back to Woods.

A crowd grouped around them when they reached the promenade, murmuring in revulsion and confusion.

'What are you doing, man?' demanded one smartly dressed observer.

'Shame on you!' said his wife.

'I sees yer keepin' some fine company these days, Detective,' mocked a familiar voice. Lavender glanced up sharply. Micky Sullivan and another shifty-looking fellow leaned on the railings, grinning at his discomfort. Their smiles didn't reach their eyes.

'Filthy heathens!' someone shouted.

Lavender ignored Sullivan, pulled out his tipstaff and held it high. 'I'm Detective Stephen Lavender from Bow Street,' he said. 'We've found these prisoners on the Isle of Dogs and I'm taking them to the forge to free them from their chains.'

'You can't parade them through the town,' another woman complained. 'Those women are barely decent!'

'I appeal to your Christian charity,' Lavender snapped in exasperation. 'These people need food, clothing and help, and I need Mr Ignatius Cugoan and the Greenwich constables to meet me at the forge so I can get justice for this atrocity.'

There was a short silence, then a small boy stepped forward. 'I'll fetch the constables for yer, sir – but it'll cost yer a penny.' Lavender rolled his eyes but nodded. The boy turned on his heel and raced away towards the town. The rest of the hostile crowd glared at him.

'Are the children of Greenwich the only ones in this town with any compassion?' Lavender snapped.

A woman stepped forward, her face rigid with disapproval. 'I'll fetch the vicar.' Pulling her shawl tighter around her shoulders, she marched away.

Lavender had hoped for a more positive response to his plea for help than this, but at least the crowd fell silent and they passed through unmolested. Micky Sullivan and his crony had disappeared. Lavender briefly wondered what he was doing in Greenwich before his attention returned to his charges.

It was only a short walk to the forge, but the chained prisoners slowed down when they passed the Royal Hospital. At first he thought their slower shuffle was the result of fatigue; then he realised they were gawping at their new surroundings. The towering stone wings of the Royal Hospital with their lofty colonnades must have been their first real glimpse of this strange new land.

The blacksmith was visibly shocked when Lavender and his line of prisoners turned up at the forge. A man of few words, he nodded gruffly when Lavender explained what he wanted, shouting over his shoulder to his wife to fetch drinking water. He wasted no time striding out to open the forge. He slid back the great wooden doors, donned a filthy leather apron over his Sunday-best clothes and searched amongst his tools for something to break off the prisoners' shackles. The forge soon echoed to the rhythmic clang of metal against metal, while a curious crowd gathered at the doors.

The blacksmith's wife pushed her way through, carrying a bucket of water and a ladle.

'Don't go near them, Lizzy!' a woman yelled from the crowd.

The blacksmith's wife ignored her neighbour and walked slowly towards the slaves. She scooped water into her ladle and offered the man at the rear of the line a drink. He grabbed it and guzzled down the water.

The crowd parted again and Ignatius Cugoan appeared. Beside him was his tall, flame-haired wife. Their faces paled at the sight before them. Jacquetta Cugoan carried a large basket of fresh bread on her arm. She followed the lead of the blacksmith's wife and walked stiffly down the line of slaves, handing out bread from her basket. The crowd at the door murmured.

Lavender shook Cugoan's hand warmly. 'Thank goodness you're here!'

'Word travels fast in a small town like this,' Cugoan said quietly. 'What can I do to help, Detective?'

'I appreciate that you probably won't speak the same language as any of these poor souls, but can you try to talk to them?'

Cugoan nodded. 'It's many years since I've used my native tongue and you're right not to be hopeful – there are hundreds of languages and dialects in Africa – but I'll try.' He moved off towards the pitiful group.

A woman appeared with an old shawl for one of the women, followed by another with a blanket for the baby and two old petticoats. The two female slaves were now free of their chains and the Greenwich women somehow got them to step into the petticoats and pulled them up over their ragged shifts.

'They're not proper skirts,' this latest Samaritan said to the silent women, 'but at least they'll cover your legs, my dears.' The black women stared back silently.

An elderly man with a troubled face and a white clerical collar around his neck appeared at Lavender's side. 'I'm the Reverend Baker,' he said. 'I've heard what's happened. What can this parish do to help?'

Lavender sighed with relief and shook his hand gratefully. 'I need someone to take care of these poor wretches,' he said, explaining the situation and how he needed to return to the Isle of Dogs immediately.

'Yes, yes,' Reverend Baker said. 'You must go and do your duty, Detective, and catch the evil felons who did this. We've a meeting room attached to the church. These poor souls can sleep there tonight. The parish will provide for their needs until a permanent home can be found for them.'

Cugoan returned to his side. 'It's hopeless I'm afraid, Detective. I can't talk with any of them. However, I'm a member of an organisation called the Sons of Africa. There are many other men like me – other freed slaves – in London. I'll write to them tonight and ask them to come and see if they can help us converse with these people.'

Lavender thanked both of them and stepped back outside the forge, relieved that his responsibility was over. It had turned cooler outside and the daylight was fading.

Fortunately, Greenwich's three burly constables soon arrived. They took in the strange sight and unusual situation at the forge and nodded grimly when Lavender explained what they had to do. He led them back to Greenwich Beach and they clambered aboard the boat waiting to take them to the Isle of Dogs.

Chapter Thirty-Two

Woods and Eddie were sitting calmly in the tumbledown old farm building when Lavender and the constables returned.

'Thank God you're both safe!'

Beside them, two scowling prisoners dangled from handcuffs in the animal stalls.

Woods grinned and winked. 'Meet the Packet Knucklers, sir. They were no trouble once Eddie stuck a branch into their spineless backs.'

'Packet Knucklers?'

'Yes, and these fellahs have been really helpful. Their ship's called the *Margaret Eve*. She's moored in the West India Docks. They're under the command of a Captain Bull and—'

'Nidar?'

'Yes, he's there.' Woods handed Lavender's pistol back to him.

Grim satisfaction spread through Lavender. His fingers curled around the barrel of the weapon in anticipation. 'What are we waiting for, then?'

'Oi!' yelled one of the captives from the animal stalls. 'What about us? Yous can't leave us alone in this stinkin' 'ell 'ole!' The irons on his wrist rattled.

'We'll send men to fetch them tonight,' Lavender said.

'One minute, sir.' Woods strode out of the building and reappeared a few moments later with the two buckets of foul human waste he'd previously removed. He dumped them close to the complaining men. 'So you don't like the stench in here, do you, fellahs?' he shouted. 'Well, try livin' with this for a while like them poor souls had to do.'

The two prisoners retched and howled with protest. Tears streamed down their cheeks.

'Don't let me forget about them,' Lavender said as they secured the door of the building with the wooden plank.

'I won't be in a hurry to remind you,' Woods growled. 'Serves them bastards right.'

The West India Docks loomed out of the mist. They were an impressive sight. Behind the high wall, thirty-eight huge warehouses, each one as broad as a cathedral, lined the sides of the two basins. A thick forest of masts and spars reached up towards the darkening sky from the mass of ships moored at the wharves. The basins creaked and groaned with the noise of straining timber and rope.

They sought entry through one of the guarded gates at the locks and were taken to a grim-faced dock manager in one of the massive customs warehouses. A mountainous pile of rum barrels surrounded them.

'Ay,' the manager said. 'I know the *Margaret Eve*. She's been loadin' cargo for a voyage to Charleston in the Carolinas. I knew she were a former slaver because of the stench of 'er.'

'She still is a slaver,' Lavender said sharply. 'We need to board her, arrest the crew and impound the ship and her cargo. How many men can you muster to help us?'

'About a dozen. I'll fetch them now.'

'Do they have pistols?' Lavender asked. 'I expect them to resist arrest.' The manager nodded and left.

Fifteen hard-faced and powerfully built men soon joined them. Lavender explained their mission. The men nodded grimly and primed their pistols. The acrid stench of gunpowder mingled with the intoxicating aroma of rum. Metal handcuffs were distributed and glinted in the weak light of their lanterns. There were twenty of them now – and Eddie.

'You're stayin' here, Eddie,' Woods said to his son.

'No, Da, please! You said I were a Bow Street constable . . .'

'Your father's right,' Lavender said. 'You've done more than enough to help us today and we're grateful for that – but you must stay here now.'

The men moved stealthily towards the *Margaret Eve*. There was little activity on the foggy quayside, but the docks were full of noise. They heard drunken laughter and muffled, sometimes foreign conversations from the ships they passed. Somewhere a seaman played a mournful tune on a harmonica. Above their heads, wooden cranes creaked in the breeze and tangled rigging slapped against the beams.

Only one gangplank descended from the stern of the towering ship onto the wharf. With pistols drawn, they stormed up it and quickly overcame the two men set to watch. 'Spread out!' Lavender yelled. 'Find the rest of the crew!'

Suddenly a shot came down from the masts above. The man beside Lavender clutched his ear and crumpled to the deck, screaming. Lavender raised his pistol and searched for a target, waiting for the next telltale flash of blue powder in the fog-shrouded rigging. But he saw nothing.

The others beside him were less cautious. A volley of shots was discharged into the sky, surrounding him with a haze of smoke. The body of a man crashed down onto the deck with a sickening crunch.

'Reload, quickly!'

The sound of pistol fire brought the Packet Knucklers up onto the deck from the hatches. Armed with pistols and knives, they hurled themselves at the officers and guards. Lavender fired into the body of a huge sailor who bore down upon him. His attacker slumped forward at his feet, clutching his stomach and screaming in agony. Lavender stepped back hastily to reload.

Scuffles broke out and more shots were fired. The stench of gunpowder stung the back of Lavender's throat.

'Search the holds!' yelled the dock manager. 'Find the rest of these bastards and get 'em all up here!'

Woods pointed towards the far end of the ship. 'There, sir. Two men – fleein'.'

Lavender caught a glimpse of the back of a broad, long-haired and heavily bearded man disappearing into the shadows. The fair-haired man at his side turned around and locked eyes with Lavender.

'It's Nidar!'

He raced forward across the main deck, with Woods and the Greenwich constables at his heels. But the bow of the ship was empty.

'Here, sir!' Woods leaned over the port side and pointed at the swinging rope ladder and the small rowing boat slipping away into the mist. Another identical rowing boat bobbed on the black water at the bottom of the ladder.

Lavender swung his leg over the side and climbed down. 'Quickly!' he yelled. 'We'll never find them again if they get into the shadows of the other tall ships. There's too many places to hide.'

He dropped down into the rocking boat, regained his balance and sat down with the oars. Woods landed heavily in the boat and it rocked again. Another blue flash lit up the dark sky above the rowing boat they were pursuing. Woods crumpled into the stern, cursing.

'Ned!' Lavender scrambled across to his white-faced constable.

Woods clutched his left arm. Dark liquid oozed between his fingers.

'The bastards!' Lavender glanced around furiously, but the other rowing boat had disappeared into the shifting mist. He stood up, aimed into the spot where he'd seen the blue flash, and fired. His eyes strained against the dark but he saw nothing to tell him his shot had found a mark. All he could hear was the banging, crashing and yelling on the deck above.

'Get him, sir!' Woods' face contorted with pain. 'Don't worry about me. Go after him!'

Lavender dropped to his haunches, pulled out his powder and reloaded. The three Greenwich constables were scrambling down the ladder to join them.

'Keep your heads down!' Lavender ordered as they dropped into the boat. 'Nidar's out there!'

'We saw them disappearin' in that direction, sir.'

They untied the rope and pushed away from the ship. The giant hulls of the moored ships formed an oppressive wall around them. Woods grimaced and clutched his arm.

The other rowing boat suddenly came into sight, floating quietly in the centre of the basin. It was abandoned. Both oars rested idle in the oarlocks.

'It may be a trap,' Lavender snapped.

They glided cautiously forward. The large, bearded man lay prostrate in the bottom of the boat. His left eye and the left side of his face were a mass of bloodied pulp. On his chest, his pistol lay idle, smoke still curling from its barrel.

'It's Captain Bull,' said one of the constables.

Lavender glanced around frantically. 'Where the devil is Nidar?'

The black water gleamed and slapped gently against the hulls of the tall ships. The surface was smooth. Nidar the serpent had slid into the water and vanished with barely a ripple.

'There's a lot of places to hide around here,' one of the constables said.

Lavender silently agreed with him. It was hopeless; Nidar had escaped again.

Woods hauled himself up to peer over the side of their boat into the other one. 'You're losing your touch, sir,' he croaked. 'That's not between his eyes like normal; you were a bit to the left.'

'Ned, lie back and save your strength. We've got to get you to a surgeon.' Fighting back his frustration and anger, Lavender told the constables to take them back to the wharf. Ned needed urgent medical attention.

Woods lay back with his eyes closed, his round moon of a face mirroring the pale orb in the black, velvet sky above. 'That gypsy girl were right all along,' he murmured. 'She said I were to avoid a horned and hairy beast wi' a ring through its nose. Well, that Captain Bull don't have a ring or horns – but he were hairy all right.'

'Ned – save your strength!'

Lavender's words were wasted. Woods was unconscious in the bottom of the boat.

Chapter Thirty-Three

Monday 11th May, 1812
Bow Street Magistrates' Court and Police Office

The pistol shot didn't shatter the bone but it's caused significant damage to Ned's left arm and he's weak from loss of blood. He won't be riding a horse again for a while.'

Magistrate Read, Vickery and Adkins listened quietly while Lavender recounted the details of the previous day's events. The three men looked grim and Lavender was exhausted. He'd barely slept. His elation at confounding Nidar's slaving business and impounding his ship had been overshadowed by his worry about Ned.

'Once I got Ned and Eddie back home, I fetched Sir Richard Allison to examine the injury.'

'Ooh, I'll wager Woods didn't like that!' Adkins said. 'He loathes Sir Richard.'

Lavender managed a wry smile. 'No, he didn't like it one bit. He chose that moment to regain vigorous consciousness. Betsy and his sons had to hold him down while Allison examined him. He accused Sir Richard of arriving to harvest his bodily organs while he was still breathing.'

Despite the tension in the room, all the men managed a small smile or short laugh.

'Is the wound clean?' Read asked.

'So far. Sir Richard doubts it will be infected.'

Read sat back, visibly relieved. 'Let's hope Woods has a quick and thorough recovery. I shall ask Mrs Read to call at their home to see if there's any further assistance we can give to the family.'

Lavender nodded. 'Magdalena went there this morning to help Betsy with the children.'

'It was good of Sir Richard to give his time in the middle of the night,' Read said. 'Did he charge you?'

'He owes us a favour. That negro skeleton Woods and I recovered – which Sir Richard took without permission – is rare and valuable. His rivals at St Thomas' Hospital would have paid us a considerable sum for such a specimen. I only had to mention this before he went to fetch his medical bag. No fee was mentioned after that.'

'Good,' Read said. 'Right, so what happened back in the West India Docks when you left?'

'The guards impounded the ship and arrested the crew. There's about twenty of them. Three were shot dead – including the captain, Captain Bull – and one of the dock guards was wounded. They intend to bring the remaining prisoners to Bow Street for questioning today.'

'Who owns the ship?'

'It's registered to a South American company headed by Capitán Don Fernando el Cerdo – but it's Nidar's ship.'

'*El Cerdo?*'

'Yes, it's Spanish for "pig". My wife uses the word all the time when she's talking about the French. According to Homer, the pig was another form taken by Proteus the shape-shifting Greek sea god.'

The side of Read's mouth curled sarcastically. 'At least the villain is consistent in the clues he leaves us.'

'They found a cramped and squalid section in the hold of the *Margaret Eve*,' Lavender continued, 'complete with shackles. With the testimony of the two men Woods and young Eddie captured, we've more than enough evidence to charge them with illegal participation in the slave trade.'

'Good,' Read said again. 'Then you can help me with the charges this morning, Lavender, before you resume your surveillance of John Bellingham.'

Lavender opened his mouth to protest, but Read silenced him with a wave of his hand. 'Vickery? I want you to scour the rookery for Nidar. Take all the men you need. Adkins? Go back to your relative at the Port of London and find out if there are any more ships on the Thames registered to Capitán Don Fernando el Cerdo.'

'But I should help, sir! I'm the only one who knows what the cove looks like.'

'Not any more, Lavender. You and Ned Woods weren't the only ones who were busy yesterday.'

Read picked up a copy of *The Day* from his desk and held it out to his officers to read. On the front page of the news-sheet was a bold advert:

REWARD
Fifty guineas
For information leading to the arrest of the
murderer and highway robber,
NIDAR,
alias Captain James Leon &
Doctor Pardus.

The advert contained the description of Nidar that Lavender and Woods had given Read on Saturday.

'I contacted Vincent Dowling at *The Day* yesterday and gave him this information,' Read said. 'Lord Yarmouth and Mr Rothschild have agreed to pay the reward between them. I appreciate that most of the population of St Giles are illiterate, but the news of the reward will already be out on the streets – along with Nidar's description. He'll no longer be able to skulk around the streets of the capital with impunity. We'll find him.'

'You'll need my help too,' Lavender said desperately.

'No,' Read said. 'You might not want to leave London at the moment, Stephen – and I can understand and accommodate your wish. Your trip to Dublin shall be postponed. But this scoundrel Nidar has a dangerous obsession with you and you've just given him a devilish shock.'

'What do you mean?'

'The man has taunted you with his nefarious highway robberies and the murder of Baron Danvers – but I don't believe for one minute he ever thought his vile slaving business would be discovered and his ship impounded. He didn't know – none of us knew – that you and Woods were sneaking around Greenwich, piecing back together the skeleton of one of the dead slaves he'd slung into an unmarked grave.'

'I'm sorry about the disobedience, sir,' Lavender said, 'but I was fascinated by the mystery.'

Read shrugged. 'Those freed slaves will be grateful for your curiosity for the rest of their lives, once they understand what the devil is happening to them. Who am I to penalise you and Ned for such a Christian act?'

'Thank you, sir.'

'But Nidar will never forgive you. He's unstable, dangerous and undoubtedly furious.'

'And wet,' Adkins smirked. 'He had to slip overboard and swim for it, thanks to you, Lavender.'

'Let's hope the bugger drowned,' Vickery growled.

'As I said,' Read continued, 'you've stung him – badly – and he'll want revenge. You and Woods did well yesterday, very well – but solving this mystery has nearly cost Woods his arm. If you set foot in St Giles, it may cost you your life. I want you out of Nidar's way today – and back on the trail of John Bellingham.'

Lavender sighed and nodded reluctantly. Read's words made sense and if he'd had a better night's sleep he might have come to the same conclusion himself. 'Three of our horses are still stabled at the forge in Greenwich,' he said. 'I brought Ned back in a cart loaned from the docks.'

'Is Woods' eldest son as good a horseman as his father?'

'Eddie? Yes, almost.'

'Good. I'll send word to the family. You said the boy is looking for work?' Lavender nodded. 'We're a man short in the stables. The pay won't be much but I'm sure every penny will be welcome while Woods recovers from his injury, and from what you've told me, this young man has a great future ahead of him as a Bow Street constable. His first job will be to retrieve your horses from Greenwich.'

Lavender didn't know if this was what Eddie Woods wanted, but he probably wouldn't have a choice now. The family would need the extra income while Ned was out of action. It was a small piece of good news in a bleak day. He sat up straighter. 'Nidar's probably got a second ship closer to us,' he said. 'The *Margaret Eve* in the West India Docks is too far from St Giles to have been his main base.'

'In which case, we'll find it. Is there anything else we need to know?'

'Yes. Micky Sullivan was in Greenwich yesterday afternoon. I don't know why.'

Read frowned. 'It may just be coincidence. We've enough to do today without chasing shadows. Forget Sullivan and concentrate on finding Nidar. Right, gentlemen – to work.'

◆　◆　◆

John Bellingham emerged from the house on New Millman Street just after two o'clock. Lavender sighed with relief. He'd grown stiff and bored waiting for the man to appear. Bellingham's landlady, Mrs Robarts, and her young son left the house with him. According to Vickery, Bellingham's behaviour had done little to excite interest or alarm over the last two days. Vickery had followed Bellingham to his tailor again on Saturday, where the merchant had purchased a smart kerseymere waistcoat of yellow with fine black stripes and a new pair of pantaloons. Bellingham wore his new clothes beneath his brown coat as he escorted Mrs Robarts up towards Guilford Street. She hung on his arm and gazed up at her lodger with undisguised adoration.

Lavender stepped out of the shadowy alley and followed the small group through the crowds. When they reached St James's Square, they disappeared inside the entrance of the European museum. It began to drizzle. Lavender pulled up the collar of his coat and sought shelter beneath the awning of a shop opposite while he waited for them to reappear.

A bedraggled and impatient horse stamped and snorted between the shafts of a coal wagon close by. Lavender empathised with the animal's frustration and wondered again if this surveillance was a waste of time. Lavender struggled to see Bellingham as a dangerous assassin. By the time the small party reappeared, Lavender was cold, wet and thoroughly fed up.

Bellingham's next stop was Challenier's Drapers, a small shop half hidden in the shade of Sidney's Alley, off Leicester Square. The two bow windows displayed a brightly coloured array of oriental silks and cotton bobbins in every shade of the rainbow. Their cheerfulness didn't lift Lavender's mood. *Drapers, tailors and cobblers*, he grumbled to himself. *I'm touring the shops while my colleagues risk their lives searching for a real villain.*

When Bellingham and Mrs Robarts reappeared, they talked briefly outside the shop, and Bellingham gave Mrs Robarts a piece of paper. *A banknote, perhaps?*

The merchant looked paler and more strained than when he'd first entered the shop. *Had something happened in there?* They parted company: Mrs Robarts and her boy turned north towards her home; Bellingham headed south towards the river. Lavender followed him.

The persistent drizzle turned into heavy rain and Lavender cursed Magistrate Read and his damned surveillance. Through the high buildings around Westminster, he saw a shaft of weak sunlight hovering on the horizon over the south bank of the Thames. All around him, wet shoppers and pedestrians quickened their pace.

The ancient facade of the Palace of Westminster rose above the rooftops, and Lavender wondered if Bellingham was heading for the public gallery in the House of Commons again. A distant church clock struck a solitary note. Lavender pulled out his pocket watch. It was a quarter off five. Today Parliament was debating the Orders in Council, the controversial government legislation that had caused international trade from the Baltic to the Americas to grind to a halt. The debate promised to be rowdy. Lavender shrugged. At least they would be out of the rain in the public gallery and well away from the British Ambassador to Russia.

When they passed the construction site near Henry VIII's old palace, the crush of pedestrians on the narrowed pavement became worse. The churning wheels of a passing brewery dray suddenly sprayed the crowd with ice-cold water. Like everyone else in the squealing crowd, Lavender leapt to one side in a futile attempt to evade a soaking and crashed into a little girl, who fell over.

Mortified at his clumsiness, he bent down to pick up the wailing child before she was trampled underfoot. Fortunately, she wasn't injured and he snatched her out of harm's way just in time. He apologised to her mother and searched frantically in the sea of bobbing hats and heads for Bellingham – but the merchant had disappeared from sight.

Lavender strode through Parliament Square, crossed Palace Yard and ran up the steps of St Stephen's entrance into the House of Commons, scanning the crowds of smartly dressed men in hats and topcoats for his quarry.

The tall folding doors of the inner chamber of the house were already closed and the sound of raised but muffled voices came from the other side. The debate about the Orders in Council had already started. There was no sign of Bellingham in the lobby. Lavender turned towards the staircase leading up to the public gallery.

A familiar blue flash flared and the sharp retort of a pistol shot rebounded off the high ceiling around the packed lobby. For a split second, he thought he was mistaken; then the acrid smell of gunpowder hit his nostrils.

A desperate voice cried out in the stunned silence of the lobby: 'Murder! I'm murdered!'

An almighty roar of shock, fear and anger erupted from the crowd. Everyone moved at once. Some headed towards the source of the pistol shot; others turned to flee, dropping hats, wigs and piles of documents in panic. The strong smell of sweat replaced the stench of gunpowder.

Lavender pushed forward against the frantic tide of the men trying to flee the room.

'Oh my God! It's the Prime Minister!'

The Right Honourable Spencer Perceval lay bleeding and unconscious in the arms of William Smith, the MP for Norwich. Perceval's face was already deathly white and drained of blood. His fair, boyish hair fell forward over his closed eyes. A crimson stain spread like a blooming rose across the white brocade of his waistcoat.

Crouched beside Perceval, Francis Phillips, the elderly and white-wigged MP for Yarmouth, had whipped off his cravat and pressed it into Perceval's chest, desperately trying to stem the gushing blood. Tears rolled down Phillips' hooked nose and dripped onto the dying man.

'Who did this? Where's the assassin?' Lavender asked. No one replied.

'Close the doors!' he yelled. 'Stop anyone leaving!'

But men continued to run in and out of the lobby. The news had spread to the inner chamber and the doors to the Commons flew open. More Members of Parliament spilled out into the seething and chaotic crowd.

Lavender cursed. 'Who did this?' he yelled again.

'There's the man!' One of the officials pointed an unsteady hand towards a figure in a brown coat slumped on a bench at the side of the hall. The villain was still here, a smoking pistol dangling idly from his large hand.

Lavender drew his own pistol and advanced. 'I'm Detective Lavender from Bow Street – drop your weapon on the floor!'

The man remained motionless. Vincent Dowling suddenly appeared out of nowhere and snatched the pistol from the assassin's hand.

Lavender rushed to his assistance. He seized the murderer's collar and jerked up his drooping head. John Bellingham's pallid and sweating face stared up at him. Lavender's guts lurched with shock.

The man he was meant to be following had just shot the Prime Minister.

Chapter Thirty-Four

W ho is he?' someone yelled behind Lavender.
'My name is John Bellingham,' the murderer said. 'It's a private injury – I know what I have done. It was a denial of justice.'

A denial of justice? He'd killed a man because his petition for compensation had failed? Was he mad?

'Villain!'

'Why did you destroy so good a man?' Francis Phillips, on the floor by the dying minister, was distraught.

'I'm sorry for it. I wish I were in Mr Perceval's place.'

Those who heard Bellingham's words gasped, then their shock turned to anger. They hauled Bellingham to his feet and tore at his clothes.

Lavender snapped back into action, moved forward and searched Bellingham. New growls of anger emanated from the throats of the enraged men when he pulled a second loaded pistol out of a secret pocket sewn inside the lining of his coat. *Oh, God – that first trip to the tailor's . . .*

Other hands reached forward, ripped Bellingham's coat and yanked out other possessions: money, a pair of opera glasses, a pocketknife, a pencil and a sheaf of papers. Lavender pulled out his handcuffs but was pushed aside by a burly man.

'I know of this villain!' It was General Isaac Gascoyne, Bellingham's Member of Parliament. His voice boomed louder than the rest. 'He's sent me many petitions for his damnable cause!'

Others took up the cry: 'I've seen him too!'

'The scoundrel petitioned me also!'

Gascoyne grabbed Bellingham by the arm and swung him round with his arm up his back.

Bellingham's voice rose in distress and his forehead gleamed with perspiration. 'You need not press me, sir. I submit myself to justice!'

Lavender held out the clanking metal handcuffs. 'Then submit yourself to these, sir.' His intervention worked; the crowd and Gascoyne fell back when Lavender snapped the cuffs into place around Bellingham's wrists.

'Let's take him before the magistrates!' someone yelled. 'We'll examine him before the bar in the chamber of the House of Commons.'

'Let's just hang the villain,' another voice growled.

'I think not, gentlemen,' said a familiar voice. Harvey Combe MP, the senior magistrate for Middlesex, pushed himself forward. 'First, we need to arrest him and formally charge him with murder.' Lavender knew him for a man of decision and leadership. 'Bring the scoundrel to the sergeant-at-arms' office; he has a prison apartment there.'

Combe led the way. Lavender and Dowling pushed the manacled Bellingham out of the lobby, past the baying mob. Some fell into step behind them. Other men carried the limp form of Spencer Perceval away.

Dowling turned to the prisoner when the group stopped at the bottom of a narrow staircase. 'Why, man? Why kill the Prime Minister?'

'I have been thwarted, misrepresented and ill used,' Bellingham replied. 'There was no *malice prepense* in my mind when I fired my pistol. I disclaim all personal or intentional malice against Mr Perceval.'

No 'malice prepense'? This was the plea of those accused of manslaughter. No judge or jury in the land would believe this attack on

Spencer Perceval was accidental. The presence of the secret pocket with the second pistol in the lining of his coat was enough to convince anyone this barbarous act was premeditated.

'Don't question him,' Magistrate Combe snapped. 'He needs to be arrested and cautioned before he's questioned.'

But Bellingham suddenly became talkative. 'The public shall see what I have suffered and they shall know my crime is nothing compared to the crime of the government.'

'Silence!' Combe spun round, his face contorted with anger. Bellingham fell silent.

Lavender pushed the merchant up the stairs in front of him. *Bellingham was stark raving mad.*

Combe led them up a narrow corridor to the sergeant's office, a small and airless room. Lavender broke out into a sweat in the crush as everyone tried to cram inside. He beckoned to the sergeant to take his place beside the prisoner and approached Combe. 'I need to fetch more officers from Bow Street and we need to search the prisoner's lodgings for evidence.'

Combe nodded and Lavender stepped outside gratefully. The corridor was packed with men demanding entry, insisting that they were witnesses.

One man's voice rose above all the others. 'I have a message from Mr Francis Phillips.'

The crowd paused and a hush descended.

'He regrets to inform you that Mr Perceval has just died in his arms. A doctor arrived, but it was too late to save him.'

The furious babble erupted again and Lavender turned away, sickened. He felt a hand on his arm. It was Vincent Dowling. The journalist pulled him to the shadows of an empty section of the corridor. 'Were you following him, Lavender?'

'There was an accident – a small girl – I stopped to help her . . .' Lavender's voice trailed away with guilt and despair as the enormity of his failure hit him.

An innocent man had died because of his mistake. If Dowling printed the story, it would ruin him and the reputation of Bow Street Police Office. They only existed because of their stipend from Parliament, and now he'd let a madman strike down the leader of that Parliament.

Dowling swallowed hard and frowned. 'Magistrate Read told me you thought he intended to harm Lord Leveson-Gower.'

More men brushed passed them on their way to the sergeant's office. Lavender raised his hands in a gesture of helplessness. 'That seemed the logical conclusion. I should've been more alert . . .'

Dowling shook his head sadly. His lank hair swayed. 'Don't blame yourself, Lavender. No one could foresee that he would do this. It only takes a second to kill someone with a pistol if the intent is there. Bellingham's insane.' He turned and disappeared back into the crowd.

Dowling's words were a little comfort, but not much. Lavender strode down the stairs, sent an urgent message to Bow Street via one of the clerks, then forced his way through the lobby to the stone steps leading down to Old Palace Yard.

The recent rain had brought a sweetness to the air. Across the yard, the fluted sides of Henry VII's chapel were in deep shadow. The gothic arches of its tall windows and soaring pinnacles on the roof reached up to the overcast sky as if beseeching heaven for some help to understand the insane bloodlust and evil of mankind.

The respite brought to him by the fresh air was short-lived. Desperately, he searched his conscience. *Was there more he could have done to prevent the tragedy?*

Behind Lavender, the men in the lobby still buzzed like angry insects. In the yard in front of him, a small crowd had gathered. The news of Spencer Perceval's assassination was already spreading across the city like a malevolent breeze.

A gang of rowdy men suddenly appeared behind the onlookers in front of the palace. They were grinning and swung bottles of ale by their sides. Lavender's heart sank when he realised they had come to gloat. One of them recognised him and pointed him out to the others. He stood up straighter and averted his eyes.

'Detective Lavender!' a voice called out. 'Standin' there to protect the Prime Minister, are ye?'

''E's a bit late, if 'e is!' yelled another. Raucous laughter followed. Lavender set his jaw and glared defiantly over their heads.

A new and shocking thought suddenly struck him like a kick in the stomach: *Nidar.*

Nidar had bragged that he was about to do 'something big'. Was this it? Had he played a part in the assassination? Did he know Bellingham from Liverpool? Bellingham was obviously unstable. His obsession made him vulnerable to coercion; the perilous state of his finances made him desperate. Nidar was a dangerous trickster, charming and ruthlessly determined. He thought back to the shadowy figure who'd given Bellingham money in the tavern and cursed himself for missing the opportunity to identify the merchant's financier. His surveillance of Bellingham had been one disaster after another.

By the time Magistrate Read, Vickery and Adkins clambered out of a carriage and strode up the steps towards him, the crowd had swelled to double the size. Boisterous and drunk, the rag-tag and scum of the Seven Dials and the rookery of St Giles poured into the Palace Yard. The slums of London were emptying into this small corner of Westminster. The decent folks hurriedly left. Carriage drivers struggled to get through to the main entrance. The constant stream of peers and Members of Parliament who arrived at the Palace glanced nervously over their shoulders when they alighted from their coaches and scurried up the steps into the House of Commons. Lavender frowned when he realised that the prison wagon from Newgate would stand out like a sore thumb amongst the gleaming carriages of the nobility.

'We'll have to call the militia.' Read was out of breath when he reached Lavender's side. 'They're already rioting in the Seven Dials.

Bonfires have been lit. They're carousing in the streets and looting the shops – and it's not even dark yet.' Read pulled his officers into the shadows of the great, carved stone doorway and lowered his voice. 'What the devil happened here, Lavender?'

Lavender explained. 'I fell behind Bellingham, sir. I lost sight of him in the crush. I thought he'd gone up to the public gallery. If only I'd stuck closer . . . I wasn't quick enough . . .'

Anger flashed across Read's face. 'For God's sake, Lavender! The reputation of Bow Street Police Office will be ruined once it becomes common knowledge that we were trailing this depraved murderer and couldn't stop him.' Lavender winced at the criticism. 'Has anyone asked why you were here today?'

'Only Vincent Dowling. He seems . . . sympathetic.'

Read's relief was visible. 'I'll try to talk to him before he writes his story. Dowling's still a Home Department man at heart. Right, what can we do to help?'

'I need Vickery to go to Bellingham's lodgings and search them for evidence. I've been asked to stay here and escort the prisoner to Newgate.' Vickery nodded, descended the steps and strode away in the direction of New Millman Street.

Lavender glanced back at the crowd in the yard. 'I'll need Adkins' help with the escort.'

Read followed his gaze to the drunken ruffians and nodded. 'Dear God. There's already so much unrest in the country. Parliament has been aware that it will only take one spark to ignite the tinderbox of revolution. Let us hope and pray this isn't that spark. I'll see Magistrate Combe and ask if Bow Street can offer any other assistance.'

'I can't get it out of my head that Bellingham may have had an accomplice in this, sir.'

Read's eyes widened. His quick mind followed Lavender's train of thought. 'Nidar? You think Nidar is involved?'

'Yes. Is this the shocking crime he planned? His "something big"? Both men are from Liverpool and we know someone financed Bellingham. Was it Nidar? Did he pay him – or blackmail him – to murder Perceval?'

'Do you have any evidence to support this theory, Detective?'

'I don't.' Lavender turned to Adkins. 'Did you have any luck tracking him down today? Are there any leads as to his whereabouts?'

Adkins shook his head. 'There's been plenty of folks rushin' to give us information about their neighbours today. We've interviewed dozens of men with northern accents – but none of them were them Packet Knucklers. There's no more ships registered to that South American Capitán on the Thames. It's like they've vanished off the face of the earth.'

'If we are to move forward with this theory,' Read said, 'we need to establish a direct connection with Bellingham, locate Nidar and find the evidence to damn him. But you're right about one thing: no crime is bigger than this.'

It was eight o'clock and growing dark before the magistrates finished questioning the prisoner. They called for Lavender and Adkins to escort Bellingham to Newgate. Palace Yard was almost impassable with the pressure of the crowd. To the east, the night sky glowed orange with the fires burning in St Giles.

When the prison wagon arrived, the crowd swarmed upon it. It quickly became obvious that the ruffians intended to shake the prisoner's hand rather than harm him.

'I didn't think there was an Englishman left that 'ad such 'eart,' yelled one fellow.

''E couldn't 'ave shot a greater rascal,' shouted another.

'The Prince Regent must be down next!'

'Get back inside!' Lavender grabbed Bellingham by the scruff of the neck and manhandled him back up the steps into St Stephen's Hall. The magistrates and Adkins scurried up behind him. Once inside, the great doors were shut.

'Call out the Horse Guards to clear the yard!' Magistrate Combe hollered at a messenger.

Lavender left Bellingham with Adkins and went to where Read stood with Combe.

'A cabinet council has been summoned,' Read informed him. He looked grey with worry. 'They've delayed the mail coaches to try to stop the news leaving London. Dispatches have been sent to every civil and military authority in Britain warning them of civil unrest. This will spread.'

'We can't get Bellingham to Newgate in this chaos,' Lavender said. 'We need less obvious transport, like a carriage.'

'Don't be a fool, Detective!' Combe snapped. 'We can't let a common murderer ride to Newgate in a gentleman's carriage!'

'We can if it's the only way,' Lavender retorted.

'Lavender is right,' Read said. 'The prison wagon attracts too much attention.'

'My carriage is at your disposal, gentlemen.' The speaker was another magistrate, the Honourable Michael Angelo Taylor. Lavender thanked him and, despite Combe's indignant protests, arrangements were made to have Angelo Taylor's carriage discreetly driven to the door.

It was another hour before the militia arrived. The Horse Guards forced the heaving crowd back out of Palace Yard. They turned into a screaming mob in seconds. Rocks rained down on the militia. Torn-up railings from St James's Park flew through the air like javelins. A cart was set ablaze, casting grotesque shadows of battling demons onto the walls of the Old Palace Yard.

'Quickly!' Lavender yelled. 'While they're distracted with the militia.'

Lavender, Adkins, Combe and Angelo Taylor hurried Bellingham down the steps and into the carriage. Lavender slammed the doors shut, closed the blinds and sat back with his loaded pistol in his hand. The vehicle lurched out of the yard. The comfort of the well-sprung coach didn't ease the tension of the journey. The streets of London were alive with rioters shouting and huzzaing for joy.

'Savages!' Magistrate Combe hissed angrily.

The horses were skittish and the drivers struggled to move forward through the crowds. They travelled in strained silence, except for one instance when a hurled beer bottle suddenly crashed and splintered against the side of the coach.

'Damn,' said Angelo Taylor. 'That'll have damaged my paintwork.'

Lavender sighed with relief when they finally rolled into the yard at Newgate gaol. He handed over custody of Bellingham to the warden and retrieved his handcuffs. Exhausted, he bid Adkins goodnight, pulled up his coat collar and set out through the mayhem towards home.

Magdalena, Mrs Hobart and an elderly whiskered man he'd never seen before waited anxiously in the kitchen.

With an outpouring of relieved and passionate Spanish, Magdalena flew into his arms when he staggered through the door. 'Thank goodness you're safe, Stephen! We heard about the assassination and the riots. Are you all right?'

He held her close for a moment, then broke away. 'Where's Teresa?'

'She's upstairs with Ned and Betsy's daughters. I brought them back here earlier to make it easier for Betsy while she nurses Ned.'

Ned. Lavender realised guiltily that he'd barely given his injured constable a thought today.

'We need to shutter up the house. The unrest may spread.'

'Here?' Magdalena exchanged a worried glance with Mrs Hobart, then pointed to the man by her side. 'This is Mr Hobart. He's come to escort his wife home to Piccadilly.'

Lavender shook his head. 'No, sir. I think you both need to stay here tonight. The militia were closing off Piccadilly when I passed through.'

The Hobarts accepted his offer and Mr Hobart offered to help him with the window shutters.

'Are the children scared?' Lavender asked.

A small smile flitted across Magdalena's strained face. 'No, but Teresa is. I've sent her to read them a bedtime story to try to distract her. She remembers only too well the rioting in Madrid after that dog Bonaparte put his brother on the throne of Spain.'

Lavender grimaced. His wife and little Teresa had experienced a brutal time in war-torn Spain. He'd promised them safety here in London – but now the capital was on fire. He'd let them down. 'How's Ned today?' he asked.

Magdalena smiled again. 'He's not an easy patient, but Betsy has his measure.'

After boarding up the lower windows of the house, Lavender ate a hasty meal before climbing wearily upstairs. He lay awake for an hour with Magdalena in his arms. They heard muffled shouting and watched the flickering orange glow of distant fires through a gap in the drapes.

It didn't seem to be coming any closer. He felt himself relax and the warmth of Magdalena's breath on his chest comforted him.

'Try to sleep, Stephen,' she murmured.

'It's been the worst day of my life,' he said. 'I still can't believe that a man who took an innocent child on an outing to a museum went on to murder another man in cold blood a few hours later.'

'There's no accounting for the behaviour of madmen,' Magdalena said simply.

'Is he mad, though? He stunned the magistrates with the calmness of his demeanour today.'

In the distance, the militia let off another volley of rifle shots. Magdalena jumped nervously. He pulled her closer.

'Madness takes different forms,' she said. 'Look at Duddles' sudden declaration to Baroness Danvers. That was a moment of madness if ever I saw one.'

Despite his wretchedness, Lavender smiled at the memory.

'Bellingham's composure is a sign of his insanity,' Magdalena continued, 'and the fact that he made no attempt to escape. He's an educated man; he knows the penalty for murder. Only a madman would think he could escape the gallows after such an atrocious crime.'

Lavender sighed heavily. 'I keep thinking I missed something today. Was there some clue I overlooked that would have warned me of his murderous intent?'

'If you think you missed something, retrace your steps tomorrow.' Her voice was sleepy now.

Just when he thought she'd drifted off to sleep she squeezed him tighter. 'Yesterday, you saved the lives of six wretched slaves and a baby, Stephen,' she whispered. 'You're amazing, my darling – but you can't save the entire world on your own. You'll always fail if you try to save the whole world.'

Chapter Thirty-Five

Tuesday 12th May, 1812
Bow Street Magistrates' Court and Police Office

Lavender overslept but still took his time over a leisurely breakfast with Magdalena and Ned's two bright-eyed, curly-haired little daughters before setting off to Bow Street. The girls had slept through the riot and were full of energy and questions. He watched Magdalena smile while she helped them with their food and felt a pang of regret they didn't have a child of their own yet. Magdalena was a wonderful mother to Sebastián, and another child would fill her days with joy during his long absences.

He'd been grateful when no baby had appeared in the first year of their marriage; he'd secretly enjoyed having Magdalena all to himself. But it had been two years now and their childlessness had become a silent void between them, an emptiness he desperately wanted to fill. He needed to spend more time at home.

A new thought struck him. Now Bellingham was detained in Newgate and Read refused to let him scour St Giles for Nidar, there wasn't much left for him to do in London. It wouldn't be long before Read packed him off to Dublin.

He sighed and pushed back his chair to leave. The shock and despair of the previous day had turned to sadness: for Spencer Perceval and his family, friends and colleagues in Parliament and for his country, which teetered on a knife edge of revolution.

Today the smell of cooked breakfasts and coal fires that usually permeated the city's streets was replaced with a heavier, more acrid smell of burning. A pall of dark smoke hovered ominously over the skyline. London was uncharacteristically quiet and several roads were blocked with burnt-out vehicles and dead horses.

Bleary-eyed militia stood in groups at street corners, eyeing everyone suspiciously. Their red coats were ripped and smoke-stained. Some were bloodied. Strained, pale-faced shopkeepers attempted to sweep away the broken glass and debris from the front of their premises and a few carpenters hammered boards over the broken windows. No one smiled. Everyone wore the dark rings of a sleepless night under their eyes.

The devastation became worse when he approached the poorer areas around Covent Garden. Every window on Long Acre was smashed and some burnt shops still smouldered.

Vickery and Adkins were already in Read's office when Lavender arrived.

'Lively night, eh, Lavender?' Adkins said.

'It was a bad riot,' Read informed them. 'Eight thousand militia were deployed into London last night and another eighteen thousand across the country in case they were needed. Numerous properties have been destroyed and looted, dozens were arrested and three people killed in the insurrection.' Lavender grimaced.

'And the Prince Regent fled to Brighton like a frightened girl,' Adkins said with a wink.

Read gave his younger officer a disapproving scowl. 'This isn't amusing, Adkins. The government's attempt to stop the spread of trouble by holding back the mail coaches failed; reports have already filtered back about significant trouble in the Midlands. Meanwhile, a witness has come forward who claims John Bellingham's father was a violent madman who died in an asylum in St Neots.'

Lavender frowned. He'd never been comfortable with the assumption that madness was inherited in families.

Read pointed to a pair of pistol bags and a small powder flask on the desk in front of him. 'Vickery was just about to explain these to us when you arrived.'

Vickery held a pistol key, a mould and some balls in his large hands. 'I found these in Bellingham's lodgings,' he explained in his slow, measured drawl. 'I'm sure the pistol key will correspond to the two pistols Bellingham carried, and if we take the ball from his second loaded pistol we'll discover that it was made in this mould.'

'This is excellent work, Vickery.' Read's voice was full of satisfaction. 'Magistrate Combe confided in me last night that, in the crush and confusion, there was only one witness who thinks he saw Bellingham fire the gun.'

Adkins snorted. 'But hundreds heard him confess to the crime!'

Read nodded. 'Yes, but if Bellingham's lawyer persuades the court that he's mad and suggests someone else murdered Perceval and dropped the pistol in Bellingham's lap when they ran away from the scene, it might not be so easy to convict him. Vickery's evidence is indisputable proof that the pistol used to kill Perceval belonged to John Bellingham.'

'Did you find anything else of interest at his lodgings?' Lavender asked.

'Only a pile of unpaid bills,' Vickery said. 'It turns out he was short of money again. His landlady told me he'd only just paid his rent. He's been in arrears for five weeks.'

Lavender frowned. 'When did he pay her?'

'Yesterday. He gave her a banknote for thirty pounds to be drawn at Mr Wilson's bank. Do you think this is significant?'

'It might be.' Lavender remembered the paper note Bellingham had given the woman outside the draper's shop the day before.

'Who signed for the banknote?' Read asked.

Lines creased across Vickery's broad forehead and he rubbed his beard. 'She never said – but now I think about it, Bellingham became agitated when I mentioned the banknote to Magistrate Combe last night.'

Lavender rose to his feet. Magdalena had been right; he needed to revisit the events of yesterday. 'I need to see that banknote. We need to know where it came from.'

Read nodded. 'Vickery and Adkins will resume their search for Nidar.'

Lavender paused. 'Did Bellingham talk of an accomplice? Did the magistrates find out anything about his finances?'

Read shook his head. 'Bellingham repeatedly declared that he worked on his own. In fact, he became heated in his denials of an accomplice.'

Lavender pulled his hat firmly down on his head and turned to go. 'Methinks the man doth protest too much.'

Rebecca Robarts was a round-faced, plain young woman of about thirty. Her eyes were red and puffy from crying and she sniffed into her handkerchief when she let Lavender into her parlour. It was a dark, formal room with uncomfortable, heavy furniture. A brick and shattered glass lay on the faded carpet. The drapes rippled in the slight breeze wafting through the broken window. She sank into a hard-backed chair and pointed to the brick. 'The neighbours did that last night,' she sobbed. 'They blame me for harbourin' a murderer! Like I told the other detective, I knew nothin' about this, sir. Nothin'!'

Lavender felt a pang of sympathy for the woman.

'If it's any consolation, ma'am, you're not the only person in London who was fooled by that scoundrel.'

Lavender stood awkwardly by the cold fireplace, waiting until her tears had dried up. He wished Woods were here. Ned was so much better at putting witnesses at ease than him.

'I need to see the banknote Bellingham left with you,' Lavender said gently.

She shook her head. 'I'm sorry. I took it to the bank first thing this mornin'. It's gone.'

Lavender's heart sank. The note would have been destroyed by the bank.

'Can you remember the name of the payee, ma'am? The person who gave Bellingham the banknote?'

She shook her head and blew her nose. 'I were so distracted, sir, I never paid attention. I'm much grieved about what happened. I'm so sorry for Mrs Perceval and her children. I thought 'e were such a nice gentleman!'

'Mrs Robarts, do you know who paid for Mr Bellingham's stay in London?'

'No. 'E said 'e were 'ere on business.'

'Did he ever bring any of his business partners to the house?'

'No.'

'Did he tell you anything about the men he met, or the meetings he had?'

'No, nothin'. 'E kept 'imself to 'imself and didn't discuss 'is business matters with me. 'E were a quiet man. I thought . . . I thought I were gettin' to know 'im a little . . .' She broke down and sobbed some more.

Lavender sighed. 'What have you done with the money from the banknote, Mrs Robarts?'

She blew her nose again. ''E owed me five weeks' rent. I promised to keep the rest safe for 'im.' Her voice rose with anger. ''E's just sent me a note from Newgate askin' for it, along with some clothes and 'is prayer book.' Her swollen face contorted with rage. 'Prayer book! 'Ow dare 'e pray to God for forgiveness after what 'e's done?'

Lavender shook his head sadly, unable to answer her question. He'd seen enough last night to know that the enigmatic murderer believed his actions were justified. 'One last question, Mrs Robarts,' he said gently. 'When did Bellingham give you the banknote?'

''E gave it to me at the draper's yesterday afternoon.'

'The draper's? Challenier's on Sidney's Alley, off Leicester Square?'

She looked up in surprise. 'Yes. 'Ow did you . . . ?'

'Did Bellingham meet someone at the draper's?'

'Yes. 'E disappeared into the back of the shop for a few minutes.'

'Did you see the man he met?'

'No, it were in a back room.'

Lavender thanked her hurriedly and left.

The doorbell gave an irritating jangle when Lavender stooped and entered the gloomy and oppressive interior of Challenier's Drapers. The stench of burning oil from the weak wall lamps mingled with the faint whiff of lanolin emanating from the rolls of Yorkshire woollen cloth leaning against one wall of the shop. On the other side, a long row of patterned Manchester cottons lined up like a parade of mismatched soldiers.

The draper, Challenier presumably, eyed him suspiciously from behind the counter, while sorting through a bowl of shiny military coat buttons. His round spectacles magnified his pale, cold and watery eyes. 'Can I help yous, sir?'

Lavender knew the draper's origins the instant he opened his mouth to speak. Years of residency in London had not taken the edge off the man's distinctive northern accent. He pulled out his tipstaff and laid it on the counter. 'I'm Detective Lavender from Bow Street Police Office.'

The draper started with surprise. 'I need to talk to you about two men who visited your shop yesterday for a short meeting.'

The shopkeeper's liquid eyes narrowed behind his spectacles and the colour drained from his face. 'What meetin'? There weren't no meetin'.'

Lavender's tone hardened. 'Don't lie to me – and roll back your sleeves.'

'What?'

'I said: roll back your sleeves.'

The draper pulled back the cheap lace protruding from the sleeves of his grey coat with a shaking hand. He pushed the material up his arms, revealing a tattoo. Lavender grabbed his wrists and turned them over, slapping his hands down on the counter.

'Oi!'

The tattoo was old and faded like Macca's but still clearly visible.

'The sign of the Packet Knucklers,' Lavender said harshly. 'I know about your crew and about Nidar. We've got plenty more like you locked up in the cells at Bow Street. So stop lying and tell me what happened here yesterday. Otherwise, you'll come with me back to Bow Street to join them.'

Challenier jerked back his arms and hastily rolled down his sleeves. Beads of perspiration formed on his forehead and top lip. 'I've done nuffin', guvnor. Nuffin'. I ain't a Packet Knuckler no more – not since I left seafarin' and settled here wi' me late wife. But Jim Proteus keeps track of 'is old crews.'

Jim. So, the man's first name was James. Unfortunately, this wouldn't help; a quarter of the men in the country were christened James. But this was progress. He'd now got a name and Challenier could testify that Bellingham had met Nidar.

'What's his full name?'

Challenier looked confused. ''E called himself Proteus back in the 'Pool, but it's Nidar down 'ere in London, I think.'

'What happened yesterday?'

''E paid me a visit last week. I swear, sir, I nearly died when the devil walked into me shop. I 'adn't seen 'im since he were a young fellah but

I knew who 'e was. I'd 'eard 'e were operatin' in London now. I were pourin' wi' sweat when 'e walked through the door, but 'e smiled that smile of 'is that don't reach 'is eyes and said 'e would use me back room to meet with a friend.'

Satisfaction filled Lavender. They'd got him. He'd found the link between Nidar and John Bellingham he needed; the bastard had financed the assassination of the Prime Minister.

'What happened yesterday?'

'It were all over in a few minutes, thank the Lord. The big fellah wi' the woman and child came into the shop, and I sent 'im round the back.'

'Did you overhear their conversation? What did you see?'

'Nuffin'! I stayed well away. It's more than me life's worth to get involved with Jim Proteus again. The big chap came out lookin' a bit upset and clutching a banknote. He left wi' the woman and Proteus vanished out the back.' He wiped away the sweat dripping from his brow with the cuff of his coat.

Lavender paused for a moment and regarded the man coldly. Would a stint in the Bow Street cells jog his memory further?

'Where does Nidar base himself?'

'I don't know. I know nuffin' about the Knucklers now – and I don't want to know anythin' about them bastards.'

'If he gets back in touch, you send me a message at Bow Street straight away, do you understand?'

The draper's watery eyes broke away from Lavender's gaze. 'Yes, sir,' he mumbled.

Lavender sighed and wondered what kind of a witness Challenier would make in court. The man was terrified of the cove. It was probably better not to pressure him too much until Nidar was behind bars. 'Don't leave London, Mr Challenier,' he said. 'We may need to talk again.'

◆ ◆ ◆

'I've got a witness who can link Nidar to John Bellingham.' Lavender sat down in a chair at Read's desk. 'I was right; Nidar gave Bellingham money and probably encouraged him to murder Perceval.' He explained what he'd learnt.

'That's excellent work, Lavender,' Read said, 'but unfortunately your witness is no use unless we can track down the villain himself, and he appears to have vanished.'

'He'll be back. Sullivan told me Nidar tended to come and go in London. He was here a few years ago causing trouble. He'll be back.'

Read nodded. 'And the next time he returns we shall be ready for him. We know what he looks like. We've got evidence linking him to the highway robberies; witnesses who can place him at the events held by both Lady Alderney and Lady Caroline Clare – and now a witness linking him to Perceval's assassination.'

'I need to interview John Bellingham. He knows how to contact Nidar—' Lavender broke off when Oswald Grey knocked at the door and strode in with a message.

Read scanned the document and frowned. 'It's from Vincent Dowling. Luckily for you – and us – he's agreed to keep silent about our involvement with Bellingham. Meanwhile, he's still following events at Newgate. I asked him to keep me informed.'

'What's happened?'

'Apparently, someone sent John Bellingham one hundred guineas this morning for his defence and expenses in prison.'

'Nidar?'

'The gift was anonymous.'

'It's got to be Nidar!'

Read shook his head. 'Not necessarily. Spencer Perceval wasn't a popular man and it's not just the lower orders who are celebrating his death. The French and the Americans will be very happy at his demise. Perceval upset every merchant in the country with his trade blockade

– not to mention every Catholic in Britain and Ireland by blocking the emancipation bill.'

'If someone has rewarded Bellingham for murdering Perceval, then it's a disgrace.'

'I agree.' Read glanced back at the note from Dowling and his frown deepened. 'There's also news from the Midlands and Yorkshire. Apparently, last night the bells were rung in Nottingham to celebrate Perceval's murder and bonfires were lit in the streets. They had to read the Riot Act.'

'How can they applaud a foul deed like this?' Lavender asked. But part of him already knew the answer. Nottingham was at the centre of the Luddite unrest.

'They openly celebrated in Leicester too. In Sheffield they roasted a whole sheep in the city centre.'

'The public reaction is almost more shocking than the murder itself.'

Read nodded, his eyes still focused on the note from Dowling. 'Because of the public unrest, the magistrates have decided to try John Bellingham as quickly as possible for the wilful murder of the Right Honourable Spencer Perceval. He'll appear in court on Friday and will probably be hanged this weekend.'

'So soon? Bellingham will be hanged before his case can be properly examined.' Lavender slammed his fist down on Read's desk in frustration. Everything jumped. Ink spurted from its bottle and ran down onto the wood. A few papers slid off one of the piles. 'What about our investigation into his accomplice?'

Read's eyes narrowed in the face of Lavender's uncharacteristic fury.

'It may not be possible to pursue this lead further, Stephen,' Read said. 'Bellingham's lawyer will barely have time to mount a defence for the man. We'll struggle to get access to the prisoner. But I'll send Vickery this afternoon to try to gain an interview.'

'This is my information,' Lavender said. 'I want to go.'

'No, Stephen,' Read said firmly. 'You'll take the rest of the day off work; you've done enough. You've worked solidly for the last eight days and you're exhausted – which is probably why you made a mistake yesterday.'

Lavender grimaced again. 'Yes. A mistake that cost a man his life.'

'Go and visit Ned Woods and take him our regards.'

Lavender sank back in his chair wearily. 'It sounds to me that the authorities aren't interested in Bellingham's accomplice. They just want to hang him and set an example to the rest of the country.'

Read sighed. 'You may be right. Dowling adds a footnote: under further questioning, John Bellingham admitted if he'd seen Lord Leveson-Gower he would have shot the Ambassador as well as Spencer Perceval. That's what the second pistol was for. So we were partially right in our suspicions about the man.'

Lavender shook his head sadly. 'It doesn't make me feel better to know that.'

Chapter Thirty-Six

A m I glad to see you!' Betsy's plump arms were covered in flour and she wore a stained apron over her gown. Her mop of curly grey hair seemed wilder than normal. She ushered Lavender down the narrow hallway towards the kitchen. 'Ned's fussing me to death! Stay a while, Stephen, and talk to him, please?'

'I'm happy to. Magdalena sends her love; she'll bring Tabby and Rachel home tomorrow.'

'Have they been good?'

'Little angels. They slept through the disturbances last night. Did you have any trouble here in Southwark?'

Betsy shook her head. 'We heard about it, of course – and the terrible shootin' of the Prime Minister. But it's been quiet here on this side of the river.'

Woods' face beamed with pleasure when he saw their visitor. He had colour in his cheeks again beneath his stubble. He sat at the large wooden table with a spoon in his right hand, enjoying a hearty bowl of stew and dumplings. Beneath his open shirt, his left arm was bandaged and strapped to his body in a sling.

'I'm glad to see you've regained your appetite, Ned,' Lavender said with a smile.

'He never lost it,' Betsy said tartly. 'He's done nothin' but eat for the last two days.' She returned to her baking at the far end of the table.

'I'm buildin' me strength back up,' Woods said with a wink.

'How's your shoulder?' Lavender asked.

Woods gently stroked his injured arm. 'Much better. The pain troubles me a little at night but it's only a scratch. It won't be long before I'm in the saddle again.'

'You'll do what that surgeon said: take your time and let it heal.' Betsy pointed menacingly at her husband with her wooden spoon. 'There's no rush for you to return to work; I've told you before, I've got a bit of money put by.' Woods grunted.

Lavender was pleased to hear about Betsy's savings. He'd worried about how the family would cope without the regular wage from Bow Street. He glanced at the bandages tying Woods' arm to his body. Betsy was right to be cautious. Ned's arm would be stiff and weak for a long time. 'Did Eddie enjoy his first day at work in the stables?' he asked.

Their faces softened into smiles.

'He loved it.' Lavender heard the relief in Betsy's voice.

'The lad enjoyed our trip out on Sunday,' Woods said with another wink. 'He's changed his mind about goin' away to sea and thinks the life of a police constable may be more excitin' than he first thought.'

'He hasn't stopped talkin' about how he arrested those villains and helped to free those poor, poor creatures,' Betsy added.

Lavender smiled. Eddie had been horrified when he'd first realised his father had been shot and had barely said a word during that long and torturous journey back to Southwark. He was glad the boy had recovered his good spirits. 'Not every day will be as exciting as Sunday,' he said. 'I hope he isn't disappointed.'

'We did well, though, didn't we, sir?' Ned asked. 'Have you heard any more from Mr Cugoan about how those slaves are farin'?'

'No, I'll drop him a line later today. Yes, Ned, we did well to solve the mystery of the severed foot. Even Magistrate Read said so.'

Woods looked pleased. 'I keep wonderin' who that poor fellah were.'

'We'll probably never find out. But one thing's for sure, whatever the circumstances of his death and unchristian burial, if it hadn't been for Ted-with-a-Head those other slaves would have been on their way to a wretched existence. He saved them from that.'

'No, Stephen,' Betsy chided softly. 'You, Ned and Eddie saved them from that.'

'So what about this cove, Nidar? Have we found him yet?' Woods asked.

Lavender frowned and explained to Ned and Betsy about Spencer Perceval's assassination and the role he believed Nidar had played in the murder. They listened quietly and shook their heads in disbelief.

'It's a wicked, wicked thing,' Betsy said.

'We need to catch this beggar – and quickly,' Woods growled.

'Vickery and Adkins are doing their best, but Nidar seems to have disappeared – no one in St Giles has come forward to claim the reward.'

They talked for a bit longer about the assassination and the rioting, then moved on to family matters and news of their mutual friends. By the time Lavender left them to return to Magdalena he felt calmer and more relaxed than he had for days. It was a relief to see Ned on the road to recovery.

He paused on London Bridge and watched the river traffic for a while, soothed by the sound of the heaving water slapping against the stone arches below him. Vessels of all shapes and sizes floated on the Thames. Somewhere out there, amongst that floating jungle of tarred wood and rope, his nemesis lay concealed.

Where are you, Nidar? Where are you hiding?

Below him a boatman hauled in oars dripping with slimy weed. He reached out for the swaying wooden ladder that led up to the jetty and climbed up.

The water drew Lavender towards it. He retraced his steps to the edge of the bridge and walked down the stairs to the wharf.

The boatman glanced at him curiously with the rope in his hand. 'Need a boat ride, guvnor?'

Lavender shook his head. 'No, thank you. I'm just taking a stroll. The river looks high today.'

The man nodded and pointed to the black high-water mark running along the stone bridge arches. 'It's been 'igh for the last four weeks thanks to all this damned rain. Mind you, it'll be 'igher tonight wi' the spring tide.'

Lavender nodded and thanked him. A shiver suddenly ran up the back of his neck, as if someone had walked over his grave. He had the uncomfortable sensation he was being watched.

He chided himself for thinking such nonsense, pulled up his coat collar and went home.

Lavender and Magdalena had just finished their evening meal and were enjoying their coffee, when a message arrived at the house for him. He glanced at the signature and scowled: *Micky Sullivan.* How did the cove know his home address?

Then he remembered their conversation at Lady Caroline's party. Sullivan had shown he knew plenty about him.

The note was short and to the point:

You asked me to pass on information regarding Nidar. Meet me tonight at nine o'clock at the ruined church of St Alphege, Greenwich, where you may learn something to your advantage.

A surge of excitement raced through Lavender. This was the breakthrough they needed. Attracted by the reward, Sullivan had obviously decided to turn informer, rid himself of his new rival and become a little richer in the process. But why meet at the ruined Saxon church? There were plenty of quiet and private locations closer to the city. He remembered their brief encounter in Greenwich two days before and wondered if Sullivan had remained in Greenwich all week. He'd find out soon enough. 'I'm sorry, Magdalena, but I need to go out for a couple of hours.'

Her face fell and she glanced at the clock on the mantelpiece. 'At this hour?'

He put Sullivan's note on the table, pushed back his chair and stood up. 'One of my informers has information about Nidar. He wants to meet at nine o'clock in Greenwich. Don't wait up for me, *querida*. I'll probably be late.'

Magdalena nodded and lifted her cheek for him to kiss as he left.

Lavender hired a horse from the stables on Tottenham Court Road and was soon trotting towards Greenwich. There was a full moon and plenty of stars in the clear sky to guide him. He remembered the boatman's words about the impending high tide tonight and avoided the narrow strip of reed-lined beach running beside the river, instead approaching the ruins from the fields behind the church.

Startled sheep scattered as he picked his way carefully through the meadow. Silhouetted against the moon, the jagged tower of the ruins was an eerie sight. Its ivy cladding rustled and whispered in the breeze. He tethered his horse to a rusty iron grille in one of the low windows of the church, lit his lantern and checked the time on his pocket watch. He was about five minutes late.

'Sullivan?' His shout echoed around the ruins and disturbed a group of sleeping waterfowl in the reeds, who rose squawking and invisible into the air. But nothing else stirred and no one replied.

Carefully, he picked his way through the blocks of fallen masonry. His eyes and ears strained against the darkness of this eerie and deserted place. The river slapped against the rocks on the shore and a bullfrog croaked mournfully to its mate. *Where the hell was Sullivan?*

A faint glimmer of light emanated from the low, arched doorway leading down to the crypt. Frowning, he stepped towards it. This place was remote enough. Sullivan didn't need to hide in the stinking bowels of the crypt to talk to him in private.

'Sullivan?'

The rising tide had already reached the doorway and cascaded down into the crypt. Cursing, he splashed through the water, stooped below the lintel of the low entrance and recoiled at the foul stench.

A small lantern glimmered weakly in one of the rough-hewn alcoves in the wall. A man's body floated face down in the water, its arms and legs spreadeagled.

'Sullivan!'

The slimy steps had become a dangerous waterfall. Lavender scrambled down them and waded towards the corpse, ignoring the cold ice-water swirling around his legs and the crunch of old bones beneath his feet.

Placing his own lantern down on the stone ledge, he tried to turn over the body, but it seemed to be stuck. He grabbed the floating head and twisted it to one side. It moved too easily; the neck had been broken. He pulled away the sandy, wet hair plastered to the side of the dead man's face. Micky Sullivan's profile came into view.

'What the devil?' Confused and shocked, Lavender reached down and tried to release the body from whatever held it so tightly to the floor.

The unmistakeable click of a pistol hammer being drawn back echoed quietly around the dark chamber.

A tall, dark-coated figure waded out of the flooded shadows in the far corner, his face obscured by the shadow of a low-brimmed hat. He held out a pistol before him in his gloved hand.

'Good evening, Lavender,' said the voice of Captain James Leon. 'I do hope you like the little surprise I've prepared for you.'

Lavender's throat went dry and his stomach lurched.

Nidar.

Instinctively, Lavender abandoned his grasp of Sullivan's lifeless corpse. His hand jerked towards the pocket containing his own pistol.

'Don't go for your weapon, Detective.' Nidar raised his pistol and pointed the cold steel barrel straight at Lavender's head.

It was no use. He'd walked straight into a deadly trap.

Chapter Thirty-Seven

Magdalena sipped her coffee and stirred restlessly in her chair. Beside her, Teresa cleared away the used crockery and cutlery onto a tray.

Magdalena felt on edge, though she didn't understand why. Was it the anguish they'd experienced last night? She remembered the nervousness she'd experienced after the massacre of Madrid, when Murat's cavalry trampled and shot thousands of innocent men, women and children. She and Teresa had escaped the city unharmed, but the horrific sights she'd witnessed in the aftermath had left her distressed for months.

Teresa paused in her work and smiled at her. 'Señor the Detective – he be home soon to his wench.'

Magdalena smiled. 'It's *woman*, Teresa – or *wife*. Not *wench* for ladies.' She pushed back her chair and rose gracefully to her feet. 'I think I'll finish my coffee in the drawing room. Please come and sit with me for a while when you've finished your chores.'

Teresa hesitated and glanced towards the door.

'Is it Mr Alfie Tummins?' Magdalena asked, kindly. 'Is he downstairs in the kitchen again?'

Teresa nodded. A smile illuminated her young face and wisps of her dark, frizzy hair escaped from the neat bun and floated around her ears.

'Well, don't be long.' Magdalena smiled, picked up her coffee cup and turned to go.

'You want this?' Teresa held out the note Stephen had received from his contact. He'd left it on the table.

Magdalena was about to tell Teresa to discard it when she caught a glimpse of the handwriting. Her stomach flew into her mouth.

'*Dios mío!*' The coffee cup and saucer clattered down onto the table. She snatched the note out of Teresa's hand.

How could this be possible? Magdalena's brain struggled to make sense of the message. The signature claimed the writer was Micky Sullivan, but the handwriting definitely belonged to that devil Captain Leon – or Nidar, as they now called him. She'd spent enough time staring at the scoundrel's writing with Lady Caroline to recognise the careless scrawl and those flourishing loops on the letter 'g'.

'What is wrong?' Teresa dabbed frantically at the spilt coffee with a napkin.

Magdalena swallowed down her fear and thought fast. Stephen needed help – and she needed help to help him. 'I'm going to fetch my cloak. Tell Mr Alfie Tummins I need him to take me to Constable Woods' house immediately.'

Teresa dumped the tray down on the table with a clatter and the two women moved towards the door. 'But why is this?'

'Señor the Detective is in danger.'

Magdalena raced upstairs for her cloak with her maid's horrified gasp ringing in her ears.

'I apologise for the miserable setting, Lavender.' Nidar's smile didn't reach his narrow-set eyes. 'But I'm delighted to have the opportunity for this little chat, especially in the company of our mutual friend, Mr Sullivan.' He gestured towards the floating corpse with the pistol.

Lavender straightened up slowly. His foot slipped on the unstable pile of bones on the floor. He felt, rather than heard, something crunch beneath his boots. *Could Nidar hear the pounding of his heart above the noise of the water cascading down into the crypt?*

'Sullivan is no friend of mine.'

Nidar scowled. 'Nonsense! I saw you both chatting together at Lady Caroline's soirée. You looked like old friends.'

Lavender half listened. He knew his only chance of survival was to launch himself at Nidar and take the weapon from him. But the floor was a death trap, unstable underfoot. Balance was difficult with the swirling water around their knees. His legs were already numb with the cold. Any sudden movement would be risky – especially with that pistol pointing at his head. But it was his only chance: he either took Nidar's weapon or his own bones would soon be added to the grisly pile beneath his feet.

'Did the two of you think you would fool Nidar?' the cove continued angrily. 'Sullivan came to me last Sunday, asking to work with me – but then he betrayed me and told you the location of my cargo and ship.'

Despite his fear, Lavender laughed. 'You're wrong. I'd no help from Sullivan. It was good detection work – and that alone – which found those poor wretches and wrecked your vile trade. I despised Micky Sullivan and would never work with him. You're delusional if you think otherwise.'

The fingers around the pistol trigger moved. Lavender braced himself for the blue flash. It would be the last thing he saw before the shot shattered his skull. *Oh, Magdalena, querida . . .*

'You're lying. Remove your pistol from your pocket and throw it away – slowly.'

Unsure why he had been spared, Lavender pulled out his weapon and hurled it into the dark corner of the chamber. It disappeared with a plop into the black water.

If Nidar wanted to talk, then let him. It gave him a few more precious moments of life and a chance of . . . what? Rescue? An impossible hope. But all men had hope even in the face of death. His only chance was to wrestle with Nidar and take the pistol from him.

'So you used Sullivan as bait to draw me here?'

'Yes, and I used *you* as bait to draw *him* here. He came quickly enough to meet you – *his friend*. Now, pull out your handcuffs.'

A wry smile curled at the corners of Lavender's mouth. 'You want me to arrest you?'

Nidar's laugh echoed around the crypt. 'I'm glad you still find amusement in the face of death, Lavender. No, I want you to cuff yourself to Sullivan.'

Lavender's face fell.

'I see you're surprised. Good. Nidar still manages to surprise you and stay one step ahead, doesn't he?' His smile broadened with manic delight. 'You were slow to realise who I was, weren't you, Lavender? But I'm impressed with how quickly you made the connection between Proteus, Pardus and Nidar. Your Greek education must have been thorough. I commend your teachers . . .'

Lavender tensed to leap. It was now or never.

A bulky figure suddenly filled the open doorway above and blocked out the pale moonlight. Lavender's heart sank as a large man, heavily swathed in scarves, splashed down the steps and waded towards them.

Nidar's grin broadened. 'You didn't think I'd be stupid enough to come alone, did you, Lavender?' The dim light cast his shadow on the dripping wall, the profile demonic. 'No. Even I am wary of the great Detective Lavender. Your reputation in St Giles is impressive.'

'You're a wanted man,' Lavender snapped. 'There's a hue and cry out for your arrest and a reward offered for your capture. You won't evade justice for long; the scum of St Giles will be happy to turn you over to Bow Street.'

Nidar shrugged. 'Yes, you've caused me some trouble there. I need to leave town for a while – but Nidar will be back.'

Lavender had heard this constant use of the third person before – from the mouths of the criminally insane in Newgate and Bedlam. Wily, supremely intelligent and with no conscience or feeling, they shifted from one persona to another, talking in different voices. Nidar was one of them, a maniac who'd risen to the top of the criminal fraternity.

'Who are you, Jim? What's your real name?'

Nidar laughed, but a muscle twitched at the corner of his right eye at the mention of his real name. 'I'm Proteus, the shape-shifting son of Poseidon, Nidar, the vile and deadly serpent of the sea, el Cerdo the pig and Leon the lion – the strongest and most feared pack leader of crime.'

'You're insane.'

Nidar threw back his head and laughed. 'And you're going to die, Lavender. All your detection, the hue and cry you've raised – it's all come to nothing. I've beaten you! The great Detective Lavender, the Chief Constable of the Bow Street Police! Your death – the one I have planned for you – will make you a laughing stock, and enhance the reputation of Nidar.'

'You won't get away with this,' he said. 'The Bow Street constables—'

'Are all tucked up in their warm little beds – especially your precious Constable Woods. How is his arm, by the way? Turning gangrenous, I hope?' Nidar gestured to his burly companion. 'Get the handcuffs.'

The thug grabbed Lavender roughly and pulled his handcuffs out of his pocket. They rattled treacherously when he held them up for his master's inspection.

'Cuff him to Sullivan.'

The thug removed the key and snapped one end of the irons around Lavender's wrist. Yanking on the chain, he forced Lavender down, reached below the water and cuffed him to Sullivan's wrist. Whatever held Sullivan's corpse down to the floor had now pulled the body under the rising water. Bent double, Lavender's own head was barely a foot above the treacherous waves. *If the water continued to rise . . . ?*

He glanced at the dark line on the walls of the crypt and his stomach lurched with renewed fear. The high-tide mark was several feet above the current position of his head. He couldn't move. The river water would continue to cascade down into the crypt and rise above his head until it reached that line. Nidar intended to drown him.

Nidar followed his gaze and grinned. 'A brilliant ruse, don't you think?' he said smugly. 'And sweet revenge for the soaking you gave me on Sunday night. The Chief Constable of the police and the former leader of London's criminal underworld – found handcuffed together in a flooded crypt. Imagine the reaction in London to this bizarre occurrence – in the news-sheets! And the rookery of St Giles! Everyone will know Nidar did this! Nidar shall be feared throughout England!'

Chapter Thirty-Eight

N ed Woods threw his spoon down into his half-finished supper
and leapt to his feet, upsetting his chair in the process. 'Fetch me
my coat!' he roared.

Eddie jumped up from his seat and raced out into the hallway. Betsy
stood up beside Ned, her face creased with anxiety and pale with shock.
Magdalena stood awkwardly before them, wringing her hands in distress.

'Ned, you can't . . .' Betsy said. 'You're injured yourself. You're still
weak . . .'

'I've got one good arm,' Woods snapped. 'And it's the one I shoot with.'

Eddie returned with his father's coat and his own. 'I'm coming
with you.'

'Help me get this damned coat over the sling,' Woods said to his wife.

Silently, Betsy helped Woods into his coat.

Magdalena felt wretched. 'I'm sorry, Betsy. I didn't know where else
to turn for help.'

'If Uncle Stephen needs us, then we're there for him.' Eddie buttoned up his coat, his young face serious. His simple comment ended
the discussion.

The other children stared in wide-eyed silence when Woods pulled
his pistol and powder out of his pocket and tossed them to Eddie.
'Load it for me, son.'

Betsy said nothing. Tears formed in her eyes.

'The carriage will be useless, Doña Magdalena,' Woods said. 'It can't get us near enough to St Alphege's. We'll take a boat and go by river. It'll be quicker.'

'The tide's against us, Da.' Eddie poured gunpowder into his father's pistol with an expert hand. 'It'll be hard goin'.'

'Not with a second set of oars and you and me rowin' together, son.'

Five minutes later, Magdalena, Woods and Eddie raced down the wharf steps and clambered into a boat on the dark river.

'We're Bow Street constables,' Eddie informed the alarmed boatman. 'We're on a mission of life and death and need to get to Greenwich immediately.'

Despite the fear gnawing at her insides, Magdalena gave a little smile at the way Ned and Betsy's troublesome son had calmly taken control.

'Huh!' the boatman muttered, pushing them away from the wharf. 'I didn't know there were women, boys and one-armed bandits in the Runners!' His sarcasm turned to genuine alarm a few moments later. Woods and Eddie hauled on the pair of oars they shared with such ferocity that the boat powered across the surging water. It rose and fell sharply against the swell of the incoming tide and water splashed inside. 'Oy! You'll drown the lot of us if we keep goin' at this speed!'

'See the bucket under your seat, Doña Magdalena?' Woods asked. 'Use it to bail us out.'

Grateful to have something to do, Magdalena tore her eyes away from the twinkling lights on the riverbank and reached for the small wooden pail. The work distracted her from her fear for Stephen and helped ward off the shivering that threatened to engulf her.

Please, God, they would get there in time . . .

'You've not won, Jim,' Lavender said quietly. 'Even if I die, others will still hunt you down. They're good men, great detectives. They know what you look like and have evidence linking you to those highway robberies – and to John Bellingham and the murder of the Prime Minister. You'll swing on the gallows at Newgate along with the rest of the common criminals.'

His nemesis just laughed and stepped closer. His eyes gleamed with madness. 'Ah, Bellingham. Such a foolish man, so easy to persuade to murder once I explained the concept of *malice prepense* to him. He wanted revenge on that Ambassador, of course – but I managed to persuade him to target his revenge on Perceval instead.'

'That was you?'

'Oh, yes. He was so gullible and soon believed Nidar when he told him they wouldn't hang him once he'd told his pathetic story to the jury. Men like him yield too easily to the desires of the moment – they're so easy to trick.'

Something stirred in Lavender's brain, a half-remembered quotation from his school days.

'And what a great outcome, eh?' Nidar continued. 'The man responsible for wrecking my trade is dead – and the country thrown into turmoil by his death!'

'So that's what it was all about, was it?' Lavender said. 'Revenge for the abolition of the slave trade?' His back ached with stooping and he couldn't feel his legs any more. His teeth chattered.

Nidar leaned forward and whispered in his ear. Lavender wanted to recoil at his proximity but he didn't flinch. 'Whoever conquers a free town and does not demolish it commits a great error and may expect to be ruined himself.'

A shudder ran through Lavender's body, followed by a severe shiver of cold. He fought to control his chattering teeth and forced his mouth into a sarcastic smile. 'You're not a Machiavellian prince, Jim. You're just a common murderer who'll dance at the end of a rope.'

Nidar slapped him hard across the face. The twitch beside the mad-man's eye had returned with a vengeance. 'I'm Nidar! This chaos in London shall be remembered as Nidar's greatest triumph!' A slow smile now crept across his features. 'Apart from your death, of course.' He stepped back, pocketed his pistol and gestured to his silent companion that it was time to leave.

The big man nodded and pointed to the glimmering lanterns. 'What about the lights?'

'Leave them,' Nidar snapped. 'Let him see his death coming.' He turned back and regarded Lavender dispassionately while the other man shrugged and climbed out of the chamber. An evil smile spread across Nidar's face. 'Perhaps when I return I'll seek out your pretty widow and offer her some comfort, eh? How do you feel about that, Lavender?'

Lavender's stomach lurched again but he managed to control his chattering teeth and steel his voice. Twisting his head, he stared straight into Nidar's eyes: 'You may have outwitted me, Jim – but you'll never outwit my wife.'

Nidar slapped him again. 'How many times do I have to tell you my name?' he hissed.

He turned and mounted the first few steps, but his desire to taunt and torture made him turn back again. 'Dante was wrong about the fiery inner circle of hell, Lavender,' he said with a grin. 'The inner circle of hell is the relentless drip of black water and its slow, deadly climb inside every one of your orifices until your lungs fill. But you'll find this out soon enough.'

His hollow laugh echoed around the chamber once more. Then he was gone.

Chapter Thirty-Nine

The lurching boat trip seemed to take forever. The black hulls of moored vessels loomed out of the river, but Magdalena barely noticed them. She focused on bailing out the water and fighting back the nausea rising in her stomach from the pitching of the boat. The metal oarlocks creaked and the timber groaned as they raced against the swell of the tidal river.

Suddenly the constant rolling stopped and they seemed to pick up speed.

'The tide's turned!' Eddie yelled. 'It's slack water.'

Magdalena heard the exhaustion in the boy's voice, but he, Woods and the boatman attacked the oars with renewed vigour.

The bankside lights and the number of moored vessels thinned out as they left the Port of London and turned south down the meandering river.

'Greenwich Reach,' the boatman said.

'We're nearly there, Doña Magdalena!' Woods' voice was no more than a grunt.

Magdalena tried not to think of the damage Ned was doing to his injured body with this incredible exertion. She stared ahead. Her eyes tried to pick out the entrance of Deptford Creek and the ruined church Stephen had described to her. Thank God, it was a clear and starry night with a full, bright moon. *Please, God, Stephen is still alive to see those stars.*

Woods glanced over his shoulder. 'That's the mouth of Deptford Creek.'

Magdalena followed his glance towards the gaping black hole in the riverbank, where the tributary poured into the Thames. On the far bank, the jagged tower of St Alphege's was just visible, silhouetted against the moon.

Suddenly, another large ship loomed out of the darkness, rocking at anchor. A small boat rowed towards it. The clouds shifted and the moonlight illuminated the faces of the two men in the boat.

'It's Nidar!' She rose to her feet, raised her pearl-handled pistol and fired off a shot before she'd even had time to think.

A scream rent the still air. Their boat swayed violently with her sudden movement. She lost her balance and fell back down.

Woods swore loudly. He and the others struggled to control the rocking boat.

'I hit him! I hit him!' she yelled in delight.

'Heaven and hell, woman!' Woods hauled in his oar, reached in his pocket for his own pistol and twisted round to face the other boat. 'Don't do that again!'

But Magdalena was already reloading her pistol.

No fire was returned. The occupants of the other boat seemed more interested in reaching the safety of their moored vessel. 'Leave them,' Woods yelled. 'Let's get to St Alphege's.'

Their boat shot up the narrow shingle beach beside the old church and jerked to a halt. The three men and Magdalena scrambled over the side and waded through the mud and reeds towards the flooded ruins.

Oblivious to the cold water soaking her legs, Magdalena prayed harder than she'd ever prayed before in her life, begging God to forgive her sins and her previous indifference to His existence, imploring Him for His help.

◆ ◆ ◆

Shivering wracked Lavender's body and threatened to dislodge his foothold. His shackled right arm was now submerged under the water, stretched and taut. The stinking river lapped at his shoulder only a few inches below his face. Water splashed into his mouth. He nearly retched at the foul taste and spat it out.

He desperately wanted to move his frozen, numb legs and ease the pressure on his straining back. But he bit back the impulse and kept his body rigid and still. If he lost his footing on the treacherous floor and fell into the water, he might not be able to stand again and would shorten what was left of his life.

Sullivan's corpse had disappeared from view. Should he duck below the water and try to free Sullivan's arm from whatever tied it to the floor of the crypt? If he could get Sullivan free from his restraints he might have the strength to pull himself and half the corpse higher. But even when the thought entered his mind he knew it was useless. Nidar wasn't stupid enough to be so careless. The maniac had planned his death down to the last detail, and if he put his head below the water he may never lift it out again.

Weariness swept through him, his eyelids felt heavy and the violent shivering of his body seemed to ease. But this cessation of his normal bodily reaction filled him with even more fear. He jerked himself awake. He mustn't drift into unconsciousness.

A strange, glimmering apparition at the far side of the crypt caught his attention.

It was Vivienne, his long-dead fiancée. Backlit with pearly moonlight, she floated towards him, her iridescent gown and long, fair hair splayed out across the surface of the water. A vision of loveliness. Compassion filled her luminous eyes. She raised her marble-pale arms and held them out towards him, inviting him to join her in death.

'Noooo . . .' His legs shifted, the pain in his body eased and he sank into the water.

Magdalena . . .

A dim light glimmered below the low, arched doorway in the outer wall of the church. Eddie raced ahead of them, bounding and splashing through the water like a young stag.

'He's down here!'

'It's the old crypt,' Magdalena said breathlessly. Water cascaded down the steps into the flooded chamber. A body floated in the swirling water below. She bit back a scream of horror.

'Stay back, Doña Magdalena!' Woods, Eddie and the boatman stooped below the lintel and clambered down the dangerous staircase.

Magdalena ignored Ned's instruction and followed the men down into the bowels of the ruined church, gasping when the freezing water rose up to her waist.

They were struggling to lift Stephen out of the water. 'Something's holdin' him under,' Ned grunted. 'He's tied down to the bottom.'

'Wait a minute!' Eddie waded to the edge of the room, grabbed one of the small lanterns from the alcove and returned quickly to his father's side. 'It's his handcuffs! He's handcuffed to—'

His face contorted in horror and he let out a string of swear words that would have earned him a sharp slap around the ear from his horrified mother. '—He's chained to another body!'

'Support his head.'

Eddie and the boatman braced themselves and took Stephen's weight, while Woods fished around in his coat pocket for his own set of cuffs with his good arm. He pulled them out and held them towards Magdalena. 'Get the key and give it to Eddie.'

She snatched out the key and thrust it at the boy. 'Will it work? Will your key open Stephen's handcuffs?'

Woods grabbed Stephen again, while Eddie reached below the water with the key. 'Same key opens every pair of cuffs at Bow Street,' Woods grunted. 'Read got a cheap batch from the ironmonger's – but don't tell the coves.'

Suddenly Stephen was free. He lurched into the arms of his constable, nearly knocking him over. They scrambled back up the stone stairs, pushing and shoving Stephen's waterlogged body between them.

'Is he dead?' a voice screamed as they fell outside into the moonlight.

'Help me, son.' With Eddie's assistance, Ned picked up Stephen with his one arm and tossed him over his broad shoulder as if he was a child. He turned and strode behind the ruins towards the higher ground of the meadow. Magdalena hurried beside him, two steps of hers to each one of Ned's.

'Is he dead?' It was only when the scream repeated itself that Magdalena realised it was her own voice.

Woods stopped on a grassy knoll and lowered Stephen awkwardly onto the dry grass. The jolt of the landing forced water out of Stephen's lungs. It shot out of his mouth. He spluttered – then coughed.

'He's alive!' Eddie yelled.

Magdalena sank down in her sodden skirts next to her husband. Ned collapsed beside her, breathing heavily.

'I'll fetch 'elp from Greenwich.' The boatman strode hurriedly towards the town.

'Turn him over, son,' Woods said. 'Get the water out.'

Eddie pushed Stephen onto his side and thumped his back. Barely conscious, Stephen retched and vomited up foul black water.

Magdalena pulled him back towards her and cradled his head in her lap, moaning her thanks to God in Spanish.

His eyelids fluttered – then opened. '*Querida* . . . ?' he whispered.

'Oh, my darling.' Tears streamed down Magdalena's face. She rocked her husband like a baby.

Wordlessly, Ned reached out his great hand and squeezed her arm. His round face was as pale as the moon above and etched with pain and exhaustion. Beneath his open coat, a dark stain seeped across his bandaged arm and the sling. Magdalena and Ned sat in silence over Stephen, watching the shallow rise and fall of his chest.

Eddie crouched beside them, glancing curiously between their strained faces, unsure of the meaning of this strange, emotional silence. In the distance a horse whinnied and stamped. Stephen moaned gently in Magdalena's arms, turned his head – and retched again.

'Go fetch his horse, son,' Ned's voice cracked. 'You can ride it back to London.'

When the boy rose and walked towards the snorting beast, Ned tore his eyes away from Stephen and turned to face her. 'I warned him, you know,' he said gruffly.

'What?'

'Back when you two first met in that coach on Barnby Moor and you helped us overcome that gang of tobymen. I warned him never to trust a filly who keeps a pistol in her boots.'

Despite the cold, the shivering and her streaming tears, Magdalena began to laugh.

Chapter Forty

Stephen vomited again, groaned and sank back against his sweat-soaked pillows. Foul black water tinged with blood splashed into the metal bowl. His stomach muscles cramped and spasmed. He drifted in and out of a restless sleep and vomited again. Clear this time – but still bloodied. He woke in the dark, unable to move for the pain and bathed in sweat. *Would it never end?*

Magdalena. *Teresa.*

Magdalena talking with a dark-suited man at the end of the bed. Magdalena mixing a white powder in a glass of water. Their muted words escaped him.

Dreams. Horrific, dark dreams. Dreams of dark water. Nidar. Nidar's leering face beneath the water, bubbles escaping from his laughing mouth. Nidar's leering face above him, pushing him under the dark water with a claw-like hand.

'Sebastián! He's after Sebastián!'

Magdalena's gentle arms pulled him back down into the sweat-soaked bed. Back down to the water . . . the freezing black water.

Betsy fed him broth. His mother held the bowl when he vomited again. His father . . . *what the devil was his father doing there? And why did he look so old and pale?*

'He's after Sebastián!'

'Easy son, easy.' His father's trembling hand mopped his brow. 'Sebastián's safe at his boardin' school.'

'*Fever from intestinal infection . . .*'

The food always came back up again. He swatted away the hands trying to feed him. Torturous pain – worse than death itself. Always retching. Blood in the bowl.

Caroline Clare. *Lady Caroline sitting beside his bed? Magdalena wouldn't like that . . .*

'*Inflammation and rupture of the intestines. Lesions.*'

More nightmarish visions. Cold, cruel eyes in a grinning face.

'Caroline Clare's here,' he whispered to Magdalena. 'Here – in our bedroom.'

She leaned over him, her face a mixture of weariness and amusement. 'I know, my darling. You've told me three times. But I've looked everywhere and I can't find her in the closet or in any of the drawers. Is she under the sheets with you?'

The white powder brought relief. A deep and dreamless sleep.

He grabbed Teresa's arm when she mixed it with water. 'More! Give me more!'

She battered his hand with the teaspoon. It stung. 'No! You'll become addled!'

He withdrew his bruised hand, marvelling at the thinness of the wrist and its weakness. *He couldn't even fight with a girl . . .*

Betsy was there. 'You've done well today, Stephen. You've kept down your porridge. Now you're going to have broth.'

'I don't want broth. It hurts.'

Strong, unsympathetic arms lifted him upright, then forced food down his throat. 'I've spent hours making this broth, Stephen, and you'll eat it.' *Who'd lifted him? Was it Betsy or Ned? Who was talking? Had Ned made the broth?*

'Teresa won't give me the morphine,' he whined. 'She hit me with a teaspoon.'

Magdalena floated over him, her dark eyes luminous with humour. 'Good,' she said. 'Behave – or next time I'll give her the ladle to beat you.'

The pain eased to a dull ache. The sweating finally stopped. He remained conscious for longer and sat up for short periods. Desperately weak, any movement left him exhausted and wracked him with fresh intestinal pain. Even staggering to the privy was torture.

He'd no concentration for reading. Magdalena sat beside the bed and read to him. Her beautiful, accented voice lulled him to sleep. Peaceful sleep now. He managed a weak smile at her occasional mistakes with the English texts. His parents visited him again. His sisters.

'Magistrate Read called by the house to ask how you were,' Magdalena said. 'But you were asleep, so he went away again.'

He pulled himself up and swung his thin legs over the side of the bed, wincing at the pain. 'I've got to get back to work.'

She was by his side in an instant, a gentle hand on his bony shoulder. 'Not in your nightshirt, Stephen.'

'I need to get dressed.'

'Yes, let's try to get you dressed today. Maybe we should go downstairs for a while?'

'I'm going to work.'

'We'll see . . .'

An hour later, he was sitting in his armchair in the drawing room, exhausted. Magdalena sat with her embroidery on her knee. There was something wrong with his clothes: his shirt hung off him and the cravat was too loose around his neck.

He woke up with a start and rubbed his eyes. 'How long have I been ill?'

'Nearly three weeks.'

'Three weeks! What the devil's been happening? Have they caught Nidar?'

'You swallowed a lot of foul river water, Stephen,' she said gently. 'You've had a terrible infection and fever.'

'I'd worked that out,' he snapped. 'I am a detective.'

She paused for a moment, as she would with a naughty child. 'The doctor said you'll probably be well enough to return to work in a week or so, provided you continue to eat and build up your strength.'

'Another week! I'll die of boredom if I have to sit still for another week!'

Her face flushed and some emotion brought tears to her eyes. 'Well, Ned is coming to visit you in an hour; that should ease your boredom.'

He regretted his harsh tone. She looked strained – and thinner herself. She rose slowly to her feet. Her flush died away and was replaced with a whitish pallor tinged with green. 'Excuse me, Stephen, I feel nauseous.' She left hastily.

He stared after her departing figure, aghast. *Had he passed on his infection to Magdalena?*

He must have nodded off to sleep again because the next moment a large hand was on his shoulder, shaking him awake. Woods' great round face beamed down at him. 'Now then, sir. How are you feelin' today?'

'Ned! How good to see you! How are *you*?'

Woods sank down onto the sofa next to Magdalena's discarded embroidery. He wasn't in uniform and his arm was still bandaged and supported with the sling.

'How's your shoulder?'

Woods glanced down at his sling and smiled. 'It had a bit of a set-back when I dragged you out of your watery grave, sir, but it should be right as rain in a week or so.'

'Another week?' Lavender frowned and wondered how long Betsy's savings would last to support the family with Ned out of work.

'It's nothing to worry about, sir. We're off up to Northamptonshire tomorrow to visit our Alby and his family for a week, anyway. I'll be back to work after that.'

A sharp pang of jealousy shot through Lavender. Ned, Betsy and their family made an annual pilgrimage to see Ned's brother every Whitsuntide. Lavender had never been comfortable sharing Ned with Alby.

Woods ignored his scowl – or didn't notice it. He reached into his coat pocket with his good arm and pulled out a couple of news-sheets. 'Mind you, we'll be busy when I get back – so you'd better make sure you recover soon.'

'Busy?'

'Yes. Take a look at this.' He handed Lavender one of the papers. It was *The Day*. Lavender's eyes swam at the small print but he managed to pick out the headline: *Daring Raid by Bow Street Constables Impounds Slave Ship*. A smaller sub-heading below read: *Brave Constable Woods injured*.

'Magistrate Read gave the story to Vincent Dowling in exchange for his silence over your involvement in the Bellingham affair.' Woods beamed. 'News-sheets all over the country have copied the story. We're national heroes.'

'Heroes?'

'Yes, Read's had loads of requests for us to go and investigate crimes – the two of us together. Some folks even offered to pay double for the services of Detective Lavender and Constable Woods together.'

'What sort of crimes?'

'Oh, unsolved murders and robberies, missin' husbands, that sort of thing.'

A wave of satisfaction swept through Lavender. Those were the kinds of mysteries he liked best.

'My bad arm means horse ridin' will be difficult for a while,' Ned continued. 'So Magistrate Read thinks I should leave the horse patrol and become your regular assistant: Assistant to the Chief of Constables.'

'Chief Constable?' Lavender grimaced. 'When did I receive a promotion? That's what Nidar called me. Where's this appellation come from?'

'I think it were *The Times*, sir. They're particularly fond of reportin' your exploits, and Read's done nothin' to dissuade them.'

'I'll have to ask him for an increase in my wages if I'm Chief of Constables,' Lavender muttered, darkly. Then he smiled again. The thought of working with Ned more often cheered him. 'I'm sorry about your shoulder, Ned – especially the extra suffering I caused you.' Ignoring his own sharp stab of pain, he leaned forward, took Woods' large hand in his own and shook it. 'I'll never forget I owe you my life.'

'Well, I had a lot of help from Doña Magdalena.' Woods smiled. 'She's become a real legend down at Bow Street now. Young Adkins asked me the other day where he could find a woman like her.'

Lavender smiled. 'Tell him God broke the mould when he made Magdalena.'

'In fact,' Woods continued, 'there's a rumour that Mrs Read intends to invite you both round to supper when you're well enough to go.'

The thought of food made Lavender wince. 'I wouldn't do justice to their cook at the moment,' he said, 'but I'm glad Magistrate Read's feeling more friendly towards my wife; it's about time he overcame his prejudice about her religion. No doubt Charity Read had something to do with this. She's always struck me as the kinder and less bigoted of the pair.'

Woods nodded. 'Doña Magdalena will probably be the first Catholic to step over their threshold.'

'What else has happened?'

'Well, they hanged John Bellingham. He stood up in court on the Friday and spent two hours tellin' the jury why he was justified in murderin' poor Spencer Perceval because no one in the government listened to his damned petition.'

Lavender sighed. 'I thought that would happen.'

'They took about five minutes to convict him – and hanged him the next day. No one were surprised at the guilty verdict except Bellingham, I think.'

'And Nidar?'

'Gone. Disappeared without a trace.'

Lavender scowled. 'He said he was going away for a while – but he'll be back.'

'But he might not be the same man,' Woods said mysteriously. 'You do know, don't you, that your wife took a shot at him when he was scurrying back to his ship?'

'Magdalena shot him? What happened?'

Woods shrugged. 'We don't know for sure – but from the squeal that followed, she definitely found a mark. Someone was hit.'

Satisfaction and hope welled up in Lavender. 'So Nidar may be injured – or possibly dead?'

Woods nodded. 'Maybe. Your wife's a better shot than either of us.'

Lavender gave a little laugh of satisfaction and thought back to the warning he'd given Nidar about underestimating Magdalena. 'I know.'

'In the meantime, things have been rather quiet in London. With Nidar gone and Micky Sullivan dead, the criminal gangs are leaderless and in disarray and have taken to squabblin' amongst themselves. We've had spates of pickpocketin' and some theft from shops to deal with, but nothin' big.'

'It won't be long before another piece of scum rises to the surface in the rookery,' Lavender muttered grimly.

'Well, we're enjoying the peace for the moment. In fact, when old Townsend returned from his work with the Bank of England, Magistrate Read felt it was safe enough to keep him at Bow Street and send the other Principal Officers back out on lucrative cases in the provinces.'

A small smile twitched at the corner of Lavender's lips. 'God help London with Townsend in charge.'

'Adkins were sent over to Dublin in your place.'

Lavender nodded. 'How are your family?'

'Good, all good. Eddie's lovin' his new job with Bow Street. That trip we made to Greenwich with him seems to have changed his mind about policin'.'

'You never intended that day to be just a pleasure outing for Eddie, did you?' Lavender said. 'It was his initiation into policing. The lad dreamed of sailing away to sea, but you were determined to keep him close.'

Woods beamed. 'Well, you can't blame me for tryin', can you, sir? And he had the best teacher in the world in you.'

Lavender smiled. 'You flatter me.'

'He made his first arrest the other day.'

'Really?'

'Yes, the builders told him the dopey chap, Windy, were an escaped convict from Botany Bay. He cuffed the fellah and marched him over to Oswald Grey in a flash.'

Lavender burst out laughing, then gripped his sides with pain. 'For God's sake, Ned! Don't make me laugh!'

Woods smiled and rubbed the grey stubble on his chin. 'Laughter's good, sir. It raises your spirits. I've hear you've been a bit low.'

'So the builders are still up to their old tricks?'

'Yes, and Read and Macca are always arguin', but the work on the new cell block and court is coming on a treat; the walls are up now. You wouldn't recognise the old place; it looks grimmer than ever. Oh, and I've also got this for you.' He reached into his coat pocket again and pulled out a letter.

Lavender shook his head when Woods tried to pass it across. 'You read it, Ned. My eyes won't focus for long.'

'I've already read it. It's from Ignatius Cugoan in Greenwich. He wrote to let us know that the slaves we rescued have been looked after by his group, the Sons of Africa. They've sent them to a farm in Norfolk where they'll learn English and useful agricultural skills.'

This was good to hear. Lavender nodded with satisfaction and the two men sat in silence for a moment, thinking back to that dreadful moment when they'd stumbled across those pitiful captives.

'I often wonder . . .' Woods said slowly. 'How poor Ted-with-a-Head lost his foot? You don't suppose . . . you don't think he lost his mind and cut it off himself to try to get rid of the leg irons, do you?'

Lavender winced and thought back to the bloodied, rusty scythe he'd seen in the reeds beside the derelict farm. An agricultural accident – or self-inflicted harm?

'I wouldn't dwell on it, Ned. We'll never know the truth about what happened to him. It'll have to be enough for us to know that if he hadn't lost his foot in such an unusual way, six other poor slaves and a baby would still be living a life of hell.'

'We did well to follow up that case, didn't we, sir?' Woods asked.

'Yes, Ned, we did.'

Woods grinned and stood up.

'You're leaving, so soon?'

'I have to, I'm afraid. I've got to help Betsy pack for this trip to Alby's.' Another pang of jealousy shot through Lavender.

'But I'll shake your hand first, if I may, sir? Woods said. He grinned and his eyes twinkled.

'Why?'

'Betsy said I were to say nothin' unless you told me – but I'd like to shake your hand before I go. Just so you know that I'm pleased for you and Doña Magdalena.'

Lavender frowned, confused. 'I think Magdalena may be ill, Ned. She's nauseous. I think she's caught my infection.'

Woods laughed and grasped him by the hand. 'Back rubs,' he said with a wink. 'They never fail.'

'Back rubs don't cure nausea.'

Woods winked again. 'No, but sometimes they cause it.' He left before Lavender could question him further.

By the time Magdalena reappeared, Lavender was on the edge of his seat.

'What have you told Betsy that you haven't told me? What's the big mystery?'

Magdalena smiled. The years dropped away from her face. She looked excited, like a young girl, and radiant. She leaned down and kissed him gently on the top of his head. 'It's early days yet, Stephen,' she whispered, 'but I know the signs.'

'Early days for what? What signs?'

'You'll be a father by next spring. I'm carrying our child.'

Author's Notes

'It was around midnight before Bellingham could finally be taken out . . . to Newgate Prison . . . He was accompanied by . . . Stephen Lavender the Chief Constable of Police . . .'

The Times, 13th May, 1812

As my Detective Lavender Mystery series moved forward to the year 1812, it was inevitable my interest would be drawn to the assassination of the British Prime Minister, Spencer Perceval, on 11th May.

I was fascinated to learn that the real-life Stephen Lavender, on whom my fictional hero is based, was involved in the aftermath of the shocking murder. He, along with fellow Principal Officers John Vickery and Harry Adkins, gathered the evidence required to convict Bellingham. The connection Vickery made between the pistol ball used to kill Bellingham and the small machine used to make it which he found in Bellingham's lodgings, is often cited as the first example in a UK courtroom of ballistic forensic analysis. My research also revealed the threatening letter Bellingham sent to the Bow Street magistrates, and I spent a lot of time pondering how they would have reacted to it.

However, the mystery writer in me soon realised that the assassination wasn't intriguing enough to form the main plot of a novel. There was no mystery about 'whodunit' and no detection needed to find the killer. Bellingham remained at the scene of the crime, admitted to the murder and was arrested on the spot.

But when I read Andro Linklater's excellent book, *Why Spencer Perceval Had to Die*, I found a mystery surrounding the case that, with a little imagination, I could exploit. No one knew who financed the bankrupt merchant's extended stay in London while he pursued his hopeless petition for compensation. No one ever found out who gave him the money on the day of the murder or who sent him the money while he languished in Newgate. The prospect of an accomplice wasn't explored by the authorities. They hanged him before his case was properly investigated. Riots swept the country in the aftermath of Perceval's assassination and they needed a swift and brutal response to stem the unrest. As Linklater explains, there were plenty of people and organisations, from Liverpool's blockade-busting slavers and traders to frustrated Catholics and the American government, who would have happily welcomed Spencer Perceval's death. His policies had made him hugely unpopular. John Bellingham was mentally unbalanced and ripe for exploitation by anyone with a murderous agenda.

This unresolved conspiracy theory fired my imagination and linked in with my long-held desire to give my detective a cunning and ruthless adversary. I'd felt for some time that Lavender deserved his own Moriarty, and so the character of Nidar was born.

The main mystery of this novel, the unexplained severed foot on Greenwich Beach, was inspired by an online forensics course I did with Dundee University. The detectives of the early nineteenth century had no access to the forensic methods and procedures we take for granted today. Most of their crimes were solved by looking for motive and opportunity. However, the study of bones (osteology) had advanced sufficiently for them to be able to identify the gender, age and ethnicity of skeletons. I decided this was something I could use to effect, especially when I learned that the transportation of African slaves to America by British ship owners had not ceased in 1812, despite the abolition of the slave trade.

I've known for a long time that Bow Street Magistrates' Court and Police Office was built over a medieval plague pit, and I knew the building was extended in 1812 by Magistrate Read. I couldn't resist the opportunity for the builders (based on the jovial and prank-loving fellows who transformed my own home in 2016) to uncover the grisly remains and cause mayhem with them. Another real incident I developed was the occasion (reported in *The Times*) when constables hauled a naked man out of the River Serpentine in Hyde Park.

The Sons of Africa was a real organisation whose members were mostly freed slaves. Sadly, The Gallery of Women Artists is a figment of my imagination, but I like to imagine it could have been real. Characters drawn from real life include the artist William Turner and everyone connected with the Perceval assassination, including Bellingham's landlady, the draper, Challenier, and Vincent Dowling, the journalist on *The Day*.

I have many people to thank for their help and support during the writing and publication of this novel, including my family, who put up with my extended stay in my writing cave, and the fantastic editorial team at Thomas & Mercer. I also would like to thank my Alpha-Readers, Sam Blain, Babs Morton, Jean Gill, Jane Harlond, Claire Stibbe, Sandra Mangan and Kristin Gleeson, for the love and support they continue to give me. And I want to pay tribute to my brilliant cover designer, Lisa Horton, who never fails to delight me with her skill.

Finally, to you, the reader, thank you for reading my book. If you enjoyed it, please leave a review on Amazon.

Karen Charlton
www.karencharlton.com
22nd April, 2017
Marske, North Yorkshire

Bibliography

David J. Cox, *A Certain Share of Low Cunning: A History of the Bow Street Runners 1792–1839* (Willan Publishing, 2010)

Percy Fitzgerald, *Chronicles of Bow Street Police-Office: Volume One* (Cambridge University Press, 2011)

David C. Hanrahan, *The Assassination of the Prime Minister* (The History Press, 2011)

Stephen Hart, *Cant: A Gentleman's Guide – The Language of Rogues in Georgian London* (Improbable Fictions, 2014)

Andro Linklater, *Why Spencer Perceval Had to Die* (Bloomsbury Publishing, 2012)

About the Author

Photo © 2014 Jean Gill

Karen Charlton writes historical mysteries and is also the author of a non-fiction genealogy book, *Seeking Our Eagle*. She has published short stories and numerous articles and reviews in newspapers and magazines. An English graduate and former teacher, Karen has led writing workshops and has spoken at a number of literary events across the north of England, where she lives. Karen now writes full-time.

A stalwart of the village pub quiz and a member of a winning team on the BBC quiz show *Eggheads*, Karen also enjoys the theatre and won a Yorkshire Tourist Board award for her Murder Mystery Weekends.

Find out more about Karen's work at www.karencharlton.com.